EBENEZER

THE TRUE LIFE STORY OF EBENEZER SCROOGE

Douglas A. Bass

MIM PUBLISHING

Ebenezer: The True Life Story of Ebenezer Scrooge

Douglas A. Bass

No part of this publication may be reproduced in whole or in part, or stored in a retrieval system, or transmitted in any form or by any means, electronic, mechanical, photocopying, or otherwise, without the written permission of the publisher. Requests for permission to make copies of any part of this book should be submitted online at:

ebenezerbook2017@gmail.com

This book is a work of fiction. Names, characters, businesses, organizations, places, events, and incidents either are the product of the author's imagination or are used fictitiously. Any resemblance to actual persons, living or dead, events, or locales is entirely coincidental.

Paperback Edition ISBN-13: 978-0-9990231-0-5

Kindle Edition ISBN-13: 978-0-9990231-1-2

Hardcover Edition ISBN-13: 978-0-9990231-2-9

Copyright © 2017 Douglas A. Bass

All rights reserved.

Library of Congress Control Number: 2017908610

Published by MIM Publishing

Cover artwork by Salvatore DiVincenzo

Printed in USA

For Sheila.

My love. My life.
Without whom this novel could never be, nor could I.

CONTENTS

Prologue — i

Part I: Before the Spirits — vi

Part II: Visits from the Spirits — 254

Part III: After the Spirits — 327

Epilogue — 377

PROLOGUE

I am quite an old man. Quite old and quite ill. It is possible that I have seen my last sunrise and my last sunset. All that my life was meant to be or not meant to be has been. This bedchamber is likely to be my last earthly shell, as it is now more likely that I will visit the other side of eternity than the hallway just outside my door before the new dawn arrives.

Don't be sad; I see the woe in your eyes and written within the crevasses of your forehead. I am not. Sad, that is. I have lived a good life. A good, long life. A great deal longer than anyone thought I would when I was a mere, undersized, crippled lad. I am certain that the undertaker peered in my window on more than one occasion to see if there he would find a crutch without an owner. The gravedigger had his shovel at the ready. The stonemason awaited the word so that he may chisel in the date of my surely inevitable demise.

Had it not been for the efforts and attention of one reformed sinner, one wretched soul that broke free from his self-forged manacles, I likely would have satisfied all of those who expected my early exit from this mortal coil. Had one man not defied the odds and overcome a greater threat to his existence than even I myself was facing, a coffin that could have been fashioned from a mere sapling would have assuredly cradled me as my final resting place long, long ago. Had he not allowed the miracle – and yes! there is surely no other word to describe it – to transform his essence, his very being, why, we would not be having this conversation right now.

No, there is no reason for you to call for the nurse. Please, do not seek her. I need no medication. I am quite lucid. In fact, I see the world more clearly now than perhaps I ever have. I see you more clearly than even you see yourself. I see the fear in your eyes. I know not whether it is for me due to where I shall soon be going, or if it is for you due to where you shall be remaining.

And so I shall tell you why I have summoned you here. Why I have asked for you, and specifically you, to come to my bedside before I breathe my last. I possess within this ancient frame a story that must be told. In point of fact, it is a story that has already been told and told quite well. It is a story that inspired many. A story that touched more. A story that continues to reach out to the world and embrace all newcomers with its wondrous tale. So why must I tell you a story already told?

Because it is time for the world to know the truth.

Yes, the fanciful yarn that is now within the public consciousness is a lovely one. And, yes, there are facets, indeed a great many, that are true to the actual events. But to understand greatness, one must deconstruct the caricature and discover the man hidden beneath.

Why?

Because only by recognizing that this man lived, he breathed, he loved, he had pain – oh, yes, so much pain – just like all of us, can we look to him as an example of what we, ourselves, can achieve. If he is a mythical creature, an archetype, as he now exists in the public mind, transformed from miser to magnificent in a wonderful fiction, we cannot touch what he achieved. We can only look at it from afar. We can marvel at it, yes, but he remains out of reach.

He should not remain so. He should be with all of us, showing us that greatness can come to any one of us at any time. It is just a matter of opening one's eyes and one's heart. Just as he did. Just as we all can.

Of course, by now I am sure you realize who the man is to whom I refer. I speak of my dear Uncle, passed these many years. I think of him often. And you may think me mad, or may attribute it to a decaying mind, but of late I have seen him. We have spoken, sure as I am speaking with you right now. It was he who charged me with the solemn duty to reveal what he had recounted while he lay upon his own deathbed and I sat where you sit now. It was he who I know was present when I first did so at the sainted man's funeral. And it was he who just last eve told me it was time to correct that which is incorrect, to make clear what is now opaque, to bring the truth to all with ears willing to hear so that his message can shine through with no distractions.

What is that message, you say?

It is never too late. It is *never* too late. Until we are gone and regrets are all that remain in our wake. Don't worry if you steer your ship into rocky shoals. It is the escape from same that makes all the difference. And there is always, always, always an escape back to the deep, calm, peaceful seas from whence we came and where we are all destined to go. If we are willing to make the choice to go there. And we can all make that choice.

So if knowing the truth, rather than the fantastic tale we have been told, will bring us to this all important realization, why did I not right the wrong when it was first released to the world? Why have I not since then come forward with what I know to be so instead of allowing the fanciful fiction to take root in the minds of the people all around the globe?

It is quite simple.

I saw all the good it was doing, even in its abridged form. Even in its inaccurate form. Almost immediately, it captured the hearts of all who were privileged enough to read it or have it related to them. The version of my Uncle's tale that swept the world gave joy and hope, and transformed the season. Why, I dare say the yuletide as I have seen it with my own eyes since the time of its publication mirrors the one I visualized as I read those words, almost as if the imaginary world of one man's mind poured out from those written pages and splashed upon our reality in vivid color and dynamism. And for that, I was very grateful! The story of my uncle's life, distorted as it may have been, was bringing a blessing to the world in a manner I concluded he would have been pleased to see.

So I remained silent.

But no more. My Uncle sees what lies ahead for us on the earthly plain and he shudders. He will not tell me more, but surely you can sense the change in the air. The world's governments are taking sides. Are arming with new weapons of death. Are taking us to the precipice of potentially the most devastating conflagration ever seen.

Hope is needed. The retelling of an old tale won't bring it. Believing that the amazing transformation of his heart only occurred because he was somehow special, or different, or a myth certainly won't bring it. Only by recognizing that hope is within the grasp of each and every one of us can we recapture the magic. Only by hearing the truth can we be saved.

What is the truth?

It is as I have said. He lived. He was not a gargoyle on a church. He was actually quite a hopeful child. And loving. And in need of love. Are any of us so different?

Some of what was presented about him was true. Yes, he had a beloved sister, but no, she was not the younger of the siblings. He had a true love, and yes, he lost her, but cannot lost love ever be found? He did have an all-consuming greed and need, but has the world really been given the opportunity to see what would truly sate that hunger and slake that thirst? And, indeed, he was vexed by the Christmas season, but does anyone truly understand what he meant when he denigrated something as a "humbug"?

I can see in your countenance what you are most desirous to discover. Was he really visited? Was he really taken on a journey through space and time? Did the Spirits really exist? I will tell you. I will tell you so that you know all. So that you can share all you learn.

Yes. Yes, my boy. *Yes.*

But that answer is too simple. It is not as you have come to believe. It is far more wonderful. In my estimation, it is far more indeed! What he saw, what he learned, ah so much more!

I will confess that I have always been puzzled that after hearing the tale as it has been presented no one has questioned why such a person as he would reform his life so thoroughly based upon what it is said he experienced. We are told he is an unremitting, greedy, grasping miser who cares for no one and nothing except from where the next shilling lining his pocket was to come. We are also led to believe he has nothing but contempt for the rest of society, whom he sees as parasites and obstacles. If so, why would such a person feel dismay upon learning that such contemptible beings cared nothing for him, and even rejoiced, upon learning of his death? Would this not confirm his loathing for these inferior insects? Instead, we are expected to accept that he was devastated by this revelation. Nonsense!

Furthermore, in the story we have all come to embrace, my dear Uncle seems unaware that death awaits all of us if we travel far enough into our future. Foolishness! He breaks down in tears, promising not to be the man he was upon seeing his own grave? Why such poppycock? He was a very intelligent man and he knew of mortality. Of course he did! Imagine if this tale were of a man we were led to believe was a saint his entire life. At the end of his journey, would he not also be shown a gravestone with his name on it by a spirit of things yet to come? Or are we to believe that a man's good deeds bless him with immortality? Utter rubbish!

In addition, while we are on the subject, what would his travels to the past have accomplished had the good author been accurate in his retelling? We see a lonely young boy, a happy young apprenticed gentleman, and a foolish fiancé. Yes, upon reflection, one could describe him in these terms as a broad summation of select vignettes of his life. But how would recounting such episodes alter the man? What would spur a rational being to wholesale change based upon the scenes of his life we are told he was shown? I say, nothing. I repeat: Nothing!

I would be remiss if I did not address the false narrative regarding the impact I played in my Uncle's reformation. We are to believe that he simply saw my small, crippled frame and his heart melted like icicles from an eave on an unusually warm day. And after we have already been shown his utter contempt for young people, no older than I, playing in the streets or singing seasonal carols. Are we to believe my Uncle had a tenderness for the ill and infirmed? After we were told that he wished the unfortunate of society should die and decrease the surplus population?

Ah, but you are saying, it was not that I was ill, but that I was surely to die before the calendar once again brought us to the twenty-fifth of December, one year hence. Again, I say, would the man as described by the good author really have cared? We are to believe that his foundation was shaken and utterly in tumult. I submit that the man described in the early pages of that publication would see my impending departure from among the living as an economic boon for my family in that my father's meager resources would be now spread among a fewer number of mouths to feed.

Contradict me, an old man lying on his deathbed, if you dare! Tell me I have not more accurately described a more consistent reaction for the monster painted at the outset of the novella with which we are all familiar. No? I thought not.

So how will the tale I am about to relate be different and, consequently, inspire the hope our world so desperately needs? I intend to show you who my Uncle was, who he really was. You will see why his life took the course it did. You will understand what he needed to make a course correction through the storm of his own creation. You will be given the gift of knowing exactly what he was actually shown on that fateful night in his sixty-fifth year of life. You will know why such visits were necessary and what they taught him. And why, but for this miracle, he could learn no other way.

So listen carefully, my child, as I speak my last. This is why I have summoned you here tonight. I charge you as my successor in this noble privilege of reintroducing the world to this great man. Hear my tale. Record it. Present it as you best see fit when I am gone. And whenever you revisit it, always know that as I entrusted you with this privilege, my heart was filled with love for you.

Let us begin…

As spoken by Timothy Robert Cratchit to his grandson, George Ebenezer Cratchit, on the night of his passing, 11 July 1913.

PART I

BEFORE THE SPIRITS

1

On the twenty-fifth of December, in the year of our Lord seventeen hundred and seventy-eight, a light snow fell outside the windows of the Scrooge family home. Calm and serene, the very portrait of a beautiful Christmas morning in the English countryside. But within those walls it was anything but calm. Tense, anticipating anxiety shrouded the house as Elias Scrooge paced the hallway, awaiting the arrival of his second child into this world.

Following at his heels was five-year-old Nancy. She was dressed in her fine white nightgown and held tight to her baby doll that her mother had made for her. Even at this tender age, she was always interested in presenting herself as neatly and properly as possible. For this reason, her father affectionately dubbed her "Fancy Nancy", which was usually shortened to "Fan". Everyone, her friends, her family, all had taken to calling her Fan. She was very proud of the moniker her daddy had placed upon her.

Now she was trailing her father up and down the hallway as she watched him chew his fingernails down to the nubs. She had never seen him behave thusly. Elias Scrooge was always a sensible man and always in control of his faculties. But something about today was making him act in a most peculiar fashion.

Elias prided himself on his prudence. He was a successful businessman, not wealthy, but comfortably supporting his young family. His home was spacious and his land ample. His wife and daughter always had the finest to wear and never feared going hungry. He had the respect of those he worked with, those he worked against, and those who worked for him. By all accounts, he had made good in this world.

True, not all was ideal at this moment in time. Elias' trade interests with the American colonies were being threatened by the current rebellion being waged on those distant shores. He was certain it was just a matter of time before such nonsense was squashed and he could return to his normal practices with his normal trade partners. For the time being, he shifted his interests so that he was participating in supplying the noble Redcoats who were forced to sail so far from home to maintain the integrity of His Majesty's realm. How insolent, those colonists, was his considered opinion. To think that individuals privileged enough to be born under the umbrella of the greatest empire the world had ever seen would perpetrate such violence against our good King George and take aim at his crown. Was it not enough that there seemed to be endless conflicts on the Continent that kept our young men busy at war? Must we contend with internal strife as well? It all seemed so uncivilized to Elias.

Christmas was always a special time in the Scrooge home. His dear Elizabeth, who was now on the other side of his bedroom door with the midwife and her sister, Nancy, after whom Fan was named, always took special pride in adorning the home in holiday splendor at this time of year. Everywhere he looked was awash in red and green. And the feast, oh the feast, that would await them on Christmas night was a meal that made Elias' mouth water in anticipation for an entire month as soon as the calendar turned from November to December. His was truly a blessed life, he was aware, but it was never as obvious and evident as at Christmas.

And now, Christmas was about to become even more special to the Scrooges because they were about to be given the greatest of gifts one can receive on this glorious day. They were about to welcome a new baby into the home. Fan was about to get the baby brother or sister she had been asking for ever since she was three years old. Elias and Elizabeth were about to have a new bouncing bundle of joy to fill their home with more love.

And there was a great deal of love in that home, to be sure. Elias and Elizabeth met at a Christmas party hosted by her father in her family's home. Elias had been invited by Elizabeth's brother, Christopher, with whom Elias had some business dealings which led to their friendship. He could always remember the moment the bolt of lightning struck him and Cupid's arrow pierced his virgin heart. The music was playing and Elizabeth was dancing merrily. He looked up and their eyes met. She too felt the electricity and she could not avert her gaze. As a result, her concentration faltered for a moment, her feet got tangled up with the gentleman with whom she was dancing, and she ended up sprawling to the ground in a most unladylike fashion. Elias ran to her side to see if she was injured. Elizabeth looked deeply into his eyes and assured him that, other than her pride, she was perfectly well as she tried to hide her embarrassment. He smiled at her and reached out his hand to assist her in arising. From that moment to this one, they have been as necessary to each other's existence as the very air we breathe and the food we consume. After six months of courting, Elias asked for and received permission to make Elizabeth his bride. That was seven years ago.

The home became more filled with love when young Nancy Elizabeth Scrooge was born just two years later. She had her father wrapped around her little finger from the moment he came into the room and laid eyes on her. He could not believe how much luck the good Lord had blessed him with. Two beautiful women with whom to be madly in love. And he was surely that. He always maintained a soft spot for his lovely Elizabeth and his Fancy Nancy. They could do no wrong in his eyes. And nothing brought out his ferocious side as when he thought either of them were threatened in any way. Woe be to the man who hurt his precious ladies. Woe indeed!

And so as he paced outside of that same bedroom door where Fan had entered the world five years earlier, his shoes clicking on the hardwood floor and echoing throughout the hallway, he could not wait to meet the newest member of the Scrooge family. Each scream that he heard emanate from behind those walls made the muscles in his stomach tighten in both excitement and sympathy. He knew that Original Sin compelled that the arrival of a child be accompanied by these necessary sounds, but he ached each time he heard the evidence that his sweet Elizabeth was in pain.

When the sounds became more frequent, Elias knew that the time was fast approaching. He glanced down at his little Fan and saw the confusion in her eyes, wondering if her mummy was okay. He had to step aside from his own emotions to reassure his little girl that all was well and soon would be even better. Soon Mummy would present us with a Christmas gift that we would never forget.

A new baby would soon be here!

2

"Almost there, sweetie," Elias heard through the walls from the reassuring voice of Sally, the midwife.

"Just squeeze my hand tighter," came the disembodied voice of Nancy a moment later. "You're doing splendidly."

Still the screams of pain continued, interspersed with the sounds of grunting and panting. Was it this bad when Fan entered the world?, Elias wondered to himself. He thought not.

"Bear down, lovie. I can see the head. Looks like you are going to have another ginger in the family. Bear down. Now, push, sweetie, push! My, there's a lot of blood. Nancy, love, be a lamb and fetch more towels." The sound of feet rushing back and forth through the next room wafted through the doorframe.

"That's good. That's very good, Elizabeth. The baby is almost here."

Suddenly there was a change in the air.

"Something's wrong! Something's wrong!" It was Elizabeth. Her voice was panicked.

"Mummy?" said Fan, and she burst out into tears.

Elias bent down on one knee and placed his hand gently on Fan's wet face. Although he was just as frightened as she after hearing his wife's alarmed cry, he knew to be strong for his beloved daughter.

"Fan," – More cries, "Oh no, oh no, oh no!" emanating from the next room – "all is well. I know it sounds frightening, but this is quite normal. All *is* well. It shall all be over soon." As he spoke, Elias motioned behind Fan's back with his free hand for his servant, James, to fetch her and take her away.

"Fan, go with James. He will bring you to the dining room and will give you something sweet to eat," said Elias, barely able to contain his own panic, but keeping his voice steady nonetheless.

James led Fan away, down the staircase, and Elias turned his attention to the closed door behind which lay his precious Elizabeth. He knew she did not cry out thusly when Fan was born. She cried out, yes, but not in fear. Not with a conviction of doom. Not as now.

Elias turned and reached for the doorknob.

"Elizabeth," Nancy cooed, "all is well."

It froze Elias momentarily and his blood ran cold to hear his sister-in-law repeat the same words he had just spoken to Fan because he knew he did not truly believe his own statement and it was based on nothing more than fervent hope. He suspected the same was true of Nancy's words.

"The head is out! One more push should do it, sweetie. Come now. You can do it!" said Sally.

"You can do it," encouraged Nancy.

As Elizabeth squeezed the muscles of her abdomen in a final push, Elias turned the knob and entered the bedchamber. What he saw terrified him to his very soul.

Elizabeth was on her back, unmoving and unspeaking, her skin pallid as a corpse, her head tossed back upon the pillows behind her. Sally was holding the new child, but all Elias could focus on were her hands. Her blood-soaked, red hands. It was as if she had plunged them into a bucket of crimson paint. They were not merely wet, but were coated and dripping.

Elias rushed to Elizabeth's side. She was breathing, but barely. Her pulse felt faint to his touch. Her skin cold and clammy.

Chaos reigned within the room, although everything surrounding Elias and Elizabeth appeared to occur in a world where time has been reduced to a speed one thousand times slower than is normal. Elias was vaguely aware that Nancy was rushing to the door to find someone to summon a doctor. He could hear from what seemed like the end of a tunnel miles away the cries of a newborn, but the sound did not register as coherent within his brain. The bedsheets were soaked in blood, which now smeared Elias' coat and trousers.

But within that bubble in which existed only Elias and his Elizabeth, they seemed insulated from the exterior world. Elias kissed the back of Elizabeth's hand that he was clutching so tightly with both of his own. With that, she stirred and looked up at him. Her countenance was one of peace.

She smiled.

"Bring me our child, Elias," Elizabeth spoke in barely a whisper.

Elias' eyes were as wide as saucers. His heart pounded within his chest. Unthinking, his head nodded back and forth upon his neck. He looked over to Sally and motioned for her to bring the babe.

Sally complied and when she reached Elizabeth, she put the child in his mother's arms, but kept her hand behind the child's head to keep him safe and steady.

"Oh, look Elias," said Elizabeth sweetly. "We have a boy." She squeezed her son to her breast with as much strength as she could muster, which was but a pittance.

Elias looked to his child for the first time and saw his angelic face. Staring back at him -- unquestionably and undeniably -- were Elizabeth's clear, blue eyes.

Elias looked back to Elizabeth.

"What shall we name him?" she whispered.

"I-I do not know," Elias stammered, as tears he fought with all of his being began to well within his eyes.

"Let me look at him and perhaps he shall tell us," escaped from Elizabeth's lips. Elias looked to Sally, still holding the boy's head, and she moved the baby so that he was now face to face with his mum.

Elizabeth smiled.

"Ebenezer," she said, continuing to smile. "His soul tells me his name is Ebenezer."

"All right, then, my love. Ebenezer it is," said Elias, still only looking at Elizabeth and not at the boy.

"Young Ebenezer needs another name to go along with it, befitting the great man that he will grow to be," said Elizabeth, her eyelids now clearly becoming too heavy to remain fully opened. "What is your middle name, my strong little man?" she asked Ebenezer.

Ebenezer let out a little sigh and locked eyes with his mother.

"Aldustous. Our child's name is Ebenezer Aldustous Scrooge. A fine name," Elizabeth spoke almost inaudibly, but proudly.

"Yes, a fine name," said Elias weakly.

"A fine name," repeated Sally softly, as she stepped back to give the family an intimacy she sensed would not come again.

"Hold your boy, Elias. Hold your Ebenezer," urged an almost silent Elizabeth. "I entrust him to your arms."

Elias, wishing to please his wife, turned his attention to the small, naked being laying upon Elizabeth's chest. He picked up the child in his hands, with his left hand under the boy's bottom and his right behind the boy's neck and head. Elias stared at Ebenezer for a long moment. Ebenezer's eyes met his father's and they stared at one another, transfixed in each other's gaze.

Elias felt a pang within his core and looked away, turning his attention back to Elizabeth in the bed.

"My dear—," he began. But then he realized. Elizabeth's eyes, while slightly open, were no longer seeing. Her nightclothes were no longer slowly rising and falling upon her chest. Her final moments had passed. Her last sight was of her two men -- her two Scrooge men -- looking each other in the eye. There was the trace of a smile upon her pale, cold lips.

Elias did not see Elizabeth slip from the here to the hereafter. He did not kiss her one final time. He did not express his love for her as their parting words. Instead he was looking at a baby. A stranger to his home and his life. One who was supposed to usher in the greatest joy, but instead ushered in the greatest pain.

Suddenly, Elias could no longer bring himself to touch the child.

"Take him!" he demanded of Sally. She did so.

"Elizabeth! My dear, dear Elizabeth!" Elias wailed, as he embraced her now still body and shook with sobs.

Sally came back over and placed her hand on Elias' shoulder.

"Mr. Scrooge, my deepest and most sorrowful condolences."

"Go, and leave me," he growled. "And take *that* with you as you exit."

"Mr. Scrooge," said Sally, slightly taken aback despite her understanding of his grief. "It is time to let God have what He has chosen to take for Himself, and for you to care for your children, whom He has chosen for you."

"I said leave me! I care nothing for a God, nor a child, that robs me of my love!" spat Elias, still holding Elizabeth with both arms.

"Mr. Scrooge!" gasped Sally. "Such blasphemy will not render Elizabeth's soul more at peace and such vitriol toward your son is inexcusable!"

"Elizabeth was my sun!" cried Elias. "And my moon! And my stars! Oh, Elizabeth, why do you leave me now?!"

Nancy returned to the doorway of the room, out of breath after having rushed to send for the doctor. She saw the scene before her, and began to weep softly. She slowly entered and walked towards Elias and Elizabeth, still locked in their final embrace.

"Oh, Elias," said Nancy. "We have lost our dear Elizabeth. There shall never be another like her."

"No," whispered Elias. "There shall never be."

He finally released his wife and lay her in a comfortable position on the bed. He and Nancy stood, staring at her and weeping. Their attention was so focused on Elizabeth's body that they did not hear Fan enter the room.

"Is Mummy with God now?" she asked softly from beneath the doorframe.

Elias and Nancy spun around upon hearing the young voice. They watched as Fan slowly walked towards her mother, but she did not cry. She leaned in and kissed her mother's forehead and made an observation.

"Mummy is smiling. She must be happy in Heaven."

Elias and Nancy looked at each other in surprise, not knowing exactly what to do with the unexpectedly stoic little girl before them.

They watched as she walked over to Sally, still in the back of the room, holding the baby in her arms.

Fan looked at him and then peered up at Sally.

"What is his name?"

"It is Ebenezer, little miss. He is your new brother."

Fan examined Ebenezer with her eyes, slowly looking him up and down. Ebenezer stared right back at his big sister. Fan put her hand gently on Ebenezer's forehead and leaned in to him.

"I am your sister, Nancy Elizabeth Scrooge, but you may call me Fan. I shall love you all the days of my life. We do not have a Mummy, but you will always have me. I swear it."

With that, Ebenezer closed his eyes and fell into a peaceful sleep.

And that is how Ebenezer Scrooge entered this world.

3

An outside observer could be excused if he mistook Ebenezer for an orphan in his early years, such was the time spent with and affection given to the young boy by his one remaining parent. The Scrooge family was split in a regretful, rueful dichotomy. On the one side was Elias, a doleful man who could no longer focus his attention or energies on much other than his own pain and who found the rare elusive smile only when elicited by his beloved daughter. On the other was Ebenezer, the very epitome of youthful exuberance and hopefulness – an angelic vision with eyes as blue as the ocean after a storm and hair the ruddy color of a sunset sky on a crisp autumn eve – who's basic needs such as feeding, bathing and clothing were met by the hired servants of the house. And, of course, by his doting sister. Fan was always keeping her watchful eye over her little brother, acting more mother than sister despite being a mere five years his senior.

Elias could not accept the loss of his dear, sweet Elizabeth. With each passing day, he became more withdrawn. He often would not come to the table for his meals, preferring instead to lay in his bed, now far too large and empty. On many such occasions, young Fan would entreat the servants to assist her in bringing up trays of food to him so that the two of them could have an intimate sup together. Even when his appetite would not stir within him, and even when his mournful eyes simply wished to gaze blindly into the abyss, Elias could never refuse his Fan.

Except with regard to one topic and one topic alone.

Ebenezer.

Elias could not stand the sight of the boy. Could not stomach the odor of his skin. Could not tolerate the sound of his cries. Could not – never – look the boy in the eyes.

Whenever Fan would carry her brother near her father, Elias would snap at her to remove the child from his presence. Whenever Fan would attempt to discuss Ebenezer with her father, Elias told her to purse her insolent lips shut and not to expel any further air that carried the child's name upon it. Whenever Fan would come to embrace her father after she had been with the boy, Elias would demand she wash herself thoroughly to rid herself of the stench that he swore emanated from her very pores after having been infected with Ebenezer's touch.

These were the only times Elias ever said a cross word to his Fan. The *only* times.

But regardless of how bitter Elias had become when it came to Ebenezer, Fan never gave up hope. She believed that she could bridge the chasm of affection that existed between the two, and that someday her father would relent and allow the child into his heart, as had all others who had encountered the boy. Her efforts would continue throughout Ebenezer's entire childhood.

The gloomy transformation within Elias' nature at home, sadly, also translated into his business persona as well. Whereas he was once known as steady and reliable, after Elizabeth's passing he was quite the opposite. He could no longer concentrate on the needs of his enterprise and profits began to diminish. Relationships he had spent years forging and reinforcing began to suffer. Decisions once considered simple and routine became too difficult for him to fathom. And his ability to tolerate even the slightest interruption when he was thinking of his lost Elizabeth, which was a considerable percentage of the time, led him to dismiss worthy and valuable fellows in his employ, all to the further detriment and deterioration of his business – his sole means of supporting his family and funding his household.

Furthering his descent was the bottle. Rather than coming home directly after a day spent at his office, Elias began making detours into the local pubs. The pint and the tumbler became the new cloisters in which he attempted to find solace and relief from the endless, crushing misery that was life without Elizabeth.

It was not long before he came to rely upon spirits to get him through each day. The time he spent working his trade and the time he spent drowning his sorrows began to invert, until entire days would go by when the seat behind the desk in his office would remain empty. Despite perching on a stool at a bar for endless hours surrounded by countless others coming into and out of his field of vision, Elias was withdrawing further and further into his solitude.

Before long, his drinking followed him home as well. He was not a mean drunk; merely a sentimental one. He would spend many hours with a glass in one hand and a small portrait of his late wife that he had drawn of her during their courtship in the other.

Yes, Elias was quite the artist in his day, a skill his father discouraged because he saw no practical value in "idling away scribbling worthless pictures like a degenerate Bohemian gypsy". Despite his father's disapproval, Elias secretly continued his artistic pursuits for no other reason than something deep within him told him he must do so. It was as if the art within was tangible even before he put paint-soaked brush to canvas and it demanded to live. Even Elias himself could not explain this to his own satisfaction.

Elizabeth discovered the particular drawing he now used as a focal point during his inebriations quite by accident. He had been moved by a perfect day spent between the two of them to draw her face and her form after he retired to his own residence. He took more care with this particular illustration than any he had ever in his life before or since. He slept not a wink that night as he remained hard at work to preserve not just her image, but her essence, and with it the pure joy that enveloped him spending such effortless hours with her in the hours prior.

With one final soft stroke of his wrist, the whiskers at the tip of Elias' brush gently caressed the delicate cheek of his one true love recreated upon the small canvas before him. Elias leaned back, mesmerized by the visage staring back at him. After an eternity encapsulated within but a moment, his senses returned to the present whereupon he looked about and realized that the sun had already arisen while he had never retired. One look at his pocket watch, crafted into existence by the great Thomas Mudge himself, alerted him to the lateness of the hour. He hastily swept all of the necessary papers strewn upon his desk into his portfolio and his new creation was inadvertently included among them. He did not know this, and there it remained until his next encounter with his lovely Elizabeth.

When they next met, he arrived directly from his workplace. He had the aforementioned portfolio with him. Upon his arrival in her home after calling upon Elizabeth, her father had some business matters he wished to discuss with young Elias, as her father respected his mind and his candor. Elias placed his portfolio along with his overcoat upon a settee, excused himself from Elizabeth, and joined her father in the study. Elizabeth, fearing that Elias' coat was about to fall to the ground based on its precarious position on the piece of furniture, lifted it. When she did, the arm of his coat brushed the portfolio, causing it to spill its contents upon the floor. Elizabeth quickly bent to replace all of Elias' important papers from whence they came when she came across the portrait.

She was stunned at its beauty and moved by its passion. Elizabeth was instantly convinced that had Elias not devoted his ample intellect to industry, he could have surely been counted among one of the great masters of the artistic realm. Tears came to her eyes as she stood admiring her likeness when Elias returned to the room.

When he saw what she was holding, his first instinct was to snatch it from her possession. His father's disapproval was so ever-present in his mind that Elizabeth's discovery brought panic and shame and a flush to his cheeks. He had never shared his artwork with anyone since being admonished by his father, nor had he ever intended to. He feared her reaction.

He took a step towards her, but quickly stopped himself. She brought the picture down from before her now weeping eyes and looked at him with such a tenderness, his fears melted away.

"Did you create this exquisitely beautiful portrait?" she asked him.

"I did," he replied simply.

"I never knew you could bring something so magnificent into existence by your hand," she said, tears still cascading from her eyes.

"It was your parents who brought the something magnificent into existence," he said. "You say that you find it exquisitely beautiful. That is because you are looking at a true likeness of yourself."

"Why did you produce this splendid image?" Elizabeth asked.

"Because I was moved to do so after our last encounter. By my love for you. I love you, Elizabeth."

"I love you, as well, my darling Elias."

That was the first time the two had ever expressed their love for one another. And it was this interaction that Elias thought of as he stared at the now slightly-faded portrait of his dearly departed love when he lost himself in the drink.

4

Had it not been for Fan, Ebenezer's young childhood would have been an entirely sad and lonely one. As early as he was able to perceive, Ebenezer was acutely aware that his father held no tenderness in his heart for him. He was likewise aware that all of his basic needs were being tended to by those who were in his father's employ and he was simply one more task to complete in furtherance of receiving their monthly wage.

But Fan, oh Fan, she adored little Ebenezer right from the start. When he was an infant, she loved to feed him, to pat his back until he produced his necessary gaseous emanations that she called his "blips", and to dress him in his tiny outfits. But above all, she loved to bathe him. When complete, she loved to wrap his clean, wet, naked body in a soft towel and to breathe in his fresh aroma. To Fan, there was no scent so sweet as that of the pate of her little brother's head after a washing.

Elias' antipathy towards the boy vexed Fan terribly. When Ebenezer took his first steps, Elias was nowhere to be found. When he looked up at his father with hands outstretched, Elias simply turned or walked away. It is no wonder that after hearing his father speak it so often when his voice was directed in Ebenezer's direction, that his first word was, "no". Of course, Elias was not present to hear the utterance. And when told of it, he simply sneered and asked the servant who reported the milestone to reserve her voice for matters of importance in the house.

As he aged, Fan took great pleasure in observing as Ebenezer developed his own particular idiosyncrasies. She delighted in watching as he crawled in his own most peculiar way. He would lean upon his right forearm, which was firmly planted on the ground. He would then extend his right elbow in the direction he wished to go, he would lunge forward with that elbow and use his trailing left hand to push him along, dragging the rest of his small body behind. It took the longest time for him to learn to prop himself up upon his hands and knees to crawl. No, for months, it was thump-push-drag. Thump-push-drag. No matter how much Fan tried to encourage him to push up on those hands, Ebenezer was ever moving through life with a thump-push-drag.

From the earliest age, Ebenezer's eyes were very alert. He had a look about him that Fan knew was great intelligence. Fan could almost see in him that he was absorbing the world like a sponge to water and bringing all outside stimuli into his mind, where his surely advanced brain was working out the mysteries of this existence.

Fan took particular notice that Ebenezer's wide cerulean eyes lit up when could be heard from another room of the house his father absent-mindedly humming or whistling a tune composed by J.S. Bach or, his favorite, Joseph Haydn. Fan despaired that Father was so stubborn in his steadfast refusal to accept Ebenezer into the bosom of his affections. The two clearly shared a love of the same music, and it is exactly this kind of connection that Fan always desired to bring to her father's consciousness, but always to no avail.

As Ebenezer aged further, he charmed his big sister with his ability to learn with such ease the games that she taught him. When old enough to cease placing the pieces in his mouth, he began to play rudimentary matches of draughts, backgammon and fox and geese with Fan. It was not long before he was acquiring the basic knowledge of chess and he had a particular fascination with dominos. Out in the open air, Fan and Ebenezer were overjoyed in their games of hopscotch and Fan was amazed at how proficient Ebenezer quickly became at ball-in-cup. When he was older still, he took a liking to shuttlecock, more so than tennis, and he had an agile mind when putting together even Fan's most complex jigsaw puzzles. They spent hours trying to outmaneuver each other in Fan's board game, "A Journey Through Europe". Fan made sure that, even though Father would not see to it, Ebenezer would have a happy youth.

As much fun as the other games were, the one thing that Ebenezer loved above all else was climbing the trees in the family orchard. Why, he could scramble up the trunk and scamper so high in the branches, that it was not long before Fan could not keep up. He loved the feeling of freedom that standing upon a high bough with the wind blowing through his fine, coppery hair and looking upon the world from his lofty vantage would always bring. Ebenezer would often perch himself just out of his sister's reach when they were engaged in a round of hide-and-seek. He clapped and laughed when Fan would spot him but would be unable to touch his garment, thus preventing her from being declared the winner. Eventually, she would have to yield and give him the chance to locate her, a task at which he was usually more successful than she. Fan never tired of

Ebenezer's antics and never resented losing at games she taught him to play. They truly had a marvelous relationship and Fan was convinced that God Himself had brought them together so that they may experience the grandeur of love from the outset of life.

As happy as Fan worked to make Ebenezer feel, he still felt the sting of the absence of their father's affection for him. Ebenezer observed, often through the crack in an open doorway, Elias embrace Fan, discuss matters of importance to Fan with her, and to simply look at her with a loving eye that Ebenezer never once saw Elias cast in his direction. Ebenezer tried to ignore the pain in his heart that these moments would cause, but as a youth he had no means by which to cope with his rejection. He sometimes tried to find the attention he did not receive by his own father in the other adults in his life; the servants who attended to him. But he soon found that once the workday was done, the doors of those who lived with the Scrooges in the home would remain closed and locked when young Ebenezer would rap upon them seeking some adult emotional contact that was not premised upon the promise of a wage. He never found such.

Somewhere deep within, Ebenezer had a faint memory of a woman who bore a striking resemblance to Fan visiting the home and looking upon him with a smile. But as time passed, this visage grew more and more dim within his memory, until he was convinced that this was but a wonderful dream remembered. An illusion without substance, despite its deep, stirring significance.

Ebenezer most desired the reassuring embrace of a loving adult when the rains would come, accompanied by thunder and lightning. He had an irrational dread of the clap of a thunder stroke followed by the flash of light, which cast all of his surroundings into shadows of the most frightful and malevolent shapes. During the daylight hours, he could contain his dread, but when such a storm would arrive after dark, he had no inner strength to combat his woe. Fortunately, he had his Fan.

She learned early about Ebenezer's terror of a nighttime thunderstorm. She tried many things to calm him, to slow the rapid beating of his heart, to dry the cold perspiration upon his upper brow. Nothing worked until Fan recalled a song that their mother was fond of singing to Fan as she lay in her bed when sleep would not come. The first time Fan sang this old Celtic tune to Ebenezer, he instantly relaxed, as though mother were there herself, stroking his hair and warming his soul with her reassuring smile. Forever after, when the storm would strike, Ebenezer craved Elizabeth's song, that Fan told him was entitled, "A Mother's Prayer". It went thusly:

'Twas the night and the light
From every little star
Shone so bright at the height
Of their homes so way afar.

Now that the rain o'er the plain
Has ceased in its descent
And the sight of the night
To mine eyes is heaven sent.

The air so clear, my dear
The cool breeze upon my cheek
Free from fear, peace is near
And hope is at its peak.

Trust in Me, trust in Me
All your lives are in My hands
And you'll see that you're free
If love reigns throughout your lands.

From the lea to the sea
When all is said and done
I love each of thee, said He
God bless us, everyone.

I love each of thee, said He
God Bless Us, Everyone.

Sometimes, Ebenezer would ask Fan to sing the song a second time. She always accommodated. By the time she was complete, his pulse had returned to its normal rate, his face was calm and relaxed once more, and often he was gently dozing, oblivious to the raging tempest that had caused him so much fret just shortly before.

5

As it has been true of children throughout the ages, if they do not receive the positive attention they crave from an emotionally absent parent, they will do what is necessary to elicit the only other type of attention that is possible. Ebenezer was no different. There were times when his young mind could not accept being ignored by his father. Despite the love and attention showered upon him by his beloved Fan, it was not always enough. There is a primal need within all of us to be accepted and loved by our sire. When that need is not met, even a harsh word can be preferable to no words at all.

The summer of seventeen hundred and eighty-three, later to be known as the "Sand Summer", was particularly hot. In addition, by late June, a thick fog was reported in British waters such that boats had to stay moored in port as they were unable to navigate. The Scrooges observed that the sun appeared blood-colored by day instead of donning its usual shade.

This uncomfortable outer environment, coupled with Ebenezer's uncomfortable inner environment, were just the combustible ingredients necessary for an imminent explosion. And something about that summer lit the fuse within Ebenezer to this end. But each time, believing she was shielding her little brother from trouble, Fan was there to douse the flames of Elias' anger.

On one occasion, Ebenezer interrupted a business meeting Elias was conducting in the parlor. Elias made it clear to all in the house that this meeting was of the utmost importance and that any interruption would be met with harsh and swift retribution. During a particularly tense moment in the proceedings, Ebenezer burst in the room doing his impression of a bird of prey. An especially loud bird of prey at that.

With a red face and seething anger, Elias grabbed Ebenezer under the arm and led him away, dragging him with such force that Ebenezer's feet barely touched the ground on the way out of the room. Once outside the company of his colleagues, Elias glared down at his son, but was so angry he was at a loss for words.

Just as his voice was about to resurface, Fan flew into his field of vision crying, "Father! Father! Please do not be cross with Ebenezer. It was I who was to blame for his actions!"

Elias looked up at Fan in astonishment. He blinked.

"Pardon?" he asked.

"Yes, Father," Fan said as she reached Elias, out of breath. "Yes. Ebenezer and I were playing a game and I told him to race through the house as the bird he chose to imitate. I should have kept him from the parlor, but I did not. The blame rests with me."

Ebenezer looked up at his sister in surprise. He then looked at his father.

To Ebenezer's amazement, Elias' features began to soften. His facial contortions melted away and his cheeks resumed their natural hue. When he spoke, it was even and steady.

"Fan, that was very wrong of you. Now take the boy away and do not let him out of your sight until this evening's business is concluded." Not one word was spoken while looking at Ebenezer.

"Yes, Father," Fan said. "Come, Ebenezer, come now." And she led him away.

This was only one of many times that Fan intervened on behalf of Ebenezer to spare him from the rod. On one particular occasion, however, she was neither able to prevent the wrongdoing, nor could she save Ebenezer from the consequences. Although the consequences of this transgression were more severe than anyone could have imagined.

One afternoon in early July, young Ebenezer was feeling particularly distraught at the lack of attention his father was giving. Ebenezer spotted an ornate vase that he knew had once belonged to his great-grandmother, Elias' maternal grandmother. He also knew that Elias greatly valued this object and that it was itself very valuable. Ebenezer stared at the vase for a long moment with the realization growing stronger and stronger within him that his father cared more for the well-being of this *thing* than for him. Unable to control the fury that boiled to the surface, Ebenezer put both hands on the vase and pushed it over with all of his strength.

It crashed to the floorboards below and disintegrated into countless pieces with a mighty explosion. James, the same servant who redirected Fan on the day of Ebenezer's birth, was the first to arrive on the scene, followed quickly by Elias himself. Elias looked at the broken pieces upon the floor, then to the mount where his cherished vase had once stood, and then finally at Ebenezer's face, flush with a combination of anger and fear.

Elias took one step towards his son, and that was enough to break the spell keeping Ebenezer's feet cemented firmly to the ground as though they were stuck in hardened mortar.

Ebenezer shot out of the house like a cannonball and ran to the one place he felt most comfortable: the orchard. Without knowing if he was being pursued, but assuming he was the fox to his father's hound, he reached his favorite tree and bounded up into the embrace of its upper branches. He was out of breath and panting, gasping in deep breaths like a dehydrated nomad guzzling in his first taste of spring water at an oasis.

He noticed that it was a particularly hot and windy day. When he looked to the sun, it was that same ominous crimson tint the family had become familiar with in that odd year. And when he gazed out onto the horizon, he saw another unusual sight. A thick cloud of fog was blowing his way, riding the wind. Ebenezer was transfixed upon the haze heading towards him. He did not hear the sound of the adults rushing in his direction ordering him to descend from the tree immediately. Nor did he hear the panic in their voices.

When the cloud reached Ebenezer, it caused a searing pain within his chest. He began coughing and sputtering, but the pain would not cease. Ebenezer had never felt anything like this before in his life. Soon, his head felt very light and a sea of white began to envelop his vision, closing in from the outside of his sight and working its way inward until his entire world was nothing but white. At that moment, he lost feeling in his arms and legs as they were reduced to jelly. The last vague image he saw was the underside of the branch upon which he had just been perched, at which point all turned to darkness.

The next he knew, Ebenezer was in his bed with Fan, a servant named Thomas, Doctor O'Shea, and, surprisingly, his father, by his bedside. At first, Ebenezer believed he must be dreaming. But the pain within his chest awoke him to the realization that this was, in fact, actuality. He tried to speak, but found that he could not. He looked down and saw blood staining the front of his shirt. His right arm was in a great deal of pain and he could see it was wrapped tightly against a stiff board. The rest of his body ached and he was very confused.

Ebenezer was a victim of the "Laki Haze", along with tens of thousands throughout Europe. Many were not as lucky as young Ebenezer. Many did not escape with their lives.

Not unlike the pain buried deep within Ebenezer's bosom that had its fill before erupting that summer, Laki Mountain, located in the south of Iceland, had a pressure within it that required relief. Over an eight-month period between seventeen hundred and eighty-three and seventeen hundred and eighty-four, fissures opened up on either side of the mountain and spewed out clouds of poisonous gas. One such gas was sulfur dioxide and, as we know now, inhaling this compound causes severe damage. The gas reacts with the moisture within one's lungs and produces sulfuric acid, which literally eats away at one's insides.

It is estimated that twenty-three thousand Britons died from the Laki poisoning, with countless others injured as was young Ebenezer. As the summer progressed, in addition to being extremely hot, severe thunderstorms dropped unusually large hailstones that were reported to have been powerful enough to kill grazing cattle.

The winter did not provide relief. The same phenomena that had caused such an unusually hot summer also caused an extremely cold winter, which killed approximately eight thousand more people throughout Britain. The weather continued to the extremes for the next several years. In fact, several years later, this weather led to a surplus harvest in France that caused poverty to explode among rural workers. This, coupled with droughts and subsequent bad growing seasons, were major contributors to a sudden increase in poverty and famine that many now believe contributed to the French Revolution in seventeen hundred and eighty-nine.

As for Ebenezer, his voice returned and his broken arm healed. But the damage to his lungs was lasting. This was the beginning of his susceptibility and sensitivity to respiratory illnesses that would plague him for the remainder of his life.

All caused by the buildup of pressure that required a release. And once no force of nature could contain it any longer, the reverberations of that release would echo throughout time forever forward.

6

Elias Scrooge's despondency simply would not improve. As he slipped further and further into alcoholism, his business slipped further and further from solvency. He was blessed to have some good colleagues who saw this an opportunity to reverse all of their mutual fortunes.

Elias was well-respected for his generosity during the height of his commercial success. He would often do favors for others, even competitors at times, because he believed that Providence smiles upon those who conduct themselves in an upright manner at all times. His tender heart could be seen as a weakness to exploit, and to be sure there were those who attempted to take advantage, but in the end, the scoundrels floundered while he flourished.

The loss of Elizabeth was known throughout his professional community. His descent therefrom was also common knowledge among his colleagues. Several of these men who were harmed by the loss of commerce to the now independent North American colonies met to discuss his situation, and their own. They determined that a union of their resources could benefit the whole. And they saw The Scrooge Company as an integral member of this potential association. The question they pondered was would it be better to allow it to continue on its path to self-destruction, at which point they could pick like vultures at the carrion of what remained, or should they incorporate its rapidly fading viability into the new enterprise they envisioned.

Upon careful consideration, it was determined that Elias Scrooge still had enough contacts and goodwill that allowing his company to die simply so they could resurrect its most profitable appendages would not be of greatest benefit. Three men of great prominence, but slipping fortunes, – Robert Bruce, Daniel Davies, and Dennis McRedmond – resolved to convince Elias to set aside his declining sole proprietorship and to enter into a profitable partnership with them.

They arranged a meeting to take place at the Scrooge home, but they did not divulge the complete nature of the assembly to Elias. He believed himself to be perfectly capable of continuing along his current path and his diminished capacity of late prevented him from recognizing the irreparable damage he was doing to his company and to his future. They intended to confront him with the reality of his situation in such stark terms that he would be powerless to resist their offer.

They arrived as one at the Scrooge home at four o'clock in the afternoon. The blood-colored sun beat down upon them on this early June afternoon. All were aware of the cloud of death that was sweeping across Europe, as the weekly periodicals had been reporting of the phenomena for some time. Along with the rest of Great Britain, it was their great hope that it would dissipate before doing the same damage on His Majesty's island as it had reportedly been doing on the Continent.

Prior to arriving at his home, Elias issued a stern warning to all of his household staff, as well as to his children, that he had very crucial business to which he must attend and that he may not be disturbed for any reason whatsoever. In truth, Elias did not know exactly why the three men approaching his living quarters were doing so, but the urgency with which they requested the meeting suggested that an important opportunity was about to be placed before him. How right he was, although not in the manner in which he had envisioned.

Messrs. Bruce, Davies and McRedmond were welcomed at the door and escorted into the parlor to await Elias' appearance. Shortly thereafter, he entered the room as well. His colleagues were shocked at his appearance. His clothes were disheveled, his hair was more than a bit mussed, his eyes were bloodshot and glassy, and he bore the distinct odor of intoxicating spirits. Nonetheless, they were determined to establish a new entity on this day, and the key to this new enterprise would be acquiring the assets now held by Elias Scrooge.

"Gentlemen, thank you for your punctuality. I always say that a man who arrives when he promises is a man of respect. Can I offer any of you a beverage on this unusually warm afternoon?" Elias asked.

They all demurred, a bit uneasy with the offer. The last thing necessary at this moment was the introduction of any additional intoxicating substances into what appeared to be Elias' already inebriated system.

"No? Very well then. What can I do for all of you?" asked Elias. "I must admit that your request for this gathering was quite cryptic. Yet, I cannot say that it was not intriguing."

"Mr. Scrooge," began Robert Bruce. "We come to you with a proposition."

"A proposition, Mr. Bruce? Of what nature?" replied Elias.

"Well," said Mr. Bruce. "Of a business nature that has the potential to benefit every man in this room."

"You don't say," Elias said, looking at all the men, each in turn.

"Why, yes, Mr. Scrooge," interjected Dennis McRedmond. "We have been studying the numbers and evaluating the situation. We have come to the conclusion that in these difficult times, our strength lies in unity."

"Undoubtedly," Elias responded, despite being unclear of their meaning.

"That is why, Mr. Scrooge, we propose a… how shall I say… a merger of our mutual interests into one conglomeration that will be stronger than any of each of us currently stands alone," stated Mr. McRedmond.

"A merger?" asked Elias with an eyebrow raised.

"Yes, we envision a united and powerful partnership," said Mr. McRedmond. "Imagine, all of our forces working together as Scrooge, Bruce, Davies & McRedmond! Our present troubles would be over with the stroke of a pen!"

"Troubles? Of what troubles do you speak?" Elias asked suspiciously.

"Oh come now, man!" Daniel Davies exclaimed.

"Mr. Davies, what is the meaning of that ejaculation?" Elias asked, turning toward the frustrated man to his left.

Mr. Davies took a deep breath and collected himself.

"Elias," he said softly. "We're here to help."

"Help? Help whom? Help yourselves, perhaps!" replied Elias.

"Just look about you," Mr. Bruce interjected. "Your business suffers. Half of the staff in your home is gone. How long before the remainder leave because you cannot afford to maintain their salaries?"

"Spies! You come as friends, but have daggers concealed beneath your waistcoats!" Elias snapped.

"No, Elias, we come as friends and we are friends," Mr. Davies spoke gently. "If you do not wish to believe the facts, you must, as a good man of business, at least believe the figures. How much longer do you believe The Scrooge Company can survive if things continue as they are?"

"You wish to devour me! And to use my family name to line your pocketbooks!" Elias cried.

At that moment, four-year-old Ebenezer burst into the parlor, flapping his arms and making the most unseemly racket. He was squawking in a high pitched tone and running about like a madman.

Elias' face turned beet red and stilettos appeared in his eyes.

"How dare you interrupt us! Did I not make myself clear on this matter?!" Elias screamed. He grabbed the boy by his arm and forcefully hauled him from the room.

The men looked at one another in despair. Their efforts did not seem to be anywhere near ready to bear fruit. They believed that without

Scrooge's participation, their anticipated venture would not succeed.

From the other room, the men could hear young Fan attempting to placate her father. What a sweet child, they all thought. And to the surprise of all present, it seemed that the mere words of his daughter were enough to calm the raging beast within Elias' breast. Perhaps the youngest Scrooge's intrusion would turn to their advantage after all.

When Elias returned, he closed the door behind him, straightened his coat and pressed down upon the hair on the back of his head with both hands. He then looked up at his guests, all standing.

"My apologies for my son," Elias began. "He is a willful boy and unless under constant supervision, a disaster from the time his eyes open in the morn until they close again as he enters his evening sleep. Now, where were we?"

The men could tell that there was indeed a change in Elias. They were tempted to invite young Miss Fan into the meeting with them to keep her father's rage caged, but that would not be appropriate.

"We were discussing a mutually beneficial partnership, Elias," reminded Mr. McRedmond.

Elias sat down upon his chair. He placed his elbows upon his knees and buried his face within his hands. He exhaled loudly. He then looked up.

"I apologize for my behavior earlier. Of course, you are all correct. The business has begun to fail," said Elias.

At the word "begun", the others looked at each other, understanding without words how much of an understatement this was, but all remained silent.

"I simply have lost my drive, my will," Elias admitted. "What was once commonplace is now beyond comprehension. What was once fulfilling is now empty and bare. I cannot go on like this."

Taking a step towards Elias, Mr. McRedmond said, "Then let us help you. Let us help each other."

"Yes, it makes perfect sense. What is it that you would have me do?" Elias asked, defeated.

The men sat down and outlined the plan for the birth of the new Scrooge, Bruce, Davies & McRedmond. As it was clear that Elias would not be capable of overseeing the day-to-day business affairs, he was guaranteed a stipend based upon the profitability of the business in exchange for the use of his name and his contacts. This was a good deal for the Scrooges. It stabilized their finances, although at a level lower than they had come to be accustomed during their years of plenty. But it kept them from bankruptcy and avoided the specter of debtor's prison for Elias, a path he was surely on had his fortunes continued on the trajectory they had been moving before the fateful meeting with his new partners.

Unfortunately, the new venture was not nearly the success the partners hoped it would be. Without the Scrooge acumen at the helm, the business stayed afloat, but did not prosper. Increasingly, the small profits, in the months where profits were produced, were swallowed up in large part by the needs of the enterprise in terms of overhead. While enough was generated to keep the business running and to allow the partners to maintain appearances, Elias' allowance from the endeavor seemed to be smaller and smaller with each passing year.

As time went on, Mr. Bruce's comment about the loss of the Scrooge home staff proved prescient. Finances being what they were, Elias simply could not maintain a full household of domestics. Eventually, the only two that remained were James and the spinster cook named Sarah, and they only did so because they resided in the home and neither had families of their own for whom to provide.

More and more, Fan took up the responsibilities of the lady of the house that would have been filled by her departed mother, had she remained among the living. Fan became quite proficient at needlework and at laundering clothing. Both skills served her well in the coming years as she was able to parlay them into work for neighboring families, which placed a few more shillings into the family coffer to supplement her father's ever increasingly meager income.

The question of what to do with Ebenezer soon arose. He was nearing the age where he would need an education if he were to enter society as a gentleman. It was bad enough that he had taken his wife, Elias believed. He would not allow the boy to sully his name by being an ignorant parasite, unable to contribute to the society in which they lived. He may have been many things that Elias abhorred, but above all, he was still a Scrooge. And Scrooges made good in the world.

The answer presented itself in the form of a remembered favor. During times that were plentiful, Elias befriended Harold Stowe, headmaster of Worthington School for Boys, a preparatory institution located a full day's ride from the Scrooge home. Mr. Stowe was in need of a loan, a business in which Elias was not customarily involved. For reasons Mr. Stowe could not fully reveal, he could not obtain these funds through the more traditional channels. At the time, he was an administrator at Worthington, but if it were known that he required the loan, it could have harmed his opportunity for advancement, such was the nature of the owners of the institution.

Elias took pity and extended the loan. Mr. Stowe had a difficult time repaying his debt, but Elias exercised boundless patience. While Elias could have called in the loan and had Mr. Stowe arrested and disgraced, he did no such thing. Mr. Stowe offered his sincere gratitude and promised Elias that even after the money was repaid, he would remain in Elias' debt.

Elias realized it was time to call in this favor. He could not afford to send Ebenezer to Worthington, but it was there Elias resolved he would go. He paid a visit to Mr. Stowe and made all of the arrangements.

He then returned home and made his announcement. Ebenezer would leave in one week hence. Ebenezer and Fan were devastated. They had never been apart for even a day in Ebenezer's entire life. Fan felt that she was not just losing her beloved brother, but that she was being stripped of her own child. And with no warning at all.

"No, Father!" protested Fan when Elias told her of the news. "Worthington is simply at too great a distance!"

"It is settled. There is to be no argument. The boy will go to Worthington," said Elias resolutely.

Ebenezer stood in the corner watching this interaction, while sobbing uncontrollably. He was terrified. How would he survive without his Fan to protect him? How could his father send him so far away?

"Stop your sniveling, boy! This is why you must go to Worthington. So that they may make a meaningful man out of you," Elias snapped.

"But, Father, there are other schools much closer to home. Better we should consider those as options for Ebenezer," Fan pleaded.

"No. It is done. The boy is going to Worthington seven days from today and that is the final word on the subject! I will hear no more of this!" Elias demanded.

"At least call him by his name, Father, before you banish him from our lives! His name is not 'the boy'. His name is Ebenezer!" Fan challenged.

"Very well, then. *Ebenezer* will be off to Worthington," Elias replied, clearly having difficulty with speaking his son's first name. "It is what is best."

"No, Father. It is not what is best. It is not!" Fan cried, and she ran from the room and up to her bedchamber to wail into her pillow.

Ebenezer followed his sister, trembling in fear and disbelief. His father was really sending him away. When would he see his home again? When would he see his Fan again? The fact that he did not know the answers to these questions was more than his young mind could grasp.

The week passed far too quickly for either of the children. The day arrived. Ebenezer embraced Fan with all of his strength and they had to be pried apart by James when it was time to leave. He was packed into a carriage with all of his worldly belongings. With tears streaming down his face, Ebenezer was led away from his home and away from the only person who ever showed him unconditional love.

The year was seventeen hundred and eighty-six. Ebenezer was seven years old.

7

The carriage pulled up to the front gate with the word "Worthington" forged in an arc above the bars, spanning from one end to the other. On either side of the barrier stood a gentleman, each wearing identical blue jackets with the Worthington School crest emblazed upon the upper right chest of each. The crest featured at its center a golden lion standing upon its formidable fallen prey. Its sharp feline eyes peered out into the distance towards its next challenge to conquer, one paw already moving in the direction of its next great triumph. The upper left and lower right quadrants of the crest were a deep crimson red, and the upper right and lower left quadrants were a deep forest green. Beneath the scene, appearing to be written on an unfurling scroll were the Latin words, "*Honorum, Integritas, Virtus, Et Fortitudo, Dirige Nos In Sempiternum*". The school motto. "Honor, integrity, courage and strength to guide us forever." Upon a mighty stone pillar to the right of the gate was chiseled, "Worthington School for Boys" and beneath that moniker, "Est. 1652".

After confirming the credentials of the passenger, the sentry stationed at the gate's right end handed the folded parchment back to the driver. He nodded to his confederate. The two guards approached and grasped the bars of the gate on their respective sides and pushed the entryway open, allowing the carriage passage through. Young Ebenezer watched as his transport passed underneath the imposing "Worthington" archway and flinched when he heard the heavy iron doors slam shut behind him after his carriage had cleared the threshold. The carriage ambled down the long, tree-lined path until it reached a mighty edifice looming before it. It turned and came to a halt parallel to the entrance of this impressive structure. Ebenezer slowly stepped from his conveyance, taking a few steps toward the massive building in front of him.

As he stood with the carriage to his back and the main hall before him, Ebenezer had never felt so intimidated in his entire life. Ebenezer, already small for his age, felt absolutely dwarfed to the point of insignificance by his new surroundings. He slowly gazed around at the endless campus he found himself immersed within and could not fathom how he would ever find his way without getting lost at every turn. At that moment, the bell housed within the clock tower atop the monstrous building before him clanged sharply, startling Ebenezer so significantly that the sound of his pounding heart consumed all others within his tiny ears and drowned out the peal of the succeeding ten gongs that followed the first. Ebenezer noted that, although it was a Tuesday, there were no other boys walking the grounds. As he looked about, the carriage driver was methodically removing Ebenezer's belongings and placing them on the ground behind him.

The doors of the main hall opened and a tall, thin man with an unusually large nose wearing the same Worthington blue jacket with the emblazoned crest as had been adorned by the guards at the gate exited. He seemed to be irritated by something the moment he stepped from the shadow of the building onto the sun splashed staircase that led down to where young Ebenezer was standing, looking ever meek and mild. He briskly hurried down the steps, stopping directly in front of the boy.

"Late," the man said, looking down at the pint sized lad. He let the word hang in the air for a long moment. Ebenezer did not know how to respond, or even if he was expected to do so.

"I'm sorry, sir," Ebenezer said timidly, despite the fact that he knew he had nothing at all to do with his arrival time.

"Late," the man repeated, sharply emphasizing the "t" at the end of the word, as he shook his head back and forth. He then looked up and cast his eyes over Ebenezer's head. "No way for a Worthington man to begin."

The man continued to look out into the distance, ignoring Ebenezer before him, and making the child feel more and more uncomfortable as each silent second ticked away. Finally, after what felt like an eternity of Ebenezer looking up at the underside of this displeased man's face, the stranger looked down at him.

"So, I suppose you are the Scrooge boy," the man said. "No money, but who needs it when you are here gratis, am I not right?"

Ebenezer did not know what to say.

"Do you speak, boy?" demanded the man, with a flush in his cheeks.

"Y-yes, sir," Ebenezer replied, in a barely audible voice.

"You ought to do it then, when asked a question," the man said staring directly into Ebenezer's innocent azure eyes. "Not a very impressive start. But what can one expect from a charity subject, eh Scrooge?"

Again, Ebenezer was at a loss for words so he said nothing.

"Mute once more," the man said, with narrow eyes. "This is why giving to those who do not earn with no expectation of return will never improve this country or this world. It just rewards apathy. The liberals may allow their hearts to bleed for the idlers, but what good is accomplished by encouraging the poor to laze about? Why produce for the good of society when you can sit on your arse and drink yourself into oblivion in a world where, by so doing, your son can go to Worthington without paying the fee? Am I right, boy?"

Ebenezer, knowing an answer was expected of him this time, scrambled through the options within his mind as how best to respond. This tall, unpleasant man had just insulted both Ebenezer and his father. But conceding defeat seemed the more prudent course of action at this juncture. Ebenezer may have been young, but he was not a fool.

"Yes, sir," Ebenezer said.

"Of course I am correct. Did you doubt it for a moment?" spat the man.

"No, sir," Ebenezer said.

"Very well. Rather than stand here and continue wasting my very valuable time, I shall take you to your dormitory. I am Mr. Fairchild. By a stroke of very poor luck, I was designated to escort you on this, your first day with us. Imagine," Fairchild said more to himself than to Ebenezer, "I, whose salary depends upon the submission of tuition by each student's family, am forced to be humbled to show you, a ne'er-do-well whose family submits no tuition, to your free quarters."

With that, Fairchild turned and began walking down the path extending to the right of the main hall, simply expecting Ebenezer to follow. Ebenezer scurried behind, struggling to keep up with Fairchild's long, loping steps. As he did, he looked back over his shoulder, concerned about leaving all of his belongings sitting in the grass in front of the large building before which they were placed. He saw several young gentlemen gathering up his bags and chests. At first he was tempted to protest, but he did not want to excite the ire of Fairchild once again. Fortunately, his choice proved to be one of good judgment as he saw that these individuals were not pilfering his personal effects, but were gathering them to bring to his new living space.

When they reached their destination, Fairchild stopped and turned towards Ebenezer, who was out of breath, but still at Fairchild's heels.

"This is Kensington Hall," said Fairchild, disgusted with Ebenezer's panting, and making no effort to hide it. "It is where you will find your bed on the third floor. And in that bed you must be each night before the last chime of nine o'clock rings throughout the campus. A Worthington man is well rested and prepared to take on each day in top form. This curfew is not subject to negotiation. Failure to abide by same shall be met with swift consequences. Is that clear?"

"Yes, sir," replied Ebenezer.

"You will note that this building is empty at present," stated Fairchild.

"That is because, unlike you, the *paying* students" – Fairchild's voice dripping with contempt as he spoke the word 'paying' – "respected this fine institution enough to arrive before classes commenced over two weeks previous. They are at study, where I expect you to be at this time tomorrow. And you will have much to concentrate upon as no allowance will be made by your instructors due to your late arrival."

Ebenezer gulped softly to himself.

Fairchild looked out towards the clock tower.

"It nears half past eleven. Your colleagues will be filing into Newton Hall for the afternoon meal when the clock strikes twelve," said Fairchild. "I suggest you settle yourself in between now and then, and then join your classmates. All are required to be at their spot in the dining hall no later than five minutes past twelve. Prayer is at exactly ten minutes past. You will show reverence. A Worthington man is a penitent man. And you will eat what is placed before you. A Worthington man is healthy in mind, body and soul."

Ebenezer was overwhelmed. As his young mind was struggling to manage all that he was being told, the porters arrived with his belongings. When they came through the door, they looked to Fairchild.

"Take his items to his designated bed." To Ebenezer, he said, "Do you have any questions? No? Splendid. Follow them."

Ebenezer actually did have many questions, beginning with learning the location of Newton Hall. But before he could open his mouth, Fairchild was ordering him to follow his bags.

"Mr. Fairchild, sir," Ebenezer began, as the baggage carriers hurried past him and began their way up the staircase. "I wish to ask—"

"Scrooge," Fairchild interrupted sharply. "Ask your classmates. My dreary duty has come to its end. I have brought you where you needed to go and have instructed you as to your expectations. I have nothing more to say to you. Nothing, save this. Among my many responsibilities at this institution is that of discipline. See to it that we do not cross paths when it comes to that obligation of mine. If you do not heed this warning, you will find me in a mood not as pleasant as you have been so fortunate as to have observed me to be in today."

With that, Fairchild turned on his heel and marched out of Kensington Hall into the late morning day.

Ebenezer looked at the spot where Mr. Fairchild had stood a moment before for a long second. His head was swimming and his insides were upended. He looked to the stairway where the last of the porters were dragging his personal belongings up each step. Ebenezer then followed these young men up to the room he would call home for the next five and a half years.

8

Ebenezer entered his designated room, Room 3C, that he was to share with five strangers. The porters placed all of his personal items on and around his bed and then left him. He looked around the room. It was odd. It all looked very lived-in already. All except for the one bed in the far corner against the wall. His bed. He felt like an intruder.

He moved the bags and boxes from the bare mattress and covered the bed with the linen sheets he found beneath his belongings. He covered the bed with the blanket he saw was designated for him and he tried his best to make it look as the other beds in the room did. Ebenezer was still very disoriented so he figured his best course of action would be to imitate what was clearly acceptable using the other boys' living spaces as the example. He tried several times, but he could not make the bedsheets and blanket appear as crisp and symmetrical as the others in the room.

Finally, he gave up and drooped down atop his bed with his knees drawn up to his chest and his arms encircling his knees. He felt the depth of his solitude. He heard the roar of the silence. He was alone. Truly all alone for the first time in his life. He put his head down and began to weep.

He thought of Fan and wondered what she was doing at that very moment. He wondered if she missed him as much as he missed her. He wished fervently that she were here with him now.

Ebenezer also wondered if what Mr. Fairchild said about his father was true. Was he really a poor man whose son was here out of charity? Why did Mr. Fairchild consider Father to be idle? Did he not run a business and partner with others who did as well? It was all very confusing.

Adding to the confusion was why Mr. Fairchild was so harsh with him. If he was truly here through an act of goodwill, why such an unwelcome

welcome? Surely someone wanted him there if he was permitted entry for no cost.

What Ebenezer did not know was that the Headmaster had forgotten his gratitude towards Elias Scrooge in the intervening years that had passed since placing himself in Elias' debt. All that remained was the obligation, which, as a man of honor, he was duty-bound to satisfy. But to Headmaster Stowe, Ebenezer represented a significant threat. He had no interest in his superiors learning the true reason Ebenezer was there for free. Quite honestly, it would be better if Ebenezer left the school as soon as possible, never to return. It would have been preferable if Elias had asked for absolutely anything but what he did to even their moral account. Resurrecting Stowe's old debt menaced him deeply. For that, Stowe resented Elias, and by extension Ebenezer, intensely for it.

As a direct result, the Headmaster maligned Ebenezer to his staff prior to his arrival. He fabricated the mendacity that Ebenezer was being permitted attendance at Worthington due to the commands of his superiors. In truth, Stowe was aware of the condition in which Elias allowed himself to sink and he despised what Elias had become. This he shared with all administrators and instructors, strongly warning them about the tainted blood that ran through Ebenezer's veins. By Stowe's account, Worthington was graciously accepting an unfit student of questionable character for reasons he did not comprehend, and that the only proper course of action regarding his education was to ensure that he be pressed unremittingly to conform to Worthington standards from the moment his feet touched the hallowed ground of the school.

Ebenezer gathered himself and decided to find Newton Hall before he was late arriving to "his spot", a location that was a complete mystery to him. He exited his dormitory building and chose to walk back towards the main administration building from whence he first alighted the carriage that transported him to this place. Before reaching it, he was accosted by an older gentleman who believed Ebenezer to either be a trespasser or, worse, a student on the campus grounds when he should be in class.

"You there! Boy!" the man cried as he ran up to Ebenezer. "What do you think you are doing wandering around unescorted at this time of day?"

"I'm sorry, sir. My name is Ebenezer Scrooge and I just arrived here but a few hours past," Ebenezer explained. "I was told by Mr. Fairchild that I must be at my designated spot in Newton Hall by twelve o'clock. But I know neither where to find Newton Hall nor how to determine where my spot may be."

"Ah, yes, yes. You are the Scrooge boy we were warned about," the gentleman said, nodding his head as he adjusted his glasses to get a good look at the lad. "I am Professor Devereaux. I teach Religion at this fine institution. Do you know your Bible, boy?"

Ebenezer shifted uncomfortably before the professor. While he was familiar with the Holy Scriptures, he was by no means proficient. He did not want another adult at this institution to raise a stern eye or cast a critical word his way after his experience with Mr. Fairchild. Ebenezer opted for the truth and tensed, bracing himself for what may come after he spoke.

"Some, sir," Ebenezer said, praying desperately in his heart that this would be an acceptable answer.

Fortunately, it was.

"Well, son, you will grow to know a great deal more than 'some' after seven years in my classroom. A great deal more, I should say," Professor Devereaux said with a smile. "A Worthington man is a reverent man."

Ebenezer exhaled a breath he did not realize he was holding.

"Yes, sir."

At that response, the professor took a step back and looked at Ebenezer from the side of his eyes.

"I see that you cower when you should stand tall. True, the meek shall inherit the earth, but the strong shall always rule it. Remember that, lad," said the unusually kind man standing before Ebenezer.

"Yes, sir."

"Now," said Professor Devereaux, consulting his pocket watch, a beautiful ornate gold timepiece, the golden links of his fob dangling between his hand and the connecting point on his waistcoat. "It is nearly twelve and you must be getting to Newton Hall. Let us go and find your rightful place within."

Professor Devereaux put his hand on Ebenezer's shoulder and directed him past the main administration building where Ebenezer had first encountered Mr. Fairchild, a structure named "Bailey Hall" Ebenezer now saw, and made a left down the next connecting path. As they walked, Ebenezer remained silent, trying not to break the spell of having such warmth directed his way. This may have been the first time an adult in his life had placed hands upon him in a gesture of care and affection since his dearly departed mother had done so when he was but seconds from her womb. Certainly, this was the first instance in which he remembered it having been done so. He did not know how to react to such tenderness, as Fan was the only person who had directed it his way until this moment. He enjoyed the sensation, but at the same time, he was unable to accept it fully. It was a delightful discomfort.

They came to a large deciduous tree and turned to their right, and there, before them, just as the school bells began their noonday peal, was Newton Hall. The quadrangle fronting the building immediately began filling with boys of all ages in blue Worthington jackets, white shirts, red and green striped ties with the Worthington lion (the same as found on the crest) in the center of the tie, and blue britches of the same shade as the jackets – the Worthington uniform. The young men were swarming from all directions, hastily beating their way to the dining hall. Without thinking, Ebenezer moved ever so perceptibly closer to Professor Devereaux for protection at his unease from being suddenly but one drop in a sea of students surrounding him.

Professor Devereaux could feel the tension in Ebenezer's shoulders. He looked down at the boy at his hip and smiled.

"Buck up, young Ebenezer. Fear not. How fortunate you are! You are looking at England in the time to come. The powerful men. Be among them. Do not be subject to them," said Professor Devereaux.

Ebenezer looked up at the professor still smiling down at him, but with a serious aspect in his stare. The professor nodded his head once at Ebenezer and then turned towards Newton Hall's main doors.

"Come now, boy. Let us find your rightful place among your colleagues in the hall. And I must get to mine as well."

Professor Devereaux directed Ebenezer into the dining hall through the horde of other students, all on a mission to reach their destination in a timely manner. A Worthington man is a punctual man. The professor walked Ebenezer towards the forepart of the hall, where the other first year students were congregating. When they reached the head of the table, the professor told Ebenezer to wait for him there. He walked up to the dais, a long table that spanned the entire width of the front end of the hall designated for the instructors and administrators. At its center was a place of honor reserved for the Headmaster. Greeting his compatriots along the way, Professor Devereaux made his way to that center seat and leaned in to ask a question of Headmaster Stowe.

Ebenezer watched all of this as his insides tossed and squirmed. He did not want to look towards his new classmates because he felt that, from his present vantage, he was on display for all to scrutinize. So he kept his eyes on the one person who had shown him kindness since his departure from his sister's arms the day before.

The Headmaster heard Professor Devereaux's question and made a sour face. Ebenezer believed he saw the Headmaster's lips form the words, "He has arrived, then?" Ebenezer's stomach tightened at the instant disapproval his name seemed to elicit. The tightening strengthened when Headmaster Stowe lifted his brow in Ebenezer's direction and for an instant, the two locked eyes. The Headmaster pursed his lips, as though he were accepting an unpleasant reality, at which point Ebenezer shifted his gaze to the floor, breaking the link between them.

Headmaster Stowe looked up at Professor Devereaux and responded to the professor's question, while pointing his finger at the table to Ebenezer's left. The room continued to fill as everyone found their place.

Professor Devereaux made his way back to Ebenezer, who by then, felt the stares of his peers boring into him and the disapproval of the Headmaster lingering within his being. He felt as though he were naked and that all eyes were on him.

"Come, Ebenezer. Your table is right here," said the professor, gesturing to his left. Professor Devereaux walked Ebenezer to an empty chair between two boys taller than he.

Professor Devereaux extended his hand towards Ebenezer. Ebenezer took it and they shook.

"This is where I leave you. Good luck, Mr. Scrooge. Welcome to Worthington." With that, Professor Devereaux walked away and headed to his designated chair on the dais.

Without thinking, Ebenezer pulled out the chair to which he was assigned and he sat down. Immediately, he heard snickers and a few gasps. Ebenezer's head snapped up and he looked around, wondering what caused this reaction. It was then he realized for the first time that all of the other boys in the room were standing behind their chairs.

Ebenezer's faux pas did not escape the attention of the headmaster. Headmaster Stowe leapt forward and pointed directly at Ebenezer. Above the din of the crowd, the Headmaster's angry voice reverberated throughout the hall.

"Scrooge!!!"

Now all eyes truly were on him. The hall became silent, but for one irate voice.

"On your feet, boy! No one may be seated until permission to do so is granted! Perhaps you are too special to arrive at the outset of classes, but you are surely not above following our rules!"

Ebenezer was terrified. He was shaking. After his brief respite from hostility, here it was, back in full force. He stood.

The Headmaster continued to stare daggers at Ebenezer. With a seething voice, he spoke through clenched teeth.

"Push your chair in and stand behind it!"

Ebenezer looked around at how the other boys were positioned.

"Now!"

Ebenezer jumped. He quickly stepped behind his chair, but struck his foot on one of the legs and stumbled. Fortunately, he was able to catch himself before he fell. Unfortunately, he was unable to save the chair from upending and crashing to the floor. The echo of the clatter reverberated throughout the now silent dining hall.

The Headmaster let out a disgusted sigh.

Beet-faced and humiliated, Ebenezer lifted the chair and replaced it at its proper spot. He then took his rightful place behind the seat and placed his hands upon the top of the chair's back, as he observed the others around him doing.

"Congratulations, Mr. Scrooge," Headmaster Stowe announced, his voice steeped in sarcasm. "In the thirteen years that I have been headmaster of this finest of preparatory institutions, we have never begun our afternoon prayer later than ten minutes past the hour on the nose."

Headmaster Stowe turned towards Father McAllister, who was waiting patiently at his podium that was stationed between the dais and the student tables facing the educators.

"Would you care to tell all of us the current time, Mr. Scrooge?" demanded Headmaster Stowe, gesturing to the enormous clock at the rear of the hall.

Ebenezer peered sheepishly towards the clock.

"Well, Mr. Scrooge? You can tell time, can you not?"

Ebenezer found his voice.

"Yes, sir."

"Do it then!"

Ebenezer looked again at the clock's hands. He took a deep breath.

"It is fourteen minutes past twelve, sir," said Ebenezer meekly.

"Fourteen minutes past the hour!" the Headmaster repeated. "You have disrespected our good Father McAllister. You have deprived your fellow classmates four minutes of mealtime. And you have made a liar out of every good and honorable alumnus of this institution who has spoken the words, 'A Worthington man is a punctual man'!"

Tears welled within Ebenezer's eyes.

"I'm very sorry, sir. I meant no disrespect."

At that moment, the clock's chimes rang.

"Ah, the chimes of the quarter hour," Headmaster Stowe said, seething and staring at Ebenezer. He waited for their song to finish. He then turned to Father McAllister.

"Father McAllister, I apologize on behalf of our newest student to matriculate. Please lead us in prayer so that God may shine his light down upon us," the Headmaster stated, turning his eyes to Ebenezer once more as he spoke his final words. "Despite recent events."

"Let us pray," announced Father McAllister.

All of the boys bowed their heads and interlocked their fingers, while keeping their hands at the top of the backs of their chairs. Ebenezer did the same.

Following the prayer, the Anglican Priest invited the room to sit and enjoy their mid-day meal. Every student sat and began to eat. Ebenezer tried to avoid eye contact as he focused on his food. But he was not destined for peace.

"So you're the Scrooge we've all been hearing about. The charity boy," said the tall boy to his right. "Oi! Wallace!" – an auburn head at the other end of the table looked up from his plate – "I am sitting beside your new roommate. What do you think?"

Wallace merely grunted and returned his attention to his meal.

"I hear your father is a real sot. And mental besides," the same boy said, with a mischievous glint in his eye.

Ebenezer tried to ignore him.

"Come on now, Peter, leave him be. Has he not been through enough this afternoon?" asked the round-faced boy directly across the table from Ebenezer.

"I just want to get to know our new charity boy, that's all, Roger," said Peter innocently.

"Pay him no mind," Roger said to Ebenezer. "Hey, why are you not wearing your uniform?"

"I haven't one," Ebenezer replied.

"Everyone has one," Peter interjected with a sneering laugh. "Did you not look in your closet?"

"No."

"That is where you will find it," said Roger. "The Headmaster's mood was likely not helped by the fact that you showed up here without wearing it."

For the rest of the meal, most of the boys ignored Ebenezer and ate their food while talking to their established friends. It certainly did not help Ebenezer's transition that his father enrolled him in the school two weeks late. The others had already begun forming friendships, developing a comfort with the school, and bonding over their shared new experience.

It also did not help that Ebenezer was widely understood to be a "charity boy". Worthington was not an inexpensive choice for education. The fellows surrounding him all came from prominent families and wealth. They were taught from the earliest age to expect nothing but the best for life to offer and were instructed, even if for many it was tacitly, to look their noses down at anyone below their station.

To everyone in that room, Ebenezer was the embodiment of just that.

After the meal, the students were dismissed. All but Ebenezer went to their next class. Ebenezer was approached by an administrator by the name of Mr. Clayton. Clayton told him that it was his duty to assist Ebenezer in obtaining all of his necessary supplies and to provide him with his school schedule.

Together they went to each of the buildings housing his first year classes so that Ebenezer would be familiar with where he needed to go the following day. He was provided a map of the grounds to assist him. He was given the necessary textbooks that were being used and all of the supplies he would need for each. After being provided all of his academic needs, Mr. Clayton led Ebenezer back to his dormitory with the instructions that he was to review his materials in the hall's study room so that he may be prepared for his next day. Mr. Clayton also informed Ebenezer that the evening meal was at precisely six o'clock.

"Please do your best to acquit yourself in a more appropriate manner than the behavior we witnessed this afternoon," Mr. Clayton advised. "Charity can be revoked. Remember that."

Ebenezer agreed and Mr. Clayton left, to return to his office in Bailey Hall.

Before beginning to study the enormous volume of information he was unrealistically expected to absorb in just a few hours, Ebenezer decided to settle into his new quarters. He unpacked his belongings and placed them in the empty drawers and closet space that seemed designated for him. When he opened the closet, just as he was told at the afternoon meal, he found five sets of his school uniform. Determined not to repeat his errors from earlier, he stripped his clothes off and replaced them with the Worthington attire.

He then looked at his schedule. Each day was the same. The boys were to rise at six o'clock in the morning. The morning meal was at seven and lasted forty-five minutes. Classes were all one hour long and began precisely at eight o'clock. The mid-day meal was at noon, just as he had experienced this day. It, like all meal times, was to last forty-five minutes, with the first afternoon class commencing sharply at one o'clock. All classes ended for the day at four o'clock in the afternoon. Extra activities, such as sporting competitions, debate, law and government, and the like took place until the evening meal at six o'clock in the evening. Following that meal was study time until the nine o'clock curfew set in.

Ebenezer's class schedule was as follows:

Morning meal.
Period One: English History.
Period Two: Reading and Literature.
Period Three: Gentleman's Writing
Period Four: Arithmetic
Afternoon meal.
Period Five: Physical Education
Period Six: Economics
Period Seven: Religion.
Extra Enrichment.
Evening Meal.

Ebenezer brought some books down to the study room, where he discovered the next of his poor luck for the day. While he had loved the hours spent listening to Fan read stories to him, he had always had a difficult time reading the words himself when she tried instructing him. He was able to do so to a small degree after many efforts with the same material and Fan's endless patience and encouragement to assist him. But Fan was not present here. And the words in these books were incomprehensible to him. Panic began to set in once again. How would he study, or even know what to study? Once again, he began to cry. He began to wonder how he could have any further moisture within his eyes to expel after the deluge he had unleashed from beneath his lids since he departed from home.

The one book that he felt any comfort with was his arithmetic text. For some reason, he was always at ease with numbers.

After several hours, Ebenezer noticed that the sun had begun to lower in the sky and the shadows cast off from the trees outside of the window were getting longer. He checked the time and saw that it was half past five. Determined to avoid any further reprimand that day, he decided to make his way towards Newton Hall early. He brought his campus map and successfully navigated himself to the dining hall twenty minutes prior to meal time.

He waited in the mid-August eve and, as he would often find himself doing when he experienced a quiet moment as his time at Worthington progressed, he thought of Fan.

Once the clock chimed six, the scene from mid-day repeated and throngs of boys, aged seven to fourteen, poured out of the academic buildings and flooded their way towards the dining hall. Ebenezer was the first to enter and he made sure he was standing behind his chair when the rest of the campus filed in.

The meal was uneventful, to Ebenezer's great relief. After its conclusion, he followed the rest of the first year students back to Kensington Hall, where two-hour study was expected. This proved to be a lonely time, as the other boys were jocular with one another and had study groups already established to go over the day's work. Ebenezer was left out. He sat by himself, again looking only at the mathematics textbook because it was the only one of which he could make sense.

Finally, it was time for sleep. Ebenezer walked down the hall to Room 3C, where he discovered who his roommates would be for the remainder of the school year. Wallace Breckinridge, the hungry, yet disinterested boy from the afternoon meal. The two Georges – Remington and Kent. Francis Dodson. And the boy who shared the space directly next to Ebenezer, but seemed none too pleased about it, Howard Thrombone.

Ebenezer changed into his nightclothes and crawled into bed. He thought the worst of his day was behind him.

And that's when the thunderstorm began.

9

Ebenezer sat in his usual spot on the hard wooden bench outside of the Headmaster's office in Bailey Hall. He had been here far too often in the four months since he arrived at Worthington. So often, in fact, that Andrew Parkwood, personal secretary to the Headmaster, once snidely remarked that if Ebenezer appeared with any additional frequency, he would be eligible for salary.

Most often, Ebenezer was summoned to this office because of his low academic achievement. His reading was far behind those of his classmates, which made all of his other studies more ineffective. On a regular basis, Headmaster Stowe had to remind Ebenezer of the standards expected of each Worthington student, even for those who pay no tuition. The Headmaster had a talent for always finding a way to weave into his reprimand the fact that Ebenezer was there at the pleasure of himself and of the school. Simply because his father was a shiftless drunkard was no excuse for Ebenezer to follow his indolent path.

On one particularly serious occasion, Ebenezer's arithmetic instructor, Professor Court, appeared with him before the Headmaster. Professor Court was quite vexed, but felt it his duty as a gentleman and as a representative of the institution to express his fervent concern that Ebenezer was guilty of academic fraud. The professor's accusation stemmed from the fact that, although Ebenezer was consistently providing the correct responses on his exams, he was not arriving at the solution in the "proper" manner as instructed by the professor. In fact and in truth, the professor often did not completely grasp the means and methods that Ebenezer was using to calculate his conclusions. This led him to the determination that young Ebenezer was simply filling space with nonsense and finding a way to pilfer the ultimate correct responses from his nearby classmates.

Ebenezer insisted that he was doing no such thing. He just saw the numbers differently than the professor did and his mind put them together, or broke them apart, in a fashion contrary to the method the standard lesson plan called for. Ebenezer was telling the truth. He had a very strong mind for arithmetic and if the professor would have simply set aside his own pride and his rigid adherence to the traditional means by which a solution may be gleaned, he would have seen this. But such was his prejudice against the boy, in equal intensity with his loyalty to the Headmaster's warnings about him, that he could view the situation in no other way. He demanded satisfaction.

Headmaster Stowe, sensing an opportunity to relieve himself of his obligation to Elias Scrooge in an honorable manner, made a proposition. It was a Friday. There were no scheduled classes the following day. Immediately following the morning meal, Ebenezer was to report to Professor Court's classroom where both Professor Court and the Headmaster would be present and no one else. Ebenezer would sit in the desk in the center of the room. Professor Court would sit at his usual station at the front. The Headmaster would be immediately behind Ebenezer. Professor Court would present Ebenezer with an alternate examination, one that had not been utilized in the past. Under Professor Court's and Headmaster Stowe's unwavering watchful eyes, Ebenezer would complete the exam. If his proportion of correct answers fell below ninety percent, he would be expelled on the spot.

The next day arrived and, just as demanded, Ebenezer entered the classroom immediately after morning meal. Both Professor Court and Headmaster Stowe took their stations. Ebenezer was presented with the test. He immediately noted that it was much more complicated than any other he had seen during his coursework to date. Nonetheless, he focused his attention on the equations before him and completed the examination with ten minutes to spare.

Headmaster Stowe, confident that Ebenezer must have failed, instructed Ebenezer to remain in his seat while Professor Court tallied his score straightaway. Stowe sat back with his arms crossed, trying to hide his smile. He would breathe easier once Ebenezer Scrooge was no longer on his student rolls. No one could accuse him of dishonoring his obligation to Elias if Ebenezer violated the most sacred prohibition common to any and all reputable institutions of education.

But Stowe's smile started to fade as he watched the expression on Court's face while he was grading Ebenezer's submission. It went from confusion to concern to dismay. It seemed to Stowe that the exam took Court an unusually long time to evaluate. The Headmaster also noted, with rising alarm, that Court never put quill to parchment to indicate an incorrect response.

Finally, Professor Court looked up and asked the Headmaster to join him in the hallway. Stowe growled at Ebenezer to remain seated and silent. They exited the room and Court walked down the hall several paces past the next open doorway to ensure that his words would not be heard by Ebenezer when he spoke to the Headmaster. Stowe followed him.

"What is it, Tobias?" asked Stowe.

Court turned around.

"I do not understand it, Harold," whispered Professor Court, looking at the parchment in his hand and shaking his head. He put his hand to his mouth and continued to stare at Ebenezer's responses.

"What do you not understand?" the Headmaster asked. "How many did he answer incorrectly?"

"That is just what I do not understand," Court said in disbelief. He looked at Stowe in the eyes. "None."

"Not a one?" asked a very disappointed Stowe.

"No, Harold," Court said. "But, again, he does not use my method. The Worthington method. He goes his own way. I see the path he travels. I just do not understand how or why he travels it. I am tempted to wonder what forces act upon this boy's brain that cause it to stray so far from those of the rest of the flock."

"So what do you suggest we do?" asked Stowe.

"As a Worthington man of honor, I must humble myself and apologize to the child. He does not commit academic fraud," said Court. "And I must redouble my efforts to get the boy to conform. Simply because he achieves the appropriate result does not mean that he is doing as he should. He must still learn to obey. And he must follow the Worthington standards."

The men returned to the room to find Ebenezer still silent with his hands clasped firmly before him on the desk.

"Mr. Scrooge," began Professor Court. "I apologize for my accusations."

"May I ask, sir, how did I score?" asked Ebenezer.

Before Court could respond, Headmaster Stowe spoke.

"Your rate of incorrect responses did not exceed ten percent. Nothing further will be done at this time. You may return to your dormitory," Stowe told him curtly.

Ebenezer looked to the Headmaster and then to his arithmetic professor. Both looked somewhat ill.

"Go now, boy," Stowe instructed. "If you do not remove yourself this instant, then in that chair you shall remain for the entirety of this day."

Ebenezer rose and left the room in obedience.

That was one month prior.

But that was by no means the most serious event that placed Ebenezer in peril of expulsion. Before the first week of September had concluded, Ebenezer was at the mercy of both Headmaster Stowe and Dean of Discipline, Mr. Fairchild. This was due to Ebenezer being the victim of a malicious prank.

Ebenezer was unpopular from the start. Not just among his class of first years, but among the entirety of the student body. Many parents instructed their sons to steer clear of the charity boy. They did not want their children to sully their reputations just as such reputations were being established. More than a few attempted to convince the Headmaster to withdraw Ebenezer's acceptance of admission, but Stowe weathered the storm. He had to waltz upon a fine line to placate the donors and to avoid said donors from reaching above his head to directly pressure the Trustees who kept him comfortably employed, but he skillfully mastered that dance.

Several upperclassmen approached Ebenezer during his Additional Enrichment time spent vying in competition at shuttlecock. Fan had taught him well and he was quite adept at the sport. In fact, he regularly bested second and third year students within his grouping. Three fifth year students – Colin O'Brien, Miles Rappaport, and Liam Nelson – took Ebenezer aside and told him how impressed they were at his skills. They also told him that they appreciated how difficult his first month as a charity boy in such an institution as this had been. They told him they could help.

Ebenezer felt like he was swept up in a dream. He was so desperate for this kind of contact. These boys seemed to be the answer to his prayers. Ebenezer was willing to do virtually anything they asked.

"The Shuttlecock Cup is a very coveted trophy on this campus," Colin told him.

"Yes, that's very true," reaffirmed Liam.

"No first year student has ever won it. Not in all the years the school has existed," Colin said sincerely. "You could be the first."

"And if you were," Miles pointed out, "you would command great respect of everyone here. Students. Faculty. Even the Headmaster himself."

Liam and Colin both nodded in approval, indicating that this was true.

Ebenezer was in awe. Could this really be the answer to his loneliness?

"We can help you," Colin said. "We know how to make this happen."

"How?" asked Ebenezer, very excited.

"Well, you simply need to improve your technique," said Liam. "But you need to do it secretly. You will have no advantage if all of your competitors can watch you as you practice."

This made very good sense to Ebenezer.

"How do I improve in secret?" asked Ebenezer.

"We will work with you to ensure no one finds out how your skills are improving and surpassing even those of Reginald Dowsy, last year's champion," said Colin. His looked around to make sure no one was listening. His voice then dropped to a whisper.

"You just need to meet us here at this very spot and half past nine tonight."

Ebenezer's smile fell and his stomach rose. Half past nine?

"But that is after curfew!" Ebenezer exclaimed.

"Shh!" the three older boys all sounded, putting their hands up around Ebenezer and peering around to make sure no one heard him.

"But that is after curfew," Ebenezer repeated, this time in a whisper.

"Of course," said Colin. "How else will we be able to ensure no prying eyes will see your transformation to an unstoppable shuttlecock force?"

"I do not know," Ebenezer said unsteadily. "Mr. Fairchild was very clear with me about curfew."

"Very well, then!" spat Miles. He looked at his friends. "I told you we should not have attempted to befriend the charity boy. He has no appreciation within him!"

"No," Ebenezer pleaded. "That is not true. I have great appreciation. I simply wish to avoid trouble."

"Well, then, perhaps you would prefer to allow your life here to continue as it has," said Liam. "We were simply attempting to assist. Let us go boys. We are wasting our time here."

Ebenezer saw the three turn to leave and he made a decision.

"No, please do not depart. I will meet you here tonight."

"At half past nine?" asked Colin, turning back towards Ebenezer.

"Yes, at precisely half past nine."

"Good. It is almost time for evening meal," said Colin. "We will see you here tonight."

At that, the three exceedingly generous boys took flight and left Ebenezer.

Several hours later, while his roommates lay in their beds, Ebenezer quietly exited his. He carefully removed himself from the room and silently descended the stairs until he was at the entryway door. He pushed it open, freezing once in fright when he heard it squeak, but continuing to the exterior when he observed that his exit was undetected.

He looked to the clock tower. It was twenty minutes past nine. He scrambled down the pathway and made his way over to the pitch in eager anticipation of learning a method to ensure acceptance and inclusion.

As he stood there, in the middle of the field, he could not believe his good fortune. To think that three older boys would help him, with seemingly no concern for their own safety. Because, of course, they would be breaking curfew to assist him. And why? Because they truly were Worthington men. For the first time, Ebenezer felt a sense of pride at being at this institution and a sense of gratitude that his father had arranged for him to be here. It seemed only a matter of time before his life would change, and all because of the three new allies who entered his life.

When Ebenezer heard the chimes indicating half past the hour, he started to become nervous. Colin, Liam and Miles had not yet arrived. Ebenezer fervently hoped that they had not been waylaid in any way. He would not want his new friends to find trouble simply because of their generosity in assisting him.

It was then he saw the lantern light coming his way. Three distinct lights to be exact. Ebenezer's heart leapt! They were coming!

But as the lights approached and the faces being illuminated by those lights came into focus, Ebenezer's joy turned to dread.

It was not Colin, Liam and Miles approaching Ebenezer. Instead, it was Headmaster Stowe, his private secretary, Andrew Parkwood, and the terrifying Head of Discipline, Graham Fairchild.

"Scrooge!" said Fairchild, his teeth grinding. "I should have known."

Ebenezer froze in terror.

The boys were not his friends. They did not intend to assist him in any way. They were likely warm in their own beds having a very good laugh at Ebenezer's expense, wondering if he was actually so foolish as to wander the grounds after curfew. Wondering if he really believed that winning a meaningless trophy in shuttlecock would bring him respect and adulation.

"Come with me, boy," Headmaster Stowe ordered.

Devastated, Ebenezer drooped his shoulders, hung his head, and allowed himself to be led back to his dormitory with orders to appear at the Headmaster's office the following day before first meal for punishment. Ebenezer was told to pray the Headmaster slept well and that Mr. Fairchild enjoyed his abridged rest because creativity when it came to retribution was a quality both men had in abundance.

As it turned out, Ebenezer found that Newton Hall was a locale that required a great deal of assistance to keep it clean. For the next month, Ebenezer reported to the dining hall after his final class and was commanded to complete any menial task to which he was assigned for the following two hours prior to the evening meal instead of enjoying his Extra Enrichment activities.

Now, he again found himself on that unpleasant wooden bench on a cold Monday, the eighteenth of December. Many of the other students on campus had already departed for the two week Christmas holiday. Most of those remaining, including Ebenezer himself, were packed and ready to leave on this day. The school was to remain open, as there were some students who remained on campus through the holidays, although the vast majority of them were seventh year students who were preparing for their graduation and advancement to prestigious apprenticeships. They would often have responsibilities that would require their remaining on the grounds.

Ebenezer was finally summoned into Headmaster Stowe's office after the customary extended wait. The Headmaster believed it better for the chagrined student to be physically uncomfortable and for his anxiety to be at a maximum before bringing him forward. Ebenezer had become accustomed to these sensations.

"Mr. Scrooge," Stowe spoke, from behind his Brobdingnagian mahogany desk, looking down over his nose at Ebenezer in the small chair in front of him. "Do you know why you are here? This time?"

"No, sir."

"I have two matters to discuss with you. First and foremost, your academic performance this semester has been quite far from stellar," Stowe remarked.

"Yes, I know, sir," replied Ebenezer.

"As I have told you many times from this very vantage, I abhor laze!" Stowe boomed.

"I am not lazy, sir," said Ebenezer.

"Do not contradict me, boy! My favorite horse reads his oat bag better than you can!" Stowe yelled.

Ebenezer lowered his eyes. He tried so very hard, but his reading was quite miserable. He enjoyed what he learned when read to him and he comprehended it fully. But when left to himself to make sense of the letters on the page, they were often just a jumbled mess to him.

"I do not expect to be surprised when the results of your winter exams are made known to me," the Headmaster said. "I do not know how many times I must remind you that you are here at my pleasure. My patience with you has limits."

"Yes, sir."

Headmaster Stowe shook his head in frustration.

"As for our other matter of business. I received a post from your father."

"Yes, sir."

"He will not be coming to collect you this holiday season," said the Headmaster dryly. "Nor will he be sending anyone from your household to do so either. It seems that you shall be our guest without respite this year."

Ebenezer was shocked by this news. He was sure that someone would be coming to bring him home during this holiday. He was desperate to see Fan. In her most recent letter to him, she made no indication that they would remain apart. This must have come as an unpleasant surprise to her as well.

"Did you hear what I said, boy?" the Headmaster asked coarsely when Ebenezer remained silent.

"Yes, sir," Ebenezer said once he found his voice. "I do not understand."

"What is there to understand? They do not want you there any more than we want you here," the Headmaster said matter-of-factly. "The only difference is that we must keep you if they refuse to fetch you."

Ebenezer struggled to prevent the tears that screamed to eject from his eyes.

"Now go back to your dormitory and unpack. You are going nowhere."

Ebenezer slowly left the Headmaster's office and trod back to Kensington Hall. He could not bring himself to unpack, as he was instructed to do. He could not accept that he would be left abandoned on Christmas. On his birthday.

He sat on his bed and looked out the window hoping for a miracle.

One did not come.

10

During the next several years, Ebenezer's most anticipated day was the one on which Fan would arrive to escort him home for the two month summer holiday and Ebenezer's most dreaded day was the one when he had to say good-bye to her again at the end of that holiday. Elias never accompanied Fan to assist Ebenezer in returning home. He never sent a correspondence to Ebenezer. He never went to visit Ebenezer, nor would he permit Fan to do so, on the rare occasions when families were permitted on campus. In fact, the last direct contact he had with Worthington was the letter he penned to Headmaster Stowe informing him that Ebenezer would not be returning home for the Christmas holiday during his first year in attendance.

In point of fact, Elias could have sent an identical letter in each succeeding year as well because he never sent for Ebenezer during the Christmas holiday. He could have sent such a letter, but he did not. So each year, Ebenezer would pack his bags with the longing in his heart that a carriage would be arriving to take him home, and each year he would be disappointed. He knew from his correspondence with Fan that she stridently attempted to persuade Elias to bring her brother home to her each year during Christmas and his birthday. Each year, Ebenezer hoped this would be the year that his father relented. But, year after year, it was not to be.

While he remained a quiet child, shunned by a great deal of the student body, Ebenezer did slowly establish some friendships. None that were particularly close, but he was a good and decent boy at heart and, for some, this overcame the aversion to him. While all of his young colleagues seemed to have been born with the proverbial silver spoon in their mouths, not all of them chose to beat Ebenezer over the head with it. It relieved him of some tension that there were a few rooms in his dormitory in which he was relatively welcome. It took him some time to trust that he was actually being invited to join any other students after his experience with the fifth years in his first month of schooling, but once he did, there were rewards to be had.

Reginald Jones, for instance. He was a dark-haired little chap who had a room on the second floor. His father ran a financial institution and Reginald was fully expected to follow in the elder Jones' footsteps. His trouble was that he was not as strong in mathematics as would be preferable for such a future. Reginald was impressed with Ebenezer's proficiency in the subject. Reginald also had a bit of the rebellious streak in him and so the notion of first, befriending the school pariah, and second, learning an alternate mathematical method to the one at which he struggled, appealed to him.

Young Master Jones was a fast learner with words, Ebenezer's great weakness. The union the two formed benefited them both. After overcoming his fear of ridicule and after gaining the appreciation of Reginald due to the improvement in his mathematics comprehension, Ebenezer confided in him that he had trouble with reading. This was not a revelation to Reginald, as this deficiency was widely known throughout the class.

What was new information of which no one else was aware was that what troubled Ebenezer most about his poor reading skills was that it prevented him from fully understanding the missives sent from his sister. She was very good about ensuring that when the weekly post arrived at Worthington, more often than not, there would be a letter addressed to a one Ebenezer A. Scrooge. Ebenezer cherished these letters, but it frustrated him so that he did not know exactly what they said in total. It was as though his sister was right before him, but that her lips were silenced due to nothing more than his own shortcomings.

The two boys struck a secret deal in which Reginald would read Fan's letters to Ebenezer and Ebenezer would ensure Reginald brought acceptable grades in arithmetic home to his father. Finally, a whole new world opened up to Ebenezer. His Fan was back in his life on a regular basis. It was a wonderful feeling.

Another young lad that accepted Ebenezer as a friend was Roger Falvey, the young man who sat across from him at his first meal and attempted to blunt the brutish attack of Peter Egan. Roger did not have a cruel bone in his body and he felt pity for Ebenezer. Small, weak and clearly outnumbered, Ebenezer appealed to the philanthropist bubbling within Roger's soul. Later in life, Roger would make a career championing for the poor and underprivileged. His father would eventually disown him for it.

Roger's room was also on the third floor with Ebenezer's and he often heard the complaints in the night coming from Room 3C.

"Egad, Ebe-wheezer! Could you cut the infernal racket! We're trying to sleep!" That was the voice of George Kent.

"Yes, Ebe-sneezer! Enough or we will have the Hall Director put you out!" This time it was Howard Thrombone.

Ebenezer continued to suffer from respiratory distress caused by exposure to the poisonous gas cloud when he was a lad of four years. On many nights, it grieved him and he could not help the outcome. His roommates were often less than understanding. Especially when they were tired. The monikers, "Ebe-wheezer" and "Ebe-sneezer" would follow him until his last day at Worthington.

If one were compelled to identify the person Ebenezer connected with most closely during his time at Worthington, it actually would not have been a fellow student. It was instead a professor. Professor Devereaux.

Perhaps it was because Professor Devereaux was, during his own youth, a small boy for his age and sickly in addition. Perhaps it was the fact that he had such deep devotion in his heart that he saw in Ebenezer Scrooge the message of Matthew 19:14. Or perhaps it was simply because he appreciated that Ebenezer looked at the world slightly differently than his classmates. In any event, the professor took a special interest in the boy and they would have many a conversation outside of classroom hours about the subject of the divine.

On one occasion, Ebenezer revealed to the professor that he felt a particular sympathy for the character of Esau. Professor Devereaux probed, asking why this was so aside from the fact that they shared hair the color of rust. Ebenezer told him it was because he thought Esau was treated unfairly.

His brother, Jacob, takes advantage of him when he is starving and forces him to sell his birthright. His brother later successfully conspires with his mother to rob him of his father's blessing. When he responds with anger and threatens to kill his brother, his mother helps Jacob escape. And despite all of that, when Jacob returns years later and tries to ensure his own safety by attempting to bribe Esau with worldly goods, what should happen? Esau refuses to accept the material gifts and shows forgiveness to his brother nonetheless!

Yet, Esau is remembered as a villain who spawned the Edomites, enemies of God's Chosen People, and Jacob is remembered as the great patriarch who was the progenitor of the twelve tribes who inherit the Promised Land. It just never sat well with Ebenezer that Esau was treated thusly. He always felt that Esau was needlessly maligned.

There was one discussion that caused Professor Devereaux great concern and almost caused the bond between student and teacher to break. One day, Ebenezer confided in the professor that he had been considering Genesis very carefully and that he had come to a troubling conclusion. He determined that he could not find a way to believe in Original Sin.

Professor Devereaux was quite shocked by the admission, but decided to use the Socratic method, as was his custom, to peel away the layers of Ebenezer's disbelief.

"What is your concern with the veracity of Original Sin?" asked the professor on that cool autumn day in Ebenezer's fourth year.

"You see, Professor, I cannot discern the motivation of Adam and Eve to commit the sin," said Ebenezer earnestly and clearly troubled by his own wavering faith.

"Well, it is not that difficult. Man was born with free will. He may choose to do right or he may choose to do wrong. Adam and Eve chose to do wrong."

"But *how* could they choose to do wrong?" asked Ebenezer, with pleading eyes.

"It is as I just stated. Free will," Professor Devereaux responded.

"That does not satisfy. Free will does not motivate us to do anything. It is but a vehicle that takes us where we are motivated to go. It is like we are riding in a carriage and we come to an intersection where the only option is to go left or to go right. Free will allows us the choice to steer the horse in the direction we prefer. But it does not influence the decision as to which direction we ultimately choose," Ebenezer said.

"Well, keep in mind that man was always created with the potential to do wrong. If it were not so, free will would be meaningless. In Adam and Eve, that potential manifested," responded the professor.

"But how could that be, Professor? This is where I run into the paradox out of which I cannot escape. Adam and Eve lived in perfect communion with God. There was no sin in the world at that point to act upon their minds," said Ebenezer. "When the snake tells Eve to eat the apple, that God was lying to her, that she would not die if she did so, what would motivate her to obey the snake and disobey God's orders?"

"Once again, I say free will," maintained Professor Devereaux.

"Once again, I say it cannot be. Disobeying God is a sin. We are told it is the very first one. Therefore, if Original Sin is to believed, the very concept of disobeying God did not exist in the world at that time. It would have been as foreign to Eve as if we were to be asked to paint with the color magnamerma. Magnamerma does not exist! Therefore, we cannot paint with it. Even if we have the potential to do so should it someday exist.

"I ask myself again and again, what could have motivated Eve to do that which did not exist and disobey God? Did she care more for herself than He? This is pride. Pride is a sin. Therefore it did not exist and could not have been her motivation. Did she want what God had? This is covetousness. To covet is a sin. Therefore it did not exist and could not have been her motivation. Did she feel it unfair God had something she did not? This is envy. Envy is a sin. Again, it did not exist and could not have been her motivation!" Ebenezer exclaimed. "Help me, Professor, because I do not see how it is possible that Adam and Eve sinned unless they were born into a world where sin already existed!"

Professor Devereaux saw the sincere desperation in Ebenezer's teary eyes. And he recognized that this was a very serious question. If man did not fall, he would not need to be saved. The question with which young Ebenezer was wrestling went to the very heart of faith in the resurrection.

"Perhaps we approach this by a different angle," said Professor Devereaux. "The Bible is infallible, is it not?"

"Yes, sir."

"The Bible tells us that Adam and Eve's conduct in the Garden was the Original Sin, does it not?"

"Yes, sir."

"Well, then, *ipso facto*, Adam and Eve's disobedience was the Original Sin that has infected this world," said the Professor calmly. "We do not need to understand all of God's ways or how He has made it so. We merely need to obey."

"I hear your words, Professor. And my heart wishes to concede. But my mind creates in me doubt," said Ebenezer sadly. "What if it is not true all that the Bible leads us to believe?"

"Now, Ebenezer," said Professor Devereaux very sternly. "I have been very patient with you until now. But what you speak rings of blasphemy! And I will not listen to blasphemy in my presence! You are to banish that question from your lips for now and forevermore!"

"I shall try, Professor," said Ebenezer weakly.

"You shall do more than try, young man. Or our additional sessions shall come to an immediate halt. I do not invite the devil as my companion. You may not bring him along with you," said Professor Devereaux in as serious a tone as he could muster.

"Yes, sir," Ebenezer said, with the fear that any other response would drive this important individual in his life away.

"Good. We will not speak of this again," said the professor, closing the door on the subject forever after. It seemed to Ebenezer that things between the two of them were never quite the same after that conversation.

11

"Why are you wasting your time packing your bags, Scrooge?" taunted Howard Thrombone. Even after sharing a room into their sixth year at school, Howard's tolerance for having Ebenezer as a roommate had never improved. In truth, this was so of all the boys of Room 3C. Without Ebenezer being aware, the other five agreed to rotate beds to prevent any one of them from having to share space next to Ebenezer two years in a row. Now that they were in sixth year, it was Thrombone's second turn in the least desirable spot. He was none too pleased about it.

"What do you mean?" asked Ebenezer. "You are all packing your bags as well."

"Yes, Ebe-wheezer, but we are all heading home for the Christmas holiday," sneered Thrombone. "We all know that no one is coming for you to do the same." The other boys did not make much of an effort to mask their schadenfreude.

"You do not know that," Ebenezer protested.

"See here, Scrooge," Wallace Breckinridge piped in. "It is not as though any of us would object to seeing that sister of yours again. She is quite the shapely woman!"

The other boys snickered and nodded their heads in approval.

Ebenezer was livid.

"Watch your tongue, Breckinridge! No one disrespects my sister, Fan! No one!" Ebenezer shouted, rising from his bed, ready for a fight.

"Calm your tone, Scrooge," Thrombone said dismissively. Despite being on the verge of thirteen years old, Ebenezer was still the shortest boy in the room and his frame was the slightest. In a contest of fisticuffs, there is no doubt that he would take a pummeling, no matter the opponent.

"Yes, Scrooge," said George Remington. "Ease yourself. The lads were just having a spot of fun."

"It is not acceptable," said Ebenezer, reluctantly backing down.

"Worry not. There isn't a one of us who would dirty ourselves by touching a Scrooge woman," Remington laughed.

Ebenezer's eyes blazed in rage. If he were not sure that the other five would join forces to give him a savage beating, Ebenezer would have surely taken his chances to bloody Remington's lip. As usual, when they effectively pressed this particular button within Ebenezer, he was left powerless, hating himself for his own weakness.

"Were you going to speak, Scrooge?" Remington queried, taunting Ebenezer.

Ebenezer continued to glare at George Remington, but said nothing.

"I thought not," Remington concluded, and cast his attention back to his task of packing his belongings.

Having had their fun, all of the other boys did the same and continued preparing for their two week holiday.

The eighteenth of December, seventeen hundred and ninety-one was a difficult Sunday for Ebenezer to bear. He was forced to watch as, one by one, the other inhabitants of his room were called for to return to the warmth of their homes for the coming fortnight. As each left, Ebenezer had to endure the smug glances of every departing boy. Why his misery brought them so much pleasure was something that Ebenezer could never fathom.

Eventually, after George Kent departed from the room, Ebenezer was alone. He sat upon his bed, as he had done each year when this time of day arrived. He hoped that this would be the year that Fan was able to convince his father to allow him to return home, also as he had done each year when this time of day arrived. Sometimes even he had to wonder why he believed Fan could achieve this most gargantuan of tasks. The only answer he had for himself was a quote he recalled from his Reading and Literature class from Pope's *An Essay on Man*; "hope springs eternal in the human breast." As Ebenezer peered out the window this year, he began to suspect that Alexander Pope was a fool. Or perhaps it was he who was the fool.

The day passed into night with no sign that this year would be any different than any other he had experienced at Worthington. He lay back on his bed, staring at the ceiling. His eyelids began to progressively acquire more and more weight until, without his even realizing it, Ebenezer's eyes closed and he gently began to snore.

Ebenezer was panicked. It was dark all around and he was in the woods. He was running. Running as fast as he could. He looked up and saw the half-moon peeking out from between the branches and the dead and dying leaves on the trees. Where was he? He had no idea. He just knew he had to run.

Was something pursuing him? No. That was not it. He was running towards something. No. Someone. Who? What was this terror within his chest? Something was very wrong. Very dangerous. He just kept running down the wooded path, surrounded by so many trees.

And then he heard it. The sound. The voice.

It was Fan.

She was crying out for help. She was crying out for Ebenezer to help! But where was she?

"Fan?! Fan??!!!," Ebenezer could hear himself yelling. "I can hear you! Where are you?!"

All he heard in response was, "Ebenezer! Why won't you help me?"

His heart was pounding within his chest. He could hardly breathe. He stopped running and starting looking around in a circle. Where was Fan's voice coming from? Why could he not find her?"

"Ebenezer! Where are you? Help me! Help me please!" Fan's voice was getting desperate.

It was so strange. Her voice was clear as crystal. He should be able to see her. But her form eluded him. Where could she be? Oh, Fan! I must save Fan!, thought Ebenezer.

"I am here, Fan! Where are you? I cannot see you!" Ebenezer called out, with his hands cupping his mouth to amplify his cry.

"He's going to get me! Oh no! He has found me! If only Ebenezer were here!" Fan's terrified voice sounded.

Someone was trying to hurt Fan. No! I must stop this!, thought Ebenezer. He felt so powerless. So frustrated. So useless.

"Fan! I wish to help you. But I am all alone! I cannot find you! Please help me find you!" Ebenezer cried.

"You let him get me! You let him hurt me! You let him kill me!" Fan's voice shrieked out.

"No, Fan! I am here! I am here! I want to be with you, but I am stuck here!" Ebenezer bellowed.

"Ebenezer... Ebenezer... Ebenezer..." Fan's voice called.

Suddenly one of the branches from the nearby tree behind Ebenezer reached forward and grabbed him by the shoulder.

"Ahhhh!" screamed Ebenezer, and he jerked up from his pillow upon his bed.

Not a branch, but a hand was upon his shoulder. When he turned his head, he could not trust his eyes. It was Fan. In his room at Worthington. She was shaking him awake. And calling to him.

"Ebenezer!" Fan cried as she jumped back in fright as the scream that Ebenezer emitted exiting out of slumber startled her. "Wake up. It is morning."

Ebenezer rubbed his eyes with his hands. He still could not accept the image he was seeing before his eyes. Surely he was still dreaming. How could it be? Fan? Here? Now? Surely not.

"Fan?" Ebenezer asked hopefully. "Is it really you? Or is this a dream?"

"No, brother. It is no dream. I am here. Here to take you home!" Fan beamed.

"Home?" Ebenezer said in a daze.

"Yes, home, and not just for the Christmas holiday. You must pack all of your belongings. You are coming home for good and for all!" Fan told Ebenezer excitedly.

This was too much for Ebenezer to comprehend. What was Fan saying?

"What is this you speak, Fan?" Ebenezer asked.

"It is true, Ebenezer. It is true," Fan said. "The other day, Father awoke and came to me. He had such a changed look in his eye. I was frightened at first because I thought, 'I do not recognize him.' But then it occurred to me. He did not look like the stranger I first took him for. He looked the way he did when I was a young child. Before mother died."

"Truly?" asked Ebenezer.

"Yes. It was as though I was transported back in time to the past. To the wonderful past when our father was a jovial, loving, gentle soul," Fan reported.

"And what happened next?" asked Ebenezer.

"He told me, 'Christmas is coming soon. What do you wish that I may grant you?' I found it to be an exceedingly odd question because he knew what I would say. I have made the same request every year since you were first sent to this place. I did not realize that he was counting on my entreating him with the same unsatisfied plea that I made each year," said Fan. "So I asked, 'May Ebenezer please come home for the Christmas holiday this year?' What he said next surprised me."

"He said 'yes'," Ebenezer said in amazement.

"No," replied Fan.

"No?" asked Ebenezer, very confused.

"He said, 'No, Ebenezer may not come home for Christmas'. I was shocked at first to hear him say your name, and with such ease," said Fan. "Before I could protest, he said to me, 'Ebenezer may not come home for Christmas. He may come home for all time.' He said this while beaming at me with a smile I had not seen since my earliest days. I had forgotten that Father had so many teeth!"

"How do you account for this?" asked Ebenezer.

"I do not know and I do not care!" cried Fan. "All that is important to me is that he sent me to fetch you and bring you home forthwith. He sent me with this note for Headmaster Stowe that I was to deliver personally."

The letter read:

> *Dear Headmaster Stowe:*
>
> *Please accept this notice that effective immediately, my son, Ebenezer Aldustous Scrooge, is withdrawn from Worthington School for Boys. Please augment your records to reflect same.*
>
> *Thank you for your courtesies.*
>
> *I am grateful for your attention to these matters.*
>
> *Sincerely yours,*
> *Elias Scrooge*

"That is why I could not come to you during the weekend. I needed to ensure that the Headmaster would be in his office to receive this correspondence in hand," said Fan. "So pack the rest of your belongings, dear brother. I have a coach waiting just outside your dormitory doors to take us both home."

Ebenezer, now fully accepting that this miracle for which he had prayed for so long was actually for truth, rushed to collect all of his personals so that he may exit Worthington as soon as possible. Fan assisted and in short time, they were ready to call for assistance from the coach below to collect Ebenezer's bags and chests and load them for the return journey. While the coachmen were attending to this task, Ebenezer and Fan rushed down the path to Bailey Hall to seek out Headmaster Stowe. This would be the first time Ebenezer looked forward to a meeting with the school's top administrator.

Andrew Parkwood was surprised to see Ebenezer approach his desk accompanied by a lovely young woman of eighteen years. To his mind, he had no notice that the lad had been summoned by the Headmaster. He soon learned that this appearance was not by appointment. Ebenezer showed Mr. Parkwood his father's letter.

Parkwood looked at it and blinked in surprise. He had to read it twice to make sure he believed the words. Immediately after, he knocked on the Headmaster's closed door and entered when he heard the voice from within cry, "Come!"

Parkwood brought the letter to Stowe.

"You will not believe what you are about to read," Parkwood told him.

Stowe took Elias' note and read it. Undeniable relief appeared on his face.

"Very well, Parkwood. Send in the boy," stated the Headmaster.

Parkwood returned to his desk to find Ebenezer and Fan still waiting. He told Ebenezer that he was to go in to see the Headmaster. Ebenezer's heart fell. He feared that the Headmaster was not accepting his discharge. Ebenezer did not know if the Headmaster had that power, but it grieved him nonetheless.

Fan could read the worry in Ebenezer's eyes and guessed its meaning.

"Fear not, Ebenezer. It is done. The Headmaster cannot keep you here. I am taking you home," Fan said reassuringly.

Still not thoroughly convinced that Fan spoke the truth, Ebenezer slowly entered the Headmaster's office.

"So, Scrooge, it looks as though you will not be continuing your studies here at Worthington," said Headmaster Stowe.

"No, sir."

"I just wished to see you one last time and to wish you well."

Ebenezer was confused. He had never known the Headmaster to speak a kind word to him.

"Thank you, sir."

"Now be gone. Make good in this world. Do not embarrass Worthington by your actions."

Those were the last words Headmaster Harold Stowe spoke to Ebenezer. He then put his head down and his attention returned to a document upon his desk. He did not even say a pleasant farewell.

"Yes, sir," Ebenezer said, and once he realized that this was the final word he would hear, he dismissed himself. He walked to Fan and together they exited Bailey Hall.

By this time, the coach was packed and ready. The siblings stepped up and sat within their designated seats together. They heard the driver give the signal to the horses and heard the crack of the reins upon the beasts' backs. The coach slowly made its way off of the campus, down the main pathway to the heavy iron Worthington gates. The guards opened the doors and Ebenezer watched from out the window as he passed through the threshold for the last time.

For the first time in his life, Ebenezer was filled with hope and with joy. He was back with his dear sister Fan. He would be troubled by

Worthington School for Boys no more. And most shockingly of all, his father asked for him to come home. Why, he did not know. At that moment, he did not trouble himself even asking the question.

The coach then began the long journey back to the Scrooge home. In its rear, the Scrooge offspring chattered excitedly to one another throughout the day and into the night. The cadence of the horses and the excitement of the day finally bested Ebenezer's will to remain awake.

He fell asleep nuzzled into his sister's bosom, her arms enveloping him. A smile danced upon his face.

12

The coach pulled up to the Scrooge home early on Tuesday, the twentieth of December. Fan roused Ebenezer from his sleep as he dozed gently next to her. He had not released his grip on his sister throughout the night. Each time she shifted, he moved with her, as though they were one. Even in his unconscious state, he did not wish to be apart from his Fan for even a moment.

Ebenezer's eyes fluttered open and he shielded them from the streaming sunshine with his hand. He sat upright and stretched, letting out a mighty yawn. He looked to his right out of the window and was treated to a sight he had not been permitted to experience for six years. He saw his home in the glimmering winter light.

"We are here, dear brother," Fan said to him. "We are home."

The front door opened and James emerged to assist the two young Scrooges. As he approached, Fan and Ebenezer alit from the carriage. James greeted each of them.

"Welcome home Miss Fan. Master Ebenezer. I trust you had a pleasant ride," said James.

"Hello James," said Fan. "Where is Father? I expected to see him when we arrived."

"He is upstairs in his bedchamber. He asked not to be disturbed. He stated that he was working on an important task," replied James.

The coachmen began unloading Ebenezer's bags and trunks. James directed them to the front foyer, where he instructed them to leave all of the items. Fan and Ebenezer followed them in. Ebenezer stood in the main entranceway and looked about in awe. Could this be true? Could he really be here? Was he really home?

Fan noticed the look in Ebenezer's eye and beamed down at him.

"Come, Ebenezer. Let us find Father," said Fan. "I assure you that you will be amazed by how he has transformed."

Ebenezer was hopeful, but still skeptical. He wished to his very core that Fan's words were true. It was just so very hard to believe.

The two ascended the stairs and went directly to their father's bedroom door, with Fan leading the way. As they approached their destination, Fan called out.

"Father! Father! We are home! We are here!"

Still no response from behind his closed door. Father must be quite hard at work, indeed, Fan thought.

With Ebenezer at her heels, Fan turned the doorknob with her left hand and began to push the door open while she knocked with her right.

"Father, why do you not reply? I have been calling you –" Fan began, but suddenly stopped as she opened the door to its full breadth and eyed the scene before her.

Elias was sprawled out upon the floor beside his writing desk. The chair beside him was on its side. His eyes were wide open. His face was contorted in a gruesome mask of fright and pain. His hands were curled inward, like talons, clutching his chest. There was the pungent acrid smell of urine in the room. He made no sound. No breath escaped his lips. His heart had beat its last.

"Father!" Fan shrieked, running to his still body.

Ebenezer heard Fan's cry as he stood at her back, still beyond the threshold of the doorway. Instantly he knew its meaning. Father was dead. There would be no reconciliation. He would not hear his father speak a gentle word to him. The very last word Ebenezer will have recalled hearing from his father matched the very first word he recalled hearing from his father.

In context, the event took place on the penultimate day of July, this year. Ebenezer's personal belongings were all packed within the carriage and he was preparing for his sixth departure for Worthington. He approached his father's room, standing in the identical spot as he now stood, while Fan, in a most distressed state, stood before Father within the room. She was informing Father that Ebenezer was about to leave for school. If history were to be her guide, Fan said sarcastically, Father would not see Ebenezer again for ten months. She asked him if he wished to say farewell to his son.

The one word Ebenezer heard clearly.

"No."

As Ebenezer stood outside of his father's door now, he reflected that the "No" from four months prior would be the last communication he would have from his father to echo throughout his memory forever.

Perhaps it would have been better if this was true.

It was not.

Ebenezer slowly entered the room and found Fan on the floor, cradling their father's head. His face was turned toward the doorframe. His eyes were still opened. Fan was hysterical, dropping her tears upon his still cheek and they landing in such a spot that it gave the impression that he was staring directly at Ebenezer with undeniable pain in his eyes and weeping.

Ebenezer stared back at his father. He felt numb. He could not cry. He hardly knew this man. To the extent a word was directed his way, it was usually one of anger or frustration. To the extent he felt his father's touch, it was usually in the throes of punishment. He was now an orphan. But as he stood there, it occurred to him that he had always been.

"Ebenezer!" Fan cried when she spotted him. "Call for help! Father is ill!"

Ebenezer continued staring at the scene without moving.

"Ebenezer!" Fan screamed again. "Did you not hear me?! Call for assistance!" Fan yelled, wild-eyed.

But no assistance could benefit Elias Scrooge. That time had passed. James heard the commotion from downstairs and ran to the room. When he saw Fan on the floor holding Elias, he hurriedly brushed past Ebenezer and walked over to her. He knelt down and looked her in the eye.

"Miss Fan," James said gently. "He is with your mum now."

Fan looked up at James. Slowly the reality washed over her body. She nodded her head absently. She released her grip upon Elias' head and placed it gently down.

Fan allowed herself to be helped up by James and led from the room. Ebenezer was now left alone with his father. He could say anything he wished and he would get no rebuke. He could unburden himself of any and all resentment that had accumulated throughout his years and he would get no challenge. He could even forgive his father, a path he was sure the good Professor Devereaux would advise he do, and he would get no rejection.

Instead, he said nothing.

His attention was drawn to the papers on the desk at which his father was clearly working when his heart gave out. Ebenezer walked to it and looked down.

He saw a square envelope identified as being intended for Fan tied with a lovely red bow around it. It sat covering a drawing of what appeared to be a young person, but the subject remained a mystery because the envelope covered the face.

Ebenezer lifted the envelope and gazed down upon what he considered to be the most lovely portrait he had ever seen. It was of Fan, but not Fan as she appeared now. Fan as she appeared in years past, when she was a young child. It was undeniably Fan. Ebenezer was transfixed by its beauty. He had never before seen a picture that seemed to capture a moment in time so perfectly.

His father had drawn this? It seemed impossible. Fan had told Ebenezer his father had the talent for artistry, but he had never seen his father display it during his lifetime. In fact, the only drawing that he knew his father to be responsible for was the faded one of his mother which Elias would stare at for hours when the bottle was his only companion. But he was so protective of the drawing that he let no one else look upon it. Ebenezer only knew that his father was gazing at an illustration of his mother because Fan told him that was what was rendered upon the paper he held. It is no wonder his father did not want to be disturbed. This drawing must have required a great deal of time and concentration.

Although it was addressed to Fan, Ebenezer could not resist examining the envelope that expressly stated upon it, "Do not open until X-mas". He looked down at his father at his feet and decided that this directive no longer applied.

As he was looking over the envelope, he took a small step forward and felt a small object beneath his toe. He bent down and saw that it was a quill, still wet with ink. His father must have been in the midst of writing something else when his heart gave out.

And that is when Ebenezer noticed the parchment that had apparently been dropped beneath the desk. Ebenezer assumed his father had been working on this when he, and the paper along with him, fell to the floor. He picked it up and rose to his feet. Although he was still a poor reader, after a few attempts he was able to understand the only lines that were written upon this page. His heart sank as he read its content.

He turned his back to his father lying still upon the floor and exited the room. He followed the sounds of his sister's sobs to join she and James down the stairs.

Ebenezer brought the two letters, Fan's beautifully wrapped one and his unfinished monstrous one, to the sitting room where James was attempting to console Fan. When Fan saw Ebenezer enter, she looked up from through her tears and suddenly felt ashamed. She should not have allowed herself to be led downstairs without first attending to her brother.

"Oh, Ebenezer," Fan said, her voice breaking. "Come here."

She stretched out her arms.

Instead of falling into her awaiting hug, Ebenezer showed her the envelope meant for her. He kept the letter with his name upon it concealed.

"Look, Fan. Father wrote you a letter for Christmas," Ebenezer said.

He walked over to her and handed her the envelope.

She looked at it and without thinking, her fingers began to remove the beautifully tied ribbon that encased it. She then opened the letter and began to read silently. As she did, she cupped her right hand to her mouth as the tears poured anew from her eyes, some dripping onto the page below.

When she finished, she looked up through her watery eyes at Ebenezer.

"What does it say?" he asked.

"I-I cannot," Fan said, overwhelmed.

"James, would you please read it?" asked Ebenezer.

James looked to Fan for permission and she silently assented with a nod. She handed the letter to him and he began to read aloud.

> *My beloved Fan,*
>
> *As I put ink to paper, I ponder what an extraordinary woman you have become. I think back to these years that we have been alone, without your sainted mother with us and I am forced to conclude that had I not had you, I would not have been able to endure. You are the light of my life and you never cease to make me proud. My love for you grows with each passing day.*
>
> *I know I have not always been the father you deserve. I hope from this day forward I may strive to alter that deficiency. You have always been kind enough to see past my faults. I shall endeavor to save you from this exercise forevermore.*
>
> *I wish you the merriest of Christmases and the happiest of New Years'. May we make 1792 one to remember!*
>
> *All my love, all my life,*
>
> *Father*

James concluded and handed the letter back to Fan. She carefully folded it and slowly placed it back in its envelope. She looked up at Ebenezer.

"Father truly had a tender heart," said Fan. "I wish you could have seen more of it yourself."

"I do not know how tender it was when directed at me," said Ebenezer, sullenly.

"Nonsense. He just did not know how to show his affection for you," said Fan.

At that, Ebenezer revealed the letter that was meant for him.

"What is that?" asked Fan.

"It is Father's Christmas correspondence to me," said Ebenezer sadly. He handed it to James.

"Go on. Read that one as well," encouraged Ebenezer.

James read the few words on the page and looked at Ebenezer.

"I think not, young Master Scrooge," said James, obviously trying to spare Ebenezer's feelings. "It is incomplete and, as such, incomprehensible."

"I read it James. I know that I am not strong with words, but I was able to read those ones. It may be incomplete, but it is fully comprehensible," said Ebenezer. "Read it."

With a great deal of unease, James complied.

My son Ebenezer,

I have hated you for your entire life. In granting you life, my Elizabeth sacrificed her own and I have never been able to forgive you

This is where the communication ended.

Fan rose and looked to Ebenezer. She took a step towards him. He took a step away.

"Ebenezer, listen to me carefully. Father wanted you home. He wanted you with him. That is why we are here now. I do not know what he was thinking when he wrote these words, but I am sure this represents nothing more than an incomplete and poorly expressed thought. Perhaps, Father was in the last moments of the illness that took him from us. We just do not know," said Fan, taking another step towards her little brother in an attempt to embrace him.

"No, Fan. You know that I love you, but you are not speaking the truth," said Ebenezer, putting his hand up to stymie her advance. "I do not know why Father summoned me home, but while it is clear that his last thoughts were apparently of me, they were not thoughts of affection. You, he loved. But me, he hated."

Ebenezer then turned and ran from the house.

"Ebenezer! No! It is not true!" Fan called after him.

But he was gone.

Just when the Scrooge family was meant to be mended, it had fallen apart further. Although it would have been impossible for Ebenezer to believe at that moment as he sat perched on a high branch in his favorite tree, his life was about to swing upward. Miserliness, illiteracy and death would somehow conspire together to result in Ebenezer experiencing a sense of real family for the first time. And, perhaps more importantly, it would lead to the introduction of Ebenezer to the only woman in his life who would ever supplant Fan as foremost in his heart.

13

After Elias Scrooge was placed in the ground next to his beloved Elizabeth, Ebenezer and Fan were brought back to the family home. The question of what would happen to the two of them was at the fore. While Fan was a lady of eighteen years, and while she had had her share of suitors, she was not interested in marriage to any of them. Her focus as she aged was in taking care of the Scrooge home, tending to her rapidly deteriorating father, and worrying about her younger brother. Nothing was able to rank higher in her evaluation, not even a man.

Father had accumulated some debts, but between his stipend from the partnership to which he was tenuously connected and the additional funds earned by Fan's needlework and laundering services, he was able to stay one half step ahead of them and maintain his household. Upon his death, his partners felt no obligation to continue making payments to the Scrooge children and so they dissolved the existing partnership and created it anew without the Scrooge name. That decision would make it impossible for Fan to meet the monthly expenses, including the care and upkeep of the property grounds, the salaries of James and Sarah the cook, and the day-to-day costs of preserving the home.

Furthermore, the few creditors that Elias did have came from out the woodwork to demand immediate satisfaction. There was but one option for survival. The Scrooge home and land would have to be sold. Fan and Ebenezer could not stay.

Following the funeral, Ebenezer and Fan were called to be present at the reading of their father's Last Will and Testament. It was clear from the start that he had not amended it for many a year. It discussed ownership and distribution of The Scrooge Company, an entity that ceased to exist in its independent form before Ebenezer began his first day at Worthington. It also called for bequeathing assets that Elias no longer owned upon his death.

With respect to his children, all in attendance were dealt a surprise regarding Elias' plans for each. He wished that if Fan were not of age or, if of age, not married at the time of his passing, that his wife's sister, Nancy, welcome her into her home. While it had been many years since Nancy and her husband, Laurence, had moved to London and had last seen their niece, Elias added a sum of money to go along with Fan into Nancy's account. Of course, the funds of which the Will spoke no longer existed at the time of the reading, but this did not dissuade Nancy from accepting the request.

With regard to Ebenezer, it was not Elias' wish that he remain with Fan. Expressing a reluctance in the text of the Will to saddle his sister-in-law with the care and shelter of both of his children, Elias instead reached from beyond the grave to appoint his own older brother, Stephen, to take charge of the boy. Elias and Stephen were not close by any measure and had not even spoken a word to one another since before Ebenezer's birth. But kin was kin and Elias thought it best for Ebenezer to go with an uncle he had never met.

Once again, the Scrooge children were to be separated. And just when they were finally being reunited. They had so looked forward to the upcoming year. It was an entire year before Ebenezer would be of age to begin his apprenticeship and Ebenezer would attend a school close enough to home that would afford him the pleasure of sleeping in his own bed each night. In so doing, he and Fan would see each other every day. With this new arrangement, it was questionable if Ebenezer would ever have daily contact with his sister again. As he heard the words issue from the solicitor's mouth, he felt hope drain further and further away that he had any chance to enjoy a happy life.

Stephen Scrooge was a dour man, but he took his responsibilities very seriously. While he was not interested in becoming father to his brother's son, he would not reject his duty. That being said, he also would not allow a dead man to tie his purse strings without his consent.

Before the sun set, Stephen sought out Ebenezer and told him to bid farewell to Fan and this house. They would be leaving immediately and heading back to his estate outside of London. Ebenezer was shocked by the quick departure plans. Once again, his world was going to be turned upside down and he was powerless to prevent it.

Fan held Ebenezer close and tried to reassure him.

"Now, Ebenezer, we shall not be so far apart. We will visit often and remain intertwined in each other's hearts and lives," Fan told him as he wet her bodice with his tears, holding onto her as though this was to be their last embrace.

Fan did all she could to remain strong for her brother, but inside a crypt could have been constructed for her soul. To have been reunited so few days before and now disjointed once more. It was not just.

"Come, Ebenezer," ordered Stephen. "Your Aunt Constance awaits us in the carriage. We go."

Fan kissed the top of Ebenezer's red head, smiled at him warmly, and released him to their uncle. Why his father felt he could not send Ebenezer with his Aunt Nancy so that he may be with Fan caused him great consternation. The only conclusion he could reach was that his Aunt Nancy did not want him, whereas Uncle Stephen, being Elias' older brother, could not turn down the obligation. Ebenezer's heart turned quite cold toward Nancy that day.

Ebenezer allowed himself to be led within the carriage and the elder Scrooge brother gave the order to the driver for them to depart. They had a long journey ahead and Stephen wished to be home by first light. He had business that required his attention and the youngest four of his children who were in need of tending.

The carriage headed out and Ebenezer watched from the window as his home receded into the distance. He would never see it again.

14

Ebenezer sat on the bed in the servant's quarters where he was assigned upon arriving at his Uncle Stephen and Aunt Constance's estate. There was ample room for him and his window looked out upon the snowy grounds. It was lovely, but it lacked heart. It lacked welcome. It lacked family.

And why should it not? Ebenezer was placed on the primary floor away from the main living space within the home. His cousins all slept in spacious bedchambers upstairs, where his aunt and uncle also lay their heads. The family quarters. That is where this house was a home. Not where Ebenezer was deposited.

It was not as though a room was not available within the hearth of the home so that he could not retire for the night among this branch of the Scrooge family. Four of the children – Edward, Patrick, John, and Stephen, Jr. – lived in the house. The eldest two, both daughters – Mary Rose and Chastity – were married and each had already made Stephen and Constance grandparents one time apiece. As a result, the girls' rooms were vacant and in fine condition. Furthermore, there was the bedroom suite that had remained unused since Constance's mother had passed away. Any of these bedrooms were an option, if only Stephen and Constance chose to make it so. They did not.

In fact, Ebenezer was given strict instructions that he was not to unpack his clothing and that the furniture for the storage of same was off limits to him. He was told in no uncertain terms that he would not be staying for a long duration. While an obligation to the dead was one that Stephen did not take lightly, he explained to Ebenezer that his responsibility ended once he could furnish the boy the means by which to be prepared for an independent future.

He then uttered the one word that caused Ebenezer's blood to run cold within his veins.

"Worthington," declared Stephen when Ebenezer asked what was to become of him. "Classes resume this Monday hence and you shall return to complete your education."

But Worthington School for Boys was not what fate held in store for Ebenezer.

As Ebenezer shivered in fear in the sterile room beneath the slightly musty covers in the foreign bed that night, his Uncle Stephen was hard at work writing a letter to Headmaster Harold Stowe by candlelight. He wished to retract the letter of withdrawal that his brother had sent. He explained that it had been dispatched in error by a very ill man and informed the Headmaster of Elias' passing. The letter concluded with a request for confirmation that his nephew's studies were to continue.

He handed this letter to his servant, Lemuel, with strict instructions that he was to ride to the school immediately and personally deliver the correspondence to the Headmaster. He was to await a reply and to bring it back forthwith. Lemuel told Stephen that he understood. He took the stable's fastest horse, Hermes, and galloped off into the snow.

The following day, Ebenezer arose early, having not slept well at all through the night. He exited his temporary room and wandered the halls of this enormous home. It was eerily quiet. Nothing and no one was stirring. He could see through the windows that snow had accumulated over the night, but that the clouds were not emitting any at present. He looked at the portraits on the walls, all of whom seemed to contain subjects that bore some resemblance to his recently departed father. He presumed these were other Scrooges from days past, but he had no way of knowing specifically who they might be. He found his way to a tall door that was slightly ajar and he pushed it open.

He found himself in a grand library. He had never seen so many books accumulated in one location before. He walked over to the far shelf and looked at the titles. Some looked quite old. As much as he felt in awe within this space, he also felt uncomfortable. It was as if this room were mocking him. So many words surrounding him that would cause him struggle if he were to try to read them. Ebenezer so envied those who found ease in that skill. Ebenezer had a deep appreciation for the imagination and listening to his sister recount to him tales such as *Robinson Crusoe* and *Arabian Nights* were some of his fondest memories. He craved the ability to bring those adventures to life for himself. If only the letters upon the page would cooperate.

As he was lost in the pleasant memory of Fan's sweet voice wafting over a book she held in hand, he did not notice his cousin Patrick enter the room.

"What are you doing in here?" asked Patrick.

Patrick's voice awoke Ebenezer from his daydream with a start.

"I'm sorry?" Ebenezer asked.

"I said, what are you doing in here?" asked his cousin, one year younger than he.

"I am doing nothing," said Ebenezer, not knowing exactly what to say. He feared that he was about to be exposed to trouble.

"There is nothing to fear, cousin. I am simply curious," said Patrick in a friendly tone. Then he added, "I am quite sorry about the loss of your father. I never knew him."

"In truth, neither did I," said Ebenezer absently, revealing a more earnest truth than he had intended.

Patrick considered Ebenezer's statement, but made no comment about it. Instead, he asked Ebenezer about school.

"Are you looking forward to returning to Worthington?" Patrick queried.

"Yes, quite," Ebenezer lied. He saw no reason to reveal his difficulties to this stranger who happened to share his surname. "It is lovely this time of year. And I truly enjoy my studies."

"I go to Amberrose Academy. *'Potentia et omnimodam'*. In truth, I don't care for it much," Patrick replied, frowning. "I envy you. I wish that I could remain at school throughout the year as you do. Instead, I return by coach each evening after final class."

"Envy me? Why is that?" Ebenezer asked, incredulous that anyone would envy him and especially for his poor fortune to have been forced to attend Worthington since before his eighth birthday.

"Freedom, cousin. Freedom!" said Patrick passionately. "I would gladly gnaw off my left hand and sacrifice it to Heaven – please do not reveal to my father that I blasphemed – if I could be removed from under the thumb of Stephen Scrooge for but a day. Tell me, is it as marvelous as I dream?"

"It is marvelous," Ebenezer blandly agreed, again lying and hoping his prevarication was not detected.

He need not have worried. Patrick was in a world of his own, considering the magic of living on one's own without an ever-present father and an overbearing mother breathing down his shirt collar at all moments of the waking day. How ironic that Ebenezer would have been in paradise if his own father had taken such an interest in his life and if his mother had been alive to do the same.

Patrick informed Ebenezer that the Scrooges were planning to entertain several of Stephen's business colleagues during the evening. Ebenezer replied that this sounded like an interesting event. Patrick rolled his eyes at his cousin.

"Ebenezer, you truly have been sheltered. How lucky for you that you have never had to experience such an evening before. How unlucky for you that you must do so now," Patrick said, smiling. "Prepare yourself for 'The Speech'."

"What is that?" asked Ebenezer.

"Father will line us all up before the first guest arrives. 'Now, I fully expect all of you to conduct yourselves as proper gentlemen, worthy of the name, Scrooge. If my expectations are not met, there is a switch with each of your names upon it awaiting you in the morning'," Patrick recited, doing his best impression of his father. He completed the imitation by pacing back and forth before Ebenezer, squinting his eyes, and puckering his lips outward as though one had just put to mouth a tart citrus fruit. When he was complete, he beamed at Ebenezer expectantly.

Ebenezer simply stared at him, a blank expression upon his face.

"Oh well," said Patrick, not getting the reception that he had hoped for. "Prepare yourself."

The boys spent the day together as Stephen and Constance busied themselves in preparation for the evening's event. Patrick invited Ebenezer up to the second floor where he saw, for the first time, what he was missing by being banished to the servant's quarters. The rooms were ornate and filled with all things a young lad could desire. Patrick reminded Ebenezer that Christmas had just passed and, despite all other things negative he could say about his parents, their generosity during the yuletide was not one of them.

Ebenezer tried to hide his emotion. He had never received a Christmas present from his father before. He always awaited with great anticipation his Christmas and birthday letter that Fan would send. But he could never participate in the conversation of his fellow classmates when they would return from the holiday break discussing all that they had received for Christmas. Nor could he avoid such conversations. Howard Thrombone took particular glee in asking Ebenezer what he had received each year when the subject arose in Room 3C. Ebenezer would always have to admit that he received nothing and would have to absorb the taunts of the other boys who would laugh that St. Nicholas had made Ebenezer a permanent member of the Naughty List.

That evening, just as Patrick had prognosticated, all of the boys, including Ebenezer, were lined up and spoken to by Stephen. Ebenezer was amazed at how closely Stephen followed the script that Patrick outlined earlier in the day, including the concluding threat of the switch. Ebenezer was forced to suppress a smile as Patrick stood next to him and, when he knew his father's eyes were on another of his brothers, surreptitiously tapped Ebenezer's leg. The clear message was, "You see, I told you so."

The evening was more dry than even Patrick had predicted. Ebenezer stuck to Patrick's side and followed his lead in all things. By some miracle, in Ebenezer's estimation, he escaped the event unscathed and unpunished. In fact, even though he could feel his uncle's eyes upon him for most of the night, not one word of reprimand was hurtled in his direction. Even more unbelievable to Ebenezer, at evening's end, Uncle Stephen approached Ebenezer and told him that he had conducted himself in fine manner. It was the greatest praise an adult Scrooge had ever bestowed upon Ebenezer and he was very proud. The other boys scoffed at the compliment, considering it a woeful understatement.

The very next day, Ebenezer awoke to the sound of his door being forcefully opened. His uncle stood in the doorway with a very stern expression on his face. In his hand was a letter Ebenezer would soon learn was Uncle Stephen's response from Headmaster Stowe.

"Ebenezer, get on your feet and follow me," said Uncle Stephen.

Ebenezer, now fully awake from fright, obeyed. He followed his uncle to a sitting room where Stephen tossed the letter in his hand down upon a table. He motioned for Ebenezer to pick it up. He did so.

"What is the meaning of this?" Uncle Stephen demanded.

Ebenezer looked at the letter but his fear, coupled with his reading deficiency, prevented him from ascertaining the meaning of the words on the page. Stephen noted Ebenezer's difficulty and his silence.

"Yes, yes. I had forgotten that I have an illiterate for a nephew," said Uncle Stephen callously. "Shame must have robbed me of my memory of such fact."

Ebenezer lowered his head and his cheeks flushed red.

"This memorandum you hold in your hand informs me that you are not welcome back at Worthington School for Boys under the prior arrangement that your father negotiated. They will only allow your attendance if I pay from my own pocket the full tuition, room and board fee for this and next year!" Uncle Stephen boomed. "Do you know what this means?"

"No, sir," said Ebenezer, trying to make himself as small as possible.

"It means that you are not going back to Worthington. My funds will not be looted simply because my dearly departed brother, God rest his soul, chose to send his son to a school run by a scoundrel!" Stephen shouted, red-faced. "How dare he not accept the termination of your withdrawal letter! Why, the ink has still not dried on the words my late brother penned!"

Ebenezer did not know what to say.

"Fortunately, I have a solution," said Uncle Stephen, calming down and lowering his voice. "You will begin your apprenticeship one year early."

Ebenezer was shocked. Where was he to be sent now?

"The only question to be answered is to whom you shall be apprenticed," said Stephen. "And what trade you shall take up."

Ebenezer continued to look up at his uncle silently.

"Many owe me favors," said Stephen to himself. "But three spring to mind who I know to be currently accepting. I am sure that they would all allow a lad of thirteen to begin work with them.

"There is Oliver Keating. He is a solicitor. I wonder if your mind is sharp enough to handle the difficult concepts associated with our legal traditions," Stephen stated, looking at Ebenezer. "No, I think not. Your reading skills are so poor, he would send you back to me before the sun rose on a second morn.

"Hmmm. Perhaps Richard Healy. He is a carpenter. An honest trade. Does not require agile mind or a nose to be firmly planted in books," Stephen considered. "But, no, look at you. Thirteen years old and scrawny as an underfed cat. You would not have the strength to survive a week under Richard's tutelage.

"Aha! I have got it. It is perfect!" Stephen cried, and without even telling Ebenezer where he would be sent for the next phase of his life, Stephen dashed from the room, leaving Ebenezer standing alone and confused.

He went to his study and drafted an Apprenticeship Indenture for Ebenezer's signature to rest beside his own as the boy's legal guardian. When it was completed, Ebenezer was summoned.

"Ebenezer, it is my understanding that you are quite proficient at arithmetic. It is perhaps your only strength. Is that correct?" Stephen asked.

"Yes, sir," said Ebenezer, not quite sure if he had just been complimented or insulted, but feeling that he was in no position to pose the question or to suggest that he had other talents aside from solving equations.

"Good. Then sign here." Stephen placed the contract in front of Ebenezer and showed him a line with a grand "X" at its fore. "You do know how to sign your name, do you not?"

"Yes, sir," said Ebenezer, taking the quill from his uncle's hand, this time certain that he had been insulted by his boorish relation for a second time in as many utterances directed his way.

"Do it then," ordered his uncle.

Without reading the document that was thrust before him, Ebenezer executed his signature in the best penmanship he could muster.

It was done.

"Go collect your personals, boy. We leave within the hour for London," commanded Stephen.

Ebenezer did as he was instructed.

Before the clock chimed, signaling the next hour, Ebenezer and his Uncle Stephen were in a carriage on their way to the Accounting Offices of Francis Fezziwig.

15

$\mathcal{F}$rancis Fezziwig was a rotund man with cherry-colored cheeks and a permanent smile affixed to his face. He was of average height, but whenever he was present, he was the biggest man in the room. Everyone knew he was in attendance and, in short time, everyone was glad for it.

Fezziwig never did anything small; it was always to excess. His appetite for food and drink was eclipsed only by his appetite for pleasure. His voice was loud, but never excessive. All knew when he entered at any function. His presence was palpable, but never overbearing. He laughed easily and was generous with compliments. And his laugh was of the infectious variety. It was a difficult task indeed to remain solemn when Francis Fezziwig was near.

His personality was imbued with its own gravity. Others were uncontrollably drawn to him. He had a story for any situation and he was expert at relating his tales. It was impossible not to be transfixed when Francis Fezziwig spun one of his notorious yarns. Often his denouement would prove to be indelicate, but as he presented it, they were never coarse. His narrations had the power to successfully thaw the inhibitions of even the most rigidly proper of ladies and have them all atwitter despite their better judgment.

Mealtime was an event for Francis Fezziwig. He did not just eat. He devoured. But he took care to savor every morsel to its fullest. Every bite was a new encounter with pure joy. He swam in ecstasy as the flavors danced upon his tongue. His delight was unmistakable and all around him soon found themselves emulating his feasting behavior. Ample time was needed to complete each course as he would never hurry the experience, but it never felt to his dinner companions as though they were wasting any valuable time.

Fezziwig loved music. The jauntier, the better. And he was especially fond of up tempo tunes suitable for dancing. There was no greater happiness for Fezziwig than prancing to a lively melody with a woman. It made no difference whether she be round or slight, taller than he or petite, beautiful to view or plain and common. Fezziwig simply loved women. Their touch, their aroma, the lilt of their voice. Everything.

But there was one woman who stood out high above the rest. His one true love, his companion thorough all of life's triumphs and tribulations, his wife of twenty-one years, Margaret. They were a perfect match. She could equal him in all things of any import. Their personalities meshed like a lock and key. Their sensibilities were of the same ilk. And their love for one another was that of fairy tales. Once upon a time they met and they have, since that day, been living happily ever after. They were two halves of a whole.

Margaret was a corpulent force of nature. She, like her husband, loved life to its fullest. She squeezed every drop of pleasure from any experience in which she found herself. When Francis completed the punchline to one of his uproarious witticisms, Margaret's laugh was always the loudest in the crowd. When the music began, she was the first to the dance floor. When the chance for an adventure reared its head, she was the first to explore the possibilities.

The relationship between the Fezziwigs was as strong as steel. She never felt the sting of envy when she saw her husband twirl a different lady on the floor. She enjoyed watching his broad smile, knowing that when the music came to a halt, the room emptied, and the lights grew dim, it was she with whom he would be retiring to the boudoir. And their mutual lust for life was not reserved for their public appearances. They made love each time as though it was their first. They took time to explore each other's ample bodies and both were committed to the achievement of the other's pleasure before they permitted their session to conclude. The rhythmic squeak of their bedsprings deep into the night was a common song echoing throughout the chambers of the Fezziwig home on more nights than not.

The only deficiency in the Fezziwigs' lives was that they were unable to conceive a child. Both loved children with their whole hearts and it grieved them that they could not produce any of their own. But, being who they were, they did not dwell on this problem. Instead, they doted on the children of friends and neighbors. If a nearby child were ill, one could be sure the Fezziwigs would know of it and appear at that family's door bearing gifts and good cheer. When a male child from their community grew old enough and was sent to war, the Fezziwigs sent correspondence encouraging his spirit and wishing him a quick and safe return.

Francis Fezziwig's accounting business provided another avenue to satisfy their need to be surrounded by the young. He would take in new apprentices as often as he was able. These boys lodged in the Fezziwig home in the most comfortable rooms the Fezziwigs could provide. The Fezziwigs would attend to all of their needs and make them feel as though they were family. They saw each of these young men as surrogate sons and this was reflected in the responsibility they took upon themselves to ensure each of the boys would have a financially successful life, a strong moral center and assurances that the Fezziwig doors would always be open to them, even after their apprenticeship service was complete. This bred loyalty on the part of the apprentices towards their benefactors that could be found nowhere else in all of Great Britain.

It was into this environment that young Ebenezer was being brought on the thirtieth of December, seventeen hundred and ninety-one. Stephen and Ebenezer first made a stop at the accounting office where Stephen knew Fezziwig would be at that time of day. They entered and an employee made his way to the rear of the main floor when they asked to speak to the good proprietor. Stephen and Ebenezer waited by the door, until the young man returned and directed them to follow him.

Before they made it across the floor to his office, Francis Fezziwig emerged wearing a bright green suit. Fezziwig loved the color green. He made it a point to wear something of green at all times. He did not care what shade. He simply could not present himself outside of his doors if his trademark green was not somewhere upon his body. He felt it was the cheeriest of the colors and he wished to always be adorned in such friendly tint. He also believed it brought out the inner merriment of those he encountered. On this day, his suit made him appear like a large, grinning toad. And clearly, there was truth to Fezziwig's theory. It was difficult to look upon him without smiling and feeling an instant sense of warmth.

Fezziwig approached Stephen with his hands outstretched in an anticipatory handshake. The two men met and indeed engaged in a hearty shake. Fezziwig looked from Stephen to Ebenezer and back to Stephen again.

"Mr. Scrooge, it is marvelous to see you again!" Fezziwig beamed. "Who do you bring with you on this fine day?"

"This is my nephew, Ebenezer Scrooge," said Stephen. To Ebenezer he directed, "Greet good Mr. Fezziwig."

"Hello, sir," said Ebenezer, extending his hand as he saw his uncle do.

Fezziwig grabbed Ebenezer's outstretched hand and shook it with such gusto that Ebenezer feared he might break it off.

"It is a great pleasure to meet you, Ebenezer," said Fezziwig, looking directly into the boy's eyes.

Peering back and forth between them again, Fezziwig asked, "How may I assist you fine gentlemen on this brisk winter's day?"

"Francis, I wish to entrust my nephew into your care and instruction. He was recently orphaned. In fact, the tragedy occurred just this Tuesday last when my dear brother, Elias, was taken to meet the Creator. I was bestowed with the responsibility to see to it that Ebenezer here has a prosperous future. I can think of no better place for him to begin that journey than here. With you," Stephen stated.

He produced the Apprenticeship Indenture papers and handed them to Fezziwig.

"You will see that all is in order. All that is required is your assent and signature," said Stephen. "I need not remind you of our previous arrangement at which time I saw fit to accommodate your needs."

"No, of course you need not," said Fezziwig as he examined the papers in his hand, still smiling as was his norm.

He looked up at Stephen.

"Yes, yes. Of course I will be happy to take on young Ebenezer. It is an unusual time of year to begin one's training, true, but that shall not be an obstacle for us, will it lad?" he said, looking at Ebenezer.

"No, sir."

"I can certainly use a new boy of fourteen once the next page of the calendar turns and we enter the new year," said Fezziwig in his usual good spirits.

"Let it be known, Francis," said Stephen. "Ebenezer is thirteen, but I hardly see how one year should make a difference to a man like you."

Fezziwig considered that for a moment.

"Thirteen, you say?" Fezziwig asked.

"Yes, but it is none but a trifle. The boy's education has come to an end and he is need of a wise guiding hand such as your own to help lead him forward," Stephen said. "And you will find that he is quite extraordinary in the field of arithmetic. It is a good match."

"Yes, it is as you say," Fezziwig said, smiling down at Ebenezer. "What is a year? I can see that this is a young man destined to surpass all expectations. Come with me back to my office so that I may locate a writing utensil and I may sign your contract."

"Excellent," Stephen said triumphantly. The three walked back to Fezziwig's office, where he dipped his quill in ink and jotted his name down in large, flowing letters. Even one in need of spectacles would not require their use to read it.

"Well, we will need to get his belongings to my home and to get the boy settled in," declared Fezziwig.

"There is room in our coach if you wish to join us," offered Stephen.

"I believe I shall," replied Fezziwig. Before exiting the establishment, Fezziwig went to one of his assistants and informed him to keep watch until he returned.

The two men and the boy took the short ride from the office to the Fezziwig home together. When they arrived, Fezziwig had his wife summoned and Margaret came out to greet her guests. Fezziwig explained to her that young Ebenezer here was going to be their newest apprentice and that he needed to be shown to his room. Margaret was busting with joy.

"Why, he's so handsome!" she said.

"How do you do, ma'am," Ebenezer said.

"And so polite!" Margaret shrieked in delight. She then grabbed him and enveloped him in a mighty hug, pressing him so tightly to her bosom that for several moments, he could not find breath.

She released him and invited him to follow her to his new room. He was instructed not to worry about his belongings and that they would be brought up later.

Stephen looked sternly at Ebenezer.

"Mind Mr. and Mrs. Fezziwig and be ever vigilant in your work ahead," Stephen said.

"Yes, sir," Ebenezer said, looking up at his uncle.

"Now go," Stephen said, nodding towards Margaret, who was simply beaming with pleasure and squeezing her plump fingers into fleshy fists in excitement.

Ebenezer followed Margaret up the stairs to the living quarters, leaving his uncle and new master behind to conclude the final details of the transaction.

"You come at such a wonderful time, Ebenezer," said Margaret, as they ascended the stairs. "Tomorrow is New Year's Eve and Francis does not permit work on such day. All of the other boys will be here so you may get to know them. In the evening, we shall have a party. Are you aware of the famous Fezziwig parties?"

"No, ma'am."

"Well then I will not spoil it for you. You shall see for yourself," Margaret said smiling.

They approached a closed door and Margaret turned the knob, permitting Ebenezer entry.

There were three beds in this room, of which one appeared not to have an owner.

"The boys are all hard at work right now and won't be home until supper," Margaret informed Ebenezer. "In this room, you will share your space with Percy Sellick and Dick Wilkins. They are lovely boys. Percy just turned sixteen years old in November and Dick is, or was until now, our youngest at fourteen."

Ebenezer looked around, uneasily. Sharing a room with other boys was not an agreeable situation at Worthington. He worried about how he would be received.

"What is the matter, Ebenezer?" asked Margaret, genuinely concerned about the look on his face.

"Not a thing, ma'am," Ebenezer lied.

"Now, Ebenezer, we do not do that here. We do not hide our truth. I can see that something troubles you. Is the room not to your liking?" Margaret asked.

"No, ma'am, it is not that at all. It is just—" Ebenezer began.

"Just what, Ebenezer?"

"What if the other lads do not like me?" Ebenezer asked, feeling foolish admitting this great fear.

"Ebenezer, they will love you. They are wonderful boys. In no time at all, you will see that you will all be great friends," Margaret said, touching her hand to Ebenezer's cheek. "I promise."

Ebenezer still was not certain, but there was something in Margaret's touch that reassured him.

"Now, come, I will show you the rest of the house," Margaret said, taking Ebenezer by the hand. "This room over here is where our older boys sleep. Their names are Randolph White and Michael Ericson. They will be wonderful mentors to you. And down the hall, come this way, is my and Mr. Fezziwig's bedroom. If you need anything in the night, you do not hesitate to find one of us. Do you understand?"

"Yes, ma'am."

Ebenezer did not know what to make of this kindness. He had never experienced it so overtly before, except when it was shown to him by Fan.

Margaret led Ebenezer throughout the rest of the house, providing a bit of narrative regarding every room. She introduced him to the servants who worked for the Fezziwigs. She took him outside to show him the grounds and pointed out a great garden with a maze formed by the hedges she had her husband install. She told Ebenezer how much she loved flowers and just needed to have a place at her home where she could wander through and look at them blooming for her.

With each additional word and each passing moment, Ebenezer felt more and more at ease. Margaret invited him to join her for a mid-day meal and the two sat and discussed. Ebenezer revealed the passing of his father and his separation from his sister. Margaret was almost in tears and assured Ebenezer that he and his sister would see a great deal of one another. She would see to it.

For the remainder of the meal, Margaret did most of the talking. Ebenezer enjoyed listening to this woman. She made him feel a way he could not quite describe. His emotional vocabulary had very few points of reference for such a nurturing adult. It is no wonder he could not recognize the stirrings of security within his being.

After the meal, Margaret told Ebenezer that his personals should have been brought up to his room. He could take some time settling himself in, while they awaited the rest of the household's return. Ebenezer obeyed and went to his designated sleeping quarters.

To his surprise, Margaret came up with him and helped him unpack his belongings. She continued a steady stream of one-sided conversation while they worked. Ebenezer remained mostly silent.

When they were through, Margaret asked Ebenezer if he liked reading books. This question stung Ebenezer as though a cold bucket of water had just been splashed in his face. He was about to say that he did, but he remembered Margaret's earlier admonition.

"I do not read well," Ebenezer admitted.

"No?"

"I love stories," Ebenezer said quickly. "My sister used to read books to me and I love how the words made me feel when she spoke them aloud. But when I try to read them myself, the letters simply get jumbled up and make little sense to me. I can usually do it if given enough time to go over them many times, but it is very frustrating."

"Is that so?" said Margaret. "Well, Ebenezer, listen here and listen good. We are going to make it so that you can read and write better than William Shakespeare himself. What do you think about that?"

"I do not know, ma'am. My Reading and Literature professors told me I had little hope," Ebenezer said sadly.

"They said no such thing!" Margaret said in disappointment and shock. "Well, mark my words. Before this date next year, we will have you reading like you never have before."

Ebenezer wanted to believe this. He felt an excitement in the pit of his stomach for the prospect. He just hoped it would prove true.

"Now, you say you love stories. Have you ever heard the one of *Gulliver's Travels*?" asked Margaret.

"No, ma'am," Ebenezer said.

"Well, you sit right there while I retrieve it and I will return shortly. I will read it to you," Margaret said. "And next year, you will read it to me. Do we have an accord?"

Ebenezer smiled.

"Yes, ma'am."

When Margaret returned to the room, she read to Ebenezer for hours, entrancing him in the land of Lilliput. Preoccupied with their task, they did not realize that Mr. Fezziwig and the rest of the apprentice boys had returned from their day at work. Percy Sellick and Dick Wilkins stood in the doorway of their room for a few silent moments, listening to Margaret's voice tell of how Gulliver was battling the Blefuscudian navy and stealing their fleet.

"I love that story," Dick said.

Margaret turned around and smiled at the two boys.

"Who do we have here, Mrs. Fezziwig?" asked Percy.

"Percy Sellick. Dick Wilkins. Allow me to introduce our newest apprentice," Margaret said. "Ebenezer Scrooge."

Ebenezer rose to his feet and was suddenly concerned. But he need not have been. Percy and Dick walked over to Ebenezer and shook his hand.

"Very pleased to meet you," Dick said.

"Very good to know you," Percy said.

"Very pleased to meet you both as well," Ebenezer replied.

"Come, boys, let us go down to the dining room where our supper is sure to be ready. And let us introduce Ebenezer to Randolph and Michael," said Margaret.

With that, they all exited the bedroom and made their way down the stairs where a wonderful meal was awaiting them all.

16

The guests began to arrive shortly after eight o'clock in the evening. Francis and Margaret Fezziwig had kept busy throughout the day overseeing all of the arrangements. All of the boys had been hard at work assisting the servants in readying for the festivities. Everyone was expected to contribute in the Fezziwig home. Despite their responsibilities, it was a merry time for all as no one allowed the preparations to be a chore. There was a great deal of laughter and everyone's spirits were high. It was New Year's Eve. A great party was about to take place.

As for Ebenezer, he was not quite sure what to make of it all. He had never been surrounded by so much warmth and congeniality. It almost did not seem real to him at all. His nature was such that, if left to his own devices, he would have remained quietly in the corner. But the others would not allow that to be.

All of the boys wished Ebenezer to join in the gaiety. They peppered him with questions to determine what foods he liked, what music he preferred, and what memories he held dear. They included in him in all of their levity and would not allow him to withdraw into a state of reticence. He found it very difficult to relax under these circumstances as his past experience taught him to maintain his guard around others near his age. It took the greater part of the day, but the other apprentices began to chisel away at his apprehension by the time the party was to begin.

It was not long before the house was filled with revelry. It seemed that no one wished to miss a celebration at the Fezziwig home. And it seemed that all of London was invited. Businessmen, politicians, and tradesmen of all kinds were among the jolly crowd. The food was delicious, the drinks flowed freely and the music was first rate. Every soul in attendance was enjoying themselves. Even Ebenezer was beginning to calm.

As usual, the largest crowd was gathered around Fezziwig himself as he regaled the masses with uproarious tale after tale. Ebenezer and Dick walked past him on their way to refill their glasses as he was in the midst of telling one of his favorite new jokes.

"… and when his head of security came to King Louis XVI after the storming of the Bastille crying, 'Sire, sire… the people are revolting!" the noble king replied, 'Well of course they are *revolting*, my good man. They are French!'," Fezziwig boomed, and the crowd surrounding him burst out in raucous laughter.

"My my, Fezziwig. You are too much," came one voice.

"Yes, too much indeed!" another voice agreed.

While Ebenezer was sipping his drink and chatting with Dick Wilkins, he noticed a new figure enter the room. He was a tall man of sturdy build. At his side was a lovely lady who, at that moment, was being greeted by another woman. When she moved to her left to join her friend, Ebenezer saw a young lady no older that he, who had been standing behind this woman, appear as if by magic.

Ebenezer was instantly transfixed. This graceful being immediately became the only image in the room. She had light brown hair, in large curls that ran down her shoulders. Her eyes were the color of sapphire and they were such pools of beauty that Ebenezer believed he could swim in them forever. She was of perfectly proportioned build and she wore the most lovely blue and silver dress. He had never seen a more beautiful face. Who was this flawless angel that had just floated into his life?

"Did you hear me, Ebenezer? I said I am going to get something further to eat," Dick said, elbowing Ebenezer awake.

"I'm sorry?" Ebenezer asked absently, still not completely comprehending his companion.

"What is it you are looking at?" Dick said, craning his neck around Ebenezer. "Ohhh. I see. Would you care to meet her?"

Ebenezer flushed red.

"M-meet whom?" he stammered, trying to hide his embarrassment.

"Meet whom indeed!" Dick laughed. "Well, if you do not wish to, my apologies."

Dick pretended to begin to walk away.

Ebenezer stopped him by quickly putting a hand on his shoulder.

"No, no. I see to whom you refer now," Ebenezer said, still not able to keep his eyes off of this mysterious girl. "Well, I would not want to be rude."

"Of course you would not," chuckled Dick. "Come with me. She is our neighbor. I will introduce you."

Dick hurried ahead but the crush of the crowd kept Ebenezer from keeping up with him. When Ebenezer finally arrived at his destination, Dick was speaking with the lovely young lady.

"Ah, there he is. Finally," Dick said. He turned to the young woman. "Allow me to introduce you to Ebenezer Scrooge."

She genuflected gently.

"How do you do," her sweet voice spoke. "I am Annabelle Marie Benson."

Ebenezer was spellbound. He was having trouble forming words. His tongue felt as though it had grown four sizes within his excessively dry mouth. Finally, he found his voice.

"I-I am Ebenezer Scrooge," he said, with a modest bow.

"Yes, I know," she chuckled lightly. "Dick here has just told me so."

"I am Ebenezer Scrooge," Ebenezer repeated, nodding his head.

Turning to Dick, Annabelle said, "Does he speak any other words?"

Dick laughed and said, "I shall leave you two alone so that you may find out."

Ebenezer's eyes went wide with fear as his new friend left him standing before this vision of beauty to whom he was rapidly proving to be a fool.

"So do you go by Ebenezer or is there something else that you would prefer to be called," Annabelle asked.

"No, I am known as Ebenezer," Ebenezer said.

"He speaks further words! How marvelous!" Annabelle teased. "Most but my parents know me as Belle."

Ebenezer did not know what to say. Within his own mind, he was screaming at himself that he was presenting himself as such the simpleton. He did not know what to do. He was flummoxed. No person had ever had this effect on him before.

"Oh no," Belle said in feigned disappointment. "I have exhausted all of his words. I suppose I will have to escort myself to the table over yonder if my hunger is to be satisfied."

Ebenezer snapped to attention.

"No, Miss Belle. I will be happy to accompany you," Ebenezer said. "I myself was just considering that I would like something more to eat."

"Splendid," Belle said. "Please lead the way."

For the remainder of the night, Ebenezer found himself following Belle around the party as though she held him by an invisible tether. She was not the least bit disappointed by the attention.

At approximately eleven o'clock, the two were standing in the corner on the opposite side of the room from the musicians so that they could hear each other most clearly without the music in their ears. They both held goblets and were sipping their drinks as they spoke.

"You have very lovely hair," Belle commented. She boldly reached forward and stroked it between her fingers. At her touch, Ebenezer's stomach leapt to the height of his Adam's Apple. "I so like the shade of red."

"Th-thank you," Ebenezer stuttered. "I believe it derives from my mother, but I never knew her so I cannot be sure. Neither my father nor my sister own red hair."

"Well, it is wonderful. The only problem is that you wear it too short," Belle said, pouting. "You would look smashing if you let it grow to cover the nape of your neck."

At that very instant, Ebenezer resolved he would do so.

"Come now, my guests!" It was Fezziwig's voice. "It is time for all to show what they can do on the dance floor. We shall 'Cross the Channel'!"

Everyone seemed to know what Fezziwig meant except for Ebenezer. Cross the Channel? Belle looked very excited.

"Come!" she said, taking Ebenezer by the hand and leading him to the center of the floor. Her touch sent an electric wave up Ebenezer's arm.

The men and women were separating into two lines facing one another, and creating a wide lane between them. The musicians were playing a bouncy tune of rapid tempo. Fezziwig grabbed Margaret and brought her to the head of the gap that had been created, while his guests clapped along to the beat of the music.

"Go on, Fezziwig! Show us what you can do!" shouted one.

"I certainly will!" Fezziwig said, taking Margaret by the hand as the two held each other and danced in circles.

"No more for Arthur," Fezziwig stage whispered to his guests, as he pointed at Belle's father. "He thinks the woman to his left is his wife! Hands off, Arthur. Beemerman is the jealous type! Ha!"

The crowd roared and continued their clapping.

"Shall we, my dear?" Margaret asked her husband.

"We shall!" he replied.

With that, the two of them danced their way down the lane between his guests encouraging them on. There were hoots and hollers. A grand time was being had by all.

After the Fezziwigs had made their way down the "Channel", they took their place at the bottom of the line and the next couple, the Stollers, who were now at the head of the lane, came together and they danced down the pathway. Ebenezer could see that this was what was meant by "Crossing the Channel" and he suddenly grew very nervous.

He could not dance.

And with each couple working their way down the line, this inability was getting closer and closer to being exposed to the room. He looked across the "Channel" and saw lovely Belle laughing and clapping as she watched Michael Ericson dancing down the lane with Madeline Baker.

Nearer and nearer his turn came. His mind raced. How could he escape this certain embarrassment? What could he do?

And then there was no more time to contemplate.

It was his turn.

His and Belle's.

She dove in towards him and grabbed him by the hands. At her touch, to his horror, he noticed that his palms had exuded so much perspiration in anticipation of his humiliation, it was as though a dam holding back a powerful river had burst. He fully expected to see a splash of water when Belle made contact, but to his relief, none came.

He finally decided he had to do something or she would pull him directly off of his feet. What ensued was Belle whirling and twirling with reckless abandon, loving every moment of her journey down the floor. Ebenezer, on the other hand, maneuvered himself in such way that it most resembled a drunken horse galloping through the mire. The crowd howled in glee at Ebenezer's antics as most believed he was simply trying to amuse.

When he reached the end of the path and returned to his side of the lane, his initial emotion was one of shame and mortification. But when he raised his eyes and saw Belle smiling at him, not in derision, but in pleasure, his humiliation fell away and he returned her smile.

The party continued in this grand fashion for the remainder of the hour until Fezziwig announced that it was one minute until midnight. He instructed everyone to pair up and find that special someone with whom they wished to enter the new year. He dashed to the side of Margaret.

Ebenezer was embarrassed once again. He desperately wanted to approach Belle, but he now felt as if all eyes would be on him if he did so. He need not have worried because she approached him just as the musicians began the countdown from ten seconds. The entire room counted with them.

"Ten!"

Belle smiled at Ebenezer.

"Nine!"

She took his hand in her own.

"Eight!"

She squeezed his hand.

"Seven!"

She looked deeply into his eyes.

"Six!"

His insides flipped to and fro.

"Five!"

Belle took Ebenezer's other hand in hers.

"Four!"

They stared at each other, facing one another directly.

"Three!"

Seventeen hundred and ninety-two was almost here. Ebenezer could not believe how it was about to begin.

"Two!"

Belle bounced in place, still keeping her eyes firmly affixed to Ebenezer's.

"One!"

The moment had arrived.

"Happy New Year!" everyone shouted, and the musicians struck up a tune. The married couples all shared a kiss. None as passionate as the Fezziwigs. Many others embraced. Glasses clinked as toasts were raised. Hearty slaps on the back were exchanged between the men.

Ebenezer and Belle were still holding each other's hands and facing one another.

Belle leaned in and whispered to Ebenezer.

"Happy New Year, Ebenezer Scrooge."

She then kissed him on the cheek. It was the first time any girl other than Fan had done so. The wet spot that remained after she pulled her head back was the only sensation Ebenezer could process. She beamed at him. He smiled back, not knowing what to say or do.

Shortly thereafter, the party broke up. All had to return home. The following day was Sunday and the clergy of London would not find making merry an acceptable excuse for missing church. Belle made sure to say goodbye to Ebenezer with hopes they would see each other again in the near future. She reminded him that she lived at the property adjacent to the Fezziwigs so she would never be very far away.

"Belle, it is time for us to depart," her father told her.

Ebenezer said goodbye to Belle as her father led her away. He watched with disappointment as the Bensons exited the Fezziwig home. As soon as she was out of his sight, he began to doubt that this remarkable evening had actually taken place outside of his own imagination.

When the last of the guests had bid their farewells, the boys were all instructed to go directly to their bedrooms for a long and healthy sleep. Cleaning up could wait until morning, or rather, later in the morning, as seventeen hundred and ninety-two was already over one hour old.

The boys obeyed. Michael and Randolph went to their room and closed the door. Percy, Dick and Ebenezer went to theirs.

After they changed into their nightclothes and climbed into bed, it began.

"So, Ebenezer," said Percy with a twinkle in his eye. "Did you enjoy your first Fezziwig party?"

"Yes, Ebenezer," Dick chimed in. "Was there anything in particular that you found to your liking?"

Both boys laughed.

Ebenezer said nothing. He thought they were being unkind to him, just as his roommates at Worthington would have done. He rolled over and turned his back to the room.

"Oh come on now, Ebenezer," Dick said. "We are just having a spot of fun with you."

Ebenezer rolled back and looked in Dick's direction. He was trying to decide if what he was hearing was true.

"Yes. We are actually quite impressed," said Percy. "She is very pretty."

Ebenezer now looked toward Percy. He was still not sure whether they were being sincere. But he could not disagree. She was the most beautiful girl he had ever laid eyes upon.

"Are you going to say nothing about your triumph?" asked Dick. "Come now, man! We need to hear."

Ebenezer finally accepted that he was not the subject of a joke and calmed himself.

"She really is quite extraordinary," Ebenezer said wistfully.

The boys continued to talk about Ebenezer's adventurous evening for another hour before, one by one, they dropped off to sleep.

Ebenezer was the last to do so.

And the last image that burned on the backs of his eyelids before he was swept into unconsciousness was that of Annabelle Marie Benson.

Belle.

17

Flowers and children are not so very different. This was the philosophy of Margaret Fezziwig. If you give them the proper attention, provide generously for their needs, speak to them kindly and often, and allow them to feel that they are truly wanted, they will bloom in ways that are marvelously beautiful to behold. This is how she tended to her garden and how she approached her relationship with the apprentice boys. In the year seventeen hundred and ninety-two, the flower in her garden that required the most care was Ebenezer Scrooge.

When he first arrived, it seemed to Margaret that she had never met a more cautious child. He seemed to choose all that he spoke with extreme consideration and she noted a perceptible wincing as he awaited the reception his words would garner. No matter how kind the other lads would be towards Ebenezer, she could tell that his mind raced to ascertain the underlying meaning of what was said to him before reacting. What would be understood by most as good-natured teasing was the most difficult type of communication for Ebenezer to accept. His first impulse was always to assume he had just been rebuked and his small frame would shrink further still. On more than one occasion, Margaret had to conduct a private conversation with the others to remind them to be delicate with young Ebenezer. She did not know all of the details of his life up to this point, but it was clear that trauma was a constant companion. And one that he would not abandon very easily.

In the first month of his stay with the Fezziwigs, Margaret began his reading lessons in the evenings after he returned from the counting house. It was clear that Ebenezer did not want the other boys to know of his difficulty and so Margaret and he established a ruse by which the others were informed he was simply taking dancing lessons and, as such, they could not be disturbed. This was plausible, as all of the boys took such lessons at one point or another during their stay. The Fezziwigs felt it very important that the boys be proficient at dance due to the particular value it would play in their social interactions forever after.

In fact, it was not entirely a lie. Three nights a week, Ebenezer would meet with Margaret in the ballroom where the New Year's party had been held. For one hour, they would conduct the reading lessons. The other was reserved for his dancing.

When Margaret had Ebenezer read to her to assess where his problem may lie, she discovered quickly that his mind would not accept full words or sentences as they sat upon the page. His mind simply viewed the world of words differently than most, much like it assessed numbers in a manner his educators at Worthington could not understand. Whereas this difference translated into a true acumen in arithmetic, it sadly had the opposite effect on his reading ability. However, once Margaret connected these two concepts, Ebenezer would be given a gift he had never experienced in his life to date. He would be taught to read in a manner tailored to his way of thinking.

Margaret decided to appeal to Ebenezer's mathematical mind and turned reading into a series of equations to be deciphered. She would break down each of the words into their individual components. She focused upon the sounds each component would generate regardless of how they were combined into any given word. She had him add or subtract components to result in a complete element. Once his brain was no longer looking to the entire word or sentence and becoming overwhelmed, he was able to recognize the individual segments and he was able to assimilate how they interacted with one another. Margaret converted reading into a series of mathematical formulas to be solved, rather than a string of words to be read. And miraculously, as far as Ebenezer was concerned, the jumble of confusing letters began to coalesce and make proper sense.

From there, he was able to expand this technique to entire sentences so that he was able to understand the interaction between the different words. Considerably later, he would even be able to anticipate the words that would follow. After many months of ardent study, Ebenezer was reading entire paragraphs placed before him on his first pass.

He felt euphoric. He felt a confidence he did not know could exist within the human frame. He also became greedy. His first stumbling block on his road to true literacy was his own impatience. He wished to be given more and more difficult tasks, but Margaret did not want to rush his development. Upon his insistence, she relented, but her inclination to maintain a steady and reasonable pace was proven correct. When he was unable to put into practice all that he had learned immediately, his frustration emerged. He took several significant steps backwards before Margaret was able to assuage his pride and bring him back to an appropriate learning stride.

But Margaret never gave up on him. Her patience was boundless. Even when she knew that providing the advanced materials would not prove fruitful, she recognized that this was something Ebenezer would have to learn for himself. Only by allowing him to stumble, she recognized, would he be in a position to later run. And then fly. She believed in him, even when he had doubts about himself. Her encouragement never wavered.

His dance skills came along much more quickly than his reading ones. Ebenezer had always possessed a love of music. To be able to move to its rhythms so gracefully was a great pleasure for him. Before long, he could not determine which of the two lessons he anticipated more; the reading or the dancing.

In truth, the other apprentice boys knew of Ebenezer's troubles with reading. It was quite clear as he sat at his desk at the counting house. But not a one gave him any indication that they were aware and not a one used such information as a weapon. Ebenezer was truly blessed to have this amalgam of individuals to be surrounding him at this crucial juncture of his life.

The year seemed to go by very quickly for Ebenezer. He thoroughly enjoyed his apprenticeship. He absorbed all he learned and found an excitement in his chest when learning it. Not only did he take immediately to the actual work placed before him, but he proved to have a talented business mind as well. Fezziwig truly appreciated the way this young man's mind worked and he never attempted to limit his means or methods. Ebenezer's experience was the complete opposite of that he suffered through at Worthington. He was given freedom to experiment with his own techniques to accomplish the tasks set before him. Even when they were unsuccessful, Fezziwig did not become cross. In truth, Fezziwig quickly recognized that he had an especially valuable asset in Ebenezer Scrooge. Should his progress continue on the trajectory his talent was taking him, thought Fezziwig, it would not be an impossible future where the sign above his establishment could read "Fezziwig and Scrooge". This was how much promise Fezziwig saw in the boy.

From a social aspect, Ebenezer also began to flourish as his barriers were slowly being eroded away. He got along well with all of the boys, but none as famously as with Dick Wilkins. Perhaps it was because they were closest in age or because of something intangible that each saw in the other, but before year's end, where you found one, you were sure to find the other. They shared a sense of humor, a taste for the same music, and even the same foods were favorites of each. Without question, they became the closest of friends. It was just one more new and positive experience Ebenezer could credit to his absorption into the Fezziwig household.

Along with this new relationship, another was also blossoming. Ebenezer and Belle saw each other as often as possible. The Fezziwigs entertained quite frequently and Arthur Benson was always on the guest list. When he would come, his family was almost always in tow. While the men were preoccupied with affairs of a business nature, Ebenezer and Belle were preoccupied with one another. He had never been able to speak so freely in front of anyone other than Fan. Belle made him comfortable in a way such that he felt as though each time she entered the room, he was home.

They also arranged many a rendezvous in the Fezziwig family garden. During the spring and summer months, they loved to sit among the sweet aromas of flowers and learn all they could about one another. Ebenezer began to notice little things that enraptured him more and more about this beauty. He enjoyed making Belle laugh because when she smiled, a dimple would appear on her right cheek. Never her left. But always her right. She also had a marvelous laugh. A sweet sound he craved.

He also enjoyed in an odd way the uneasy feeling in his stomach she elicited when she sat quietly and looked at him in the eye. It made him feel self-conscious, but at the same time, alive. He had to force himself not to look away, but he found that he was always the one to break the gaze first. She had a confidence about her that was beyond her years. As he lay in his bed in the darkness at night, he would often wonder what about him kept her attention other than the longer red hair of his that he was now growing down to just above the tops of his shoulders.

She was a dream who had infiltrated his reality. When they were together, he wished never to be apart. When they were apart, he wished only to be together.

Adding to Ebenezer's contentment, he was also happy that Margaret had kept her promise about him being permitted to visit with Fan on a regular basis. Aunt Nancy and Uncle Laurence resided not very far by carriage. The Fezziwigs encouraged Ebenezer's interaction with his sister and on many a weekend, Fan was invited to the Fezziwigs for a delicious meal. On other occasions, Ebenezer was given access to one of the family coaches, and he was driven to his aunt and uncle's home so that he may pay a call on Fan there.

One of Ebenezer's favorite visits to Nancy and Laurence's home occurred on Saturday, the fourth of August. The day before was Fan's nineteenth birthday. Due to business constraints, Uncle Laurence was unable to hold a celebration for Fan on the actual day of her birth, and so he scheduled a modest party for her the following day. All from the Fezziwig home were among those invited to show them appreciation for how well they cared for their nephew and because they welcomed their niece on her many visits.

The event was lovely. It was not as elaborate as a Fezziwig affair, but few were. Fan enjoyed herself and Ebenezer was even able to display his newfound dancing ability with his sister. She was both surprised and delighted at his aptitude with difficult steps. The event ran well past darkness before Ebenezer and his new household were compelled by the late hour to depart. A good time was had by all. In four short months, the Fezziwigs would return the favor with an invitation to Laurence and Nancy when they did something for Ebenezer that he had never experienced before.

On Monday, the twenty-fourth of December, the Fezziwigs threw Ebenezer a birthday party. And a surprise one at that.

The set up was easy. Ebenezer had never had a birthday party and so he was not expecting one. He was told that the Fezziwigs were hosting a Christmas party on Christmas Eve, which did not come as a revelation to him. Everyone in the house was in on the secret.

On Christmas Eve, much like New Year's Eve, Fezziwig did not permit work at his establishment. The apprentice boys, including Ebenezer, assisted the servants in preparing the house for the affair. While they were bursting with excitement, not a soul disclosed the true nature of the party to Ebenezer as they worked side by side with him all day. It was most difficult for Dick Wilkins, as he had become accustomed to sharing his every thought with Ebenezer in the past year. But, good lad that he was, Dick remained silent.

After the guests had all arrived, it was Belle's turn to do her part for the surprise. Fezziwig had conscripted Arthur Benson for his assistance in carrying out the plan. Although Arthur was not particularly fond of the fact that his only daughter was spending so much time with the unworthy young man whom he derisively called, "that Scrooge boy", his friendship with Francis Fezziwig demanded his cooperation. Arthur gave his permission to allow Belle to lead Ebenezer from the house at the designated time so that the Christmas party's dual purpose could be prepared.

When such time arrived, precisely at nine o'clock, Belle played her part brilliantly. Of course, she and Ebenezer had found each other almost from the instant she arrived. Ebenezer detected a lightening of the air around him and when he looked up, there she was. His heart soared. He absent-mindedly stroked the ponytail in which his long red hair was now tied. He then approached her after politely greeting her parents who stood between the two. To Ebenezer's relief, the Bensons gave him a smile – although he could not tell if they were forced smiles – and wished the boy a "Merry Christmas". Ebenezer returned the sentiment. Belle then spoke.

"My, my throat is so very dry. Good Ebenezer, would you be so kind as to show me to the nearest beverage station?" Belle asked.

"Of course, Miss Belle," Ebenezer responded, keeping one eye on her father. "If that is acceptable to you, sir."

"You may go," Arthur said, and the teenagers headed off together at a brisk, yet appropriate pace towards a punch bowl.

Arthur turned to his wife.

"I do this for the sake of Francis, his friendship, and our business relations," Arthur said as his eyes followed his daughter. "But I do not care for this infatuation that I am witness to. That Scrooge boy has nothing. Despite what Francis says of him, I do not believe he will amount to much. I understand his father was a drunkard who drank himself into an early grave. Such weakness is bred within the stock. I wouldn't want such a malady running through my bloodline."

"I fully agree, dear," replied Theresa Benson. "But they are young. And our Annabelle is bright. She will exhaust herself of the boy in due time."

"I certainly hope you are correct, my love," Arthur said, still watching Ebenezer and Belle across the room. "If she does not, we may have to intervene."

"Let us try to enjoy the party, dear," Theresa said, trying to divert her husband's attention and improve his mood.

"Yes, let's," Arthur said, and looked at Francis Fezziwig coming his way. "Fezziwig, you scalawag! How goes it!"

From their vantage, Ebenezer saw Fezziwig and Arthur Benson engaging in a hearty discussion. He relaxed a bit once he realized he was no longer under Belle's father's watchful eye.

When the clock chimed its ninth bell, Belle looked to Ebenezer with mischief in her eyes.

"Ebenezer, take me to the garden," she said. "I wish to see it on this snowy eve."

Ebenezer was not sure whether he could accommodate. He did not wish trouble with his generous hosts. But, when it came to Belle, he did not know if he had the power to decline.

"Well, Belle, I do not know..." Ebenezer stammered.

"Were you told we may not?" Belle asked, batting her eyelashes.

"No," Ebenezer said, considering the question.

"Then what stops us? I simply wish to see how the garden appears by moonlight as the snow falls upon it," Belle stated. "Would you please show me?"

That was it. Ebenezer had no capacity to deny Belle what she desired.

He took her by the hand and they exited out to the rear of the party. As soon as their feet touched the snowy grass, Dick Wilkins, who had been surreptitiously following them, came back to the ballroom and gave Fezziwig the signal.

The apprentices and servants quickly went to work. They erected a banner that read, "Happy Birthday" upon the wall and sweet cakes were brought from the kitchen. Furthermore, the presents wrapped so beautifully were brought into the room and placed before, but not beneath, the Christmas tree. The musicians were made ready. The entire preparations took fifteen minutes. When complete, Dick Wilkins was sent to retrieve Ebenezer and Belle.

He stepped outside and walked to the garden. He found the two shivering in the cold and looking deeply into each other's eyes. He could not hear what they were discussing.

Ebenezer noticed Dick before a word was spoken. He got very nervous.

"Dick, is all well?" Ebenezer asked, very worried. "What are you doing out here?"

"All is fine, my friend," Dick replied with his rehearsed response. "It is just that Mr. Benson has fallen ill and wishes to depart early. I was sent to fetch Belle."

Ebenezer was very disappointed. He did not want to be separated from Belle. It only occurred to him while they were walking back to the lit house that he had not spared a thought for Mr. Benson's welfare.

"I certainly hope your father mends quickly," Ebenezer said to Belle.

"Oh, I am sure it is nothing," Belle said. "This happens to father from time to time."

Belle did not seem as disturbed about her untimely departure as Ebenezer expected. This also led to worry. Was she beginning to tire of their time together? It was an unfathomable thought.

When they re-entered the house, Dick led the way to the ballroom. Ebenezer noted that the door was closed, which was odd. He was so busy worrying that Belle was losing interest that he did not notice the absence of music emanating from the room. In fact, he did not notice the absence of sound emanating from the room.

Dick entered first, followed by Belle. When Ebenezer walked through the threshold, the entire room said as one, "Surprise!" Ebenezer nearly jumped out of his skin in fright. He had never experienced a surprise party before.

He looked up at everyone staring his way. The music began and the crowd began singing a welcome song to him. He looked around in shock. What was happening?

Francis Fezziwig burst through the crowd and lunged at Ebenezer. He grabbed Ebenezer's hand and shook it mightily.

"Happy Birthday, my boy!" Fezziwig cried.

Everyone was laughing and cheering.

"Pardon?" Ebenezer said. He was still not certain what he was witnessing.

Belle turned around with a beaming smile upon her face. Ebenezer could not help but notice that dimple he loved so.

"Happy Birthday, Ebenezer!" she squealed.

"I-I do not understand," Ebenezer stammered.

"What is to understand, my boy?" Fezziwig asked. "Tomorrow is not just Christmas, but your birthday as well. We have all made merry this last hour in celebration of the birth of our Lord. Now we will spend some time making merry in celebration of yours!"

Ebenezer was overwhelmed. No one, aside from Fan, had ever acknowledged his birthday before. Speaking of Fan, suddenly, as if conjured from thin air, there she was!

She approached Ebenezer and gave him a mighty hug.

"Happy Birthday, dear brother!" Fan said. "Is it not wonderful? All here to honor you!"

"I do not know what to make of it all," Ebenezer admitted.

"Just enjoy it, Ebenezer," Fan said. "You deserve it."

And for the remainder of the night, Ebenezer endeavored to do just that. He accepted the slaps on the back from his fellow apprentices. He feasted on the sweets brought out that were baked just for him. He opened birthday presents that came from someone other than Fan – although he opened the one brought by her as well – for the first time in his life.

He loved all of the gifts bestowed upon him, but one stood out above the rest. It was simple, but it touched his heart. A year earlier, it would have been a wasted gesture. But now, it was the gateway to another universe and a promise fulfilled.

The gift came from Mrs. Fezziwig.

It was her copy of *Gulliver's Travels*.

Ebenezer opened it and on the first page, there was written in her hand, "Keep this book close to your heart. When you read its pages, know that I keep you close to mine."

Ebenezer began to weep, despite being surrounded by so many. Was it because of the sentiment written on the page? Or because he knew that the real gift was that he could now read that sentiment on the page? He did not rightfully know. All he knew was that he could never part with this wonderful present. He sought out Mrs. Fezziwig and they shared a tight embrace.

This book would remain with him throughout the remainder of his life.

18

During the next several years, Ebenezer continued to grow and flourish at the Fezziwigs'. This development was accompanied by growth of a different kind as well; one that Ebenezer found less desirable. Shortly after his fourteenth birthday, Ebenezer began experiencing sharp pains in his knees and back. When these pains intensified, the reason became apparent. Small Ebenezer was suffering growing pains. Before his fifteenth birthday, the difference was noticeable. Before his sixteenth, Ebenezer would experience a spurt that saw him ascend several more inches in height. It was almost as if he had been stretched by invisible hands each night while he lay in his bed asleep. Perhaps, Mrs. Fezziwig wondered aloud, he had swallowed the magic beans described in one of their favorite tales to read during his continuing lessons, "The Story of Jack Spriggins and the Enchanted Bean". By the Christmas of seventeen hundred and ninety-four, Ebenezer's days as the undersized waif he had spent his life existing as were over.

He even overtook Dick Wilkins in height before the year was out. However, he always remained thin. Regardless of what he ate, Mrs. Fezziwig feared that a stiff breeze would carry him away.

This, to Ebenezer's mind, was the good news regarding his changes. Other alterations to his appearance were not so desirable. He noticed that he was developing more and more "eruptions" upon his face. Red and often oozing, with a white head of pus at its tip. Most frequently, these would appear around his mouth and upon his forehead. Mrs. Fezziwig tried to calm Ebenezer's embarrassment by informing him that this was just a part of life at this age. This did not make Ebenezer feel any better.

Other changes were occurring as well, none of which pleased him. Ebenezer noticed that his voice would squeak at random intervals when he spoke. He discovered hair growing in places he was not prepared for hair to grow. He feared the prospect of a sharp blade being introduced to his most sensitive of areas. He feared more the potential that without such blade, his new hair would grow out of his britches at his waist or down his leg to his shoes. Ebenezer did not share these worries with Dick or anyone else. He was far too embarrassed.

Adding to his ever-growing embarrassment was that he found himself to be much more gawky and clumsy in his increasingly larger frame. He would occasionally trip over his own feet for reasons he could not fathom. His arms also often felt too long for his body. This was a confusing time of life and Ebenezer was not fond of it one bit.

Francis Fezziwig tried in earnest to help Ebenezer through this transition period. He had been through this with past apprentices and he was quite adept at approaching the subject. But no matter how he tried, Ebenezer resisted accepting that this was the fate of all young men. He also doubted that a handsome man could be waiting on the other side of all these pubescent changes.

Adding to his distress, the summer of seventeen hundred ninety-four was a difficult one for Ebenezer. The Bensons decided to take a two month holiday. Two months without seeing his sweet Belle. Two months without hearing her mellifluous voice. Two months without touching the creamy, soft skin of her hands. For Ebenezer, the two months may as well have been two centuries.

"I am sorry, dear Ebenezer," Belle said, telling him the news as they sat in the Fezziwig garden. "There is nothing I can do to prevent it."

"But two months! For a holiday!" Ebenezer cried. "It is too long."

"I agree, but what is to be done?" Belle responded. "Father has decided and there is no choice in the matter."

"But where will you go?" Ebenezer asked, trying mightily to control his emotion.

"We shall tour Ireland," Belle told him.

"Ireland?" Ebenezer said incredulously. "One does not need two months to tour Ireland. It is a small island!"

"Nevertheless, this is where I shall be," Belle said, holding Ebenezer's hand in her own.

"It is because of me, is it not?" Ebenezer said angrily. "Your father disapproves of me. He thinks me poor and worthless. He does not believe I will ever be able to care for you in the manner in which you deserve and so he takes you from me in the hopes that your feelings for me will abate in your absence."

"I do not think this is the reason for our holiday, Ebenezer," Belle said. "But even if it was…"

Belle forced Ebenezer to look in her eyes. He had been looking down at their hands.

"Even if it was his intent, it would not matter. Two months apart cannot change my feelings towards you. Nor two years. Nor two thousand years," Belle said softly. "I am yours and you are mine. We have promised it so and so it shall be."

Belle was referring to a conversation the two had had several months earlier in this very garden. Ebenezer asked Belle if she would remain faithfully his for the remainder of their days. She told him she would. He apologized that he had no money or he would give her a trinket to commemorate their vow. Belle smiled and told him that she needed no trinket. Their words were ironclad and his request was as valuable as gold.

When it was time for Ebenezer to escort Belle home, he did not want to leave. He held fast to her hands, attempting to delay their parting.

"Come, Ebenezer. Walk with me home," Belle encouraged.

Finally, Ebenezer relented, feeling a powerlessness he had not experienced since his days at Worthington. They walked in silence across the Fezziwig land until they reached that owned by the Bensons. Ebenezer took Belle up to her front door. He stood there, internally struggling with a mix of emotions; rage and despair, sadness and fear. His hands shook as he released his grip and their fingers slid apart.

Belle turned to her door, and shuddered. She then turned back to Ebenezer. Tears filled her blue eyes. For all of the strength she was projecting, now, at this moment of separation, her will failed her. She threw herself into his arms and they shared a long and tight embrace.

"Oh, my sweet Ebenezer. I shall miss you so," Belle wept.

"I shall miss you." It was now Ebenezer's turn to feign strength.

Belle looked deep into Ebenezer's eyes and then did something scandalous. She kissed him upon the cheek. But not fully and only upon the cheek. She leaned in and brushed the corner of his lips with her kiss. It was the first time either of them had experienced that sensation. The forbidden contact sent a rush of excitement throughout both of their bodies.

Belle pulled back, for a moment worried that Ebenezer would be aghast at the inappropriate affection. She had nothing to fear. If anything, it was good that they were at her father's doorstep. Had they been ensconced in the garden away from all prying eyes, Ebenezer may not have been able to overcome the overwhelming urge he had at that moment to press his full lips upon hers, as though they were married.

"Farewell, my Ebenezer," she whispered.

"Farewell, my Annabelle," Ebenezer whispered back. It was a rare occurrence indeed when Ebenezer called Belle by her full given name.

With that, Belle entered her house and Ebenezer was left to wander back sadly to the Fezziwigs'.

It was at this vulnerable time that Ebenezer formed another significant relationship that would mold his life. Ebenezer was at his desk working fervently away on one particularly hot afternoon. Fezziwig approached him and asked that he run an errand. Fezziwig was low on ink and the usual messenger boy was absent from his station. He had been ill for several days and so it is likely this was the cause. In fact, Fezziwig was concerned enough for the boy's welfare that he planned to pay a visit before the day was done to check on his health.

Fezziwig presented Ebenezer with a change purse containing considerable funds for the order. He trusted Ebenezer implicitly, which is why Ebenezer was sent on this task. Ebenezer, of course, accepted and, after garnering all of the necessary information, left for the ink supplier's shop across the city.

Ebenezer did not really care for London very much. He was much more comfortable in the open spaces as where he was raised as a boy. He found the city too crowded with too many people for his comfort. Some, like Dick Wilkins, found London to be very exciting. All of the hustle and the bustle. Not Ebenezer. He found that a day spent on the London streets made him long for an evening spent in the quiet Fezziwig garden.

Ebenezer alit from the cab and paid the fare when he reached his destination. Before he entered the shop, several younger boys came running down the cobblestone and, unable to avoid Ebenezer, bumped into him hard enough to almost knock him from his feet as they passed. They were dirty and smelled of the street.

One of the boys turned around and tipped his cap at Ebenezer.

"Begging your pardon. Ever so sorry," he said.

Ebenezer brushed himself off.

"Quite all right," Ebenezer said.

The boy then rushed to join his two friends who were not polite enough to apologize.

Before Ebenezer could step into the ink supplier's shop, he heard a booming voice.

"Halt right there, you worthless guttersnipes!"

Ebenezer's head jerked up toward the sound that thundered above the din of the city traffic. He saw a man of considerable height and size seizing one of the impolite boys by the scruff of his collar. The man dragged the child almost off of his feet towards the very spot where Ebenezer was standing, transfixed by the scene.

The other two boys ran off and abandoned their friend.

When the man arrived with his quarry struggling in vain within the grip of the mighty man's fist, he shoved the child in Ebenezer's direction so that he could look at Ebenezer.

"Did you run into this young man?" the man demanded of the boy in his grasp.

Ebenezer thought this was a very nice gesture, but a bit much to elicit a simple apology.

"Answer me, boy!" the man instructed when he received no response.

"Yes!" the boy finally relented.

"Thank you, sir, but this is quite unnecessary," Ebenezer said. "I am not injured in any way by the boy's actions."

"No?" asked the man. "Check your pocket and see if all you brought with you on your journey remains in your possession."

Ebenezer did not know what this man meant, but he checked his pockets. To his astonishment, Fezziwig's change purse was gone!

The man reached into the boy's vest and produced the missing change purse.

"Are you perhaps a little light, my friend?" the man asked Ebenezer.

"Why, you little ragamuffin!" Ebenezer exclaimed, taking back the purse.

"Now, boy, I shall release you on the condition that you shall never take what does not belong to you ever again. If you assent, and I find you to have lied to me, things will not go so smoothly for you if we meet again," the man said severely. "Are we in accord?"

"Yes, sir," the no longer squirming boy said. As soon as the large man released his grip, the boy bolted from the scene and disappeared around the corner.

Ebenezer looked at his rescuer.

"Thank you, sir. I cannot tell you how much I appreciate your intervention," Ebenezer said, offering his hand. "This money belongs to my master and I would be quite distressed if I had to go to him and tell him I had lost it all."

"It is not a problem at all, my good man. Allow me to introduce myself. I am Victor Ferguson," the man said, shaking Ebenezer's outstretched hand. "It is good fortune that I happened to be looking to hail a cab when you stepped from yours. I saw the entire incident unfold."

"It is good fortune for me indeed! I am Ebenezer Scrooge," Ebenezer said.

"I must say," Ferguson stated. "You look quite familiar to me. Who is your master?"

"Mr. Francis Fezziwig, the accountant," Ebenezer replied.

"Ah yes, of course. That is why I recognize you," Ferguson said. "Everyone is fond of Mr. Fezziwig. I must have seen you in his company."

"Do you know Mr. Fezziwig?" Ebenezer asked.

"No, not formally, but I have always wished to make his acquaintance," Ferguson replied.

"Well, I think he would be most pleased to meet you after the service you have just done for him," said Ebenezer. "Perhaps after I order Mr. Fezziwig's ink, I could introduce you, if you are not too busy that is."

"That would be splendid! I truly appreciate your generous offer. I will accompany you," Ferguson said with a broad smile.

After accomplishing his task, Ebenezer shared a cab with Mr. Ferguson back to the Fezziwig office. Ferguson told Ebenezer how impressed he was that Ebenezer was more concerned for his master than for his own safety when it came to the stolen money. It was the mark of true character that Ebenezer's first thought when he learned of the theft was for Mr. Fezziwig. Ferguson commented that he wished he had a lad as valuable as Ebenezer working with him. Ebenezer blushed lightly at the compliment.

Ebenezer asked what Mr. Ferguson's business was and Ferguson told him that he invested money and made others rich. He said he found it quite a fulfilling job and one that he was proud to say at which he was quite skilled. But, he could always use some help and he would like to teach his ability to another. He asked if Ebenezer would be interested such a possibility.

"I couldn't, sir," Ebenezer replied. "I am indentured to Mr. Fezziwig until my twentieth birthday."

"I see," said Ferguson.

"Even if I were not," Ebenezer said, "I could not. The Fezziwigs are very good to me."

"I appreciate that kind of loyalty, my good lad. Although, I would never dream of taking you from your master. Only to add to your knowledge," said Ferguson. "It could prove quite lucrative for you. But perhaps wealth is not important to a fine young man as yourself. I apologize if I offended."

"No, sir," Ebenezer said, hearing the words "lucrative" and "wealth" echo within his mind. "I am not offended."

When they arrived back at Fezziwig's place of business, Ebenezer brought Mr. Ferguson directly to Mr. Fezziwig's office. Ebenezer knocked and Fezziwig welcomed him in.

"Ebenezer, my boy, how did it go?" Fezziwig asked from behind his desk as he seemed to be looking for something important upon the paper he was studying.

"It was quite eventful, actually, sir," Ebenezer replied.

Fezziwig looked up and saw the gentleman who accompanied Ebenezer into the room. Fezziwig rose to his feet and came around his desk. He approached Mr. Ferguson and shook his hand.

"Who might you be, sir?" Fezziwig asked.

"This is Mr. Ferguson," Ebenezer answered. Ebenezer then told Fezziwig about the attempted theft and how Mr. Ferguson thwarted the effort.

"Well, well. You have my great thanks, sir," Fezziwig said, presenting one of his familiar smiles.

"It was my great pleasure, Mr. Fezziwig," said Ferguson. "I cannot abide dishonesty and cannot accept watching a fine young lad such as Ebenezer here become victimized."

"I thank you again for your words, Mr. Ferguson," Fezziwig said, nodding his head in approval. "If there is anything I can do for you in the future, please consider me your servant."

"I merely wished to meet you and shake your hand," Ferguson said. "I have been a great admirer of yours for some time, as your gatherings are legendary and your accounting office of the highest reputation. Such a man is one I would like to know, I have often said to myself. How fortunate for me that I was able to meet you at this time."

"Again, I thank you, Mr. Ferguson," Fezziwig said. "Ebenezer, before Mr. Ferguson is on his way, please collect his contact information. He shall be an honored guest the next time the Fezziwigs host an event."

"Oh no," Ferguson protested. "I could not impose."

"I insist," Fezziwig stated, holding up the palm of his hand.

"Well, thank you, sir," Ferguson relented. "I have met the great Francis Fezziwig. I have had the honor of shaking his hand. And now, I am promised to be in his company again. I shall now take my leave of you and allow you to conduct your very important business."

The two men shook hands again and Ebenezer led Mr. Ferguson to his desk. He had Ferguson write down the address at which he may be contacted. Then Ebenezer walked Mr. Ferguson out.

"Good day, Mr. Scrooge," Ferguson said, tipping his hat. "I look forward to seeing you again."

"And a good day to you, sir," Ebenezer replied.

Ebenezer did not know it at that moment, but he had just bid farewell to a man who would change his life forever.

19

The reception was a great success. Fezziwig was very pleased with the turnout and he was glad to be able to introduce Victor Ferguson to his friends and colleagues. All were regaled with the report of Mr. Ferguson's bravery. When Fezziwig recounted the event, the thieves were more numerous and more dangerous than Ebenezer remembered them to be, but a hero's tale has never been harmed by the great tradition of exaggeration.

Ebenezer watched as Ferguson smoothly glided from one circle of partygoers to another and charmed them all. Ebenezer had not seen anyone so adept at interpersonal interaction since Francis Fezziwig himself. He witnessed Ferguson to be a social chameleon; in each group, he recognized the tone and tenor of the conversation and adapted perfectly to it. In a cheery group, he was the clown. In a group discussing important business, he was serious and contemplative. When Ebenezer witnessed a lady drop her scarf, Ferguson was the first to the floor to retrieve it. He was quick to flatter with sincerity and he accepted the admiration of the attending guests with grace. He was very impressive indeed.

He made quite the impression on Arthur Benson. Arthur was commenting on how fortunate he felt that he had his son, Philip, back under his roof. Philip made his homecoming from his service in His Majesty's armed forces just after the Bensons returned from their holiday in Ireland.

"His leg is quite badly injured, but thank the good Lord, they did not have to amputate, as they first thought may be necessary," Arthur was saying when Ferguson joined the conversation.

"He must be very brave and you must be very proud," Ferguson said. "May I ask where he did battle?"

"Corsica. He sailed under the command of Lord Nelson himself," Arthur said with pride.

"Nelson only accepts the best of men," Ferguson said, impressed. "Your son brings great honor to us all."

"He does," Arthur said with a smile. "He does, indeed."

"I hope you do not think it inappropriate, sir," Ferguson said. "But I wish to raise a glass in honor of your son."

All within earshot agreed this was most proper. They raised their glasses for the toast.

"To Philip Benson. A true Englishman, a brave soldier, and his father's son. May his recovery be swift and complete!" toasted Ferguson.

"To Philip Benson!" the crowd said as one.

"I thank you, kind sir," Arthur said after the clinking of glasses. "You are truly a gentleman."

"It is nothing," Ferguson said modestly. "Your son sacrificed for the good of us all. I merely recognized such valor."

"Well, I think it is quite extraordinary. On this day when we are here to honor you, you honor me and my family," Arthur said, shaking Ferguson's hand. "Come! Let me get you another drink!"

When the party came to an end, Ferguson was filled with praise for Fezziwig and extremely grateful for his hospitality. Fezziwig told him it was the least he could do after his honorable actions with young Ebenezer. Fezziwig repeated his offer that if there was anything further he could do to show his gratitude, Ferguson need only ask.

Ferguson did have one request.

"I find Ebenezer to be quite the astute boy. More so than is usual," Ferguson said.

"I quite agree," Fezziwig replied.

"I wonder if you would mind if I could borrow his talents on occasion to assist with my investment business? The boy would learn a great deal and my load would be lightened," Ferguson queried.

"Absolutely," Fezziwig stated at once.

"Wonderful," Ferguson brightly responded.

From that day forward, Ebenezer spent one day a week in the company and under the tutelage of Victor Ferguson. Ebenezer was very excited to expand his knowledge to the investment business. And very flattered that Mr. Ferguson wished to train him at such.

Ferguson had an unusual talent for drawing Ebenezer from the shell in which he usually resided. Unlike most, he was able to get Ebenezer to reveal his most intimate thoughts with minimal prodding. A common topic was Belle.

Ferguson told Ebenezer that he noticed at that first party how Ebenezer and Belle looked at one another. Ebenezer admitted that he felt deep love for the girl and wished someday that they marry. Ebenezer disclosed their secret vow to Ferguson and his dismay that he had nothing to give to Belle to commemorate the occasion. During this conversation, Ferguson could tell that something else was bothering the lad.

"You speak of Belle and this wonderful promise you have made to one another," said Ferguson. "But I sense something is troubling you. Something prevents you from fully immersing yourself in the joy you should feel that your lady love wishes her life to be with you. What distresses you?"

"You are correct, as you always seem to be, Mr. Ferguson," said Ebenezer. "I am disturbed because I am quite certain her father does not approve of me. He thinks I am not good enough for his daughter and that I shall never be."

"I am your friend, Ebenezer, and so I cannot lie to you," said Ferguson. "You are correct. I have heard him say this. But, where there is a problem, there is always a solution."

"I do not think so in this case," Ebenezer said sadly.

"Oh, of course there is, my boy," Ferguson said. "There is one thing I know will change Arthur Benson's mind about you."

"What is that?" Ebenezer asked hopefully.

"The same thing that is of most importance to all, whether they admit it or not," Ferguson said. "Money."

"Money?" Ebenezer asked.

"Yes, of course. Money. Gold. Bullion. In whatever form you choose to describe it," Ferguson said knowingly. "It is what makes the world go 'round and, if you possessed great quantities of it, Arthur Benson's opinion would turn in your favor. This is what you desire, is it not?"

"Yes, of course," Ebenezer replied. "It is just that Mr. Fezziwig has always counseled us that there is far more to life than money. I believe the way he put it was, 'Wealth will not kiss you goodnight, gold bars will not hold you tight, paper currency will not support you in a fight, for only your loved ones will keep you feeling safe and right'."

"That is a pleasant fairy tale sufficient for women and children. But it does nothing to assist a man in the real world," Ferguson said. "Mr. Fezziwig counsels that there is more to life than money. Well, I have found this to be the common cry only of those who have plenty of it. Tell the pauper in the street that money will not cure his ills. See if he responds with such a rhyme as the one good Mr. Fezziwig recites."

Ebenezer seriously contemplated what he was being told.

"So do you wish to overcome Arthur Benson's objections to you?

Do you wish to learn how it feels to be in complete control of your own destiny? Where you need not ask anyone for anything and yet you may have all that you desire?" Ferguson asked.

"Yes," said Ebenezer with a smile.

"Good. Then you are in the right place. Making money, as you know, happens to be my bailiwick," Ferguson said. "I can help you so that when you feel the time is right, young Belle will be yours forever. But it will require focus and commitment on your part. I will need your undivided loyalty. Can I count on such?"

"Yes," Ebenezer agreed.

"Marvelous," Ferguson said.

Ebenezer proved to be an excellent student for Ferguson. And, true to his word, he would do whatever was asked of him. Soon, Ferguson secretly began to provide Ebenezer with an income if Ebenezer's work led to the lining of Ferguson's pockets. Ferguson asked that Ebenezer conceal his newfound funds from Fezziwig because he knew of Fezziwig's mindset.

Fezziwig's philosophy was that an apprentice's remuneration came in the form of the skills acquired. He considered money to be corrupting on the young mind. Better to be skilled in the long view so that later one may provide the greatest service to society than to do whatever is necessary in the short term to acquire the pound and the shilling. Ferguson did not share this perspective.

On the first day Ferguson attempted to provide Ebenezer with payment, Ebenezer objected that Mr. Fezziwig would not approve.

"Does Fezziwig's counting house profit from the work you produce?" Ferguson asked.

"Yes."

"But you are not permitted a portion of that profit," Ferguson observed.

"No."

"Then Fezziwig keeps it all for himself," Ferguson noted. "That does not seem fair to me. Easy to speak so dismissively of wealth when one has it and prevents those doing the work to acquire it for him from obtaining any of their own."

Ebenezer had to admit that this made sense. From that day forward, Ebenezer accepted his commissions. And he kept them a secret from the Fezziwigs.

Ebenezer could not deny that he liked the feeling of power that came with controlling his own funds. He liked that he was not dependent upon Mr. Fezziwig should he choose to make a purchase that he desired. He also became addicted to the art of the deal. He felt a rush from assisting Ferguson sell a client on an investment. His eyes grew wide as he watched the golden coins transferring from the sold to the seller. He liked the feeling of the weight in his pockets of his portion that he earned. He quickly took to heart the main three tenets of success Ferguson taught him: study, guile, and patience.

On the twenty third of October, in Ebenezer's sixteenth year, he entered Ferguson's office with a wide smile upon his face. He was ten minutes late, which was unheard of for Ebenezer, but Ferguson said nothing. He could see that Ebenezer came bearing news.

"Mr. Ferguson, I have followed your advice and I purchased the 'promise ring' this very morn," Ebenezer said proudly.

"Allow me to view it," Ferguson said.

Ebenezer removed the small golden band from within his pocket. He put it into Ferguson's outstretched palm.

Ferguson studied the article of jewelry for a moment and then handed it back to Ebenezer.

"Fine work, my boy," Ferguson declared. "Belle will be unable to resist it."

That night, Ebenezer and Belle arranged to meet in the Fezziwig garden. Ebenezer brought the ring and planned his surprise.

When Belle arrived, she looked lovely. Her curls bounced upon her shoulders as she approached her awaiting Ebenezer. She reached out with both hands and he took them both, drawing her near. He softly kissed her cheek, inhaling the sweet aroma of rose petals.

They spoke for several minutes about the trite and mundane. Then Ebenezer looked deeply into her eyes. At first he could not speak.

"Whatever is the matter, dear Ebenezer?" Belle asked. "You have suddenly gone so rigid."

"Belle, my love," he began. "Do you recall how last year you promised yourself to me and I to you?"

"But of course, Ebenezer. How could I forget?" Belle replied.

"At the time, I could give you nothing but my word," Ebenezer said.

"Your word has always been enough for me," Belle said.

He took the ring from out his pocket and showed it to her.

"Now, I can give you more," Ebenezer said. "I would be honored if you would take this ring to commemorate our promise to one another. If you would accept this as my solid promise to you that when my apprenticeship is over and I have made good, that I will replace it with one that will signify you have agreed to be my bride."

Belle was shocked, but delighted.

"Oh, Ebenezer. It is beautiful!" Belle said breathlessly, as Ebenezer slid it upon her finger.

"I know it is not much, but it is what I have at present," Ebenezer said. "I will make good and you shall never want for anything when we are one."

"Ebenezer, it is wonderful! I did not need anything, but I do love it," Belle said. "And you need not worry about me wanting for anything. So long as I have you, I have everything."

Ebenezer thought to himself that he would ensure that she did, indeed, have everything. And when he could provide that, her father could no longer object to their union.

20

Belle loved her Promise Ring. She wished to wear it at all times and display it for the world to see, declaring that she belonged to her dear, sweet Ebenezer. But she dared not do so. Her father had already been hinting to her in not very subtle ways that she needed to begin getting "serious" about her future. She had several suitors other than Ebenezer who would have been more than pleased to have her cast her beautiful blue eyes in their direction. They were the sons of prominent members of the community who were friends with Arthur Benson.

One evening, Arthur's resolve hardened.

He sought out his daughter and learned she was in her room. He entered without knocking, as was his habit. He owned his home and felt that privacy was the province of he who paid the bills. What he saw enraged him.

Belle was twirling around in her room, holding her left hand up to her face with a broad smile. Upon her third finger was a small gold band that did not belong. Arthur noticed it immediately, and instantly surmised from whom it was given.

"What is the meaning of this?!" he shouted.

Belle stopped mid-twirl and fell against her bed in fright. She had not heard her father enter. She quickly placed her left hand behind her back. But it was too late. Her secret was out.

"The meaning of what, Father?" Belle asked innocently. "I was merely dancing."

"Show me your hand," Arthur ordered.

Belle lifted her right hand.

"No, daughter. Your other hand," Arthur stated, unamused.

Belle's mind raced, but there was no avoiding this. She slowly brought up her left hand and Arthur's eyes fixed on her third finger.

"What is that?" Arthur asked severely.

"It is a ring, Father," Belle answered.

"I can see that it is a ring. I can also see that it is a ring that neither I nor your mother presented you," Arthur said crossly. "Where did it come from?"

"London, I believe," Belle stated.

"Do not get wise with me, child!" Arthur boomed. "From whom did it come?"

"It was given to me by Ebenezer," Belle admitted. "It signifies our promise to belong to one another."

"It does no such thing!" Arthur said slowly and angrily. "The time has come for me to fulfill my responsibility as your father."

At that, he left Belle's room and she listened as his heavy footsteps became fainter and fainter until she heard the Benson's front door open and then slam shut.

"Annabelle," Arthur began at an evening meal approximately one week later, "I was just speaking with Preston Caine and he mentioned that his boy, Roland, has taken notice of you. Now there is a fine young man. I would like to arrange a meeting for the two of you."

"For what purpose, Father?" Belle asked.

"Why to commence a courtship, of course," Arthur said.

"A courtship!" Belle said, aghast.

"Naturally. He is an appropriate suitor. Tall, well read, and well moneyed," Arthur said. "It is a good match."

"I am sorry, Father, but I do not see it as such," Belle protested. "Roland Caine is pompous, arrogant, and a bore."

"I think your opinion may be clouded by other, shall we say, less desirable interests," Arthur responded.

"And to what interests do you refer?" Belle asked, her cheeks beginning to flush red in anger.

"You know very well of whom I speak," Arthur replied. "It is time for this childish romance come to its appropriate and inevitable end. I have been patient long enough."

"There is nothing childish about my relationship with Ebenezer, Father!" Belle exclaimed. "And I do not see anything inevitable about its end!"

"Please, child," her mother admonished. "Do not speak with such harsh tones to your father. You are a lady. You must behave as such."

"But, Mother," Belle protested.

"There is to be no argument," Theresa Benson said firmly. "If your father commands that you meet with Preston Caine's boy, then you will do so. And you will be polite, and proper and resplendent. That is the last word on the subject."

"I think not!" Belle retorted, leaping from her seat. "This is my life and I shall not be coerced into an appalling union simply because it is one you prefer!"

"Annabelle!" her mother exclaimed in shock. "You will mind your tongue and your tone. And you will obey! Now sit!"

Belle looked back and forth at the scowls on her parents' faces. She had never before behaved in this manner in front of her parents. The decorum infused within her being since her earliest days took hold of her. Her wild eyes softened. Her shoulders drooped.

She returned to her seat with her parents' disapproving stares continuing to bore into her as they waited for what was expected.

"I apologize, Father. And to you as well, Mother," Belle said softly.

"That is better," Arthur said triumphantly. "And so it is settled. I will arrange a meeting for you and Master Caine. And you shall sit with him."

"Yes, Father," Belle conceded. However, she had no intention of allowing Roland Caine to continue his interest in her. She would see to it that by the end of their first encounter, his hopes for a future wife would rest with another.

Belle decided not to mention this conversation to Ebenezer. Why do so? What good could come of it? She will obey her father's wishes and meet with Roland Caine and her behavior will compel him to cancel his ambitions to make Belle his own. She saw no need to upset Ebenezer with news of this situation.

Without her knowing so, her father had every intention of ensuring that Ebenezer knew Belle would be meeting with another suitor. A few short days after the meal in which he declared Belle would meet with Roland Caine, Arthur Benson paid a visit on Ebenezer. He found Ebenezer in the Fezziwig garden on an unusually pleasant evening in November.

Ebenezer was surprised to see Mr. Benson coming his way and he stood at his approach. Ebenezer spoke first.

"Hello, sir. A good evening to you," Ebenezer said politely.

"Yes, yes. And to you as well," Arthur said dismissively. "I come to speak to you about Annabelle."

"Yes, sir," Ebenezer said, very nervously. He had a very bad feeling in his core.

"I will come directly to the point, as I see no reason to dilly dally," Arthur said. "She is meant for another. Your relationship with her has come to an end."

All of the color drained from Ebenezer's face. His knees buckled and he was forced to sit.

"Begging your pardon, sir?" It was all Ebenezer could think to say.

"Yes, I speak the truth," Arthur said.

"With respect, sir, I have not heard Annabelle express such wishes to me," Ebenezer said.

"Listen here, Scrooge," Arthur said more softly, putting his hand on Ebenezer's shoulder in an almost fatherly gesture. "Let us speak frankly. What have you to offer her? Nothing. Does she not deserve more?"

Ebenezer thought about that.

"More than what, sir?" Ebenezer asked weakly.

"More than you!" Arthur barked.

"I believe she should make her own choice on that matter, sir," Ebenezer said, with as much confidence as he could muster.

"Oh, boy," Arthur sighed. "Do you see nothing? I am telling you. She has made such choice. And it is not you."

Ebenezer could not believe what he was hearing.

"You will cease troubling her and you will cease all attempts at seeing her," Arthur said staring directly into Ebenezer's eyes. "You will allow her the life she deserves."

"Sir…" Ebenezer began.

"I see that you still do not accept what is plain before you," Arthur said, with growing frustration. "I did not wish to be cruel, but you must know the truth. She is with the other young gentleman right now, as we speak."

Ebenezer felt as if a cannon ball had just ripped through his heart. It could not be!

"No," Ebenezer said softly.

"It is so," Arthur said. "And now it is done. Trouble her no more."

Arthur then left and headed back to his home. He was very pleased with himself. It was well past time that this be done. Fezziwig was of no help in the matter. Annabelle is too willful to trust to the task. It was a father's duty to protect his daughter.

Ebenezer was dizzy and nauseated. It could not be true. His Belle could not be with another. Ebenezer decided to make his way to Belle's house and prove Arthur Benson a liar.

Ebenezer waited a sufficient time to allow Mr. Benson to return to his home so that he would not be spotted. He then carefully followed the path that Arthur Benson had just trod and snuck up to the side of the Benson abode. He peered into all windows, knowing that he would not find his Belle in the company of another young man.

Until he came to the window of the sitting room.

What he saw there made him doubt his eyesight. Belle was seated, holding a cup of tea on a saucer. And across from her was a young gentleman sipping from his own cup. He could not hear what was being said, but it was clear to Ebenezer that both participants found the conversation to be pleasant. Suddenly, Ebenezer heard his Belle let out her beautiful, euphonious laugh and he could see the emergence of her sole, adorable dimple. It was more than he could take.

Ebenezer dashed back to the Fezziwig home as fast as his legs could carry him. He entered the house and ran to his room. He found it fortunate that no one else was present and he threw his face into his pillow, into which he wept like a child. How could his Belle do this to him? How could she keep company with another?

At that moment, Ebenezer resolved to redouble his efforts to become worthy of her. He could not allow his poverty be the barrier that kept his love from his arms. They were promised to one another. She accepted his ring. No! He would not allow another take her from him. He would not give up so easily. If Arthur Benson's approval was what was needed, then Ebenezer would do anything, anything at all, to achieve it. At that moment, he felt very fortunate to have Victor Ferguson in his life.

Belle played her part well, but not well enough. Her behavior did not put off the intentions of Roland Caine. He truly was as arrogant as Belle feared and he could not recognize her disinterest in his advances. To Roland, he could not fathom his relationship with Belle being anything but a success. In fact, to his mind, she was quite fortunate indeed that of the volumes of other debutantes he could choose from, he focused his attention on her.

Belle surmised that her father had paid a visit on Ebenezer when he did not appear at their next scheduled appointment in the garden. That had never happened before. Belle marched back home and found her father in the study.

Before she could speak, he addressed her.

"Ah, my dear," said Arthur. "There you are. I had been hoping to find you."

"Oh, Father?" Belle replied.

"Yes. I am very pleased to inform you that young Master Caine has requested another meeting with you," Arthur said. "I, of course, assented."

"Father, what did you say to Ebenezer?" Belle asked, ignoring Arthur's last comment.

"Ebenezer? Whatever do you mean?" Arthur asked.

"Come now father. You are a man of truth and honor," said Belle, furious. "What did you say?"

"Well, if you must know, the boy and I did have a very fruitful chat not very long ago," Arthur said. "I merely expressed to him the truth of the situation."

"And what truth is that, may I ask?" Belle asked, shaking in rage.

"Simply that your silly association was at its end," Arthur replied casually. "And that you had committed yourself to another."

"What is that you say!" Belle exploded.

"Watch your volume, my girl," said Arthur evenly. "I love you dearly, but if the switch is necessary to curb your insolence, I am not above going to such means."

"Father, I must make myself clear," Belle said. "I love Ebenezer. I always shall. I have no interest, no interest at all, in Roland Caine. I never shall."

"Nonsense," Arthur said dismissively, with a wave of his hand. "You do not know what you are saying. Nor do you know what is best for you. That is why I am here."

Belle stormed from the room without another word. She did not know what to do. She hoped deeply in her heart that her father had not driven her Ebenezer away forever.

21

The Fezziwig Christmas party of seventeen hundred and ninety-five was in full swing. As had been the norm for the past several years, all in attendance were also aware that this party now doubled as a birthday celebration for Ebenezer, who was now knocking on the doorstep of his manhood. He was to be seventeen in one day hence.

Ebenezer had not seen Belle since his conversation with Arthur Benson in the garden, one month prior. He threw himself into his work at Fezziwig's, but he fully immersed himself in his work with Ferguson. He had come to conclude that while Fezziwig could provide a great many things, only his work with Ferguson would make him the man he needed to be to win Belle.

Ferguson noted the change in Ebenezer right away.

"I like your gumption, Ebenezer, but to what can I attribute this new look of determination in your eye?" asked Ferguson.

"Mr. Ferguson, I promised you complete loyalty and you have it. I promised to do whatever you asked, and I will," Ebenezer said. "I must learn the ways of accumulating the maximum amount of wealth in the shortest period of time."

"I see," said Ferguson, pleased. "Would this, by any chance, have anything to do with our young Miss Belle?"

"Yes, it has everything to do with her," Scrooge admitted, wild eyed. "Her father spoke with me and told me our relationship was at an end. I then saw her in the company of another. She has not accompanied Mr. Benson to our home during the last two dinner meetings Mr. Benson and Mr. Fezziwig conducted, although she had never missed one before. I must earn her love."

"I find this all most acceptable, Ebenezer," said Ferguson. "But, bear in mind, that what I will teach you may run contrary to the lessons instilled in the Fezziwig household. Are you prepared to do what is necessary?"

"Yes, sir," Ebenezer said desperately. "Absolutely, sir."

"When I say this, I mean that you will learn some very hard, and perhaps difficult truths about the real world," Ferguson said. "For example, speaking of the concept of truth, things are not always as simple as they may seem. Truth, itself, like any other commodity, finds its value only in what it can bring you. And sometimes, its absence yields the most rewards."

"I understand," Ebenezer said.

"Do you?" asked Ferguson.

"No, not fully," Ebenezer admitted. "But I accept what you say and will follow your teachings on this, and all matters."

"Very good," Ferguson said, nodding his head.

It was only then that Ebenezer realized that there was another individual in the room. Rising from his seat in the shadows, a gentleman of twenty-four years of age approached Ebenezer and Ferguson.

"So this is the boy you were telling me about?" the stranger asked.

"Indeed," smiled Ferguson. "And his spontaneous vow of loyalty exemplifies all I have told you about him."

"It certainly does," the man said. "If I did not know better, I would say that you arranged this for my benefit."

Ebenezer watched this interaction in silence.

Ferguson turned his attention to Ebenezer.

"Ebenezer Scrooge," Ferguson said. "Allow me to introduce to you, Mr. Frederick Radcliffe. He is an associate of mine and, in truth, the best student I ever had."

Ebenezer and Frederick shook hands.

"The best student, perhaps, until now, that is," Ferguson concluded, winking at Ebenezer.

For the remainder of the month, Frederick Radcliffe was always at Mr. Ferguson's office when Ebenezer arrived on his weekly loan from Fezziwig's place of business. Radcliffe and Ferguson made a very formidable team on their sales calls, Ebenezer noted. They earned more that December than Ebenezer had witnessed Ferguson earn alone in the past.

Radcliffe seemed to take a genuine interest in Ebenezer's plight regarding Belle. He committed himself to assisting in any way he could. However, without knowing the players personally, he conceded, it would be difficult to directly intervene.

Ebenezer saw a solution to that problem. Upon the approach to the

Fezziwig Christmas party, Ebenezer asked Fezziwig if he may bring a guest. Assuming the guest to be Belle, Fezziwig agreed at once. When he learned that it was a business colleague that Ebenezer met during his work with Ferguson, Fezziwig kept the invitation open. He enjoyed Mr. Ferguson's company and was more than prepared to welcome one of his friends into the Fezziwig home.

Ebenezer was overjoyed to see Fan when she arrived at the party. He had not seen much of her in the last several months. She noted a difference in her brother, but could not quite pinpoint what it was she found to be at odds with his usual demeanor. She did notice that he was not attached at the hip with Belle, as he usually would be by this time in the evening. It was then she noticed Belle was not present in the ballroom at all.

"Where is your Belle?" asked Fan.

"I cannot say for certain that she is 'my Belle'," Ebenezer said sadly.

"Whatever do you mean?" Fan asked, surprised.

"I believe she seeks out the company of another," Ebenezer said sullenly.

"I find this very hard to accept," Fan said. "Did she tell you so?"

"No. But I was witness to a tea she shared with Roland Caine," said Ebenezer.

"What did she say about this tea?" asked Fan.

"She said nothing," Ebenezer replied. "In truth, we have not spoken since."

"When was this?" Fan asked.

"Approximately one and a half months ago. In early November," Ebenezer answered.

"Why has it been so long since you have spoken?" Fan asked.

"I do not know. She has not accompanied her father for his business dealings with Mr. Fezziwig at the house. I have been quite busy myself," said Ebenezer. "We just have not."

"You should make the effort to at least send a note," Fan said. "You do not know what she is thinking. She does not know what you are thinking. This is not a good situation, brother."

"Fan, I cannot," Ebenezer said. "What if she responds to this note and informs me that she prefers Roland Caine. I do not wish to know that."

"Oh, my brother," said Fan. "You have so much to learn."

At that moment, Ferguson walked by with Radcliffe by his side.

"Ah, Mr. Ferguson. You have made it at last," Ebenezer said, his spirits brightening.

"Yes," Ferguson said. "And it is a true pleasure to see you again, Miss Fan."

"And you, Mr. Ferguson," Fan said. Ebenezer thought he detected an unpleasant look in Fan's eye.

"And Fan, this gentleman to Mr. Ferguson's left is Frederick Radcliffe. He works with Mr. Ferguson. They are quite a team," said Ebenezer. "Mr. Radcliffe, allow me to present my sister, Fan."

Fan and Frederick locked eyes.

"Well, it certainly is a pleasure to make your acquaintance, Miss Fan," Radcliffe said, not breaking his gaze from hers.

"Pleased to meet you, Mr. Radcliffe," Fan said, with a little curtsey. She too could not look away.

Ferguson noted the instant attraction.

"Come, Ebenezer. I have questions for you," said Ferguson leading him away. Radcliffe remained behind and he and Fan began a conversation.

"What questions do you have?" asked Ebenezer when they were at a safe distance away from his sister.

"In truth, I have none," responded Ferguson. "I just had the notion that those two would prefer the opportunity to more fully introduce themselves to one another without our eyes and ears intruding."

Ebenezer looked back at his sister and he saw her thoroughly enjoying her time with Radcliffe. He had never seen such a look in her eye before.

It was then that Belle entered the room.

To Ebenezer's great dismay, Roland Caine followed immediately after and took Belle's wrap from her shoulders. Ebenezer could not stand the sight and so he turned to seek out the company of Dick Wilkins, who was fully apprised of the situation.

Belle looked to find Ebenezer from the instant she entered the room. She saw him hurry away when her wrap was removed from her shoulders. She immediately followed after him.

"Ebenezer," Belle called from behind him when she was at his heels.

He pretended not to hear her voice.

"Ebenezer," she repeated. "Please, turn around and look at me."

Ebenezer let out a mighty sigh. Then he did as he was asked.

"Why do you not seem happy to see me?" Belle asked, with tears in her eyes. "It has been more than forty-five days. I remember when such a prospect would be unimaginable for us both."

"You do not accompany your father to this house anymore," Ebenezer said flatly.

"It is not because I do not wish it," Belle said. "Father has forbidden it."

"Is this true?" Ebenezer asked.

"Yes, my Ebenezer, it is," Belle responded. "Please take my hand. I have forgotten your touch."

Ebenezer desperately wanted to do nothing more. But he had another question.

"Why do you come in the company of another?" Ebenezer asked, nodding towards Roland Caine, who was obviously in search of the lady he escorted into the room.

"Ebenezer, my father commanded it," Belle replied.

"I am told you are promised to him," Ebenezer said.

"No! Heaven forbid!" Belle exclaimed. "Where did you hear such a vicious rumor?"

"From your father," Ebenezer said.

"Ebenezer, no," Belle said, pleadingly. "I belong to you. I always shall."

As she said this, she reached out and they clasped each other's hands. A wave of relief washed over Ebenezer. He missed this sensation so.

"Excuse me, but what do you think you are doing, accosting my lady?" Roland Caine's angry voice spoke.

Ebenezer looked up and saw the taller, more muscular boy staring daggers his way.

"She is not your lady," Ebenezer said, releasing Belle's hand and stepping up to Roland so that they were now chest to chest.

"You insult my honor, you scrawny street urchin," Roland said. "And for that, you shall pay the price."

Roland reared back and brought his fist crashing into Ebenezer's jaw. Ebenezer was knocked to the floor. When he touched his lip, he found it to be rapidly swelling and he saw blood on the back of his hand when he pulled it back from his aching mouth. Both his pride and his face were in pain.

Ebenezer leapt to his feet and lunged at Roland with a roar. He thrust his shoulder into Roland's chest with as much force as he could muster and grabbed the larger boy around the waist as the two boys tumbled to the ground. Ebenezer found himself atop of Roland's chest. He reached back with all of his pain and his anger and his frustration and slammed his fist down upon Roland's exposed nose. It crunched beneath Ebenezer's blow and blood began to pour from both nostrils.

Unfortunately, this only angered the young man on his back. He grabbed Ebenezer by the throat and, with one quick move, slammed Ebenezer's helpless head to the dancefloor. Roland mounted the smaller boy, placing his knees upon Ebenezer's shoulders to prevent him from offering a viable defense as Ebenezer squirmed helplessly beneath his rival's legs like a turtle upended upon its own shell. Seizing the advantage, the angry older boy then began raining vicious blows down upon Ebenezer's exposed face that Ebenezer was powerless to avoid. Somewhere, seemingly in the distance, Ebenezer thought he heard the sound of Belle screaming, but what she was saying he could not discern. The unyielding assault was finally brought to a merciful halt when the nearest men, finally recognizing the truth of what was happening between these two young combatants, dragged the furious Roland from off of Ebenezer. The two boys looked as though they had been through a war.

Roland was led away to tend to his broken nose. Ebenezer remained supine on the floor, aching everywhere. Belle dropped to her knees beside Ebenezer, crying.

Fezziwig appeared in his field of view.

"What was the meaning of this?" Fezziwig demanded.

"Please do not be cross with Ebenezer," Belle pleaded. "It was Roland who initiated the altercation."

"Is that so?" Fezziwig said, trying unsuccessfully to hide a smile, immediately understanding the situation.

Ebenezer was pulled to his feet.

"Are you alright, my boy?" Fezziwig asked, looking Ebenezer in the eye.

"Yeth, thir," Ebenezer said, his words somewhat slurred as his swollen lip and light head did not allow him to speak otherwise. Ebenezer was a bit uneasy on his feet and Fezziwig assisted him to a seat.

Fezziwig leaned in and touched his forehead to Ebenezer's.

"Women, my boy," Fezziwig said knowingly. "More dangerous than muskets."

Ebenezer just looked up at him thorough eyes that were rapidly swelling shut.

"Come, we will take you away and get you cleaned up," Fezziwig said. He had Dick help and they walked Ebenezer out of the ballroom to attend to his wounds.

To Arthur Benson's great dismay, the incident only cemented his daughter's devotion to Ebenezer. It also was the final insult that Roland Caine would accept in his pursuit of Belle. He could have any female he chose. Why waste his time with one who wished to spend her time with a gaunt skeleton-framed nothing such as Ebenezer Scrooge?

This was how Ebenezer closed the door on his sixteenth year.

22

"And who gives this woman to this man?" asked Father Collingsworth.

"I do," said Ebenezer, as he placed his sister's hand into that of her betrothed.

Her fiancé smiled as he took Fan's hand from Ebenezer and they turned as one toward the good priest so that they may complete the ceremony to form their union. In a few short minutes, Ebenezer would be in the presence of Mr. and Mrs. Frederick Radcliffe.

The courtship lasted but a few months. Fan and Fred spent long hours in each other's company and Fan never wanted the time to end. She had never been so smitten. She had been approached in the past by other fine young gentlemen who had marriage on the mind, but she always found fault in each of them. Not so when it came to her Fred. She found his conversation to be fascinating, his manners impeccable, and, in truth, she had never seen a more handsome fellow. When he enveloped her in his powerful, muscular arms, she felt a safety she had never known. For the first time in her life, Fan was truly and deeply in love.

From the initial meeting at the Fezziwig Christmas party, the two seemed inseparable. Fred formally asked permission, in writing, of her Uncle Laurence, as head of the household, to begin his courtship of Fan. This duly impressed both Uncle Laurence and Aunt Nancy. Such formality was becoming more rare in these modern times, where propriety was often the victim of so-called "progress". This was the view of Laurence Manningham in any event.

Fan and Fred spent hours in conversation. Fred told Fan of his youth, having been raised in an orphanage. He never knew his parents, nor any details of them, save one. When he was merely days old, they placed him in a basket and dropped him at the doorstep of a local church. It was a miracle that he did not expire from exposure on that very night. The next morning, a kind woman discovered the child as she passed and brought him to the clergyman within. He did not even have a name. The surname of the woman who rescued him was "Radcliffe" and so that was how it became attached as his own. "Frederick" was a name bestowed upon him after the priest brought him to Browncroft's Orphanage. Fred did not even know who originated the designation.

Fan was always saddened when she heard of Fred's youth. It reminded her too closely of her dear brother's own. She empathized deeply with Fred's sense of loneliness and mourned his abandonment. Fred told her how he watched with sadness as a child as others with whom he shared sleeping quarters were adopted and found homes. Eventually, he dispensed with even the hope that he would ever live in a home with a mother and a father. Upon hearing each new anecdote of his early years, Fan fell more and more in love as her instinct to protect intertwined with her infatuation. It frightened Fan to think that these same tales could have been recounted by own her sweet brother had she not been there to safeguard him when he was a child. She wished in her heart that she could have done the same for her Fred.

In only two short months, Fred could wait no longer and he asked Fan to be his bride. They were walking along the River Thames on a chilly February evening. Fred feigned that he had slipped and he fell to one knee. When Fan turned in concern to assist him to his feet, she found him holding up a beautiful engagement ring. It took a moment for Fan to comprehend what was happening. Her amazement was so great that she did not hear Fred make his proposal. While she stood staring down at him without a response, he flashed her a nervous smile, wondering if he was being denied. He asked a second time and upon this request, Fan burst out into tears and lunged into his arms repeating the word "yes" over and over again. She struck him with such force that the two sprawled to the ground, laughing in the snow. A passerby must have thought them both mad as he increased his gait after glancing their way.

Of course, the first person with whom she wished to share her happy news was Ebenezer. She asked that Fred direct the carriage to the Fezziwig home before taking her back to her aunt and her uncle. Fred complied and the two paid an unannounced, but very welcome, visit to the Fezziwigs. After being received into the home, Ebenezer was summoned. He was pleasantly surprised to see his sister standing before him, along with Fred by her side. She then showed him the ring and shared with him the glad tidings. Ebenezer was very pleased to witness his sister so ebullient. He hugged her tightly and gave Fred a hearty handshake.

Francis Fezziwig was his usual magnanimous self and upon learning of the impending nuptials, he instructed his servant to fetch one of his vintage bottles from the wine cellar and specifically requested it be one that had been set aside for a special occasion. All in the house shared a toast to Frederick and Fan. Fezziwig offered to host an engagement party if, in so doing, he would not offend her Uncle Laurence. Fan thanked Fezziwig for his generosity and told him that she would relate the offer back to her uncle when she returned home that night.

Uncle Laurence accepted the offer to utilize the Fezziwig home for the fete, but insisted on being permitted to reimburse Fezziwig for any and all costs that were expended on his niece's behalf. Fezziwig agreed and together they arranged the most grand engagement celebration seen in London for many a year. Glasses were raised throughout the night expressing the desire that this be a long and prosperous union.

This was a very happy time for Ebenezer. In addition to his pleasure that his sister was so overjoyed, his relationship with Belle was strong once more. After her father's failed attempted coup to dissolve their association, Belle simply chose to openly defy his wishes. While Ebenezer was still determined to obtain Arthur Benson's blessing, Belle felt no need for it.

They resumed in a more discrete and careful manner, as Ebenezer had no wish to antagonize Arthur. And Arthur, for his part, while still not accepting his daughter's decision, chose to bide his time before he would again attempt to assist her in making the proper choice. He was not through with his meddling. It was his prerogative, he felt. A father must protect his daughter. And a man must protect his family name.

As the day of the wedding approached, Fan was faced with a delicate quandary. She was grateful to her uncle for all he had done for her since her father's death. He had given her a home in which to live and treated her as though she were his own. She could not have asked for a more generous benefactor. And while it would be most appropriate that he escort her down the aisle in her last moments as an unmarried woman, Fan preferred another to be given this honor. She wished that her dear brother, Ebenezer, join her as she took her final steps as a Scrooge. She feared, however, that she would insult her uncle if she made such request. One morning, her Aunt Nancy found her struggling with the dilemma.

"What troubles you, Fan?" Aunt Nancy asked, quite concerned.

"I do not know if I can speak of it with you," Fan replied.

"Does it concern your upcoming marriage?" Aunt Nancy asked.

"Yes," said Fan, wringing her hands.

Aunt Nancy believed she knew what this was about. She herself had questions and concerns about the duties of a wife after the vows were exchanged. She smiled at her niece.

"Fear not, Fan," Aunt Nancy said. "I understand your disquiet. But I assure you, all will be well."

"I do not know," Fan said, surprised that her aunt knew of her problem. "I do not know how to tell him."

"He will understand," Aunt Nancy said, now certain that her assumption was the correct one. "He knows that this is a special experience for you."

"But do you not suspect he will be insulted when I tell him that I wish another to take his place and that I am denying him the honor?" Fan asked.

Aunt Nancy was now in shock.

"My dear, I do not believe I fully understand. Who do you prefer to escort you into womanhood?"

Fan had never heard of marriage described in exactly this way.

"Why, Ebenezer, of course," Fan responded.

"Ebenezer!" Aunt Nancy shrieked. She stumbled backwards in dismay. "What are you saying? My love, that is most inappropriate! He is your brother!"

"Yes, Aunt Nancy. That is exactly why I thought it most appropriate it be him," Fan said, perplexed by her aunt's reaction. "Since I do not have a father with whom to share this, I thought the man closest to my heart, aside from my betrothed, should be permitted the honor."

"Child!" Aunt Nancy said, now fanning herself with her hand in an effort to prevent herself from swooning. "Where have you obtained such ideas?"

"Aunt Nancy, did your father not do this with you?" Fan asked, still very confused by her aunt's intense reaction.

"Certainly not!" Aunt Nancy exclaimed.

"No?" asked Fan, very bewildered.

"Fan, my love," Aunt Nancy said grasping both of Fan's hands in her own. "I understand your desire to be in the presence of one who makes you most comfortable. But what you speak of goes against nature! It is with your husband you will experience this, and no other man. Your wifely duties are to him and him alone!"

Fan finally realized what her aunt was speaking of and understood her forceful concern. Her eyes grew wide and her face flushed red.

"Aunt Nancy!" Fan exclaimed. "We do not speak of the same problem!"

"We do not?" Aunt Nancy asked weakly.

"No! Heavens no!" Fan cried. "I am not concerned about my wedding night or my marriage bed."

"You are not?" Aunt Nancy asked, still gripping Fan's hands and feeling dizzy.

"Of course not! I worry because I wish to ask Ebenezer to walk me down the aisle instead of Uncle Laurence," Fan said. "I do not wish to insult my good uncle."

"That is what you have been speaking of?" Aunt Nancy queried, nearly falling over in relief. "Thank the good Lord!"

The two women looked at each other for a moment and then burst out into laughter together. The tension was finally broken. Aunt Nancy released Fan's hands.

"Fan, your Uncle Laurence loves you very much," Aunt Nancy said, at last. "He wants nothing but your happiness. If you tell him that you wish Ebenezer to escort you to the place of your vows, he will understand. I promise you, there will be no insult felt."

"Are you certain, Aunt Nancy?" Fan asked.

"Yes, of course," Aunt Nancy replied. "Just speak to him with honesty and all will be well."

Aunt Nancy was, of course, correct. Uncle Laurence understood completely and gave his blessing to the choice. Ebenezer was honored that he was asked and accepted without giving it a second thought.

And so, on the fourth of June, seventeen hundred and ninety-six, at precisely seventeen minutes past ten in the morning within the confines of the mighty Anglican church, Ebenezer witnessed as his sister was officially wed. She was Nancy Elizabeth Scrooge no more. She would be known forever after as Fan Radcliffe.

23

"Ebenezer? A word?"

It was Ferguson. He was calling from his office.

Ebenezer quickly scurried in.

"Yes, sir."

"Ebenezer, I think it is time that I have you take the lead on one of our sales," Ferguson said. "What do you say to that?"

Ebenezer was very excited about the prospect.

"Yes, sir. I would be happy to do so," Ebenezer replied.

"As you may or may not be aware," began Ferguson, "I have been working quite closely with our good Mr. Fezziwig and his circle of colleagues for these past several years, beginning shortly after we first made acquaintance of each other."

"No, sir. I must admit that I did not know this," Ebenezer said.

"Yes, when I have had an opportunity to enrich their pockets, and mine as well, I have presented them with various occasions of good fortune," Ferguson said.

"That is most kind of you," Ebenezer responded. "I am most pleased to learn that you have aided Mr. Fezziwig and his friends in such manner."

"It is the very least I could do," Ferguson told Ebenezer. "They welcomed me immediately without even a thought of assessing my credentials before doing so. I value such personalities. I have my entire life. When one trusts me, and so quickly, it is always the truth that we become of vital importance to one other's futures."

Ebenezer was very happy to hear that Mr. Ferguson took such an interest in Mr. Fezziwig's well-being.

"That is most generous of you," Ebenezer said.

"Yes, well, as we are speaking of the concept of generosity," Ferguson said. "I have come across a new opportunity for Mr. Fezziwig that could produce great dividends for him so long as his investment is more generous than he has been comfortable parting with in the past."

"I see," said Ebenezer.

"Under more usual circumstances, I would ask Frederick to present this fabulous option, but he is away on his honeymoon with his new bride, as you know," Ferguson said. "This investment has relatively little risk and will almost certainly quadruple the capital of whomever is fortunate enough to acquire his share early."

"Quadruple, sir?" Ebenezer said with wide eyes.

"Certainly. At a minimum," Ferguson said. "However, such a return is only possible if the input is sufficiently significant. I, myself, will be involved with my own capital."

"What is it that you wish me to do?" Ebenezer asked.

"You are to be my lucky charm," Ferguson replied. "Mr. Fezziwig has been apprehensive about committing very much to any of my endeavors to date, despite how unreserved he is in all other aspects of his personality. I have found that many of his colleagues have been taking their cue from him when it comes to my business, and they too, have consequently been more conservative in their dealings with me. Do you understand?"

"Not entirely, sir."

"Fezziwig is the key to making this venture an enormous success. And not just for him. For all who look to him," Ferguson said. "If we can convince Mr. Fezziwig to ante up at this time, the others are sure to follow. This is an opportunity that comes along perhaps once in a lifetime. It is our duty as men of business and men of honor to ensure our good Mr. Fezziwig grasps it with both hands. I want you to present it to him."

"Why entrust me with such an important task?" Ebenezer asked.

"Because I trust you. And more importantly, because Fezziwig trusts you," Ferguson replied. "I will teach you all you need to know and all you need to say. And, Ebenezer, when this strikes, and it will strike, you will be in line for the healthiest commission your eyes have ever seen."

"I shall?" Ebenezer asked.

"Yes. I will give you four and a half share. I have never before made such an offer, even to Frederick," said Ferguson. "He will likely bemoan me for what I do for you, but you need not worry about that.

"Furthermore, if Arthur Benson participates, you will be doubly blessed. You will have in your pocket more riches than you have ever considered possible to date, and you will be responsible for doing the same for the man you wish to call father-in-law. He will be sure to accept you after you enrich his coffers so. And after you can show that you are no longer a poor apprentice with nothing of your own to provide for his daughter. I tell you, this shall establish you for success.

"Do you accept?"

Ebenezer's head was swimming with the possibilities. He could provide for his Belle. He could have the approval of her father. And he could recompense Mr. Fezziwig for the kindness and generosity he has shown. All for being the one to bring an assured financial boon to Mr. Fezziwig and those he holds most dear.

"I do, Mr. Ferguson. I most certainly do!" Ebenezer said heartily, shaking the hand Ferguson had thrust in his direction.

"Good. Here is what we must do…" Ferguson began.

Victor Ferguson then laid out the entire plan by which Ebenezer was to approach Mr. Fezziwig with this golden opportunity. His primary task, as he learned, was to help Mr. Fezziwig lower his guard when it came to parting with his money. With Ferguson's assistance, he was to educate him as to the nature of the program and to secure his assent to allow Ferguson to provide the same opportunity to his wide network of colleagues.

He was also to make it clear to Fezziwig that this would be of great value to Ebenezer. That by vouching for the investment, he will be, in fact, vouching for Ebenezer himself. Ferguson was being so good as to allow the potential investors believe that this formula for success was actually first detected by Ebenezer and his keen mathematical mind. All knew of his unusual talent in this area. Now they could all profit from it handsomely.

Ferguson reminded Ebenezer of the three tenets for success.

Study.

He must learn all that Ferguson was teaching him to the fullest before attempting to bring this grand idea to Fezziwig.

Guile.

He must use whatever knowledge or advantage he had to assist in convincing Fezziwig of the wisdom of this financial plan.

Patience.

He must not rush himself in his preparation, nor Fezziwig in his decision. He must be methodical, tenacious and resolute. He must know in his heart that what he is doing is right and never waver. His future, Fezziwig's future, and the future of all with whom Fezziwig did business would forever be altered by this one all-important deal.

Ebenezer asked that Mr. Ferguson be permitted to join the Fezziwigs for supper one evening several weeks later. He was so invited. Ebenezer asked Mr. Fezziwig for a private meeting following the meal. Noting how important this appeared for Ebenezer, Mr. Fezziwig agreed. He, Ebenezer, and Ferguson made their way into the library.

Ebenezer had studied well and learned much from both of his

mentors that were now in the room with him. This was apparent as he described the means and methods that he claimed, at Mr. Ferguson's insistence, he had devised to ensure a healthy profit at a minimum of risk. Mr. Ferguson chimed in from time to time to express his wonderment at such a simple, yet marvelous plan that Ebenezer had conceived. He truly had a gifted mind. Ferguson was clear that he was getting involved at the maximum rate. Together, Ebenezer and Ferguson convinced Fezziwig of the brilliance before him.

To show his utmost confidence in Ebenezer, as Ferguson had hoped would be a motivator, Fezziwig committed a great sum to the endeavor. He also agreed to call for conferences with his closest allies and, at such, to vouch for young Ebenezer's genius. The meeting was an enormous success.

At its conclusion, Mr. Ferguson presented Mr. Fezziwig with a letter that he hoped Fezziwig would sign. It extolled the virtues of the plan and gave due credit to young Ebenezer. At the top of the paper was an interesting crest of two rams seemingly crashing their heads into one another. Fezziwig chuckled when he saw the letterhead symbol. He said that he would be happy to sign such letter as he did so.

Ebenezer could envision the adulation that all would shower upon him once this investment yielded the riches all were assured of reaping. He could see in his mind's eye Mr. Benson welcoming him into his family with a hearty slap upon the back. He could picture his sweet Belle in a beautiful white wedding gown pledging her life to him while all in attendance greeted the union with applause.

During the following several weeks, Fezziwig assisted Ferguson and Ebenezer in arranging meetings with many of his wealthy friends. To Ebenezer's great surprise, even Arthur Benson agreed to listen to the proposal. With Ferguson's assistance and Fezziwig's sponsorship, Ebenezer successfully drew in the total amount Ferguson informed him would be needed to confirm that the venture would be a success.

Ebenezer awaited with great anticipation the day on which the grand plan was to go into effect. Once it did, he wore a smile that he thought would never be erased. He had difficulty concentrating at the counting house as his mind was only on how well the engine of riches he helped set into motion was prospering. This anxiety would continue throughout the month.

For reasons Mr. Ferguson stated he could not understand, the investment was not yielding the results he had expected. And then one day, while Ebenezer was working at Mr. Ferguson's office, chaos reigned.

Ferguson came bursting out of his office in a panic.

"Ebenezer, Ebenezer," Ferguson said breathlessly. "Come at once! We must make our way to Mr. Fezziwig's financial institution where his funds are kept!"

He grabbed Ebenezer and dragged him out the front door. Ebenezer had no idea what was occurring. He was completely confused and shaken.

"Mr. Ferguson, what is happening?" Ebenezer asked as they stood on the street.

Ferguson hailed a cab and pulled Ebenezer in behind him without answering the question. Ebenezer had never seen Ferguson in a state such as this. It frightened him.

Ferguson relayed the address and told the driver to make all haste. It was an emergency.

"Mr. Ferguson, please, sir," Ebenezer pleaded. "What is afoot?"

"I will tell you, Ebenezer. It is the worst of news. Our investment is on the brink of collapse. All of the funds that have been provided us are in danger of dissipation. Only you can save it and only if we find ourselves at Mr. Fezziwig's bank immediately!" Ferguson said, wild-eyed.

"Only I?" Ebenezer asked incredulously. "How can this be? What is it that I can do?"

"You will see. You will see," Ferguson responded, keeping his eyes focused out the window.

When the cab arrived at the financial institution, the two climbed out and Ferguson rushed them in through the doors.

"Follow my lead, Ebenezer. Ask no questions. Contradict me not. You are to remain silent. When the time comes, you will do as you are instructed. We have but one opportunity to save thousands of pounds for a great number of people. Included among such people is you," Ferguson instructed. "Now wait right here."

Ferguson walked across the room and spoke with a portly banker. He handed the man a piece of paper. When the conversation was concluded, he looked back and pointed at Ebenezer. The banker nodded and together they walked back towards Ebenezer. When they reached him, the banker spoke.

"Follow me, gentlemen," he said. And they were led to a private office room.

When they sat at the table, the banker looked to Ebenezer.

"I am told that you are Mr. Fezziwig's private secretary," the banker said. "I am Mr. Wolcott."

Ebenezer was about to answer, when Mr. Ferguson shot him a look that clearly was intended to convey that he was to remain silent as he was told to do so earlier.

"Your attendant, Mr. Farnsworth here tells me that you are a mute. It seems that we are in the unusual situation where you are here to speak for another, yet you cannot speak for yourself," Mr. Wolcott said with a toothy smile. He began to laugh most heartily at his own joke.

Ebenezer said nothing, but his confusion only continued to grow. Why was this banker calling Mr. Ferguson, Mr. Farnsworth? Why was he thought to be mute? Or Mr. Fezziwig's private secretary? Mr. Fezziwig did not even have a private secretary.

"You seem quite young for the task I am told you are here to perform," Mr. Wolcott observed. "But I have learned that it is not for me to decide how a man chooses to conduct his own business. If he wishes to employ a bony mute with the face of a child to manage his financial affairs, I am in no position to argue."

Ebenezer still did not understand anything more than the fact that he promised Mr. Ferguson to remain silent.

"How much are you sent here to withdraw?" asked Mr. Wolcott.

"Allow me, please," Ferguson said, reaching into Ebenezer's pocket. Ebenezer could see from the corner of his eye that Mr. Ferguson was concealing a piece of folded parchment. He then simulated removing it from Ebenezer's pocket and handed it to Mr. Wolcott.

Mr. Wolcott studied the paper before him. He furrowed his brow and then peered up from the tops of his eyes at Ebenezer.

"This note tells me that your name is Ebenezer Scrooge. You are personal secretary for Mr. Francis Fezziwig. He appoints you with full power to withdraw all of his funds as he is planning to relocate them to a different institution. I see his signature here and it is duly notarized with appropriate seal," Mr. Wolcott stated.

Ebenezer had not one idea as to what was occurring. Mr. Ferguson placed his hand on Ebenezer's shoulder and applied steady pressure.

"Well, Mr. Scrooge, I am very sorry to be losing your employer's very sizable business," Wolcott said. "I will need your signature before I can transfer any of the funds to you."

Ebenezer looked to Mr. Ferguson who gently nodded.

Mr. Wolcott slid a parchment before Ebenezer. Ebenezer was directed to sign at the bottom of the page beside an oversized "X". Wolcott dipped a quill in ink and handed it to Ebenezer.

Ebenezer took the quill and looked down at the paper. It indeed had Mr. Fezziwig's signature at the bottom. At the top, Ebenezer noted a crest of two rams locked in battle.

Ferguson, noting Ebenezer's hesitation, spoke.

"Thank goodness our benevolent employer, Mr. Fezziwig, has sent us on this errand," Ferguson said. "Without this transaction, there would be significant financial suffering by a great many. Time is running quite short."

Ferguson then squeezed Ebenezer's shoulder a bit harder than before, a clear indication that he wished Ebenezer to sign.

Ebenezer promised complete loyalty. Simply because he could not understand the circumstance in which he now found himself did not mean he should renounce that vow. Mr. Ferguson had been nothing but good to Ebenezer. Mr. Ferguson needed his help now. He did not see how he could refuse.

Ebenezer leaned over and signed his name to the parchment.

Shortly thereafter, Ferguson exited the bank with the certificate of funds tucked neatly within his coat pocket. Ebenezer was by his side. They hailed a cab and headed back to Ferguson's office.

When they were on their way, Ebenezer spoke.

"Mr. Ferguson, I do not understand what has just transpired."

"Ebenezer, my boy, you are a hero," Ferguson said, proudly.

"I'm sorry, sir?" Ebenezer said.

"With the control of these funds, we will be able to infuse the proper amount of capital into the investment at the proper time. Of course, we will not use all of the funds. By day's end, everything will have changed for you, my boy. Everything," Ferguson stated, smiling.

"But what of Mr. Fezziwig's fortune?" Ebenezer asked.

"It shall be doubled. At a minimum," Ferguson said happily. "We will then return all of the funds, including the surplus and you will be hailed a savior. You must simply trust me."

Ebenezer decided that he had no other choice.

Alea iacta est.

The die was cast.

24

A few short days after Ebenezer's fateful journey with Ferguson, representatives from Fezziwig's bank sent him a correspondence thanking him for his past business and inquiring if there was anything that they could do to earn it back. Fezziwig was naturally puzzled by this query and responded in writing that he had not ceased his business relationship with the institution. The savings he had accumulated throughout his life were still safely stored within their vaults. He imagined that a simple error had taken place and he thought nothing more of it.

After receiving this odd correspondence, Fezziwig found that several of his suppliers refused to deliver his office's necessaries because they claimed an inability to draw upon his funds. They claimed that his credit was no more and they sought all past due expenses be paid immediately. Fezziwig thought he must be the victim of a curse or an ill-conceived, but highly elaborate joke to have two such financial errors occur in just one week's time. He resolved to make a trip to the bank that Friday before making his way to his office so that he may discuss the matter with the appropriate officials personally. It was a convenient time for him to do so as he had to collect funds in any event to pay his employees' wages.

Upon his entry into the bank, he requested to speak to the highest-ranking individual in attendance. A few short minutes later, he was greeted by the bank manager, Bernard Kent.

The two men shook hands.

"Mr. Fezziwig, I am most pleased to see you," Mr. Kent said cordially. "But I must admit that I am quite surprised to find you here."

"Why would that be, Mr. Kent?" Fezziwig asked. "I always come at this time of month to collect funds so that I may finance the wages of those in my employ."

"Yes, I acknowledge that is true to be sure," Kent said, "but after your withdrawal one week ago, I do not understand why you have come here to complete this errand. Should you not go to your current financial institution?"

Fezziwig was baffled. Did Kent just utter the word, "withdrawal"? And did he refer to Fezziwig's "current financial institution"?

"Sir, I am there at this moment. I beg your pardon, but you seem to be of a mistaken notion" Fezziwig said. "I have not been to this bank for one month and I have made no withdrawal."

Mr. Kent looked at Fezziwig for a long moment. He then smiled.

"Mr. Fezziwig, are you making sport of me?" Kent asked.

"Mr. Kent, I do not understand the content of our conversation. If you are speaking to me in jest, I ask that you please cease. I find this not to be amusing," Fezziwig said, with increasing frustration.

"Sir, I speak in all seriousness," Kent said, very puzzled at Fezziwig's tone and words. "I do not understand your intent here today."

"My intent?" asked Fezziwig, very agitated. "My intent is to withdraw the necessary funds to recompense my staff for this past month's services. As has always been my intent at this time of month. My intent is also to resolve the confusion under which my creditors seem to be suffering regarding my credit with this institution so that my place of business may be supplied with all that is necessary to keep it running efficiently and appropriately. It seems quite the simple chore."

"Yes, sir," said Kent, still very confused. "It would under other circumstances be. But you removed all of your savings from this institution one week ago. We have nothing in our coffers that belongs to you."

Fezziwig nearly fell over when he heard this.

"What is this that you are saying?" Fezziwig cried. "There must be some error. You must have another customer on your mind. As I stated earlier, I have withdrawn nothing from this bank for approximately one month. I withdrew nothing last week, and I can assure you that I certainly did not divest this institution of all of my funds at any time!"

"Mr. Fezziwig, please calm yourself," Kent said.

"Calm myself?! Calm myself?!" Fezziwig was approaching apoplexy.

"Yes, sir. This is a reputable place of business and you must conduct yourself with the appropriate decorum," Mr. Kent said. "Perhaps you should accompany me to my private office where we may continue this conversation."

Fezziwig agreed and followed Kent to his office. Kent closed his door.

Fezziwig forced his voice to appear calm and he spoke.

"Now, Mr. Kent, I apologize for my behavior, but I hope you can understand my dismay," Fezziwig said. "I stand before you and you tell me that all of the fortune I have spent a lifetime accumulating is now gone."

"Mr. Fezziwig, I am more than a bit confused," said Kent. "One week ago from this very day, you sent your personal secretary with an executed notarized authorization and he departed with your funds."

"My personal secretary?!" Fezziwig cried, once again losing his temper. "I have no personal secretary! To whom did you give all of my capital?"

"As I said, Mr. Fezziwig. It was given to your personal secretary," Kent said, trying to keep himself composed in the presence of the unhinged individual before him.

"And as I said, Mr. Kent, I have no personal secretary!" Fezziwig retorted.

"I have the necessary paperwork right here," Kent said. He produced the document in question. "As you can see, here is your authorization, here is your signature duly notarized, and here is the signature of your personal secretary, Ebenezer Scrooge."

"Ebenezer Scrooge?!" Fezziwig exclaimed, not believing his eyes. "It cannot be! Ebenezer Scrooge is my apprentice, a lad of merely seventeen years! Some imposter enters your office claiming to be Ebenezer Scrooge and you simply hand over to him my life savings? Who made this terrible blunder?"

"I see that the account was closed by Mr. Abraham Wolcott, one of our esteemed executives," replied Kent, ignoring the insinuation that one of the bank's fine personnel had made an error. "Perhaps you would feel more comfortable if he joined us for this conversation."

"I should say so!" Fezziwig stated vehemently.

"Excuse me, but for a moment," Kent said, and he exited his office.

While he was out, Fezziwig examined the document more closely. He did not understand even one aspect of it. He could see his own signature staring back at him, but he clearly had no memory of signing any such instrument. Surely it must be a clever forgery.

He also fixated on Ebenezer Scrooge's signature. It did appear to be young Ebenezer's handwriting. But why would Ebenezer sign such a document? Surely he did no such thing!

It was then that Fezziwig noticed the rams crashing horns at the top of the page. He had seen this before. His memory struggled to recall just when that was.

Mr. Kent returned to his office followed by Abraham Wolcott. Kent resumed his seat behind the desk.

"Mr. Wolcott, this is Francis Fezziwig," Kent introduced.

Abraham Wolcott extended his hand to Fezziwig. It took a moment, but Fezziwig, always the gentleman, took Wolcott's hand and shook it.

"Please gentlemen, be seated," Kent offered.

Wolcott and Fezziwig sat in the chairs before Kent's desk.

"Now, Mr. Wolcott, can you please review this document upon my desk," Kent said, handing Wolcott the withdrawal authorization.

Wolcott took the parchment in hand and read it. He then looked up.

"Do you recognize this document?" asked Kent.

"Certainly, I do," Wolcott responded.

"When did you first lay eyes upon it?" Kent asked.

"It was on this Friday last," Wolcott replied.

"Can you please explain to us the circumstances during which you viewed this document?" Kent requested.

"Of course. I was summoned to assist a customer who had this in his possession. He was a young fellow, didn't look to be more than eighteen or nineteen years of age. Very gaunt. About my height. Red hair growing down the back of his neck, tied in a ponytail," Wolcott recited. "He told me that he had important business of a sensitive nature to conduct. So I brought him into my office that he may have some privacy."

Fezziwig's blood ran cold at the description that so closely matched Ebenezer's own. It simply did not make any sense.

"Excuse me for interrupting," Fezziwig said, holding up a hand. "Was this young chap alone or did another accompany him?"

"He was quite on his own," Wolcott responded.

Fezziwig's confusion continued.

"May I continue?" asked Wolcott.

"Please do," answered Kent, as Fezziwig sat mired in his perplexity.

"In any event, the young man told me his name was Ebenezer Scrooge and that he was the personal secretary of Francis Fezziwig, the accountant. He was given specific instructions by Mr. Fezziwig to withdraw the sum total of Mr. Fezziwig's funds because he was to transfer them to a different institution. I did not think it proper to ask where the funds were to be deposited nor did Mr. Scrooge volunteer such information to me.

"He then presented me with the document you see before us that, as you can plainly see, has been properly executed by Mr. Fezziwig and duly notarized with seal. I confirmed Mr. Fezziwig's signature with that we have on file and confirmed the authenticity of the notary public from our records. All were correct and proper.

"I then had Mr. Scrooge sign in the appropriate location, which he did quite cheerfully. I next prepared the funds for transfer, gave same to Mr.

Scrooge, and wished him well. Other than the large sum extracted, it was quite routine and he seemed very pleased that the transaction proceeded as smoothly as it did."

Fezziwig became more and more bewildered as Wolcott spoke. Ebenezer came to this bank with a false document and made off with all of Fezziwig's fortune? How could this be true?

Fezziwig's mind began to race. This Friday last? Ebenezer should have been in the company of Victor Ferguson.

Ferguson! It was then that Fezziwig recalled where he had seen the letterhead consisting of the two rams. It was when Ferguson had presented the parchment to him and requested his signature on the correspondence vouching for Ebenezer's investment plan. Could Ferguson have switched letters or in some other way transferred the signature to a document other than the one Fezziwig believed he had executed? Ferguson must be behind this, Fezziwig concluded. It simply could not be Ebenezer.

"Are you quite certain the young man was alone? There was not a larger, older gentleman closer to my own age to accompany him?" Fezziwig asked.

"No, sir," replied Wolcott. "Mr. Scrooge was indeed quite alone."

Fezziwig let out a dejected sigh.

"What am I to do now to remedy the situation?" Fezziwig asked, fully expecting Mr. Kent's cooperation in devising a suitable resolution. "I can assure you that I did not send Ebenezer Scrooge, or anyone else for that matter, to defund my savings."

"I am very sorry, sir, but I am afraid there is nothing we can do for you at this time," said Mr. Kent apologetically. "As you can see, all of the paperwork is indeed in order. Mr. Wolcott followed all of the proper procedures and all formalities were met."

"Are you to say that I have no recourse?! That all for what I have worked and entrusted to this institution is lost forever? That I must go home to my wife and inform her that we awoke in secure comfort, but we shall enter sleep entirely penniless?" Fezziwig cried, rising to his feet. "And what of all of those who look to me for their livelihoods? I have a great many responsibilities. No, sir! I cannot accept this!"

Fezziwig pounded his fist on Kent's desk.

"Sir, please maintain your self-control and appropriate cordiality," Kent said as both he and Wolcott rose as well. "From the document before us and Mr. Wolcott's statement, it is quite clear what has transpired. I do not know what game you are attempting to play at here, my good man. If your funds were not redeposited according to your wishes, perhaps you should discuss this with your secretary."

"But I have no secretary!" Fezziwig bellowed. "I demand

satisfaction!"

"There is only one man from whom you can receive such," said Kent, leaning in. "Ebenezer Scrooge.

"Now as we have no further business here, and as you have chosen to no longer be a customer of this fine institution, I will bid you a good day and ask that you remove yourself from these premises before I am compelled to have you escorted out against your will," said Kent.

Fezziwig was beside himself with anger, but he forced himself to regain his calm. He closed his eyes. He took several deep breaths. He then opened his eyes to see that several large gentlemen had appeared at Mr. Kent's now open doorway. Whether Fezziwig liked it or not, he could see that he would be leaving.

"This is not the final word. I will not be made the pauper because of the negligence of this institution," said Fezziwig, as the large men approached him with malice in their eyes. "But, I go now of my own volition. I would thank you to ensure that I will not be molested in my departure."

Kent nodded at his security force and they parted to allow Fezziwig the freedom to leave the office. He did so and they shadowed him until he exited the building's front doors.

Fezziwig hailed a cab, after confirming that he had enough in his pockets to cover the fare, and instructed the driver to go directly to Ferguson's office. Both Ferguson and Ebenezer should be there at this time. He was determined to obtain some answers.

25

At the same time that Fezziwig was entering the front door of his financial establishment, Ebenezer was entering the front door of Ferguson's business establishment. Fred was already at his desk working away and he looked up when Ebenezer arrived. He and Fan had recently returned from their extended honeymoon.

Fred smiled up at Ebenezer.

"How goes it, Ebenezer?" Fred greeted.

"Well," Ebenezer replied without much conviction. He had been uneasy ever since he accompanied Ferguson the prior week. He had been eagerly awaiting the good word that the investment was saved and that Mr. Fezziwig's fortune had grown. He had hoped today would require another trip to the bank to redeposit the original funds and the additional sums that Ferguson promised would have been earned. Ferguson had called him a hero. He certainly did not feel as such.

Margaret Fezziwig had noticed Ebenezer's change of demeanor all week. He seemed to have regressed into the timid young boy she first encountered upon his entry into their household. His appetite was quite clearly arrested at mealtimes. She was very concerned and attempted to draw him out. It was a futile effort. Eventually, she decided that perhaps she needed to allow him the time and the space to resolve for himself whatever it was that was troubling him. It made her heart ache to see him in such obvious distress, but she restrained herself from pushing further. However, she resolved that should this anxious behavior continue into the following week, she would be unable to hold herself back any further. She could not stand to see one of her boys in pain.

"You say it goes 'well'?" Fred asked with a smile. "Then perhaps you should inform your face. It speaks a contrary message."

Ebenezer forced a strained smile.

"How was your honeymoon with my sister?" Ebenezer asked, trying to change the subject.

"It was grand," Fred declared. "She is quite the woman. I am a lucky fellow indeed."

"Be sure you do not forget that," Ebenezer said. "She deserves nothing less than the best."

"And I shall give it to her," Fred said. "Worry not about that."

Ebenezer looked into Ferguson's darkened office. It was odd for him not to be hard at work by this hour. Perhaps he was out meeting with a potential client and attempting to close a sale.

"Where is Mr. Ferguson?" Ebenezer asked. He was very anxious to learn that his actions the week prior led to financial success.

"I do not know," said Fred. "He was exiting as I was entering this morning. He told me that he left a memorandum for you on his desk and he was quite adamant you follow its contents precisely."

Ebenezer entered Ferguson's office, hoping desperately that the instructions were to meet him at the bank so that the surplus funds may be deposited.

They were not.

The note read:

Ebenezer,

Good morning. Today I have important tasks for you to complete. They are vital to the ultimate success of our venture. Question nothing. I promise that you will understand fully in the end.

You are to take the change purse from the top drawer of my desk. Keep that purse safe. In it, you will find sufficient means to fund your cab fare for your journey and to purchase all that I require of you. Worry yourself not where we shall meet or what you are instructed to buy.

I have seen to it that there will be a cab awaiting you outside of this very office as you read these words. The driver has all the information that you will need to complete the day's tasks.

You will exit the building and turn to your left. At the corner, you will find the designated cab waiting. In order to confirm that you are indeed the lad I sent, the driver will expect that you deliver into his hands this missive. Do so.

Now go and make haste. Aside from the driver, share this with no one. I await you with good news.

Your friend,

VF

What unusual instructions, thought Ebenezer. But the final line about good news was welcome indeed. Ebenezer hoped this meant that the investment was a success.

Ebenezer exited the office, bidding Fred a farewell, and entered the street. As instructed, he walked down the roadway to his left where he did indeed find a cab awaiting him. He looked up at the driver.

"You Scrooge?" the driver asked.

"Yes, sir," Ebenezer replied.

"I was told you would have a correspondence to hand me to confirm that you are the young man I was to escort today," said the driver. "Do you have such?"

Ebenezer presented the letter to the driver. The driver looked it over, then folded it up and put it in his pocket.

"This be the one," the driver confirmed. "Please come aboard, Mr. Scrooge."

Ebenezer climbed into the carriage.

The driver spoke.

"I understand we have quite a few errands to accomplish together today," the driver said. "The name's Jasper. Jasper Cornwallis. Most call me Wally. You may do the same."

"Pleased to meet you, Wally," Ebenezer said politely.

"Alright, Mr. Scrooge," said Wally. "It appears that we are off."

It was a very peculiar day for Ebenezer. Wally drove him throughout London and at each stop, Ebenezer was instructed to collect something of extravagant value. Wally had a list, but informed Ebenezer that he had strict instructions not to reveal what was next to accomplish until they arrived at the appropriate location. Each time that the cab stopped, Wally turned and provided Ebenezer with his specific orders.

During his travels, Ebenezer purchased a fine Italian silk shirt meant for a relatively tall, thin man. He purchased a new gold pocket watch. Two new magnificent hats. An excellent suit, clearly intended for the same man as the shirt he had purchased earlier.

At noon, Wally informed Ebenezer that as a reward for his loyalty and for assisting him by completing these necessary purchases, Ferguson wished that Ebenezer experience an extravagant meal at a first-rate restaurant for the first time in his life. At first, Ebenezer was quite uneasy in the presence of so many affluent patrons. He felt out of place and did not feel worthy of his surroundings. However, as the meal progressed and the waiters catered to his every request, he began to feel more content. None of his fellow diners gave him any sidelong glances or appeared to cast their eyes upon him in any negative way. All of the staff accepted his presence as they did each of the other customers. And his lunch was exquisite. Never before had he tasted such a delectable assortment of fine foods. By the time he was to pay the bill, he had settled in quite comfortably. He decided that he could very easily get used to this type of lifestyle.

Following his mid-day interlude, Wally brought him to a leather craftsman where he purchased a pair of the most splendid boots. At each succeeding stop, he was instructed to accumulate more items of extreme value. Ebenezer was puzzled as to why Ferguson needed this collection of expensive luxuries. The shopping spree went on all day, in all corners of the city.

Ebenezer had to admit that as unorthodox as his chore was that day, it was quite the pleasant experience. He had never had occasion to acquire such lavish items and never before in his life had he eaten as well as he did that afternoon. He imagined that this was what it must feel like to have wealth. It was an intoxicating sensation.

As the afternoon turned to evening, Ebenezer was getting restless. He was also getting nervous. Something about his tasks seemed suspicious. Why would Mr. Ferguson need all of these specific products? And why could he not himself acquire them? Furthermore, as to some of them, why did he even wish to own them? Clothing that would not fit his body? Hats that would not fit his head? Boots that would not fit upon his feet?

The more Ebenezer thought about it, the more uncomfortable he became. Ebenezer had been sent all around the city shopping like a well-kept Parisian mistress. If he did not know better, he would believe that Ferguson was sending Ebenezer out to purchase these items for himself. To what end? As a reward for the success of the investment? Was Ferguson allowing Ebenezer some enjoyment because of the windfall his efforts assisted in creating? Or, was there something more sinister at hand? This thought terrified Ebenezer so greatly that he immediately put it out of his mind.

One question that Ebenezer could not put out of his mind was: Where was Victor Ferguson?

Ebenezer's frustration rose to a boiling point and he finally disregarded the instruction not to ask Wally where they were heading next. Wally repeated to him that he was most sorry, but he could not accommodate. Ebenezer asked Wally where Mr. Ferguson was awaiting him, but Wally told him he could not answer that question. He told Ebenezer that all tasks must simply be completed in the order in which they were requested. He could not explain more, he said, because he was not privy to more information.

Ebenezer toyed with the idea of halting the day's activities and demanding that Wally take him back to Mr. Ferguson's office. However, he did not. He was so desperate to believe that once his tasks were complete, Mr. Ferguson's good news would be revealed to be the promised financial triumph that he decided, against his better judgment, to press on. The sole concession Ebenezer won from Wally was when Wally relented and told Ebenezer that he would inform him when the subsequent stop would be the last.

That time came late into the eve, to Ebenezer's great relief. But to Ebenezer's extraordinary surprise, Wally pulled up directly in front of Ferguson's business office. Right where Ebenezer began the day's journey almost ten hours prior.

"Why have we halted here?" Ebenezer asked.

"It is our last stop," Wally said simply.

"But this is where we began," Ebenezer observed, nonplussed.

"So it is," Wally replied.

Ebenezer peered out from the window of the cab.

"It appears dark inside," Ebenezer noted.

"I will wait here until I see you enter, Mr. Scrooge," Wally offered.

"Thank you, Wally," Ebenezer said, as he alit from the carriage.

He approached the front door and attempted entry. The door was locked. Perhaps, he thought to himself, Ferguson was waiting inside. Ebenezer knocked, but received no response. Ebenezer was very confused and, after his travels throughout London that day, quite exhausted. He walked back to Wally and his awaiting cab.

"No one there to greet you, Mr. Scrooge?" Wally inquired.

"No, Wally," Ebenezer said, confused and more than slightly irritated.

"No worries, young sir. I was told this may be the situation," Wally stated. "Come, let me take you home."

"But Wally," Ebenezer protested. "I have exhausted all of the funds I have been given for today's adventure. I cannot pay you."

"Think nothing of it, Mr. Scrooge," Wally said. "I have been well compensated for our travels together today. I was instructed that if we should find ourselves in this very situation that I was to bring you home. I am happy to do so."

"Thank you, Wally," Ebenezer said, and he once again climbed into the cab.

On the ride back to the Fezziwig home, Ebenezer contemplated his day's adventure. He was led throughout the city on an elaborate scavenger hunt for items of extreme value. None of the items or the pursuit for same seemed necessary for any purpose other than keeping Ebenezer busy and away from Ferguson's office for the day. But why would Mr. Ferguson wish for Ebenezer to be absent from the office? Were there not easier methods to achieve this goal? Perhaps, Ebenezer thought to himself, he was wrong to suspect ill of Mr. Ferguson and this day's escapade was as he originally surmised; as a gift for his assistance in brining wealth to Mr. Ferguson and all of his clients. Mr. Ferguson certainly valued money. It was not inconceivable that he would reward those who provided the means to amass great quantities of it.

But one fact vexed Ebenezer and he could not remove the bile that rose in his throat as he thought of it. Mr. Ferguson promised that Ebenezer's journey would end in his presence. Not only in his presence, but with glad news. It was disturbing indeed that Mr. Ferguson was not to be found when Wally halted his horses at Ebenezer's final destination.

Ebenezer was no fool. He sensed trouble. But if Mr. Ferguson had ill intent for Ebenezer, what could be done to resolve it now? Ebenezer was mired in the mix of these proceedings far too deeply. If the investment plan failed, it was Ebenezer who proposed it. It was Ebenezer who executed his name to remove the Fezziwig's fortune. He was convinced that he could not discuss this matter with anyone; not even his precious Belle. Not even his beloved Fan. He must be wrong in his suspicions. All would prove prosperous in the end, he told himself.

For if it was not, he could not even contemplate the disaster. His mind could not accept such a catastrophe. Nevertheless, he resolved to hide away all of the goods he purchased for Mr. Ferguson when he returned home. He would keep them as safe as the monies he received from Mr. Ferguson throughout his term of service with the investment businessman. If anyone were to find them, it could be perceived that Ebenezer purchased these items for himself with ill-gotten gains. He could not have that.

When they arrived back at the Fezziwig house, Ebenezer collected all of the day's merchandise, thanked Wally, and entered the front door. To Ebenezer's great relief, Fezziwig and the other apprentices still had not returned from the counting house. Ebenezer quickly brought all of Ferguson's items into his room and placed them deep within his closet. If his worries were for naught, he would simply retrieve them when Mr. Ferguson came to collect that which he requested Ebenezer purchase.

If not, well, he shuddered to consider.

26

"Ebenezer, did I hear you arrive?" Margaret Fezziwig called.

"Yes, Mrs. Fezziwig," Ebenezer called back as he hurried down to meet her. In his haste, he neglected to notice that the sleeve of the silk shirt he stashed in the back of the closet came free and lay in plain sight upon the floor.

When Ebenezer came down the stairs, Margaret greeted him with a mighty hug.

"Come," she said. "Let us await the return of Mr. Fezziwig and the rest of the boys in the dining room. They should arrive at any moment."

Margaret and Ebenezer did not have to wait long. But as soon as Fezziwig and the apprentices entered the dining room, it was clear that there was a problem. Fezziwig was not wearing his traditional smile and he seemed to have aged several years despite the fact that merely one workday had passed. His dour mood clearly infected the apprentices. All trod as if they had spent the day laboring in place of Sisyphus.

Margaret noticed right away. She ran to her husband and enveloped him in her arms. Ebenezer was left sitting alone at the table, a sharp pain in the pit of his stomach.

"My dear," she cried. "Whatever is the matter?"

"We had a very long day today," said Fezziwig, looking at Ebenezer. "Let us eat. We will discuss it later."

All of the returning apprentices sat down. Mrs. Fezziwig said grace and they all began to dine. It was a quiet meal, something unheard of in the Fezziwig household. Ebenezer was filled with a sense of dread. He hardly touched his food.

After supper, as the boys were filing out of the dining room, Fezziwig spoke.

"Ebenezer," he said. "Please remain. We must speak."

Ebenezer's entire body tensed and he returned to stand before Mr. Fezziwig.

"Is there anything I can do to assist?" Mrs. Fezziwig asked.

"No, my love," Fezziwig said. "I simply need to discuss a few matters with Ebenezer. Please, join the boys and we will be out shortly."

When they were alone, Fezziwig stared at Ebenezer for a long minute. Ebenezer fidgeted before him, becoming more and more uncomfortable by the second. Fezziwig had never acted this way before. Why would he not speak?

Finally, he did so.

"Ebenezer, please sit," Fezziwig requested calmly and softly. Ebenezer complied, and Fezziwig remained standing. Fezziwig looked down at Ebenezer.

"Ebenezer, do you know where I was today?" Fezziwig asked.

"No, sir," Ebenezer answered nervously. "Were you not at the counting house?"

"I was," Fezziwig responded. "But that was not the only location at which I stepped foot."

Fezziwig paused again.

Ebenezer looked up at his master. His right knee began shaking up and down rapidly and mindlessly.

"You seem uncomfortable," Fezziwig said coldly.

"I am, sir," Ebenezer admitted. "I do not know what is happening."

"Ebenezer, I went to my bank this morning," Fezziwig said, at last. "Or at least I went to the institution that I had always believed to be my bank. I was told in no uncertain terms that it was no longer so. Have you any idea why that would be?"

Ebenezer's mind raced. What was he to do? Clearly, Mr. Fezziwig knew of his appearance at the bank with Mr. Ferguson. His divided loyalties had come into conflict at last. Ebenezer had received no word of the investment's success. Mr. Fezziwig's demeanor suggested the opposite was the truth.

He made his choice.

"I do," said Ebenezer. "I am terribly sorry, Mr. Fezziwig, but I went with Mr. Ferguson to your bank and withdrew your funds in order to save your investment and ensure its success. Mr. Ferguson assures me that when you next receive an accounting, your financial records shall reveal a doubling of your initial deposits."

"How did you accomplish this?" Fezziwig asked so evenly it frightened Ebenezer.

"We went together, Mr. Ferguson and I. He had me present myself as a mute and so I said nothing. A withdrawal authorization was produced and I was asked to sign it in the capacity as your personal secretary. I regret to confess that I did so," Ebenezer admitted.

"Where are my funds now?" Fezziwig asked slowly.

"In truth, sir, I do not know," Ebenezer said. "Mr. Ferguson took them in order to stabilize the investment and ensure it would bear fruit for all."

Fezziwig looked at Ebenezer silently. His lips pursed. Tears were glistening in his eyes.

"Ebenezer, we have known each other a very long time," Fezziwig began.

"Yes, sir," Ebenezer acknowledged.

"I brought you into my business. I brought you into my home," Fezziwig said.

"Yes, sir," Ebenezer responded.

"I have treated you as though you were my own," Fezziwig said.

"You have, sir," Ebenezer agreed.

"I have never before known you to lie as you have just done to my very face," Fezziwig said, disappointed.

"Mr. Fezziwig, I did not lie," Ebenezer protested. "I swear it."

"You swear it?" Fezziwig said with tragic humor. "Ebenezer, I spoke with both the bank manager and the executive with whom you met, Mr. Wolcott."

"Yes, it was Mr. Wolcott we met," Ebenezer said.

"Mr. Wolcott told me that you were alone in his presence," said Fezziwig. "I confirmed this information with him twice during our unpleasant conversation."

"No!" Ebenezer exclaimed.

"Yes. He also told me that you were quite verbose for a mute," Fezziwig said. "You presented yourself as my personal secretary, you produced the false document allowing the withdrawal, and you departed with my fortune. So I ask you again, where are my funds?"

"Mr. Fezziwig, I swear on my honor, none of that is true!" Ebenezer cried.

"On your honor? On your honor? What honor?! Ebenezer, you are not a child anymore. You will be eighteen years old before the year is out. You have just admitted to me that you pilfered every last farthing that I possessed in the world," Fezziwig stated, getting more agitated. "Now you wish for me to trust your word?"

"Mr. Fezziwig, I apologize, but you must believe me," Ebenezer pleaded. "I do not know why he did so, but Mr. Wolcott was not truthful with you."

"Ebenezer, do you realize that I was unable to pay my employees' wages today?" Fezziwig asked. "They worked with diligence for this past month. They earned the proper wage that I, on *my* honor, promised to them. And I was forced to inform each of them that they would go home to their wives and families with no recompense today."

Ebenezer was unable to speak.

"Furthermore," Fezziwig continued, "I was unable to confirm for them precisely when they may expect their past month's wages. Or any future months for that matter. Under such circumstances, how do you expect that they will find it in their interests to continue in my employ?"

Ebenezer did not know how to respond.

"The question I just posed was not rhetorical," Fezziwig said severely. "I wish an answer."

"I do not know, sir," Ebenezer said, softly and completely defeated.

"Nor I," Fezziwig said, staring down at Ebenezer. "And after we are through here, I must exit this room and inform my wife that we are, at present, penniless. I must inform my domestic staff that they will suffer the same fate as my counting house staff. And I must inform my apprentices that, if I cannot resolve this problem posthaste, that there may be no business remaining for them at which to complete their apprenticeship!"

Ebenezer shrank further into his seat.

"Furthermore, my friends and colleagues will wish explanation as to why I have brought to them such an ill-conceived investment plan and vouched for its designer," said Fezziwig. "In what state do you fathom my reputation shall be once they discover they have all been swindled by a smooth speaking charlatan and his young accomplice?"

"But, sir," Ebenezer pleaded. "Mr. Ferguson assured me that this investment will create great yields for all who are involved."

"Pull your head from out your arse, boy!" Fezziwig boomed. "You are too smart to continue to believe so! Or, you are continuing to play your part for Victor Ferguson, in most unconvincing fashion! After what you did for that man one week ago, it is clear that we have all been the victim of a deception. I should not be surprised if we never see Mr. Ferguson's face darken our doorsteps ever again."

Ebenezer hung his head.

"I did not yet tell you this," Fezziwig added. "I went to the offices of the good Mr. Ferguson after my encounter at the bank. I wished to speak to him and to you. I found you neither to be present. Your new brother-in-law told me that you had gone to meet him. Perhaps to collect your spoils?"

"No, sir," Ebenezer said. "I did not see Mr. Ferguson at all today."

Before Ebenezer could explain how he spent his day, a shriek was heard outside the doors of the dining room. It was Mrs. Fezziwig.

Fezziwig bolted from the room and Ebenezer followed after him.

Mrs. Fezziwig was collapsed in a chair in the front foyer. At her feet was a letter that had just been delivered by messenger. The apprentices and the house staff came rushing towards her scream.

"What troubles you, Mrs. Fezziwig?" asked Percy Sellick, kneeling beside her and holding her hand.

Dick Wilkins picked up the fallen correspondence and read. His eyes went wide and his skin turned ashen.

Mr. Fezziwig arrived and ran to his wife.

"My darling," Fezziwig said. "What has transpired?"

She couldn't speak.

"I believe this explains Mrs. Fezziwig's distress," Dick said, handing the communication to Mr. Fezziwig. Ebenezer entered the room and Dick shot his closest friend a look of such venom, Ebenezer could almost not recognize his face.

Fezziwig read the note.

My dear boy Ebenezer,

> *You have played your part well. As you promised, Fezziwig suspected nothing and you were correct that he would assist us more than even I could have dreamed. I sincerely hope you were careful with your earnings, not just merited for this magnificent venture, but for all of your efforts throughout your tenure with me for which I bestowed upon you riches. Now that it does not appear as though dear Mr. Fezziwig will be in a position to complete your training, you know where to find me. I will be happy to work with you again.*

Your friend and partner,

VF

"What is the meaning of this?" Margaret Fezziwig asked, finally regaining her voice.

"It seems that our young Mr. Scrooge has been involved in a plot to bankrupt us," Fezziwig said.

All gasped.

"Worse still," Fezziwig began. "It appears that he may have succeeded in achieving his goal."

"Ebenezer," Margaret said incredulously. "Is this true?"

"At this point, I must admit that I do not know," said Ebenezer sadly. "I was merely attempting to aid in your prosperity."

"This missive speaks of riches you have received in the past. Did you accept financial remuneration from Mr. Ferguson and kept this information from us?" Margaret asked.

"Yes, ma'am," Ebenezer admitted.

"And what have you done with your earnings from, how does he put it in this vile correspondence, 'this magnificent venture'?" Margaret asked, further in distress.

"I have earned nothing from this, I assure you," Ebenezer said emphatically.

"You lie!" Dick chimed in. "Now the items in our closet I have just discovered have an explanation."

"What items, Dick?" asked Mr. Fezziwig.

"I shall show you," Dick said running off up the stairs.

"What will be in Dick's possession when he returns?" Fezziwig asked Ebenezer.

"Items that are not my own," Ebenezer said, bewildered as to how the goods were found out. "I was sent to purchase a great many things by Mr. Ferguson today. They belong to him and were purchased with his funds."

Dick returned with the expensive items of clothing and other objects of high price that were stowed in the closet. He handed them to Mr. Fezziwig, who immediately noted that each of the articles of clothing were meant to fit a man of Ebenezer's proportions.

"These are meant for Mr. Ferguson?" Fezziwig asked dubiously. "Yet, they would fit only you and not him!"

"I cannot explain why he sent me to purchase items in these dimensions," Ebenezer said.

"I can!" Dick cried.

"We all can, Dick," Fezziwig said sadly.

"What is to become of us?" Margaret asked weakly. She looked at all of her boys, terrified that if the worst was indeed true, that she would have to part with them.

"We will find a solution, my love," said Fezziwig. "But for now, Mr. Scrooge, I am afraid that you must go. I will give you use of our family carriage for this final journey. I do not care to know where you are going, only that you be on your way immediately."

"But Mr. Fezziwig," Ebenezer stammered.

"I said go," Fezziwig repeated. A servant opened the front door. "Your personal effects will be sent wherever you wish them to be delivered."

"Please, Mr. Fezziwig... Mrs. Fezziwig... all," Ebenezer began.

Dick Wilkins rushed forward and grabbed Ebenezer by the collar of his coat. He then forcefully dragged Ebenezer to the doorway and pushed him out into the night. Ebenezer fell to the dirt.

Ebenezer looked back up at Dick's face contorted in rage.

"I cannot believe I ever called you 'friend'," Dick said. And then he slammed the door in Ebenezer's face.

Ebenezer picked himself up and climbed into the awaiting carriage. The driver stared at him with eyes slit.

"Where to, Mr. Scrooge?" asked the angry driver.

Ebenezer could think of only one place where he would be welcomed. He told the driver to take him to the home of his sister, Fan.

As they pulled away, the last sound Ebenezer could hear emanating from within the house was the wail of Mrs. Fezziwig's cries.

27

𝕱an was very surprised to see Ebenezer at her doorstep. In an instant, she knew that something was terribly amiss.

"Ebenezer!" Fan cried, upon observing her brother's morose visage before her. "What has happened? Is someone ill?"

Ebenezer simply shook his head slowly, he on the verge of tears.

"Please, come in, come in," Fan said emphatically, putting her arms around his shoulders and directing him through the front door. He shuffled forward as his sister directed. Fan was becoming more frightened by the moment.

"Ebenezer, please speak to me," Fan pleaded. "What troubles you?"

Fred heard the commotion and entered the room.

"Fan, did I hear the front door?" Fred asked as he arrived. "Oh, Ebenezer, it is you. How goes it?"

"Fred, something is terribly wrong," a distressed Fan said to her husband. She turned her attention back to her brother, who had yet to speak. "Ebenezer, come and sit. I will get you a cup of tea. Then we must talk."

Ebenezer put his hand up weakly and shook his head while closing his eyes and bowing his head into his hands. Fan did not know how to respond. Clearly, something of great import was troubling Ebenezer. She shuddered to imagine what tidings he had to bring. She did what her instinct taught her to do. She embraced her brother and hugged him tightly to her. Together, they then sat upon the chesterfield.

Ebenezer could hold back his tears no more. He buried his face into his sister's shoulder and allowed the dam to burst. She sat, allowing him to mourn, with her arm cradling his head as she rocked him slowly back and forth, something she had not done for him since he was a young child. She waited patiently for him to find the ability to express his woe.

After several minutes, she whispered to him.

"Ebenezer, it shall all be alright," Fan said. "Please, now, tell me what is the trouble that leads you to this state."

Ebenezer sat up and looked at his sister through watery eyes. He glanced over at Fred who had been standing and watching the scene unfold.

"I am ashamed to speak this aloud," Ebenezer said at last in barely a whisper.

"Ebenezer," Fan said looking at him, holding his face in her hands and wiping away his tears with her thumbs, "there is nothing you could say that could ever harm my opinion of you. I love you, as I always have. Whatever it is that is on your mind, we will find a solution to your trouble together."

"Fan, do not promise your enduring acceptance with such haste," Ebenezer said. "You have not heard of what I have done. Your opinion may indeed be altered."

"Never!" Fan said, looking Ebenezer directly in the eye. "Did you hear me, Ebenezer? Never."

Ebenezer took a deep breath. He glanced once more at Fred, who had now sat upon a chair as he looked in Ebenezer's direction.

Ebenezer then made his full confession. He left nothing unsaid. He explained how he had been surreptitiously accepting payment from Ferguson for this past long time. He described how he allowed the investors, including Mr. Fezziwig, to believe the financial plan was of his origin and how he participated in convincing Mr. Fezziwig to become an unwitting accomplice to the scheme. He told of his trip with Ferguson to Fezziwig's bank and how he executed the withdrawal authorization under false pretenses. And he revealed what had just occurred at the Fezziwig home that very night prior to his arrival.

Fan sat and listened without a word throughout Ebenezer's entire recounting. She kept her face steady despite what she heard. Her concern remained focused on Ebenezer's well-being.

In the end, when his tale was complete, Ebenezer slumped back, deep into the divan, fully spent.

Fred was the first to speak.

"Ebenezer, I find what you say to be difficult to accept insofar as it relates to Mr. Ferguson," Fred said skeptically. "I have known him for many a year and this narrative does not comport with my experience with him."

"Fred!" snapped Fan. "Do not insinuate that my brother is a liar!"

"All I have related is the truth, Fred," Ebenezer said, nodding his head.

"Ebenezer, I am sorry, but I am concerned that you have not been fully honest with us about your role in this endeavor," Fred said, looking at his wife through slightly narrowed eyes, but saying to her nothing.

"Fred!" Fan said harshly. "Did you not hear me? I told you to mind your words when it comes to my brother's account."

"Fan, please do not speak to me thusly," Fed seethed. "I am your husband and deserve the respect that comes along with that position. As for your brother's integrity, I believe we have just heard that he has concealed his earnings from his master, he has engaged in a scheme to defraud said master and all of his colleagues of considerable sums, he has borne false witness at a major institution of finance, and he has, in essence, purloined the total assets of a man who has provided him a home and a livelihood. I do not think that under such circumstances it is unreasonable for me to suspect that the full truth is not what has just escaped his lips. Particularly when he speaks so very ill of a man I have known and respected for a great many years."

"Nevertheless…" Fan began.

Ebenezer interrupted.

"Fan, Fred, please do not argue," Ebenezer pleaded. "I understand Fred's reservations. I would share them if I were sitting in his seat."

Ebenezer turned to his brother-in-law.

"I do not know how to convince you that these words are the truth," Ebenezer said.

"Ebenezer, aside from the fact that I expect a vital portion of this tale is absent, I also do not understand your assumption that this endeavor will not ultimately result in the success Mr. Ferguson has promised," Fred said. "Leaving aside your role in removing your master's life savings under false pretenses, which is loathsome to be sure, how do we know that your economic venture will not yield the results assured by the good Mr. Ferguson?"

"Fred, did you not listen fully to Ebenezer's retelling?" Fan asked, irritated. "It is quite clear that Mr. Ferguson used Ebenezer for his own purposes and that this 'investment' was intended to benefit no one other than Mr. Ferguson himself!"

"Fan! This is the last time that I will warn you!" Fred yelled. "I will not tolerate this sort of insolence in my own home! Not from anyone and certainly not from my wife!"

"Fred, do not speak to me in this manner," Fan said indignantly.

"That is all! My patience has run its course and now it is at its end!"

Fred exclaimed standing up. "I shall leave the two of you to your slanders before I say or do something that I may later regret! And while I am gone, it is my fervent hope that you consider the proper role and place for a wife. For you have stepped well beyond such boundaries tonight!"

Fred walked across the room and exited the house, slamming the door behind him.

"Fred, no," Ebenezer said, standing and beginning to follow after.

"Ebenezer," Fan said, attempting to project a strength she did not feel. "Allow him to go. His tone and his words were entirely inappropriate. Perhaps he needs some time to himself to calm his temper and realize the error of his ways."

Ebenezer turned to Fan.

"Are you sure this is what you wish?" Ebenezer asked.

"No," Fan said, unable to hold back a tear, "but I do not see how you chasing him will result in him doing anything other than running faster from you."

Fan then took in a deep breath.

"In truth," she said, "he may have been correct as it relates to your situation. It is possible that Mr. Ferguson awaits with the good news he promised. Until you speak with him, there is no reason to abandon this hope.

"As for the rest, I cannot say that I condone your actions. They were very wrong indeed and I am quite surprised that you have committed these acts," Fan said. "But, I am sure that it was Mr. Fezziwig's anger you heard tonight and not his entire being. I doubt he intends your banishment to be permanent. On Monday, you will go with Fred to Mr. Ferguson's office and you will obtain the answers you seek. If Fred's supposition is the correct one, Mr. Ferguson will present you with the means by which to allay all of Mr. Fezziwig's financial fears."

"And if it is not?" Ebenezer asked meekly.

"We shall leap that puddle should the rains come," Fan said. "In the meanwhile, you may remain here with us for as long as you wish. Come, let us settle you in to our guest bedchamber."

Ebenezer followed his sister to an unused room in the small home. It was just a temporary living space, Fred told her upon their return from their honeymoon. While he amasses the appropriate funds necessary to purchase the house he planned for them. Mr. Ferguson had been so kind as to intervene on Fred's behalf with Arthur Benson, who owned several properties. Ferguson secured Mr. Benson's commitment to let this one to Fred for a reasonable cost.

Mr. Benson was at the time still quite taken with Mr. Ferguson. He had been so ever since their first meeting when Ferguson was so kind as to have all raise a glass to the rapid recovery of his son. As such, Benson was happy to accommodate. Despite his reservations about Ebenezer's intentions with his Annabelle, he had no qualms about Fan. He actually always found her to be most pleasant.

Later that evening, as Ebenezer lay asleep in his designated bed, he was awoken by the sound of furniture crashing in the main room. Ebenezer emerged from his guest quarters to find Fred and Fan engaged in yet another quarrel. Fred had obviously imbibed quite the quantity and it had the effect of unleashing his belligerence.

"Fred, I have never seen this side of you before!" Fan cried.

"This is your fault that I find myself in this state!" Fred retorted. "Your function is to remain loyal, demure, and when I command it, quiet. You failed in all of these roles this evening!"

"Fred, I apologize," Fan said. "But you must understand that you were insulting my brother."

"I do not care if I was insulting the King himself!" Fred growled. "Your place is by my side. Unless my memory fails me, your name is no longer Scrooge, but Radcliffe! You shall behave as though it were such!"

"You are correct, my husband," Fan conceded. "Again, I offer my sincere apology. But please, let us no longer engage in this. Your current state frightens me. My father drank himself into an early grave. I do not wish to witness my husband follow that same path."

"What you wish does not concern me!" Fred said, again becoming irrationally angry. He was standing over Fan and he raised his hand in such a manner that Ebenezer thought he may let his fist fly.

Ebenezer ran and placed himself between Fred and Fan.

"Fred, please calm yourself," Ebenezer said. "I am truly sorry for the trouble I have caused. But perhaps it is time that you allowed yourself some sleep."

Fred brought his cocked arm down. He looked at Ebenezer as he swayed uneasily on his feet.

"Very well," Fred said. "I shall retire to my bed."

"No," Ebenezer said, looking at his frightened sister, noticeably shaking. "I think it better that you rest your head in the room in which I have taken up residence. So that you may avoid ascending the stairs in your current condition. I would not wish you to stumble and become injured. I will sleep here, upon your sofa. It is most comfortable."

Fred looked as though he was about to argue once more, but after examining the staircase swaying before his drunken eyes, he decided the bedchamber on the main floor was most desirable.

"I have a better idea," Fred said to Ebenezer. "*I* shall sleep in the vacant bedroom on this floor and *you* shall sleep on this sofa."

"Splendid," Ebenezer said. "Allow me to assist you to the room."

Ebenezer walked Fred to the bed that he had recently abandoned and sat him down. Ebenezer removed Fred's boots and lay him on his side upon the pillow. Before Ebenezer had reached the doorway to complete his departure, he could hear Fred softly snoring.

Upon returning to the main sitting room, Ebenezer found Fan waiting for him. She was most distressed.

"You go to sleep," said Ebenezer. "I will remain down here and prevent Fred from joining you, should he awaken during the night. I am sorry I have caused you so much bother."

"Nonsense, Ebenezer," Fan said. "All will be well again in the morning. You will see."

Fan ascended the staircase and returned to her sleeping quarters. Ebenezer lay his head upon the sofa. Within minutes the only sound emanating from the Radcliffe house was that of Fred's snores.

28

On Monday morning, Ebenezer accompanied Fred to Ferguson's office. The carriage ride was the first opportunity that Ebenezer had to speak with Fred without his sister being present since the events of Friday night. Ebenezer was quite angered by what he perceived as near violence towards his sister. It frustrated him that Fan seemed to ensure that she was present at all times to guarantee that Ebenezer and Fred had no confrontation. Now they were finally alone.

"Fred, I wish to discuss with you the events of this past Friday night," Ebenezer said in the cab as it made its way to the Ferguson establishment.

"You are ready to tell me the truth as to your role in the financial intrigue you described, is that what you speak of?" Fred asked as he continued to peer outside the window.

Ebenezer's cheeks flushed red.

"No, that is not what I speak of," Ebenezer said, attempting to douse both his embarrassment and his fury. "I told you the complete truth, whether you accept it or not."

"What then?" Fred said, still not looking at Ebenezer.

"I speak of your unfortunate decision to raise your hand to Fan," Ebenezer said.

"I do not remember doing any such thing. And even if I did," Fred said, finally turning toward Ebenezer, "that is none of your concern. She is my wife and if I must correct her, that is my prerogative."

"Fred, I assure you that when it comes to my sister, it is indeed my concern," Ebenezer said. "And if there should be a next time that you attempt to 'correct her' by raising your hand to her, please know that I will be there and you may not find the outcome pleasing."

"Driver, please stop!" Fred called. The carriage came to a halt. Fred turned fully to Ebenezer and looked at him square in the eye.

"Brother-in-law," Fred said. "If I did not know it to be otherwise, I would conclude that you had just threatened me. Now, I know this cannot be so. For several reasons. First, you are currently seeking refuge in my house. Surely, you would not be so rude as to instigate a physical altercation with your benevolent host. Second, you must be aware that you haven't the frame nor the physique to offer a reasonable challenge to me in a battle of fisticuffs. Surely, you would not be so foolish as to attempt an assault that ends only with your certain drubbing. Third and lastly, Fan is my wife and, as such, she has promised the good Lord in the presence of witnesses, yourself included, to love, honor and obey me in my capacity as the head of my household. Surely, you do not think yourself above a mandate decreed by God Himself? Or am I mistaken?"

Ebenezer listened uncomfortably as Fred issued his thinly veiled threat, but said nothing.

"I thought not. So, since I know you did not just threaten me, I presume that I am the one in error for even considering the possibility," said Fred, coldly continuing his unblinking stare into Ebenezer's eyes, like a snake hovering over a mouse that will soon be its next meal. "For that, dear brother-in-law, I humbly apologize. Do you accept?"

Ebenezer's strength was failing him. Never before had Fred seemed so dangerous. A stalking predator and Ebenezer his helpless prey. Ebenezer wanted desperately to respond with something clever and something forceful. But no such thoughts would coalesce and he could not hide his intimidation.

"Please, brother-in-law," Fred said slowly and evenly, leaning in ever so slightly. "Forgive me so that we may continue on our way."

Ebenezer realized that only his capitulation to Fred would bring this tense exchange to an end. He could hold out no more. He yielded to the larger, older and more powerful man.

"I forgive you," Ebenezer said softly.

"Thank you. You have proven yourself wise and benevolent," Fred said, still in that same slow and deliberate tone. Without breaking his gaze from Ebenezer's eyes for even a moment, Fred called out.

"Driver! Continue!"

The passengers heard the slap of the reins upon the horses' backs and the carriage began with a jolt. Fred flashed Ebenezer a wry smile and then, finally, resumed his initial posture, gazing out the window of the cab.

Ebenezer was humiliated. His attempt to protect his sister had only succeeded in establishing his brother-in-law's dominance over him. He turned his head and looked out his own window so that Fred could not see how thoroughly his face had blanched.

When they arrived at Ferguson's place of business, Ebenezer was witness to a most distressing exchange.

"This here is the spot that I spoke of, Mr. Alexander," a rotund man in a fine suit was saying to his counterpart, who appeared older than the speaker. The large man looked vaguely familiar to Ebenezer. "It is an excellent location and you are in luck that it has just become available."

Ebenezer and Fred approached.

The older gentleman was speaking.

"What is the monthly cost that you are seeking," Mr. Alexander asked.

"Why, it's practically nothing for what you would be receiving," the large gentleman responded. He then noticed Ebenezer and Fred.

"Can I help you gentlemen?"

Ebenezer did not know what to say. Fred had no difficulty raising his voice.

"Mr. Clarington, I presume?" Fred asked.

"I am," the large gentleman replied. "And you are?"

"Excuse my rudeness," said Fred politely. "My name is Frederick Radcliffe. This gentleman here with me is my good friend, Ebenezer Scrooge. We each conduct business in this very building from time to time at the request of the lessee."

"Pleased to make your acquaintances," Clarington said. "I am, as you already seem to know, Maximillian J. T. Clarington, the owner of this building. Here with me is Mr. Ian Alexander, a prospective tenant of same. And you, based on your introduction, must work for the Ferguson fellow."

"That is correct, to be sure," Fred replied.

"Well, sir, it appears that I know more about your business interests than even you do," Clarington said. "For Mr. Ferguson paid me a visit three days past and cancelled his lease. I have confirmed that he has cleaned out all of his business and personal property from this location. If you have come in seek of a day's wage, I am afraid you have come in vain."

"Thank you for your time and your kindness," Fred said, shaking Clarington's beefy hand.

"Of course," Clarington said.

Fred directed the still silent and crestfallen Ebenezer away from the doorfront and led him down the street. From behind them, they could hear Mr. Clarington and Mr. Alexander continue their negotiation for the office space.

"Well," said Fred to Ebenezer. "It appears that we have both been deceived."

Ebenezer's last hope that this nightmare was not, in truth, reality was now dashed. Ferguson was gone. All of Fezziwig's money was gone with him. As well as that of all of the other investors. There was no salvaging the situation. Ebenezer had absolutely no idea what to do next.

He thought back to the past weekend. He realized he was now guilty of making yet another promise that could not be fulfilled.

On Saturday, he asked Fan to call on Belle so that he could attempt to explain to her the goings on that were afoot before she heard news from her father. Fan was better than her word. Not only did she bring word to Belle, she returned home and brought with her Belle to Ebenezer.

He was surprised to see her.

"Belle!" exclaimed Ebenezer. "You are here!"

"Of course. Your sister told me that there were circumstances that I must understand that involved you. She asked if I could accompany her so that you could relate them to me personally. I agreed at once," Belle said. "What is the problem, my darling?"

"I have done wrong, Belle. I have done most wrong," said Ebenezer. "But I will endeavor to correct my errors so that no one shall suffer from my inappropriate actions. Please know that I only had the best of intentions."

"Of course, my Ebenezer. I would never think otherwise," Belle said. "What has happened?"

Ebenezer was forced to relate his confession a second time. His guilt was no less at the surface upon this retelling than when he purged himself before Fred and Fan initially.

Belle told Ebenezer that she believed all that the said. Still, it was quite the shock to learn of his actions. Nevertheless, she vowed to stand beside him, come what may.

Ebenezer told her that he planned to confront Mr. Ferguson that coming Monday and swore that he would not cease until Mr. Ferguson provided him satisfaction. If the investment plan was not producing the earnings promised by then, Ebenezer would ensure that all of the monies would be returned to their rightful owners with an apology for the lack of gain. He told her that he was determined to restore his honor and all of the investors' fortunes. He also told her that he desired from the deepest recesses of his soul that the Fezziwigs would find it in their hearts to forgive and to allow him to return.

The look in Belle's eye belied her doubt that such circumstance would be possible based upon what she had heard. But she said nothing except that she desired this as well.

Now that Ferguson had vanished with all of the plunder, Ebenezer saw no hope of reconciliation with the Fezziwigs.

29

Matters grew only worse.

Fezziwig's collapse was swift and brutal.

The word of Ferguson's disappearance and absconding with all of the invested funds spread quickly. Almost as quickly as word of Fezziwig's inability to make payroll. Fezziwig spent the first Monday following the revelation about the financial scheme receiving visits and fielding questions from angry colleagues who all demanded the return of their money with which they parted based solely on his good word. His reputation was damaged more quickly and more thoroughly than even he had feared.

Additionally, most of Fezziwig's employees did not show for work on that merciless Monday, as they were out seeking employment elsewhere, just as he predicted would occur. Before the week's end, clients of the business began cancelling their association with Fezziwig's counting house. The reason given by one and all was that they did not have use of a financial services company that could not maintain its own solvency.

Within weeks, Fezziwig's business was in total free-fall. He could no longer meet all of his necessary obligations due to his reduced staff as each day fewer and fewer employees were reporting for work. As a result of this inability, additional clients cancelled their association with Fezziwig. The consequence of fewer clients was lesser income. With lesser income and no reserves, the handwriting was on the wall.

Fezziwig knew that his options were few to contain the bleeding. He swallowed his pride and went hat in hand to his friends and business associates seeking a loan to see him through these difficult times. However, it was a fruitless endeavor. Time and time again, he was turned down angrily.

"Your question must be one made in jest, Fezziwig," Raymond Potter scoffed. "It is certainly made in the worst of taste. You empty my left pocket with your apprentice's fraudulent scheme and now you wish that I offer you my right so that you may help yourself to still more?! Be gone from my sight immediately or I cannot be held responsible for your impending misfortune! I fear for your safety and my current inability for restraint."

This, in one variation or another, was the common reception Fezziwig received when he went seeking funds. Even those who were sympathetic to Fezziwig's plight, and there were a few, still declined his entreaty nonetheless. Not because of any ill they harbored in their hearts, even if they did so, but for purely practical reasons. The state of his business was such that they found it unlikely that he would ever have the means by which to repay that which he borrowed. It could truly be said that Fezziwig was between the devil and the deep blue sea.

Arthur Benson's rage over the loss of his earnings due to a plot contrived by Ebenezer Scrooge was irrepressible. He had never cared for the boy due to his obvious intention to resign his daughter to an indigent future and now it seemed that he wished the same for her father. When he learned that Ebenezer was seeking sanctuary in a house that Arthur himself owned, his fury was incandescent.

He summoned Fred Radcliffe and presented him with an ultimatum.

"Mr. Radcliffe, I understand that you presently provide safe harbor for Ebenezer Scrooge within the confines of my house that I was so good as to let you for less than market rate," Arthur said. "Is my information accurate?"

"It is, Mr. Benson," Fred replied emotionlessly.

"Very well," Arthur said with an evil smile upon his face. "Then here is the reality of which you must become aware. You will go home to your wife. You will give her the opportunity to bid farewell to her ne'er-do-well brother. And then you will put him out. If you do not follow my instructions precisely, then by the time the sun sets in tomorrow's western night sky, you and your wife will join young Mr. Scrooge in homelessness."

"I understand, Mr. Benson," said Fred. "It will be done."

When Fred arrived home, he relayed Arthur Benson's ultimatum to Fan. She was beside herself in anger, fear and dismay.

"Where shall we go?" she asked her husband.

"Whatever do mean?" replied Fred. "We shall go nowhere."

"Do I understand you to mean that we will stand together against Mr. Benson's unreasonable demand?" Fan asked, feeling very proud of her Fred.

"Certainly not," Fred responded, exasperated with his wife's childish question. "We shall accede to the wishes of our good landlord and Ebenezer will find alternate lodging, of course."

"I'm sorry?" Fan blurted. "My ears must deceive or my sanity fail. You did not just suggest that we oust Ebenezer from this home?"

"No, I did not suggest. I declared," Fred replied with a steely gaze. "Ebenezer will exit this house. And, my dear, that is the final word on the subject."

"But, Frederick," Fan pleaded. "He is my brother."

"Yes," Fred said. "And he is also an admitted charlatan and a thief. One of his victims happens to hold the deed to this house. And I will not defy his demand when it comes to the residents he permits to live in the structure his labor earned him. Now that is all that will be said on the subject."

"Fred," Fan began.

"I said that is all!" Fred screamed, slamming his hand against the nearest wall. "I say, woman, your capacity for obedience continues to confound me! One would confuse you for a man if it were not for your obvious physical qualities! I have made my decision and it is unalterable! Furthermore, due to your seeming inability to understand your function in this marriage, I will bestow upon you a critical responsibility. You will inform Ebenezer that his stay in our home has come to an end."

"No!" Fan shuddered. "I cannot."

"This matter is not open for discussion, my wife," Fred said, looming over her. "You will learn your place. I swear it!"

Ebenezer stepped into the room and overheard the concluding comments of this discussion. Neither Fred nor Fan was aware that he had entered. Ebenezer decided that he could not allow his bad decisions to harm his sister.

"Fan, I will leave," Ebenezer said.

Fan was startled at her brother's words and her body gave a judder.

"Ebenezer," she said, turning to him. "No."

"Yes, Fan," Ebenezer said, placing his hand upon her upper arm. "I cannot see you lose your home due to my errors."

"Good lad," Fred said.

Fan shot her husband a look. He responded in kind. Their silent battle persisted for a moment, and then Fan returned her attention to Ebenezer.

"But, Ebenezer, where will you go?" Fan asked.

"I will solve that problem," Ebenezer said.

Fan grabbed Ebenezer and pressed him to her in a mighty embrace.

"How can I allow this?" Fan asked, still holding her brother, realizing she would not have her way.

"It is not for you to allow," Ebenezer said, extracting himself from his sister's arms. "It is for me to do."

With that, Ebenezer walked to the front door. He looked back one final time to see his sister burst into tears and run from the room. He then opened the door and removed himself into the night.

Ebenezer walked the streets of London aimlessly. He truly did not know what to do or where to go. He had minimal funds, all of which he now realized were ill-gotten gains appropriated by nefarious means. He had no home. He had no job. He had no friends. And it was growing darker.

Ebenezer was at a loss. He simply continued to meander with no destination.

Suddenly, the heavens opened and it began to rain. Then pour. Within moments, Ebenezer's clothes were soaked and his respiratory disorder reared its unfortunate head. He began to wheeze and cough.

He was vaguely aware of the sound of hoof steps clip-clopping behind him and drawing nearer. A cab pulled up directly next to him and came to a stop. The door swung open.

Ebenezer looked up, about to tell the driver that he had no use for his services. Before he could speak, his eyes fell upon the passenger who was offering him a ride. His shock stole his voice.

It was Victor Ferguson.

30

"Come in, my boy," Ferguson called to Ebenezer.

Ebenezer continued to stare at this phantom from his recent past. He had difficulty believing his senses. This person who had used him to ruin the life of the only man who had ever shown him the care and affection usually bestowed by a father was now smiling down at him. Ebenezer felt ill. He wished to scream. He wished to rend Ferguson limb from limb. His anger simmered to a boil.

Still he could not speak.

"Ebenezer, what good does it you to stand and catch your death when I am here offering a dry refuge from this dreary night?" asked Ferguson with mocking eyes. "Come, join me. Let us talk."

"There is nothing that we have to say to one another," Ebenezer spat.

"*Au contraire, mon ami*," Ferguson replied. "There is a great deal for us to discuss. Now come, don't be a fool. Step from the rain. Find shelter with me."

Ebenezer sneezed. He could not deny that remaining exposed to this weather could surely mean his end. Despite his disgust for the odious individual sitting before him, the dry cab called to him. Out of options, he stepped cautiously into the carriage and out of the rain.

"Close the door behind you," Ferguson suggested.

Ebenezer did so.

To the driver, Ferguson ordered: "Continue!" The cab recommenced on its way.

Ferguson then spoke to Ebenezer.

"Now, here take this and dry yourself off," Ferguson said, handing

Ebenezer a towel. Rain droplets were cascading from his hair down his face and dripping off of the tip of his nose. Ebenezer took the towel and began to mop his face.

"Excellent. Now does that not feel better?" Ferguson asked, still smiling with every word.

A thunder clap exploded seemingly directly overhead. Ebenezer flinched noticeably at the sound. He had still never fully recovered from his childhood phobia.

"Well, I see that you do not wish to speak. That is fine. You may listen instead," Ferguson said. "I come bearing happy news for you. I am in need of an assistant. An apprentice, you might say. Can you surmise who it is that I have chosen?"

Ebenezer continued staring at Ferguson, but refused to play his game.

"Come now, Ebenezer. This question is an easy one," Ferguson said, continuing to toy with him. "No? You do not wish to venture a guess? Very well, then. I will tell you. It is you."

Ebenezer finally could hold back no more.

"Surely you jest, Ferguson," Ebenezer said, emphasizing his choice to delete the "mister" from Ferguson's title.

Ferguson's smile only widened.

"Not at all, my boy," Ferguson said. "I offer you a vocation. I offer you a warm, dry roof over your head and a soft, comfortable bed upon which to sleep. I offer you the opportunity to earn. I offer you the only chance you have to win your fair Belle."

"You have overplayed your hand, Ferguson," Ebenezer retorted. "I have already won my Belle. You cannot dangle that carrot before me."

"Hah! You still have spirit! I am pleased to see it," Ferguson said. "Sadly, you still do not have the proper sense that God has instilled within the common barn owl. Ebenezer, your precious Belle derives of wealth. She has a prominent father who has a powerful distaste for you. Look now at your situation. You are alone. You have no home. You are virtually destitute. You have no hope of survival on your own. Had I not fortuitously come along and recognized your form, you may have been at this very moment dying in the street."

"What point do you wish to make?" Ebenezer asked, irritated at both Ferguson's assessment and the fact that it was undeniably accurate.

"Belle will tire of you," Ferguson said. "Now that she knows what you have done for me, she will never trust you again either."

"She will stand beside me, through this and all," Ebenezer said forcefully.

Ferguson chuckled condescendingly.

"And just what makes you believe that is true?" he asked, as though he knew what answer he would receive.

"Because she loves me," Ebenezer responded.

"Ah yes, love," Ferguson responded, obviously thoroughly enjoying what he perceived as Ebenezer's naiveté. "Allow me to welcome you into a little secret those of us who live in the real world know of love."

Ebenezer stared at Ferguson. Ferguson leaned in towards Ebenezer. He looked to his left and to his right dramatically as though he were ensuring no one else could hear what he was about to reveal.

"It's humbug," Ferguson whispered, with a wink of his eye.

Ebenezer shook his head and looked away.

"You do not believe me?" Ferguson asked. "That is fine. You will. In time, I promise you. You will."

In truth, it was not that Ebenezer did not believe Ferguson. It was that he did not wish to believe him. It was his deepest fear. That Belle would someday turn her back. It is why he was so obsessed with establishing himself as worthy of her affections.

"So, what say you?" Ferguson asked. "Tell me that of which I am already aware. Tell me that you will continue this journey with me and you will re-pledge your allegiance to me, as you once did."

Ebenezer did not know how to respond. In his mind, he imagined reaching forward and incapacitating Ferguson with extreme prejudice; then bringing him to Mr. Fezziwig and all of his deceived colleagues on the proverbial silver platter so that they may all share in the pleasure of tearing him to pieces.

The thunder cracked once again overhead, waking Ebenezer from this daydream. He wanted the cab to halt and he step out and be done with the repulsive man to his left. Rather, in truth, he wanted to want the cab to halt. But he could not bring himself to speak the words.

After a moment of Ebenezer's silence, Ferguson's eyes narrowed.

He called to the driver.

"Halt!"

The cab came to a stop.

"Ebenezer, look out that window," Ferguson ordered. "My offer expires one minute after I complete what I am about to say. You may come with me. You will achieve riches, you will achieve knowledge, and you will achieve Belle. Or, you may step back into the rain on this darkened night. In that event, you will end up a vagrant, you will end up alone, and I assure you that long after you will wish it to be so, you will end up dead. When this carriage begins moving again, you will either be with me riding towards your bright future or you will be out there, going nowhere and achieving nothing. Make your choice."

Ebenezer studied the wet world outside the window. He considered his infelicitous situation. He fought the creeping certainty that Ferguson was correct in his prognostication about Belle's future needs and desires.

He wished nothing more than to conjure even one reasonable alternate option. He could come up with none. He sighed heavily and sadly.

"Your time is up," Ferguson stated. "Your decision is at hand. Do we ride?"

Ebenezer hung his head.

"Yes," he said softly, consummating his deal with the devil. "We ride."

"Excellent!" Ferguson expressed, cuffing Ebenezer playfully on the shoulder.

To the driver: "Continue! Onward to home!"

And so Ebenezer stared blindly out into the night beyond his window, listening to the rhythmic clip-clop of the horses' hooves upon the cobblestone, as he was being driven down to the abode that would be home for the next two years. On this wet and steamy August night, Ebenezer could not shake the sensation that he was being driven directly into the bowels of hell itself.

31

For the next two years, Ebenezer lived his life within the shadows. It could be no other way. Because his business dealings in London were not yet concluded, Ferguson had to keep a low public profile to avoid detection if he wished to continue his operations within the city. Ebenezer was advised to do the same. Whether he wished to accept it or not, there were a great many powerful men who would like nothing more than to discover Ebenezer alone and unguarded. A beating may be the least of Ebenezer's troubles. It was not an impossibility that he could find himself one unfortunate night hanging from the end of a rope with a jubilant crowd at his feet. Ferguson explained that he had been witness to this many times in the past. Ebenezer wished it was otherwise, but he was forced to accept that Ferguson was most likely speaking the truth.

During his second stint in Ferguson's employ, Ebenezer was drawn deeply into the full world of Ferguson's intrigue. Ebenezer discovered that Ferguson's interests extended far beyond investment swindles. He learned that his new master's hands were immersed in a great many pots.

Ebenezer was quite astounded to discover that Ferguson's associates were not all of the obviously nefarious quality. In fact, the percentage of such individuals was quite minimal. During the many perilous errands on which he would be sent, he often found himself in the presence of seemingly upstanding members of society. On more than one occasion, Ebenezer was even sent with messages or money to the halls of Parliament itself. During his first such assignment, he nearly fell from his feet in shock when his contact met him in the designated location, removed his wig, placed Ebenezer's delivered missive beneath it, and returned to the debate being conducted regarding current legislation on the floor.

Eventually, Ebenezer took it for fact that the criminal element existed in all segments of society, but none were more dangerous than those who wore the mask of decency. While the thug who greets you with a scowl may cause you to bleed as he takes a few shillings, the real danger came from the gentleman who greets you with a smile who will bleed you dry as he takes every last pound. Ferguson's "real world" of which he so often spoke was one that Ebenezer came first to fear, then to loathe, then to accept, and then, frightfully, to resemble.

Right from the start, Ferguson made it clear to Ebenezer that his primary duty was to ensure Ferguson's own safety. He explained it thusly.

"Ebenezer, are you familiar with the pharaohs and emperors of old?" Ferguson asked on Ebenezer's first morning in residence at Ferguson's lair.

"I do not understand your query," Ebenezer responded.

"They were very interesting men. Very powerful," Ferguson said. "And with power comes a great many things. Riches. Women. Respect. But, unfortunately, it also breeds enemies. Do you understand?"

Ebenezer just stared at Ferguson.

"The pharaohs and emperors knew that their enemies were all about," explained Ferguson. That is why, before they would dine, they had food tasters who would swallow their cuisine and sip their drink before the leader did so himself. He would watch them. If they showed even the slightest hint of illness, or if they should die on the spot, he would know to avoid the repast and he would live on to see another day."

"Why do you tell me this?" asked Ebenezer, feeling uneasy.

"Because this is, in essence, what you shall be for me," Ferguson stated. "No, do not worry. I will not have you tasting for poisons before my every meal. But you will be sent to meet with many undesirables. Among them shall be those I do not yet know well enough to confirm my security or those who wish to meet in locations where I do not have an established escape. If you come out alive, I will know it is safe for me to venture inward."

Ebenezer stared at Ferguson, trying to determine if he was being truthful or playing another game with him.

"Feel flattered, Ebenezer," Ferguson said with a broad smile. "The food taster was a prestigious profession. He was well compensated and his life was made most pleasant. For each day could be his last. Do you not see the parallel in your own situation?"

Being sent on dangerous undertakings was not the most disagreeable aspect of Ebenezer's new life. It was the fact that he, once again, found himself lying to those closest to him. He could not reveal to Belle or Fan his new arrangement. Whereas they were both kind enough to excuse his first dalliance with Ferguson due to his ignorance as to his role in the dishonorable man's wicked scheme, Ebenezer could not expect them to accept his current alliance while in full knowledge for whom he was acting. Ferguson ensured that Ebenezer was fully aware of the certain ramifications should the truth be revealed to either of them. Ebenezer struggled to devise any circumstance within his mind by which the two most important women in his life could understand his current employment, but he could think of none. It was undeniable that Ferguson owned him fully.

However, Ferguson informed him that he was not entirely cold-hearted. He would not require Ebenezer to eliminate these vital relationships from his life. In fact, he would facilitate Ebenezer's interactions with both his sister and his lady love.

Ferguson needed Ebenezer to conduct his work within the shadows. But he also needed a public face to operate for him within the light. It was no great surprise to Ebenezer who Ferguson chose to fill this capacity.

Fred remained untainted by Ferguson's investment ruse. He presented himself as among the cheated. On the surface, he commiserated with all of the other unfortunate investors. His reputation remained intact.

Fred informed his wife that Ebenezer had found employment and lodging, but that he wished to remain out of sight due to the anger so many felt towards him. He would be the intermediary that would bring Ebenezer for his visits with Fan. He would also arrange for Belle to visit the Radcliffe home so that Ebenezer could engage with his beloved. Due to her father's intense resentment, their relationship must, for now, remain entirely underground.

As a result of he being the only link to Fan and Belle, Ebenezer quickly realized that he was at the mercy of Fred as much as he was at the mercy of Ferguson. Each deception in which he participated dug his grave deeper and deeper. Before he realized it, he was in so deeply, there was no escape.

As his time with Ferguson progressed, Ebenezer proved to be a valuable asset. He learned quickly and Ferguson's contacts rapidly came to like him. Ebenezer's fear that Ferguson or Fred would reveal his secret employment to Belle or Fan kept him loyal and subservient. Eventually, living in a world surrounded by the corrupt, as introduced to him by Ferguson, became as normal to Ebenezer as once the world surrounded by the decent, as introduced to him by Fezziwig, had been.

As Ebenezer became more compliant, Ferguson began rewarding him with words of wisdom. For example, Ferguson taught Ebenezer to distrust banks, a lesson that had been launched when he participated in removing Fezziwig's life savings.

"It is only the imbecile who allows his wealth to be held and controlled by another," Ferguson said to Ebenezer one day. "Personal safes and vaults are the only places one's riches should reside. And one should never commit all of his funds to one location any more than he should rely on but one source of income. Some say to expect the best and prepare for the worst. I say this is codswallop! Expect the worst and prepare for the worst. In this world, it is the only way to survive."

Ferguson also instructed Ebenezer to maintain a healthy fear of relationships.

"Sometimes your enemy is easy to detect. More often, however, he is not," Ferguson said. "He shakes your hand. He speaks to you with a smile. He calls you 'partner'. He knows your wife and your children. He eats your food at your table. This is the man you must fear, for if you do not, he may be the last man you ever see."

One of the most lasting lessons Ferguson imparted to Ebenezer related to the keys to success.

"Ebenezer, do you recall when I taught you the three essentials for a successful life?" Ferguson asked, as they ate their evening meal one night.

"Yes, of course," Ebenezer said, as he cut himself another slice of meat. "Study, guile and patience."

"Correct," Ferguson replied, most pleased with his young student. "Add to this list two further. Thrift and leverage."

"Oh?" Ebenezer inquired with eyebrows raised.

"Thrift. A foolish man acquires a shilling and it is gone before the day is done. What has he to show for it? Nothing. Perhaps a useless bauble. A wise man turns that shilling into two. And he maintains both, only parting with either if absolutely critical. Thrift requires that which most men never possess. Self-control. Never spend more than is necessary to accomplish your goal. Never lose sight of that goal. And never get emotional when it comes to money," Ferguson tutored.

Ebenezer listened.

"Leverage. Always have the upper hand in all situations. Never hesitate to use it," Ferguson schooled. "If you do not have the leverage, acquire it before you engage. It is always obtainable. It is simply a matter of following the straightforward formula of which you are already aware. Study. Guile. Patience. This method will be successful every time."

One conversation turned to the subject of Fezziwig.

"Fezziwig, much as it pains me to inform you of this, was a great fool," Ferguson explained.

"He was no such thing," Ebenezer retorted.

"Oh yes, Ebenezer. The very definition," Ferguson said. "He was guided by trust, truth and love. These are simply tools for manipulating others. By now you should have discovered this to be so. If not, I fear for your life each time you leave this residence. Those who learn this lesson prosper. Those who do not turn out like our dear Mr. Fezziwig."

Ebenezer did not want to believe this.

"You will take your lesson from his example if you are wise," Ferguson imparted.

"What do you mean by this?" Ebenezer asked. He did not like where this was going.

"Belle," Ferguson said.

"What about Belle?" Ebenezer asked, getting more uneasy.

"I say this to you as a friend, Ebenezer," Ferguson said with a smile.

"You are not my friend," Ebenezer retorted.

"I am. The best one you shall ever have," Ferguson replied. "One day you will realize this is true."

Ebenezer scoffed.

"Do not trust Belle with your whole heart," Ferguson counseled. "Doing so will make you blind to the truth, even when it stares at you an inch from your nose."

Ebenezer listened, but seethed.

"I see you are angry. That is simply the battle that rages within you. Your emotion wishes that you shut your eyes and stick your head within the sand. Resist that. Resist it with all of your being, Ebenezer," Ferguson said. "Follow your intellect. It is imploring you to realize that what I say is true. She has already spent time with Roland Caine. Others pursue her. And her father does not approve of you. To ignore these facts is to make you the architect of your own destruction."

This most recent bit of advice struck Ebenezer very close to the heart. Meeting with Belle at Fan's home, each time in defiance of her father's wishes had become most taxing on their relationship. While it was undoubtedly exciting at first to carry on this private affair, as time passed, it simply became a stress that neither could ignore.

Furthermore, because the world believed that Belle had given up Ebenezer, it was impossible for her to prevent her father from arranging courtship meetings with suitors that she was compelled to attend. Ebenezer was being driven mad with jealousy each time he knew his Belle was in the company of another, even if it was only to maintain appearances until he could re-emerge after he had amassed enough of a fortune to care for her properly. He feared that before this day should arrive, Belle's pretended affection for another man may be revealed as genuine.

Ebenezer's troubles with Belle were not the only romantic difficulties for those who were born with the surname Scrooge. Fan and Fred were attempting to conceive, but were having no success. Fred blamed Fan for this inability and he began spending more and more time at the local pub. He would often come home surly, perfumed in whiskey and spoiling for a dispute.

From time to time, when Ebenezer would be invited to their home, he would notice bruises on Fan that had not been there the visit previous.

She always had an explanation for same, but Ebenezer was suspicious that these were the result of Fred's promised "corrections". Fan compelled Ebenezer to withhold making any accusations or asking any questions of Fred. This caused Ebenezer great distress, but he complied with his sister's wishes. He would spend the remainder of his life wishing that he had not.

Adding to Ebenezer's stresses during his time indentured to Ferguson was his guilt as it related to Fezziwig. During this period, Fezziwig's business completely collapsed. He was forced to sell his home and his property to pay his debts. Good man that he was, he attempted to the best of his ability to make every individual to whom he owed whole. Shortly thereafter, both he and Mrs. Fezziwig disappeared entirely. Ebenezer had no idea to where they had gone.

Ebenezer resolved that he would find a way to recompense Mr. Fezziwig for all he had done for him and to right the wrong he had done to him. Ebenezer had no idea how he would accomplish this, particularly while he was under the thumb of Ferguson and while he lived in constant fear that Fred would reveal his terrible secrets to Fan and Belle. He took to praying each night before permitting himself the luxury of sleep. He was out of answers. It was time to seek them from above.

It is said that the Lord works in mysterious ways. Ebenezer was about to learn how true this aphorism could be.

32

The fifteenth of May, seventeen hundred and ninety-eight was one Ebenezer would not soon forget. He was sent out by Ferguson to collect information from Martin Witherspoon, a well-compensated and reliable agent, about a land swindle he intended to initiate. Ferguson's eye had been trained upon a certain coastal property owned by Jeremy and Rebecca Waterman of Devonshire. He had attempted its purchase through a prior intermediary but had been rebuffed by the stubborn landowners. He now sought to compel the sale through his own means.

After his meeting with Witherspoon, Ebenezer made his way back to Ferguson's home. It had been several weeks since he had last seen Fan or Belle and he was anxious to arrange for the next time that he may do so. He planned to discuss this issue with Ferguson before revealing what he had learned about the Waterman estate.

When he arrived at the front entrance, he knew immediately that something was wrong. The door was ajar and swaying with the breeze. Ferguson would never allow his home to remain unsecured. Ebenezer entered with caution.

Ebenezer crept slowly and quietly through the silent house. He dared not cry out in the event his instinct was correct and danger was afoot. Nothing seemed out of place and had the front door not presented itself in such a suspicious state, Ebenezer would have had no reason for alarm. He slunk around each corner of the main floor, fully expecting an intruder to leap out at him at any moment. But there was no intruder. At least not one who had yet made his presence known.

Ebenezer kept his senses at full alert as he entered his own sleeping quarters. It was just as Ebenezer had left it when he departed that morning. If anyone had been in here, he thought to himself, they had done an excellent job of covering their tracks.

He continued his noiseless examination of the house when he came upon Ferguson's bedchambers. The door was closed, as it normally would be. Ferguson always kept his door locked, whether he be in it or not. Ebenezer was about to continue his investigation of the abode when something within stopped him. He took a step back and gazed at the closed door before him.

He reached forward and grasped the doorknob. He twisted the knob clockwise and to his great surprise, it turned in his hand. He pushed the door open and stared at the scene before him.

Victor Ferguson was on the floor, immersed in a pool of his own blood. He was not moving. He was not breathing. His nose was badly mangled and his left cheek showed signs of serious trauma. Ebenezer bent down on one knee, seeing his own reflection in the puddle made by Ferguson's internal bodily fluids. He reached forward and touched the skin on Ferguson's dented cheek. It was cold against Ebenezer's fingertips.

Victor Ferguson was dead.

A later confession by a one Ezra Tyler would reveal what had occurred. Mr. Tyler had made the unfortunate decision to engage in a business deal initiated by Ferguson. The insult to his honor to which this encounter had led had proven to be two-fold. Not only did Ferguson render Tyler a much poorer man financially, he also transformed him into a cuckold as well.

On the same day that Tyler discovered that his money had been stolen, he arrived home to find Ferguson in his bed with his wife, mid-coitus. He chased the naked man from his home but before he could locate his firearm, Ferguson had escaped. Never before had Victor Ferguson been so careless. He valued his vigilance. During his final moments upon this earth, he was surely reminded as to why he did so.

Tyler then did what no man prior had been able to accomplish. He tracked down Ferguson. It was the one mystery that was never solved about the affair. Even as the hangman tightened the noose, he refused to disclose his means by which he accomplished this task.

When Tyler arrived at the Ferguson shelter, he stealthily broke his way into the house through a rear entrance. He found the refuge to be vacant. He took his position in the dark. And he lay in wait.

Two hours later, Ferguson entered the house, entirely unaware that he was not the first person to have done so that afternoon. He was in a jovial mood as one of his schemes had just come to fruition that very day and he was laden with riches to entrust to the vault hidden in his bedchamber beneath the floor.

He removed his coat and ambled down to his room. He took the key from his pocket and unlocked his door. He then entered and placed the sack that contained his latest booty down upon his desk. He knelt on the floor and pulled up the rug, revealing the safe hidden beneath. He entered the appropriate combination and unlatched the hatch. As he stood to retrieve the purse from his desk he looked up and realized for the first time that he was not alone.

Standing in the doorway was a very angry, but very self-satisfied Ezra Tyler holding a pistol aimed directly at Ferguson's heart.

Ferguson was about to speak in an attempt to diffuse the situation, but Tyler was not about to listen to anything Ferguson had to say.

"Keep your mouth shut if you know what is good for you, Mr. Ferguson!" Tyler demanded.

Ferguson did as instructed and raised his hands to show that he was no threat. All the while, his mind was racing to discover a means by which to turn the circumstances to his advantage.

"You abuse my trust. You steal my earnings. And you despoil my wife," Tyler said. "There is no hope for you now. I simply wanted you to know who it was that ended your life before I did so. I wished to see the look of recognition in your eyes before the deed was done."

Seeing the determination in his gaze, Ferguson took one step forward and smiled genially.

"Mr. Tyler –"

But that was as far as he was able to get.

A shot rang out and Ferguson fell immediately to the floor.

Tyler slowly walked up to his fallen prey. Ferguson was still breathing, although it was labored and wet. Tyler suspected that his bullet had penetrated Ferguson's lung.

He leaned down and whispered into Ferguson's ear.

"No one disrespects a Tyler and lives to tell the tale."

He then removed the second pistol he had hidden in his waistband, placed it directly against Ferguson's chest above his heart, and pulled the trigger.

Ferguson's body gave a mighty jolt as the sound of the gunshot was muffled within his clothing and his chest cavity. This was the killer blow.

Tyler stood over the recently deceased Mr. Ferguson feeling very content. His honor was restored. His disrespect avenged. He turned to leave when the image of Victor Ferguson penetrating his beloved wife flashed before his eyes.

He then turned around, reared back with his boot, and kicked Victor Ferguson square in the face. When he peered down, he was pleased to see that Mr. Ferguson's handsome face was handsome no more. Ferguson's nose was distorted and his cheek had rather caved in. Now Tyler felt that his work was complete. He dipped a pouch that he had brought for the occasion into his quarry's spilled blood and collected some before leaving.

Without even giving a thought to the open safe on the floor, Tyler exited the room and closed the door behind him. He chose to remove himself from the house through the front entranceway, but with this, he was less careful. Having thought he fully secured the door, he walked triumphantly into the crisp late afternoon and made his way home.

He had two more tasks to accomplish to fully satisfy his injured pride. When he walked through his door, he found his wife waiting for him when he returned. She was terrified. He dipped his hand within the pouch he had brought to the scene of the crime and, with the blood of her lover on his hand, he slapped her directly across the face, smearing Ferguson's discarded blood all over her cheek. He told her the source of her new coating. He then demanded she cook him his supper lest she suffer the same fate. After she did so, he dined like a king. He slept more comfortably that night than ever he could remember.

The next day, he went to the local constable and confessed his crime. For his honor to be fully restored, he felt that all the world must know what he had done. Had he not done so, it is unclear as to when the corpse would have been discovered.

As Ebenezer stood over the dead Mr. Ferguson, he was not as disinterested in the open safe as Mr. Tyler had been previously. What Ebenezer saw on the floor that evening was his freedom. Victor Ferguson gone from his life and a small fortune for his taking to begin his life anew.

Ebenezer emptied its entire contents and added to his newfound fortune the gold pieces he found in the change purse upon Ferguson's desk from that day's spoils. He closed the safe and returned the rug to its location prior, concealing the vault. He looked once more at Ferguson and his eyes narrowed. He could not control himself and he spit in Ferguson's deformed face.

Ebenezer then exited Ferguson's room and closed the door, returning it to the state in which he found it. He left the home, following the path that Tyler had trod just hours before. However, Ebenezer was more careful than Tyler had been and he ensured that the front door was, in fact, closed.

Ebenezer stepped out into the brisk night and took a deep breath, smiling. He felt as though he had escaped from prison. It was time for him to begin living his own life.

With that thought, he hailed a cab and, after he climbed aboard, trotted off into the night.

33

𝕰benezer considered going directly to visit with Fan and inform her of his newfound freedom. However, upon reflection, he decided that he needed to establish a plan before making any rash moves. He needed to determine where he would live and what he would do with Ferguson's funds to begin establishing his foothold into a secure future. He also did not wish Fred to be made aware of Ferguson's death before Ebenezer had a chance to decide how he would ensure that there was no possibility that the crime could be traced to him. Ebenezer had no doubt in his mind that Fred would take any opportunity to sever any ties that connected him to Ferguson in order to protect himself. The strongest link between the two men rested with Ebenezer.

Therefore, Ebenezer had the driver take him to the nearest boardinghouse. He requested a room in which he could remain for one week. If he needed more time than this, he certainly had the means to do so. If he required less, he had lost nothing.

He paid the fee and was led to his new temporary home. When he was alone with the door closed, he sat upon the bed and took a deep breath. He could not believe how much his life had changed just within the last hour. It was overwhelming.

As Ebenezer considered his options, he realized that he would be unable to publicly present himself in the business community at this point in time. There were still those who would do him harm because of his role in Ferguson's investment scheme. He would need to establish himself as self-sufficient and would need to employ some of the lessons he learned from Ferguson to ensure his safety. The most important of which was leverage. With leverage over his enemies and over those who could be useful as valuable friends, he would be able to emerge from the dark and take his rightful place where he knew he belonged.

In the meanwhile, he determined that he had but two options to achieve this goal. The first, and likely wisest, had him leave London, and perhaps all of Britain, and take up residence in a location where his name was unknown. He could establish his business, whatever that would be, in the Low Countries or perhaps Russia. He had never ventured to such places, but he surmised that there he would be safe to walk the streets without fear.

Despite the reasonableness of this option, Ebenezer rejected it out of hand. He could not imagine living his life entirely away from Fan and Belle. Months, or more likely years, would be required to see this plan to fruition. He had already spent more time away from his sister than he cared to recall during his stint at Worthington. And he could not leave Belle to the machinations of her father. As it was, Ebenezer was more than uncomfortable that Belle had spent the last two years as the subject of courtship by others. Fortunately, Arthur Benson had been respectful of her rejections of all comers to date. Ebenezer knew that this would not last forever. If he left the country, he was certain she would marry another. He could not stomach the thought.

All that remained was subterfuge. He could not conduct business in his own name; it would have to be in that of another. To his disadvantage, he did not have an individual such as himself or Fred as Ferguson had to run his errands and assist with his deals. As such, this was the less desirable of the options from the perspective of ease in execution. But he could see no other way.

With it settled that Ebenezer would not leave London, the next logical step required him to determine how he would make his fortune. Ferguson's funds could take him a long distance if he invested them properly. He remembered Ferguson's advice. A fool acquires a shilling and it is gone before sunset. A wise man turns that shilling into two. All it required was study, guile, patience, thrift and leverage. Ebenezer had learned his lessons well. It was now time to employ them. Once successful, he would never feel the sting of poverty again, he would never be under the control of another, and he would never be apart from his Belle forevermore. Wealth was the key to his happiness.

As he pondered his situation and considered his skills, he looked about and realized that the answer was staring him directly in the face. If he purchased real estate that was suitable for use as boardinghouses or other rental property, a fortune could be had. It would provide a steady stream of income, if done correctly, for a modicum of cost. He could purchase the property using an assumed name. His potential employee pool would not be of the class that would be connected to those who sought to do him ill. If he found that the rental income was not sufficient, he could sell the property at a profit and then begin anew. Ebenezer had learned much during his biennial tutelage under Victor Ferguson. He felt quite confident that he could convert real estate ownership to his great advantage.

Ebenezer knew also not to rely solely and exclusively on one means of income. He would use his knowledge he acquired of the markets to invest some of Ferguson's fortune. This too could be accomplished anonymously. Ebenezer had mastered the acquisition of information. Often he had been compelled to use that knowledge to fill Ferguson's pockets. Now he could use that skill to line his own.

Ebenezer had also learned much from Ferguson's death and he resolved that regardless of how difficult times may become, he would not resort to emulating Ferguson's criminal ways in order to extract himself from trouble. Nor would he do so to advance himself or his interests. Ebenezer was certain that Ferguson met his end at the hands of an unscrupulous business associate. A random burglar would not have left behind all of the valuables in the house. Victor Ferguson was murdered. That is why the intruder entered the home. Ebenezer was sure this was true.

When Ebenezer awoke the next morning, he immediately initiated his plan. He first purchased for himself a small and inexpensive home under a fictitious name in which to live. He also located a boardinghouse that he decided was appropriate for his needs. He offered ten percent over market value to secure the sale. With the deed in his pocket, he had begun his journey into a larger world. Before the year was out, he would acquire two more properties with rooms to let. He also speculated in the commodities market and used his knowledge and skill at procuring the necessary information to triple his investment before his twentieth birthday.

His quest to obtain wealth had truly begun.

With resources now at his disposal for the first time in his life, Ebenezer resolved to immediately right his greatest wrong. During his time attached to Ferguson, Ebenezer had come into contact with a fellow named D. V. Hagenwood who was particularly adept at locating those who do not wish to be found. Ebenezer sought out this individual and employed him to discover the whereabouts of Francis and Margaret Fezziwig. Ebenezer's guilt about how he had participated in their downfall ate at him night and day.

After Ezra Tyler confessed to the murder of Victor Ferguson, a weight was lifted from Ebenezer's shoulders. Fred could no longer use Ferguson's death to hang Ebenezer. However, he still possessed the fact that Ebenezer spent the conclusion of his teenaged years working for

Ferguson as the sword of Damocles hanging precariously over Ebenezer's head. He used this leverage to his advantage.

Knowing that it would not be long before Ebenezer would show up at his doorstep to visit with his wife, Fred exercised patience. That day occurred within a week of Ferguson's death. Ebenezer arrived unannounced.

"Ebenezer!" Fan cried as she saw her brother at her door. "It has been far too long! Why have you not visited sooner?"

"I could not, Fan. Not until now," Ebenezer said. "But I am here."

They embraced and she invited him in.

They sat on the divan and Ebenezer informed his sister that he had begun a new chapter in his life. He said that he had embarked on a new business venture. One that had more promise than any he had ever experienced before. Fan was very excited for Ebenezer and asked him what it was in which he was now engaged. Ebenezer remained vague, exactly how he had responded to such questions during the previous two years. He maintained the same rationale; that there were those who would do him harm if his business interests were known. He also wished to protect Fan because he knew that many, including Arthur Benson himself, had called on her inquiring if she knew where her brother was residing and for whom he was working. By continuing to keep the details of his life opaque, Fan would never be put in a position where she could be compelled to either lie, which he knew she abhorred, or to tell the truth, which would only lead to her becoming complicit in harming her brother.

Before his visit was complete, Fred made his entrance. He asked Fan to excuse the men so that they may speak privately. Fan was never pleased with the notion of Fred and Ebenezer conferring alone because she knew of the friction that had grown between them. Additionally, she was always in fear that Ebenezer would voice his concerns for her safety, despite his promise never to imply such was at risk. However, when Fred told her that they would either conduct their meeting within the house or outside of it depending on her compliance with his wishes, she relented and left the room. Ebenezer noted that Fan seemed much less inclined to disobey Fred than she had been at the outset of their marriage. When Fred was present, the vibrant spirit that she had always possessed seemed dimmer somehow.

"Ebenezer, my dear brother-in-law," Fred began. "It seems that you, sir, are out of a job and a home. Yet, here you sit, having arrived at my door presumably after paying the fare of a hired coachman. I wonder from where you began your travels and how you produced the necessary remuneration."

"What is it that you wish, Fred?" Ebenezer asked annoyed.

"I do not know how you accomplished this," Fred said, "but I know you have come into some means. I suspect it has something to do with the recent unfortunate passing of our common colleague. I have asked my contacts throughout the city and am satisfied that you are in no one's employ save your own. As such, we are about to strike a bargain."

"What is the nature of this bargain of which you speak?" Ebenezer asked, disappointed that even with Ferguson gone, he still had one oppressor remaining.

"You and I are to become partners, Ebenezer," Fred said. "You will fully disclose to me your current business interests, you will show me where you reside, and you will share with me fifty percent of your earnings."

"You must be mad!" Ebenezer exclaimed.

"Quite the contrary," Fred said calmly. "If you do not accede, I will inform both my wife and your beloved the name of whom you have been working these past two years. I will inform them of the nature of your work. And I will strongly hint that Ezra Tyler, that feeble fool we read about in the periodicals this week, had an unnamed and heretofore unidentified accomplice. Can you deduce who that may be?"

Ebenezer considered what he was hearing. He attempted to think his way out of Fred's trap.

"If you attempt to sink me, you will only succeed in scuttling your own ship as well," Ebenezer said. "From where could your information derive if not from your own association with the late Mr. Ferguson?"

"Worry not about that, brother-in-law," Fred said confidently, with a smile. "Be certain that I have already taken all necessary precautions. Your argument falls flat. That is all you need know. I would not test your luck if I were in your shoes."

Ebenezer could not tell if Fred was bluffing.

The two continued their game of parry and riposte, with Fred, the more accomplished scoundrel, winning the day. In what he called a show of mercy, Fred reduced his initial demand. In the end, Ebenezer agreed to share twenty-five percent of his earnings and allowed Fred to accompany him back to his home so that the location would no longer be his secret. Despite the danger of Fred learning the truth, Ebenezer chose to conceal all of his interests from Fred except for his most lucrative boardinghouse investment. He did not believe that Fred would accept anything less. Fred at first suspected Ebenezer was not being truthful, but his arrogance proved to be his Achilles heel. He ultimately decided that he had such control over his younger counterpart, that Ebenezer would be too frightened to hold back any information about his earnings.

From that day forward, Ebenezer was forced to conduct his business much more carefully. Not only must he worry that Fred would disclose his previous employment to Belle and Fan, but Fred could now also inform the angry swindled investors where he resided and the source of his income. There was but one obvious release hatch from the spider web Fred had Ebenezer ensnared within. Sadly, Ebenezer could not see it. Not yet. He would remain as Fred's unwilling partner because he could not recognize the solution that had been available from the start.

Ebenezer's relationship with Belle continued to struggle. He could not control his rage when she met with other men. She could not control her frustration that he would not simply marry her and they escape together. He promised that he would marry her once he had acquired enough wealth to be worthy of her affections and to ensure that she may hold her head high in society even as she was known to one and all as Mrs. Ebenezer Scrooge. She scolded him that he valued wealth and possessions too highly. Clearly, he informed her on many an occasion, she did not understand the ways of the world.

On one warm day in July as they met at Fred and Fan's home, Ebenezer finally informed Belle that he had left his previous employment and was now engaged in making his way on his own. He told her that it should not be long before he had enough to allow them to marry. His only request was that she not inquire about his business.

Belle hesitated to accept this condition.

"Ebenezer, if we are to be together, we cannot withhold information about our lives from one another," Belle said.

"All you need know is that I am working hard to create the life you deserve," Ebenezer replied.

This was always his response, but Belle's patience was growing thin. As summer turned to autumn and autumn to winter, Ebenezer continued to insist that he had not produced enough. When the calendar's page read seventeen hundred and ninety-nine, Ebenezer's pursuit of "enough" had still not come to an end. Belle's increasingly frequent insistence on discovering Ebenezer's source of earnings and his equally insistent denial to reveal same pushed them further and further apart.

Belle believed that Ebenezer could not see that his quest for the accumulation of wealth had overtaken his initial reason for the quest. What Belle did not know was that Ebenezer had discovered the method by which he could re-enter society with her by his side. His plan required him to amass enough prosperity that he would have the means by which to repay the losses of those he assisted in swindling as well as having enough to care for Belle in the manner to which she was accustomed. If only he were wise enough to realize that he should have shared this information with Belle. Instead, he pressed himself harder and harder, continuing his single-minded focus to expand his business interests and increase his financial holdings.

Six months into the final year of the century, Ebenezer felt himself blessed with a marvelous day. It was the fourth of June, Fred and Fan's third wedding anniversary. Ebenezer realized that he had finally acquired the means sufficient to repay Arthur Benson to compensate him for all of his losses in the investment swindle. Ebenezer also received word that very morning that D. V. Hagenwood had finally located Mr. Fezziwig after his long absence from Ebenezer's life. Ebenezer planned to provide Mr. Fezziwig with a rich payment as well as to promise him an ongoing dividend from whatever it was that Ebenezer would accumulate from that day forward. Mr. Hagenwood's message informed Ebenezer to meet him at three o'clock in the afternoon at their prearranged location.

Ebenezer planned to visit Fan in the morning to wish her a happy anniversary and to tell her of all of his grand news. From there, his travels would take him to the doorstep of Arthur Benson with a bagful of money and a sincere apology. He hoped that this would allow him to resume his courtship with Belle in the free and open air. The corners and shadows had clearly had a stifling effect on their love for one another. He could not wait to allow it to breathe unimpeded once again. Ebenezer expected that after this victory was won, he would meet with Mr. Hagenwood and take the first steps towards reconciling with the Fezziwigs.

Yes indeed, thought Ebenezer with a smile as he attracted the attention of a cab driver. This shall be a glorious day. It shall be one that I will never forget.

He was correct by half.

34

Ebenezer alit from the carriage and wished the driver a merry day. His spirits were bright. With a jaunty step, he made his way to Fan's front door and made his presence known.

Fan answered the door with a bright smile of her own. She too, Ebenezer could discern right away, was having a glorious day. The siblings exchanged their cheerful greetings, embraced, and Ebenezer followed Fan into the house.

"I would like to wish you a happy anniversary, Fan," Ebenezer began as they sat.

"Why, thank you, Ebenezer," said Fan, looking brighter than she had in longer than he could remember. "It is a very happy day indeed. I am so glad that you are here. I was, whether you believe me or not, preparing a message when you arrived asking that you come. And, by Providence, here you are!"

"I have not seen you so jolly in many a visit," Ebenezer said. "I am pleased to be witness to this joyfulness."

"And why should I not be joyful, dear Ebenezer," Fan asked, "when I have news such as this to share with you."

"I have news as well, but I can see that mine must wait," Ebenezer said. "I am most intrigued. What have you to say?"

"It is a miracle, Ebenezer. A miracle!" Fan said, beginning to cry, but maintaining the broad smile upon her face.

"What is a miracle, Fan?" Ebenezer asked expectantly.

"Shortly after the new century commences, I shall make you an uncle!" Fan exclaimed.

Ebenezer was stunned into silence for a moment.

"What is that you say?" Ebenezer asked.

"Yes, Ebenezer, it is true. I am with child!" Fan squealed. "After so long that we have waited, Fred and I shall at last be parents! I thought it not possible, but God is great indeed and He has blessed my womb! I had suspected several weeks ago, but had disappointments in the past and so I waited to be sure. And then I decided announcing to Fred on this day would be the perfect anniversary present! Sadly, he exited too early for me to share this news with him before he began his workday. And so you are the first to know!"

Ebenezer's initial shock subsided and he broke out into a great smile.

"Congratulations, my sister!" he said, reaching for her to give her a mighty hug, but then choosing to give her but a dainty squeeze for fear that he may harm her or the child growing within now that she was in such delicate condition.

"Oh, grip me as always you have done, my silly brother," Fan said, laughing. "I shall not break!"

Ebenezer chuckled, but was still unsure how safe it would be to smother his sister with the love he wished to express. He squeezed a bit tighter, but still withheld all of his might.

"That is simply marvelous tidings, Fan. Simply marvelous!" Ebenezer said as they broke their embrace. He looked at his sister's beaming face. He could almost not accept the truth. His darling sister would be a mum. No one was more suited for the job, he was sure of this. She was more mum than sister to him for his entire life. He knew that this child was lucky indeed.

"Oh, where are my manners?" Fan exclaimed. "I have told you of my announcement, but you have brought news of your own. Forgive me, brother. What word have you to bring?"

"There are no need for apologies, Fan," said Ebenezer. "I do have happy news, although it will not compare with what you have just revealed to me. You have simply added to the greatness of this day."

"What have you to say?" Fan asked.

"I have the means to repay Mr. Benson that which I was responsible for his losing through the scheme of Mr. Ferguson. I have brought it with me and plan to present it to him this very day and beg his forgiveness. It is my fervent hope that he will accept and will allow Belle and I to continue our romance in the light of day," Ebenezer stated.

"That is wonderful!" Fan cried. "I am certain he will do so."

"Ah, but there is more," Ebenezer said. "Today shall be a day I shall not soon forget. Something I have anticipated for years is about to come to fruition."

"What could this be?" Fan asked.

"The Fezziwigs have been found," Ebenezer said, holding Fan's hands in his own. "I will go to see them on this day. I will present them with the vast funds that I can now afford to repay. And I shall promise them more, so much more, as I acquire it."

"Ebenezer!" Fan exclaimed. "That is sensational! How did you accomplish this?"

"I hired a man reliable for such tasks," Ebenezer explained. "I began to lose hope as time progressed, but he has delivered!"

"Where are they?" Fan asked. "No one has seen them for more than two years."

"I do not yet know," Ebenezer said. "But I will learn their location when the clock strikes three this afternoon. I shall meet my man and he will provide the information I have dreamed of for so long."

"I am so very happy for you, Ebenezer," Fan said.

"And I for you, Fan," Ebenezer replied. "But now I must go. I must visit with Arthur Benson so that my day may remain on schedule."

"Go then, Ebenezer," Fan implored. "I shall call for you after I inform Fred of our fabulous situation. I expect that we shall require a grand celebration and you must attend."

"Of course I shall, Fan," Ebenezer said, as he rose and walked to the door.

They bid each other a fine remainder of the day, each wishing the other luck with their tasks ahead, and Ebenezer returned to the cab he had asked to remain waiting for him. He then headed off to the Benson property.

On the way, Ebenezer allowed himself the pleasure of foreseeing himself as an uncle. He determined to be a wonderful uncle; one who would do anything for Fan's child. Now he had more glad tidings to share with Belle. Her father will be made whole. Their love may be expressed in the open. The Fezziwigs have been found. And now, he was to become an uncle. This already breathtaking day was proving to be more glorious than he believed possible when he awoke that morning.

When he arrived at the Benson's, he once again asked the driver to await his return. He did not know how long this visit would last, but he did not wish to gamble with fate and arrive at his designated rendezvous with Mr. Hagenwood even one minute late.

Ebenezer walked towards the front door, but as he passed a window, something odd caught his eye. He peered into the sitting room and there, to his great surprise and consternation, was Belle making merry with a gentleman Ebenezer did not recognize. His blood boiled. She had not informed him that her father had arranged a meeting for her today. She always gave him foreknowledge of such an event. Why did she conceal this one today? And why did she seem so pleased by this man's advances?

Ebenezer saw the man laughing and then he did something truly indecent. He leaned forward and placed his hand upon Belle's arm! And Belle did not recoil! She allowed this flirtatious excuse for contact to continue! Could it be that she was truly enjoying this man's company?

It was then Ebenezer noticed the dimple. Yes, the dimple on her right cheek was in full view and was mocking him. This was not a ruse. Belle's enjoyment was not counterfeit. This was unacceptable!

Well, if this be who she choose, Ebenezer thought, so be it! His face was beet red from his chin to his hairline. His eyes were as narrow as slits. His hands were balled into fists. If she should choose to act the jezebel, Ebenezer fumed, who was he to restrain her?

Ebenezer was unable to control his rage. He looked at the sack of riches in his hands and determined that Arthur Benson, the man who sired this unabashed coquette, would not see his money today. If she be engaged in this courtship on this day without pre-informing him, Ebenezer reasoned, how could he trust that this was the first time this has occurred? Perhaps this is a common happening as he worked day and night in an effort to provide her a luxurious life. If that be so, this family did not merit his appeal or his recompense. Not on this day. Perhaps, never.

Ebenezer marched back to the cab and violently threw the sack of coins to the floor.

"Is everything alright, sir?" asked the driver.

"No, it most certainly is not," Ebenezer responded through teeth gritted.

"To where would you like to be off, sir?"

It was too early to meet Mr. Hagenwood. Ebenezer had expected to be with the Bensons for at least an hour. He accounted for such. He realized that he needed to cool his head before seeing Hagenwood. He took a deep breath and blew it out. One was not enough. He repeated the exercise two more times before his blood began to return to a more hospitable temperature.

"Drive us around London, please," Ebenezer said. "Assume I am a first-time visitor. Just ensure that I am at our next destination by no later than five minutes of three."

The driver obliged.

While riding in the carriage, Ebenezer fought with himself mightily. He did not wish to stew over the indecent display he had witnessed at the Benson home. He forced himself to focus his attention on the glad news Fan imparted and the amazing fortune he was about to receive. Before the day was done, he would see the Fezziwigs again. He would make right what he once made wrong. His gnawing guilt that had consumed him for so long would finally be assuaged.

At exactly five minutes of three in the afternoon, Ebenezer alit from the carriage. He was shaking with anticipation. His anger at Belle was, for the moment, put aside. He stood and looked out into the distance, imagining what he may say when he first encountered the Fezziwigs. He hoped they would greet him kindly.

As he was lost in his thoughts, a short, dark-haired man walked up to him.

"Greetings, Mr. Scrooge," Hagenwood said.

Ebenezer was startled at the voice and looked down to see his contact standing before him.

"Mr. Hagenwood," Ebenezer said, grinning. "I am most pleased to see you."

"Have you my final payment?" Hagenwood asked.

Ebenezer reached into his coat pocket and produced an envelope. He gave it to Hagenwood, who examined it carefully. Satisfied that he was properly compensated, Hagenwood deposited it into his pocket.

"Do you have the location for me?" Ebenezer asked, lightly hopping back and forth from one foot to the other.

"I do, Mr. Scrooge," said Hagenwood, but he hesitated.

"Well, then tell me, man! I can handle the suspense no more," Ebenezer beseeched.

D. V. Hagenwood spoke one word. It caused Ebenezer's smile to vanish and his face to fall.

"Marshalsea."

Ebenezer took in a sharp breath.

"But that is a debtor's prison!" Ebenezer exclaimed.

"It is," Hagenwood responded.

In fact, Marshalsea was not just a debtor's prison. It was a notoriously foul debtor's prison. Located in Southwark, just south of the River Thames, it was a dirty and dishonorable institution. For those inmates who could afford the fees charged, they had access to certain amenities. The most valuable of the privileges available was the right to exit the prison's walls during the day so that they could earn enough to repay their creditors, which would allow them to shorten and ultimately terminate their sentences. For those who could not afford the fees, they would be crammed into one of nine small rooms with dozens of others. Because they could not earn a salary while locked away, not only would their creditors remain unpaid, but the prison fees for which they were responsible would accumulate, placing them in an impossible situation. Often inmates would find themselves held captive for years, even if their initial debts were minimal.

Those who eventually found a way to repay their debts along with the prison fees would prove to be the fortunate ones. The poorest often starved and were subject to torture at the hands of their jailors. For many, they exited on their backs and were deposited in the local churchyard.

"I must go to him immediately!" Ebenezer shouted, his body cold and numb from this information. "But first, please, tell me where Mrs. Fezziwig has been found."

"I am very sorry, but she was not," Hagenwood replied. "Her whereabouts are unknown. I utilized all of my resources, but she has vanished."

"Perhaps Mr. Fezziwig will be able to supply that information," Ebenezer spoke to himself. He turned back to Hagenwood and shook his hand.

"Thank you, Mr. Hagenwood," Ebenezer said, already heading back to the awaiting carriage.

"Any time you need anything further, Mr. Scrooge, you know where to find me," Hagenwood said, and walked off.

Back in the cab once more, Ebenezer frantically extolled the driver to make haste to Marshalsea Debtor's Prison. He did so and once there, Ebenezer practically flew from the carriage to the main gate. He informed the guard that it was imperative that he speak with the warden. The guard pretended not to understand the question until Ebenezer placed a gold coin within the palm of his hand. Miraculously, his comprehension emerged.

He left Ebenezer waiting at the gate, nervous and anxious. He peered at the exterior of the facility. He could not accept that his actions led Mr. Fezziwig to this dreadful place.

When the guard returned, he informed Ebenezer that the warden was available, but he would not show him the way until another coin was deposited in his hand. Ebenezer followed the guard through the labyrinth of the institution's interior until he found himself at the door of the warden, Daniel Brewster. The guard knocked for him.

"Enter!" a sharp voice called out.

Ebenezer walked into the office and found a solidly-built man, slightly shorter than he, with broad shoulders and strong hands. He had dark hair, dark eyes and a dark, cold glare.

"What is it that you want, sir?" Brewster barked. "I am a busy man. I am not usually in the practice of entertaining visits from strangers."

"I am very sorry, sir," Ebenezer said as politely as he was able to muster. "I come to pay the debt of one of the unfortunates you keep housed within these walls."

"Ah," Brewster said, his eyes brightening at the mention of money. "And exactly which of my wretched flock shall be the recipient of such good fortune?"

"I come to pay the debt of Francis Fezziwig," Ebenezer said.

"Fezziwig, Fezziwig..." Brewster mulled. "The name does not ring familiar."

Ebenezer

Ebenezer shook his head in disgust. Corruption all the way to the top of a government facility. Why should he be surprised? Ebenezer reached into his pouch and handed the warden his obviously required bribe.

Upon accepting the funds, Brewster went to his desk and looked in his manifest.

"Fezziwig, you say?" he asked, as he searched the register.

"Yes, sir," Ebenezer said. "Francis Fezziwig."

"We have no Fezziwig here," Brewster said coming to the end of his search. Ebenezer's eyes brightened. Perhaps Hagenwood was wrong. Perhaps Mr. Fezziwig had not been resigned to this dreary place.

"Wait," Brewster said, holding up his hand. "I must check the red book."

Brewster pulled from his desk a thick book with a red binder. Ebenezer could not see what it read on its cover before Brewster flipped it open. He ran his finger down the page approximately one third of the way through the red tome. His finger came to a stop and he looked up.

"Francis Fezziwig, you say?" Brewster confirmed.

"Yes, sir," Ebenezer replied.

"Dead," Brewster informed as nonchalantly as if he were reporting the time of day.

Ebenezer was immediately nauseated. This could not be. It must be a mistake.

"Pardon me, sir?" Ebenezer replied, hoping that his ears deceived.

"Yes, indeed," Brewster said, peering at the words beneath his finger on the page. "Dead. The twenty-seventh of February. Seventeen hundred and ninety-seven. Unknown causes."

Ebenezer's head became light and his legs went weak. He put his hand to his face. Mr. Fezziwig was dead. Over two years prior. How could this be? All Ebenezer could think was that this was entirely his fault.

"You sir!" Brewster said harshly. "Is there anything further that you require? If not, I must ask you to leave. I have much to accomplish."

"No," Ebenezer said wearily. "I require nothing more."

"Then go," Brewster ordered. "Reynolds! Are you still by my door?"

"Yes, warden," the guard responded.

"Escort Mr..." Brewster began, seeking Ebenezer's name.

"Scrooge," he said softly.

"Escort Mr. Scrooge out of here and off of our grounds," Brewster commanded.

"Yes, warden," Reynolds said. He took Ebenezer by the arm and led him back through the halls from where he first entered until they reached the front gate. Ebenezer was directed out the door and into the street.

Ebenezer slowly walked back to his cab, still in shock and dismay. Fezziwig was dead. It did not seem possible. The vibrant, gregarious soul who lit up every room in which he entered was gone. The world was a darker place for it.

Ebenezer climbed back into the cab and sat staring at his hands.

"Where to next, Mr. Scrooge?" the driver asked.

Only one name came to mind as Ebenezer sat reeling in this state.

"Fan," he whispered.

The driver could not hear him.

"Say again, please sir?" the driver asked.

Ebenezer told him to go back to Fred and Fan's house. It seemed like an eternity had passed since he was there just a few hours prior. The day held so much promise when he entered her doors in the morning. He was going to resolve his debt with Arthur Benson. He was going to engage with Belle in the light of day. He was going to reconcile with the Fezziwigs. How did everything turn so sour?

Belle was in the company of another. Mr. Fezziwig was long dead. Mrs. Fezziwig was impossible to locate, perhaps dead herself.

Ebenezer hoped that Fan would be able to work her magic and help him through these tragedies.

When he reached Fan's home, something seemed awry. There were three men at her doorstep. Ebenezer observed that they were not arriving, but leaving. One was clearly a doctor. His countenance did not speak of one who was merely visiting in concern for Fan's prenatal health. When Ebenezer approached closer, he saw what was clearly fresh blood on his clothing.

"What has happened?" Ebenezer asked, frightened.

"Who are you?" asked the doctor, as all three men stared at him.

"I am Fan's brother. I wish to know if she is hurt?" Ebenezer said, staring at the blood.

"She will be fine," the doctor replied. "She suffered a nasty fall down the staircase of her home. But she is awake and alert and, despite her appearance that may suggest otherwise, she will heal."

Ebenezer heard the words "fall down the staircase" and nothing more. He pushed past the men and ran to be by sister's side. On the way, he found Fred in the sitting room with a snifter in his hand, sipping a brandy.

"What have you done?" Ebenezer hissed.

"I have done nothing, brother-in-law," Fred said calmly. "Except to return to my home to find my wife at the base of the staircase, unconscious and bleeding profusely. I called for the doctor. He and his associates arrived, assisted Fan to our bed, and he bandaged her wounds. I was told she would be fine."

"You lie," Ebenezer said, fuming. "I know you lie."

"I do no such thing," Fred said. "You may ask her yourself, although she remembers nothing of the incident."

Ebenezer turned and bolted up the stairs, taking them two at a time. When he reached the top, before he could proceed to Fan's bedroom, Fred's words stopped him.

"Oh, Ebenezer, I must congratulate you," Fred said.

Ebenezer turned and looked down at Fred.

"You are to become an uncle," Fred told him, with an evil look in his eye. He then casually turned and walked down the hall, returning his attention to his drink.

Ebenezer watched him walk away, listening to his heels clicking on the floor. He then snapped from his trance and rushed to his sister's bedside.

35

𝔍an's doctor was correct. Her wounds did heal. Slowly, but they did heal. But her fall, if that is indeed what occurred, left her in a weakened condition. She was never quite the same after her injury.

Furthermore, her pregnancy was a difficult one. She was quite ill from the time she had awoken from her terrible accident through the month of August and into September. After almost five months of being in a family way she weighed less than she had before her childbearing had begun.

Ebenezer regularly checked in on his sister. To his disgust, Fred was rarely at home. Based upon his odor and his equilibrium when he would return, it was no secret where he had been spending his time. Ebenezer began to suspect that he need worry about with whom Fred was spending his time as well. More than once, Ebenezer detected the faint scent of perfume emanating from Fred's clothing while noting the late hour at which he stumbled through the front door.

It infuriated Ebenezer that he believed his sister was being mistreated and disrespected. But she always implored him to avoid confrontations with Fred and told him that she was sure that Fred was simply exhibiting the nerves of impending fatherhood. She was certain that once the baby was born, all would be well in the household. Ebenezer did not share her conviction.

Additionally, Ebenezer was convinced that Fred was responsible for Fan's injury on the stairway. But because Fan could not remember the accident and because she was steadfast that Fred's version of events was the correct one, Ebenezer had no proof. He felt powerless to protect his sister, and now his unborn niece or nephew, as Fan stubbornly stood by her husband.

All the while, Ebenezer was still distraught over learning of Fezziwig's death. It was an open wound that could never close. He felt himself a murderer, having pushed Fezziwig to his ultimate demise.

To cope with these frustrations, Ebenezer threw himself into his enterprises, which now also included owning minority holdings in several substantial businesses. He had begun to repay the swindled investors of Ferguson's scheme through intermediaries. All were now aware that Ebenezer Scrooge was operating somewhere in London, but because he showed his good faith in attempting to resolve their losses, animosity towards his name was softening. His plan for re-entering society was working.

At least it was working with most. Due to his anger regarding what he had witnessed during Belle's secret courtship meeting on the fourth of June, Ebenezer still had paid Arthur Benson nothing. Perhaps he should have done so because Arthur's patience with Belle's consistent rejection of appropriate suitors was at an end. And he was no fool. Knowing that Ebenezer was near, he realized that Belle fancied herself meant for him. He decided that it was time for his daughter to marry and to marry well. He resolved that he would be in his grave before he would allow Belle to carry the surname Scrooge.

Arthur organized a gala to take place at his home that he promised would rival any that the disgraced Francis Fezziwig had thrown in the past. On the fourteenth of September, seventeen hundred and ninety-nine, Arthur Benson invited one and all to a masquerade ball. He pledged that he had an announcement at the end of the evening that would itself be worth attendance.

Ebenezer learned of this party. He was fascinated by the fact that it was a masquerade ball. He determined to secretly attend hidden behind a mask. What he did not know was that this was precisely what Arthur Benson had hoped he would do.

Arthur Benson was good friends with Thaddeus Weatherby, who had made his fortune in shipbuilding. The young man Ebenezer had witnessed in the Benson home associating with Belle was Thaddeus' son, Nathaniel. The two men agreed that their children should wed. The fact that Nathaniel had not yet asked and that Belle had not yet agreed was of no consequence to them. They conspired together to ensure that this union would take place. Their minds were set on it.

After the party had been in full cry for several hours, Ebenezer entered the room in search of Belle. With all concealed behind masks, it was not an easy task, but he knew her well. He knew her gait. He knew her laugh. He knew her voice. He even knew her aroma. It did not take long for Ebenezer to correctly identify the woman whom he had loved since he was thirteen years old.

He approached her from behind as she was in the process of taking a respite from the dance floor and was indulging in a beverage.

"Good madam," he said as he touched her shoulder. "Would you care to dance?"

Belle immediately knew who it was.

"Ebenezer," she whispered as she turned to face him. "You take a great risk in coming here."

"My risk is not as great as you may think," Ebenezer said. "In fact, it diminishes every day."

"Where have you been?" Belle asked. "It has been nearly a month since I have seen you!"

"I have been hard at work," Ebenezer replied.

"That is always your response," Belle pouted. "I think that you are still cross about my meeting in June with Nathaniel Weatherby."

Ebenezer said nothing to contradict.

"We have been through this more times than I can recount," Belle said with exasperation. "I was given no advanced warning of his visit that day, nor was I aware that you were skulking about outside my window. I care nothing for him. But, my love, hear this. If I continue to wait for you, I shall surely awaken one morning as an old, shriveled spinster. Why will you not save me from this fate?"

"I shall, my dear," Ebenezer replied. "The time approaches when I will have enough to re-enter society and to properly provide for your needs and your reputation."

"Aargh!!!" Belle exclaimed, throwing up her hands. "Enough. Enough. I have heard this refrain for longer than I can remember! I fear you shall never have enough! Well, at the moment, I have had enough! Do not follow me. I wish to be alone!"

Belle marched off, leaving Ebenezer staring after her.

Arthur Benson was clandestinely observing this interaction. He smiled and knew the time had come. He walked up to the raised stage erected for the musicians and asked that they assist in obtaining everyone's attention. He motioned for Thaddeus Weatherby to collect Nathaniel and remain near.

"Ladies and gentlemen," Arthur began. "I am so pleased you have been able to join us this evening. I promised you a grand announcement and the time has come. I ask that everyone please take a drink in hand."

Ebenezer took a glass from a tray a nearby servant was holding. He watched Arthur Benson from the corner of his eye. He sensed he would not appreciate what he was about to hear.

"Now where is my precious Annabelle?" Arthur called out.

"I am here, Father," Belle replied.

"Please come up, my dear," Arthur requested. Belle did as she was asked.

"Ladies and gentlemen, it brings me great pleasure to announce to you that the Bensons are about to embark on a new merger," Arthur said with a wink and a smile. "A short while ago, Nathaniel Weatherby, here to my right, asked my lovely daughter, Annabelle Marie, to be his bride. And I am pleased to report that she happily accepted! So you see, the true masquerade tonight is that this has been an engagement party from the start! Cheers! Please, drink to their health and everlasting happiness!"

Sounds of pleasure swept throughout the crowd and the tinging of clinking glasses filled the room.

Ebenezer stood frozen, glaring at Belle.

Belle and Nathaniel were in shock, but decorum prevented them from doing anything other than thanking the wave of well-wishers.

Arthur and Thaddeus smiled brightly at each other, having successfully enacted their plan. They clinked glasses and patted each other on the backs.

Ebenezer finally awoke from his catatonia and beat a hasty retreat from the room. He exited the house and quickly had his carriage driver take him home.

All the while, Belle was attempting to locate Ebenezer in the crowd, but the pandemonium prevented her from witnessing his departure. She was burning with embarrassment and anger at her father. He intentionally placed her in an extremely delicate position. She planned a lengthy confrontation once the house was free of guests.

"You will do as you are told," Arthur Benson said to Belle later that evening when she initiated her rebellion. "And there is nothing more to say on the matter."

"Father, I do not love him," Belle pleaded.

"I do not speak of love. I speak of marriage," Arthur replied casually.

"Father, please," Belle implored. "I cannot marry Nathaniel Weatherby. I love another."

"That Scrooge boy," Arthur said dismissively. "I know it all too well. I should have put a stop to that before it even began. I am too soft-hearted. That has always been my problem."

"I will marry Ebenezer," Belle said defiantly.

"Annabelle. My love," Arthur said softly. "There is no purpose to this argument. I am your father and the head of this household. I have made a decision. It is the right decision. It is the only decision. And it is what will occur. Now, it is late and you need your rest. Leave me and get some sleep. Tomorrow shall be a busy day. We will get the blessing of our priest at church for your impending nuptials. And we will begin preparations."

"Father, you do not listen to a word I say!" Belle complained.

"That is correct. I am the father. You are the daughter. I do not listen to what you decree. You listen, and obey, my commands," Arthur explained patiently. Arthur Benson refused to lose his temper. He refused to raise his voice. And he refused to back down.

Belle was becoming more and more frustrated. She was getting nowhere with her father. And she was feeling more worried that the decision truly was not hers to make.

She resolved that there was but one solution. She would go to Ebenezer the next day after church and explain to him the predicament in which they found themselves. Either he abandon his foolish quest for "enough" and they elope immediately, or he risk losing her forever.

Church the following morning was an especially uncomfortable experience for Belle. She sat beside her father to her right and Nathaniel Weatherby to her left. The entire congregation was made aware of their engagement from the pulpit, making it that much more difficult to undo. Arthur was doing a masterful job of ensnaring his daughter in this Gordian knot of a marriage before she was even compelled to speak the words, "I do".

After the service, and after Belle was forced to thank the myriad of parishioners who congratulated her and her intended, Arthur had her promise Father Morrison that he would officiate at her marriage ceremony. Now she had made a commitment to a man of God. Her entanglement was becoming more and more complete.

Later in the day, Belle was finally able to extricate herself from her father's watchful eye. An unexpected matter of business that required Arthur's attention arose and he was compelled to travel to his office. Belle took the opportunity to make her way to the one place she was certain Ebenezer would be this day after the events of the night before. She took a carriage to Fan and Fred's home. But she did not go alone.

Belle was quite correct that Ebenezer was, in fact, with his sister. Fan had yet another restless night and nausea-filled morning. Ebenezer sat by her bedside and recounted the miserable events of the evening previous. He felt angry, betrayed and heartbroken. Fan shook her head and smiled ruefully.

"Ebenezer," she said. "You see nothing. You are so intelligent in so many facets, but I swear it that in love, you have not matured past your thirteenth year."

"What is that to mean?" Ebenezer asked, surprised at his sister's words.

"Do you not recognize what has happened?" Fan asked.

"I believe I do," Ebenezer said resolutely.

"No, you clearly do not," Fan responded. "Belle did not agree to any engagement. Her father organized the ruse to force her hand. He presses his will upon her."

"Are you certain that you are correct?" Ebenezer asked skeptically.

"Of course," Fan replied. "You are always so quick to assume the worst of people, Ebenezer. Your pessimism has only grown as you have aged. You must trust if you are to have love in your life."

"Fan, I must protest your description of me. I am surely no pessimist. I am, however, a proud realist," Ebenezer said. "I see the world as it truly is, beneath the shroud that it attempts to fool the naïve into believing it is."

"No, my brother," Fan said kindly. "You see a shroud where none exists. You conjure the evil that you are convinced hides within. And you fear the fantasy of your own creation."

"I love you, Fan," Ebenezer said. "And I do not wish to argue. But it is you who cannot see that which is plainly before you."

At that moment, there was a knock at the front door. The Scrooge siblings decided to put a halt to their conversation and Ebenezer walked down the stairs to greet Fan's visitor.

Ebenezer opened the door and there, standing before him, was Belle.

"Ah, Mrs. Weatherby, I presume," Ebenezer said sarcastically.

"Ebenezer, we must talk," Belle said, ignoring Ebenezer's inappropriate comment, as she pushed her way past him into the house.

"What is there to say?" Ebenezer asked, following her in, his pain commandeering his lips. "Is there a particular gift that you wish I bring to your wedding?"

"Ebenezer!" Belle bellowed. "Enough of your childish ways! I am here with a serious dilemma and one for which we must determine a solution! You must know that I have not consented to this engagement!"

"I did not hear you contest it!" Ebenezer retorted.

"What would you have me do? Contradict my father in a room filled with people after he had just made his statement? Why, that would be tantamount to publicly declaring him to be a liar!" Belle exclaimed.

"Is he not a liar?!" Ebenezer demanded. "Or did he speak the truth?"

"Ebenezer, I am not about to declare my father a liar before a crowd of his closest associates and friends," Belle said. "That would be most inappropriate, and you know this to be true!"

"I note that you did not answer my query," Ebenezer retorted.

Belle shook her head back and forth as anger flashed across her face.

"What has happened to you, Ebenezer? You are not the young man with whom I fell in love," Belle stated, piercing Ebenezer's heart with her words.

"Perhaps I am not," Ebenezer responded. "Perhaps I am wiser, more worldly and less willing to be made the fool! Why have you come here?"

"I came here so that we may discuss a solution to this problem my father has created," Belle said. "But perhaps you do not seek such solution."

"The solution seems simple, if what you claim is the truth," Ebenezer said. "Reveal to the world that you are not betrothed to that Weatherby dolt and expose your father as the fraud that he is!"

"It is not as simple as you wish it to be," Belle stated, trying to ignore the nagging pain in her pit as she was forced to listen as her father was, yet again, disrespected. "But I agree that his mendacity must be disclosed in another manner."

"What manner would that be?" Ebenezer asked.

"We must marry. Immediately. Today," Belle said. "It is the only way to prevent me from walking to the altar with Nathaniel Weatherby."

"Belle, you know this to be impossible," Ebenezer stated, frustrated with Belle's incomprehension. "I have told you time and again that I must accumulate enough wealth before our wedding day may come. Only by doing so can we avoid scurrying around in the shadows like diseased rats. I will not allow you to live in such a manner!"

"I do not believe that you speak the truth to me, Ebenezer! It pains me to admit this, but now I know it is true. You do not intend to marry me. Another idol has replaced me in your heart," Belle said, tears in her eyes.

"What idol do you speak of?" Ebenezer said, highly insulted.

"A golden one," Belle said. "I know now as I look in your eyes that you shall never believe yourself to have enough. You say that you seek riches for me, but you refuse to hear my words when I tell you I need no riches. You say that you have a grand plan to legitimize our standing in this community, but there is no grand plan. You are different. You have changed. Your refusal to commit your life to me on this day tells all."

"The rubbish you speak!" Ebenezer cried. "Of course I have changed. I am a grown man. While you remain a child. Content to accede to the wishes of your father or to compel an impossible situation. You present me with a foolish girl's ultimatum. Hastily marry you and destroy both your reputation and your stability or watch as you give yourself to another. Well, I say no! You will not place me between Scylla and Charybdis!"

Belle stopped. She took a step backwards, keeping her sad eyes trained on Ebenezer's fiery ones. She let out a mournful sigh.

"Very well. As you would have it," she said softly. "I release you."

Ebenezer was taken aback. It was as though Belle had smacked him directly across the face.

"Have I ever sought your release?" Ebenezer asked angrily.

"Not with your words," Belle said in the same sad tone as before.

"With what then?" Ebenezer demanded.

"Ebenezer, I understand. Our promise is an old one. Made when we were but children. When you were poor and content to be so," Belle said quietly. "I see all now. Tell me true. Would you seek me out if we had met only yesterday?"

"You think I would not?" Ebenezer asked, highly offended.

"Ah, now it is you who does not answer the query," Belle noted.

Ebenezer was shaking in rage, pain, and confusion. How could she question his love and devotion after all he had done for her? And now she wishes their relationship should terminate? Simply because he wishes to maintain her honor, respect and place in society? How dare she!

Belle reached into the pocket of her dress. She produced the small gold ring that Ebenezer had given her so long ago. It signified their promise to always be together. She believed it no longer belonged in her possession.

"Here, Ebenezer," Belle said, holding out the ring as she attempted mightily to keep her tears at bay. "Take this. Keep it. When you gaze upon it, I hope you remember me fondly."

Ebenezer made no move.

Belle reached forward and took his hand within hers. She turned it so that his palm faced upward. And she pressed the ring into the center of his hand. She then closed his fingers around it.

"Goodbye Ebenezer. May you be happy in the life you have chosen," Belle said, her voice cracking.

Ebenezer was still frozen.

Belle exited Fan's home, closing the door behind her and she ran to the carriage awaiting her return.

Ebenezer remained still as a statue. He looked down at his hand and unfurled his fingers. He stared at the Promise Ring that no longer carried with it any significance.

He began to regret his hostility. Perhaps Belle truly could not resist her father. Perhaps she truly had no interest in marriage to another man. He decided that he must stop her. He could not allow her to walk out of his life. If an immediate marriage was the only means by which to keep her firmly affixed to his side, so be it. He must tell her right away before she escaped forever.

Ebenezer ran to the front door and thrust it open. He opened his mouth to speak when he witnessed a sight that rendered him mute. His eyes widened in shock.

There before him, Belle was in the arms of another man! Her face was buried in his waistcoat and so she did not see Ebenezer standing there in the doorway. The man had his back facing Ebenezer so he could not be certain of his identity. But Ebenezer knew who he surely was.

It was Nathaniel Weatherby!

Ebenezer's eyes narrowed and his heart grew cold. He looked down at the ring in his hand and he pressed it deep within his pocket. Fine! If this is how she wishes it to be, then this is how it shall be! Ebenezer stomped back into the house without even closing the front door. He walked down the hall to regain his composure before heading upstairs to recount this dastardly tale to Fan.

From out the window, had he been watching, Ebenezer would have seen Belle walk to and climb aboard the carriage. The gentleman who had accompanied her followed behind with a pronounced limp. The driver assisted him as he climbed aboard as well. The driver then directed the horses to make their way back to the Benson home, removing Belle from Ebenezer's presence and his life.

36

As the year marched onward towards its end, Ebenezer spent more and more time by Fan's bedside. Her physical condition continued to deteriorate as her pregnancy progressed. She had been receiving regular visits from her doctor who suggested that she remain in bed for as many hours in the day as possible so as not to tax her limited strength. Ebenezer was eagerly anticipating the day when she would finally give birth and this extended assault on her body would come to an end. Ebenezer had never heard of a woman having such a difficult time with pregnancy.

Through it all, Fan maintained high spirits. Her only concern was for the baby. Whenever her physician would examine her, she would always ask if the child's health was well. Of course, there was no way for the doctor to know with certainty, but, despite the troubles Fan was experiencing, he seemed to believe that the infant within was progressing normally. This always made Fan smile and relax. Ebenezer began to suspect that the doctor was simply revealing to Fan what he knew she wished to hear.

Aside from his concern for his sister, Ebenezer was fully consumed with his work. He buried his despondency over the loss of Belle deep within and shut his ears to the rumors he continued to hear swirling about her imminent marriage. His finances continued to thrive as his sister's health continued to wilt. Between maintaining his bottom line and maintaining his presence by Fan's side, he had time for nothing else. This is how he preferred it.

Fred had not become any more the interested husband or soon-to-be father than he had been when Fan first announced the coming of the child. Ebenezer's anger towards Fred had hit its zenith. He had absolutely no use for the man whatsoever. Certain that he was spending his time and the family money on the drink and unchaste women, Ebenezer privately resolved that once the baby had arrived that he would remove Fan from Fred's home and install her and baby within his own. While divorce was a sin, Ebenezer reasoned that God surely made exceptions in extreme circumstances such as these. Ebenezer could not accept that the Holy One would prefer his sister and her offspring suffer when a loving alternative was available. And if Fred should object, well, Ebenezer brooded, so be it. Ebenezer's days of being intimidated by that carousing sot had come to an end. In Ebenezer's present state of emotion, it would have been perilous indeed for Fred to cross him. Ebenezer had already stood with two dead men at his feet. What difference made it, Ebenezer considered, if there was a third?

Fan made Ebenezer promise her that he would come for a visit on Christmas Day. Fan insisted that she see her brother on his and the Lord's birthday. Ebenezer had no use for either this year as it simply reminded him of his times at the Fezziwig festivities and, of course, it reminded him of Belle. He had planned to work the entire day and to drown out the noise of the season with the scratch of his quill. But, as always, and especially because of her condition, Ebenezer relented and assured Fan that he would be there. As his only stipulation, he urged Fan to promise in return that she would call for her doctor to examine her. It had been more than a fortnight since she had last been evaluated and Ebenezer desired assurances that her health was stable. He also wished to privately discuss Fan's health with the doctor away from her bedside with the expectation that the man of medicine would be more truthful when her ears could not hear his words. Fan agreed to Ebenezer's condition.

When the twenty-fifth of December arrived, Ebenezer fulfilled his promise to both Fan and to himself. He spent the morning hard at work, examining several other potential business opportunities that had recently become available to him. When he heard the clock strike noon, he reluctantly put his work aside and hailed a cab to take him to Fan's home.

Along the way, he saw quite the spectacle. Shopfronts and houses were decorated for the season. Small assemblies of vocalists were on many a street corner, singing carols for the yuletide. Delivery men were bustling to and fro dispatching orders placed for Christmas goose and other meats to be consumed that evening on many a table. The mood of the city was light. The theme was goodwill toward man. Ebenezer could not help wondering where this generous spirit was to be found the other three hundred sixty four days of the year.

Ebenezer arrived at Fan's home and allowed himself in. He was under no illusion that Fred would be present to answer the door if he knocked, nor would he subject his sister to the rigors of removing herself from her bed to permit him entry. Fan had bestowed upon Ebenezer a key months ago so that he may avoid all of this trouble if he found the door locked. On this day, it was not.

"Fan, I am here!" Ebenezer called as he walked through the threshold.

He could hear screaming coming from the direction of his sister's bedroom. Was there an intruder in the home? Was someone harming his Fan? Or was Fred "correcting" her by the violent means Ebenezer was convinced he employed?

"Fan! I am coming!" Ebenezer cried, as he ran up the stairs.

When he arrived at her room, he was met by the sight of Fan in her bed with a man standing between her open legs that were spread wide and bent at the knees. His first thought was that his sister was in the process of being violated. He reached forward, prepared to kill the man assaulting her with his bare hands if necessary. It was then he realized what he perceived was simply the product of his worst imaginings projected upon the scene before him. Instead, the truth was that the man standing before her was Dr. Briggs and Fan was in the process of giving birth.

"What is going on here?!" Ebenezer cried.

The doctor turned and recognized Ebenezer.

"I have called for the midwife to assist me. Please remain in the hallway and send her in when she arrives," Dr. Briggs said. His hands and apron were covered in Fan's blood. She continued to scream, clearly in a great deal of pain.

"Is Fan alright?" Ebenezer asked, his eyes wide in fear.

"She will be fine. But you cannot be here. Allow me to do my work," the doctor ordered.

"But why is this happening? The baby is not due to be born for another month hence?" Ebenezer asked, unable to remove himself from the spot. His sister was suffering. How could he leave her in such a state?

"We can discuss the intricacies of childbirth and gestation periods later!" Dr. Briggs said impatiently. "Please be gone! And send to me the midwife when she arrives."

Ebenezer slowly exited the room. Fan's cries continued. Ebenezer could not remove from his mind's eye the image of her blood covering the doctor. He had knowledge that women must bleed during childbirth, but this seemed excessive. Had she spilled this much blood due to an accident or injury, Ebenezer could not imagine a physician would inform him to worry not.

Shortly thereafter, the midwife arrived. Ebenezer directed her to Fan's room, not that its location was any great secret. Fan's cries and moans had not subsided. Ebenezer was convinced that something was terribly wrong. However, once again, he felt powerless to alleviate his sister's suffering. He was forced to do that which he found most uncomfortable in this world. He was forced to trust another. To make matters more difficult, he had to trust another with the health and well-being of the one person most important to him in his life. It was a most disagreeable situation.

As Ebenezer paced the hallway, his anger grew that Fred was not here. As usual, when his sister needed him to be the husband he promised to be, he was once again absent. Ebenezer could only thank the heavens above that he had insisted that the doctor visit. Had he not done so, Fan would have been left in this state alone with no help to be found until Ebenezer himself arrived.

While the doctor was attending to Fan, Ebenezer exited the house and walked himself to the home of Fan's neighbor, Charles Chesterfield. Ebenezer introduced himself as the two men had never actually spoken despite having seen one another from time to time during Ebenezer's visits. Mr. Chesterfield's wife, Claire, had been kind enough to look in on Fan on occasion and had brought with her various treats that she thought Fan would enjoy.

Ebenezer told Mr. Chesterfield what was occurring in the house next door and he asked if Mr. Chesterfield would be good enough on this Christmas Day to retrieve Fred. Ebenezer was certain Fred was at one of the local pubs. It was a sad state of affairs that such establishments would be operating on this day, Mr. Chesterfield observed. Ebenezer was inclined to agree. Mr. Chesterfield agreed to the task and he left on his errand, explaining to his wife where he was going. She insisted on accompanying Ebenezer back to Fan's home to stay with him during the ordeal. The Chesterfields' children were all grown and so there was no one remaining behind that she needed to care for.

Despite preferring to return to his sister's house alone, Ebenezer thanked Mrs. Chesterfield for her gracious offer and together they headed back into Fan's home.

When they arrived and passed through the door, Ebenezer's fear grew sevenfold. Fan was still crying out in distress. The midwife that had arrived before Ebenezer visited the Chesterfields' was now standing where Dr. Briggs had been previous. Hearing Ebenezer return to the hallway, Dr. Briggs left Fan's room to speak with him.

"I do not want you to worry," Dr. Briggs began, "but Fan has lost a great deal of blood. She is also, as I am sure you are aware, in a great deal of discomfort. Furthermore…"

"Furthermore what, doctor?" Ebenezer demanded.

"The baby is in breech," the doctor stated.

"I am not familiar with this term," Ebenezer said.

"It means that the baby is coming out the wrong way. It should be his head I see first," the doctor explained. "Instead, this child leads with his buttocks."

"Is this a problem?" Ebenezer asked.

"It very well could be," Dr. Briggs stated. "The greatest danger is that his umbilical cord could wrap itself around the child's neck, strangling the baby before he is even fully born."

"What is to be done?" Ebenezer asked frantically.

"Right now, Miss Hines, the midwife, is attempting to turn the child while he is still within his mother," the doctor said. "We are hoping this will be successful and the child will survive."

"And what of Fan?" Ebenezer asked, terrified.

"She is in a great deal of pain. And I cannot lie and tell you that what Miss Hines is attempting does not cause her more. But we are doing all we can to safeguard the lives and safety of both mother and child," Dr. Briggs replied.

Ebenezer was about to ask why the doctor chose to mention the need to safeguard Fan's life, but decided he did not wish to hear more. He just wanted this process to be over and for both Fan and baby to be well.

"Now, I must go back in the room," Dr. Briggs said. "Please stay out here and try to remain calm."

With that, Dr. Briggs re-entered Fan's bedroom as her wails continued to emanate from therein.

"Calm?" Ebenezer exclaimed. "How does he expect me to remain calm?"

Mrs. Chesterfield took Ebenezer's hand and looked him in the eye.

"Mr. Scrooge, please come with me. I will make you a cup of tea and we will get through this together," she said with a kind smile.

"I do not know if I should leave Fan alone," Ebenezer said.

"She is not alone. She is in good hands," Mrs. Chesterfield said. "Please, come with me. I assure you, all will be well. I had six children of my own. Each of my children have had children. It is not an easy process, but with God's help, it all turns out well."

Ebenezer allowed himself to be led downstairs to the kitchen where Mrs. Chesterfield made them each a cup of tea. She spoke with him, trying to salve his nerves and to remove his mind from the situation occurring in the bedroom above their heads.

Ebenezer and Mrs. Chesterfield had been sitting together for almost an hour when Dr. Briggs appeared before them. His apron was now covered with blood. Ebenezer would not have been surprised if Dr. Briggs informed him that he had just returned from a slaughterhouse.

"Please come," Dr. Briggs said solemnly. "The child is here. But…"

Ebenezer did not hear the "but". He rushed up the stairs and found the door to be closed. He heard the cry of an infant from behind the entranceway. He entered and saw what he would later realize was an unusual sight. The baby was in the arms of the midwife. He was quite small, which did not surprise Ebenezer due to the fact that the child arrived so much earlier than expected.

He then turned his attention to Fan's bed. It was then that it registered that he had not heard Fan's voice for quite some time. He was confused because, at first, he did not see Fan. Surely she had not stood and walked away. And then he realized that he was looking directly at her.

It is simply that the bedsheet was pulled up, covering her entire body, including her face.

"I'm terribly sorry, Mr. Scrooge," Miss Hines said woefully.

Nothing was making any sense. Why was Fan beneath her bedsheet? Why was her baby not within her arms? What was going on?

"Pardon?" Ebenezer asked, in a daze.

It was then Dr. Briggs entered the room. He was followed by Mrs. Chesterfield. Her hand was over her mouth, concealing her trembling, grief-stricken lips beneath.

"There was nothing more we could do for her," Dr. Briggs said softly. Mrs. Chesterfield wept quietly.

No!, Ebenezer thought. This could not be!

But it was.

Fan was dead.

It took a moment, but the reality crashed into Ebenezer like a ship thrown upon the rocks during the most violent of storms. He found that he could not breathe. He fell to his knees. All of his strength left him. His sobs began to pour out of him in buckets. He wailed loudly, awash in sorrow.

Ebenezer was in ultimate agony.

The three others in the room decided to leave him to have his final moments with his sister alone. They stepped outside of the room respectfully, bringing the baby with them.

Ebenezer ran to his sister's side and pulled down the bedsheet. She seemed peaceful; she could have been asleep. But her beautiful eyes would open no more. Ebenezer embraced her and rocked her back and forth as she had done for him so many times in the past. His tears surged from his eyes as his entire body shook uncontrollably. He could not accept that his Fan was gone.

As Ebenezer mourned privately within the room, the others conversed in the hallway.

"The child is gorgeous," Mrs. Chesterfield observed. "Boy or girl?"

"He is a boy," Miss Hines replied.

"Does he have a name?" Mrs. Chesterfield asked.

"He does. It is Frederick," said Miss Hines.

"Did mother and child have any time together?" Mrs. Chesterfield asked.

"They did, thank the good Lord," Miss Hines replied. "I placed the child upon Mrs. Radcliffe's chest and they stared at each other. She spoke to him, too quietly for me to hear. I then leaned in and asked her what she wished to name the boy. She responded, but in too faint a whisper at first. I asked again, and she said 'Frederick'. She named him for the father."

At that, Ebenezer emerged from the room, shuffling slowly forward. He was in a stupor.

Thinking that it may assist his spirits, Miss Hines asked if he would like to meet his new nephew. She told him that the child's name was Frederick.

Ebenezer looked her way and then down at the baby in her arms.

"Frederick?" Ebenezer asked. His countenance then grew dark.

"Yes, sir," Miss Hines confirmed. "Would you like to hold him?"

Ebenezer did not respond.

He simply walked past Miss Hines, shrugging off the attempts by Dr. Briggs and Mrs. Chesterfield to console him. He walked down the stairs, across the room, and out the front door. It was now early evening. As he looked to the heavens, allowing the light snow to fall upon his face, he contemplated that he was now truly and utterly alone in the world.

A teenaged boy walked past him and tipped his cap as he went by.

"A Merry Christmas to you, sir!" the boy said cheerfully.

Ebenezer glared at the boy.

Through gritted teeth beneath narrow eyes, Ebenezer softly growled one word that only he could hear.

"Humbug!"

37

The bells pealed twelve times outside of his window. Ebenezer sat at his desk staring at the same page that he had been mindlessly gazing at for over two hours, yet it was not penetrating his eyes any more now than it had when he first looked upon it. After the sound of the last chime died away, Ebenezer peered up. The date was now the first of January, eighteen hundred. The new century had officially begun. And Ebenezer entered it alone.

He sat in the quiet, pondering the events of the last several days and months.

Fezziwig was gone, long since dead. His last sight had been that of the walls within the debtor's prison to which Ebenezer's own actions had resigned him.

Belle was gone. Married to Nathaniel Weatherby on the seventh of December. Moved across the sea to the Americas one week later, accompanying her husband who had been assigned by his father to oversee the construction of the new Weatherby shipyard in Boston, Massachusetts.

Fan was gone. Lay into her eternal resting place three days prior. Her child, young Frederick, was entrusted to the care of his Great Aunt Nancy and Great Uncle Laurence, just as his mother had been. Fred, the father, did not attend the funeral. And as of this moment, his whereabouts were entirely unknown.

Disturbingly, it was later learned that shortly following his marriage to Fan, Fred had visited the Society for Equitable Assurances on Lives and Survivorship, the esteemed institution founded by Edward Rowe Mores over thirty years prior. He purchased what was known as a term life insurance policy on the life of his new bride that promised a considerable distribution should she pass away within ten years of the policy's purchase.

Generally used as a protection for widows and children to provide for them in the event of the death of the breadwinner of the family, Fred clearly saw the opportunity to use this financial tool in a different way. One wonders what the bald man with the club foot, the Actuary, William Morgan, thought when Fred presented his request for such a policy. Whatever that may have been, the policy was written, the premiums paid, and the proceeds distributed.

It would never be made clear what Fred's intent was in purchasing such a policy of limited duration on the life of his young bride. The implications were disconcerting.

Ebenezer resolved that he would no longer be consigned to the fringes of society. Through diligence and relentless, single-minded drive, within five years, Ebenezer amassed enough of a fortune to repay all of the swindled investors of the Ferguson scheme. He settled all accounts, including, eventually, that of Arthur Benson. Ebenezer had the most difficulty compelling himself to satisfy his debt to Mr. Benson as his pain regarding the loss of his Belle was one he still struggled to suppress.

Ebenezer paid him last, but unlike the others, he did so in person.

"Ebenezer Scrooge," Arthur sneered upon his entrance into his own sitting room where Ebenezer awaited him after being granted admittance to the Benson home. It was the thirteenth of April, eighteen hundred and five.

Ebenezer turned from the window to face Arthur. This was the very window through which Ebenezer had first seen Belle engaged in lively conversation with Nathaniel Weatherby the first time Ebenezer came to execute this day's errand. Ebenezer was quite aware of it.

"How dare you bring yourself within my home," Arthur spat. "Although I am glad to see that you have finally rid yourself of that ridiculous pony tail." In fact, Ebenezer had sliced off his long locks on the very day Belle exited from his life.

"I have something that belongs to you," Ebenezer said, his voice as dead as a doornail. He then reached out and presented Arthur with the recompense he had intended to make so many years ago.

Arthur took the money and counted it. He then looked up at Ebenezer. He contemplated his next words carefully. Before he could speak, Ebenezer did so.

"My debt to you is now paid," Ebenezer said. "I owe you nothing and you no longer have reason to disparage me. Know that I am in London. My office shall soon open."

"I see," Arthur said.

"You have never believed that I would ever amount to anything more than a poor, worthless vagabond," said Ebenezer. "You were wrong to discount me. I came today with two purposes. First, as I have already accomplished, to place you in status quo ante. Second, I have come to inform you of your future. The day will come when I will bury you! You made an enemy of the wrong man. You will rue the day you chose to tangle with Ebenezer Scrooge."

"Leave my home, you insolent twit!" Arthur said, scoffing at the threat.

"Gladly. The odor offends," Ebenezer said as he walked to the front door. Before he exited, he turned and spoke one more time.

"Remember what I say," Ebenezer warned. "Enjoy what you have at present. It will not last forever."

Before Arthur could speak another word, Ebenezer left the house and was on his way.

Ebenezer arrived home to find his Aunt Nancy at his door, toting five-year-old Fred, Jr. with her. Ebenezer was exasperated. He regretted allowing her to learn his address. As he walked up to her, he threw up his hands.

"Aunt Nancy, what are you doing here?" Ebenezer asked.

"I brought your nephew to see you," she replied calmly.

Ebenezer took his aunt by the arm and directed her away from the child. He spoke so that the boy could not hear his words.

"How many times must we go through this?" Ebenezer asked her. "No matter how much I protest, you persist on forcing this child upon me. I am a busy man and I do not have time for such things!"

"You do not have time for your family?" Aunt Nancy questioned. "No man should ever consider himself so busy."

In truth, Ebenezer felt nothing but pain each time he looked at the boy. He carried his father's name, which infuriated Ebenezer, and his mother's face, which devastated him. It had been over five years since she had passed, but for Ebenezer the ache within his very being had not subsided. Each day he awoke to discover that he had forgotten another piece of his sister. This was yet another reminder of the cruelty of life. As he stood there, he could not quite recall the exact tone of her voice or touch of her hand or scent of her hair. What he could remember was that she was his one and only rock keeping him safe and sheltered from a malevolent world. And that she had been stolen from his life, never to return. Rational or not, this child standing before him, currently with his finger planted firmly up his left nostril Ebenezer noted with impatience, was the living embodiment of the day he lost her and every day thereafter that she was, and would be, absent from his life.

Nancy had no time for his self-pity. She had endeavored for five years to break this wall of grief that Ebenezer had erected around his heart so that his nephew would be permitted entry. She continued to remind him that little Fred was all we had left of Fan. She told him that to reject Fred was to turn his back on his sister. She charged that by abandoning Fred, he was no better than the boy's father.

Ebenezer had grown weary of these arguments and of his aunt's unannounced visits with the boy. Right or wrong, pain often speaks louder than reason.

Ebenezer felt that he had done right by the boy. He had established a trust for the boy's benefit, one that he fed with additional funds each month and which he managed with care. By the time Fred was a man, he should have quite the start in life. Ebenezer noted that most do not have such advantage.

"Are you not going to invite us in?" Aunt Nancy asked with an angry undertone.

"Very well," Ebenezer relented. "For a short while. But I truly have more work to do than hours in which to get it done. Therefore, this visit must be a limited one."

As always, Nancy attempted to have Ebenezer engage with the boy and Ebenezer attempted to dodge all such interaction. Despite his uncle's obvious disdain for him, little Fred clearly had a special interest in Ebenezer. He always smiled at the older man, he followed wherever Ebenezer tried to hide and he was eager to hug Ebenezer's legs whenever he was quicker attempting to grab his uncle than Ebenezer was in preventing such contact.

It was not that Ebenezer disliked the boy. It is just that it was far too painful to allow himself to feel anything for him. This was something Aunt Nancy refused to understand.

Ebenezer reveled in his life lived out in the open without the burden of the Ferguson scheme hanging over his head any longer. He opened his office, at which he found it much easier to conduct his business and manage his diverse holdings. He became an employer and found pleasure in exerting his will over others. After having been under the control of Ferguson, been intimidated by Fred, and been forced into the shadows by the swindled investors, it was refreshing for Ebenezer to be free to conduct his affairs as he saw fit.

As time progressed, and his success grew, his power and standing within the community grew with it. What did not improve was his reputation. Due to the means by which he conducted his business, and due to his past associations, he was known as one who was ruthless and one could not be trusted. He was slandered as a miser and a recluse. But these murmurings were always done in the dark. No one would dare say such things to his face. In fact, Ebenezer was quite oblivious of the reputation that he had gained. To his mind, the fear he instilled was read by him as respect. The lack of social interaction others sought with him was understood as intimidation. He believed himself quite well liked and, after a lifetime of having been shunned by others, he took great pride in this assessment. It encouraged him to continue down the path he had charted for himself. Business first, business last, business always!

Ebenezer maintained his tenacious pursuit of wealth throughout his twenties and into his thirties. The only sensation resembling joy that he could experience was parting his quarry with their money and having it placed within his own pocket. The only conversation worth having was one that advanced his financial interests. Friends were the only luxury he felt he could not afford. Every moment he let opportunity escape was a moment another was ensnaring it. That was his fervent belief. Let others attend the theater. He would own the theater and charge them for their pleasures. Let others relent on the Sabbath day. He would take what they left behind. Let others take a holiday. He would commandeer their customers and clients so that they had none when they returned.

Ebenezer was an extraordinarily difficult man for whom to work. He expected his employees to work as hard as he did and to share his philosophy about enterprise. Few could keep up with his zeal and fewer had the interest. He did not compensate any greater than any other employer in the city, but his voracious demands vastly surpassed that of even his nearest competitor.

It was not until eighteen hundred and twelve, when Ebenezer was introduced to a gentleman five years his junior, that he was first presented with a man who could perhaps eclipse him in business acumen, stamina and ruthlessness. The younger man walked with vigor across the meeting room floor at the Executive's Club, the sole social organization of which Ebenezer was a member, purposefully seeking out the thirty-three year old entrepreneur sitting by the fire and reading the *London Times*. He approached and cleared his throat so that Ebenezer would take notice of him.

Ebenezer lowered his newspaper.

"May I help you?" Ebenezer asked.

"Are you Ebenezer Scrooge?" the younger man asked.

"I am," Ebenezer replied.

"I just wanted to look you in the eye, sir," the man said. "And for you to look in mine."

"And so we have done. May I get back to my reading?" Ebenezer asked dismissively.

"You may. But as you do, know this," the man said. "You have just stared into the face of the man who is going to drive you into poverty. Good day, sir."

The younger man then turned on his heel and exited via the same path by which he had entered. There was a jaunt in his step as though he had just won a great victory. Ebenezer watched him with a furrowed brow as he left, listening to the sound of his footsteps clacking confidently down the vast hallway he was traversing as though he owned not only the entire building, but the entire city block upon which this structure was situated. When he reached the great atrium that led to the front entrance, he pivoted to his right and exited from view.

Ebenezer Scrooge had just met Jacob Marley.

38

𝕵acob Marley was born on the seventeenth of February, seventeen hundred and eighty-four. His childhood was one of privilege. His father, Aaron Marley, taught him from as early an age as possible that sleep is for the weak, "cannot" is a word for the feeble-minded, and enough is never enough. He also taught him that success is earned by he who knows more than the next man and he who can ingratiate himself with the most powerful and influential among the crowd. Confidence is a virtue, while arrogance is anathema. The man destined for greatness knows the difference. And the most important lesson of all: Failure is not an option.

This is not to say that Jacob was told not to take chances in an effort to accomplish more, and in more innovative ways, than the competitor. Jacob was permitted, and in fact even encouraged, to experience small defeats that he could use as tools to lead him to ultimate success. He was not granted the right, however, to allow a defeat to stop him or be counted as his final effort.

As part of his education, his father had him read at least three periodicals per day to instill the ability to contribute to any conversation in any crowd in which he should find himself. His mantra was that the response was always "no" if one dares not query. And that the only question that proves one a fool is the one not asked. Assumption was more deadly than consumption.

Jacob was also molded by his mother. Edna Marley was a severe woman who never smiled. Growing up, Jacob was to know his lessons, his languages, and his Bible. He mastered all with ease.

Jacob learned well. If he had a flaw, it was the fact that he learned too easily and was frustrated that others were not as intelligent as he. He could not understand nor accept when people could not see the rightness of his position immediately, despite the fact that most usually came to view him as correct. It seemed to him a waste of time to cater to lesser minds, but to his credit, these thoughts were always kept masked.

Jacob grew to be his father's most valuable apprentice. He quickly surpassed the elder Marley in the esteem of their customers, clients and colleagues. By the time he was in his early twenties, he was the de facto chief of Marley & Sons. He had three older brothers, but none took to the business as did Jacob. He was poised for ultimate success and believed he deserved nothing less.

Without question, he had a sharp mind and a keen sense of business. He had no romantic interests and his only social interactions were to increase his fortune. He worked harder and longer than any other man. There was no time for congratulations in Jacob's opinion and nothing was a victory. It was all the next step to the financial greatness he would never stop chasing.

Jacob worked every day of the week to stay ahead of those he perceived to be his financial enemies. Some openly denounced his working on the Lord's Day, but privately they entrusted their future to his nimble mind. The name "Marley" came to be known throughout London as synonymous with tenacity and hard work. And most importantly, success.

He was extraordinarily personable, despite only socializing for business purposes. He was well liked and knowledgeable about all of the news of the day. His father's insistence that he be aware of all topics of interest to his target audience was well learned. He was also an eloquent speaker. He had the innate ability to transfix any gathering with his topic of choice. This had a great deal to do with his inherent knowledge of the perfect subject matter for any given congregation.

When his father passed away suddenly in eighteen hundred and twelve, Jacob was twenty-eight years old and ready to take on the most formidable competitor in the market: Ebenezer Scrooge.

As of the date of his father's death, Jacob was of slender build, not as thin as Ebenezer, but two inches taller. He had thick black hair and dark brown eyes. Very alert eyes. His ears were always open, listening for opportunity.

One such opening involved Arthur Benson. For the better part of the two years after Jacob introduced himself in such audacious manner, Ebenezer was engaged in a one-man war against Arthur Benson with the financial ruin of Benson deemed the only acceptable ultimate victory. Ebenezer had become a direct competitor of Arthur Benson's and was gobbling up market share with relative ease and startling speed. He was fully intent on fulfilling his promise to punish Benson for both his treatment of Ebenezer and his role in removing Belle from Ebenezer's life.

Jacob Marley saw his opportunity to engage Ebenezer indirectly in a proxy war with Arthur Benson's livelihood as the battlefield. While Jacob had been making inroads in breaking Ebenezer's seeming invincibility in the business community, he needed a notable victory to truly make his mark. Arthur Benson's situation was the perfect chance to do so.

Jacob paid a visit to Arthur's office one snowy day on the twenty-first of November, eighteen hundred and fourteen.

"Mr. Benson," Jacob said as he shook Arthur's hand. "A great honor to meet you, sir. I am Jacob Marley of Marley & Sons."

"To what do I owe the pleasure, Mr. Marley?" Arthur asked, recognizing the young man before him.

"I will get directly to the point, as I know you are a busy and important man," Jacob said as both men sat. "I understand that your business has been suffering some significant setbacks of recent. Mine is in need of diversification and I have a store of capital that I am determined to put to good use before the week is done. I have always been interested in engaging in the textile industry, but I would prefer not to begin from the foundation. As a result, I believe you and I have a great deal to discuss. Would you agree?"

"I would. Proceed," Arthur said, intrigued.

"I would like to purchase a one-half interest in your company. We will be partners, with all profits shared equally," Jacob said. "You, of course, would remain as the primary operator of the company, as you have the knowledge and experience."

This offer seemed too favorable to Arthur. He was immediately suspicious.

"And why do I deserve such generosity from you?" asked Arthur.

"Ah, I can see I am speaking with a shrewd man indeed," Jacob smiled. "From my perspective, it is you who would be the generous party. For funds that I would otherwise spend in any event, I ensure myself a guaranteed success and a quick return."

"Please, sir," Arthur said. "I can see that you are young only in age. You have done your proper due diligence. You know that if things do not improve in the very near future, the Benson doors may close, imploding upon its own weight. At that point, you could potentially take by force the whole that which you now offer to share by half. So I ask again, why do I deserve such generosity from you?"

Jacob was impressed. He had gotten so very bored manipulating the destinies of the ignorant and the weak. Despite having inherited his business from his father, he was of the firm belief that a man should build what he owns with his own two hands. The class of the entitled heir to their father's fortunes weakened the business community and the country as a whole in Jacob's considered opinion. Arthur Benson was clearly not cut from this cloth.

"Very well, Mr. Benson," Jacob said. "You win this round. I shall reveal the truth. You and I share a common foe. At the moment, he bests us both. What you have, you are losing. What I have, I am not gaining quickly enough."

"Who is this foe?" Arthur asked.

"Now you bait me to provide that of which you already know," Jacob said. "But since you have been so good as to indulge me on this fine Monday morning, I will reciprocate and answer your query. Our common enemy is Ebenezer Scrooge."

"Yes, you have done your due diligence," Arthur said, impressed with this young man before him. In many ways, he was reminded of himself at that age. Or perhaps he only saw he whom he wished he had been at that age.

"Do we have an accord?" Jacob asked, extending his hand.

"We do," Arthur said, accepting Jacob's hand and providing him a hearty handshake.

"Excellent," Jacob said. "In that case, there is no time to waste. We shall begin our new venture immediately. I shall return later this morning promptly at half past eleven. I shall bring you my share of the funds along with a contract memorializing our merger. After you execute said contract and accept my investment, we shall share a mid-day meal together where we shall map out our strategy to take Marley and Benson to the top of the textile industry."

Arthur enjoyed the brash confidence this young man exhibited, both in assuming his involvement would bring Benson's business to new heights and in mentioning his own name first in establishing the hierarchy between them.

Arthur grew to be more impressed with his new young partner as the years progressed. Within six months, Benson's business stabilized. By the first anniversary of their handshake, it turned a corner and actually began to wrest back some of the market that Ebenezer had seized from his control. By the second anniversary, it was clear that Ebenezer's grand plan of sending Benson to the poorhouse had effectively been thwarted.

Jacob Marley had scored his first major victory over his targeted rival. And he was just getting started.

39

Eighteen hundred and sixteen was a year that for Ebenezer was most vexing. He found himself rebuffed both professionally and personally. He would enter the following year with an even colder and more hardened heart.

The relatively new Marley and Benson merger was successful in preventing Arthur Benson's complete destruction. In fact, to Ebenezer's unremitting consternation, the merger saved Benson Textiles and re-established it as a viable and growing concern. Marley & Sons had been taking nibbles out of Ebenezer's business interests for several years, but this was the first time it had scored such a coup over the E. A. Scrooge Company. The entire business community took notice. Ebenezer was livid.

Ebenezer's fury was three-fold. First, he was most distressed that a fissure was exposed in his powerful conglomerate. Second, he was enraged to have been made a liar as it related to his promise to bankrupt Arthur Benson. And third, his ego was bruised by being bested by the brash neophyte who threatened his financial future in the Executive's Club four years prior. Ebenezer clearly had a new enemy. His name was Jacob Marley.

To shore up the strength of his own business, Ebenezer added moneylending to his list of services. Ebenezer was most fond of interest. And he soon developed a reputation for utilizing all resources at his disposal to ensure his repayment. If the owed monies were not forthcoming, he had no reservation about seizing any and all assets the debtor possessed, including the very homes in which they and their families resided. And if there were no such assets available, Ebenezer became notorious for filling the cells of such dreadful locales such as Coldbath Fields Prison (known commonly as the Steel), Fleet Prison, Giltspur Street

Compter, and King's Bench Prison, to name a few.

Jacob Marley was not deterred by any moves made by Ebenezer Scrooge. If anything, he was emboldened by them. After his success with Benson, he believed himself to have the momentum to take on the E. A. Scrooge Company directly. It was not long before it seemed that the entire city of London was divided into one of two camps; either one supported the Marley & Sons surge or the E. A. Scrooge Company juggernaut. Without realizing it, this intense rivalry yielded positive results for both men. They sharpened their skills, strengthened their holdings, and improved their businesses.

However, neither could see the beneficial unintended consequences of the all-out war each had waged upon the other. Not yet.

During this period, Ebenezer had to contend with another thorn in his side. This one was of the internal variety. After relentless pestering and prodding by his Aunt Nancy, Ebenezer finally relented and allowed fourteen-year-old Fred to apprentice for him. The only conditions were that Fred was to obey every command given by his uncle without question and that he was to continue to live with Nancy and Laurence. It was not long before Ebenezer realized that only one of his demands would be met. Ebenezer's home remained his own.

Fred proved to be a challenging student. He could never accept a precept without full explanation. Even then, it was always open to challenge. He could not perceive the value of withholding mercy and simply making cold calculations to drive business decisions. He relentlessly resisted his uncle's participation in the execution of arrest warrants for debtors. It seemed that Fred was deliberately incapable of reforming his liberal attitudes that themselves may keep the poor in their houses, but would surely, if they were Scrooge Company policy, send Ebenezer to the poorhouse.

Through it all, Fred clearly had a great love for his uncle. He viewed him as misguided and believed his priorities to be focused incorrectly, but beneath it all, Fred always saw a good man struggling to burst forth out from the anger and resentment under which it was so thoroughly submerged. Fred always had a smile and a cheery disposition, even when disobeying his uncle's wishes. He was adept at disagreeing without being disagreeable.

Ebenezer had a great many conversations with his Aunt Nancy about his desire to relieve himself of the burden of Fred's apprenticeship. She always reminded him that he took an oath to see this period of tutelage to its natural end. As a man of honor, Ebenezer was forced to concede the point, but he rued the day he allowed himself to make this bargain with his aunt.

As it would turn out, Ebenezer would not suffer Fred's daily company for very long. In the winter of eighteen hundred and sixteen, shortly after it became apparent that Arthur Benson was destined to die a wealthy man, Fred decided that the world of industry and commerce was not where his future lay. One week before his seventeenth birthday, he asked for a meeting with his uncle.

"Uncle Ebenezer," Fred said, sitting in a chair before his uncle's desk. "Thank you for meeting with me. I must ask you a question and I am certain that I will receive nothing but your complete honesty."

"Of course," Ebenezer said.

"Please tell me how you assess my apprenticeship," Fred requested.

"Very well," Ebenezer said without hesitation. "I find you frustrating, recalcitrant, and resistant to all things practical. I believe a sense of business is one you have never possessed, nor will you ever acquire. If I were to count the hours I have spent attempting to force some decent knowledge into your very thick skull only to be astonished by the impenetrability of same, I would find myself struggling to extract myself from severe malaise. In sum, had I not been present at your birth, I would be forced to conclude that we do not share the same bloodline."

"I understand. That makes my decision very clear and allows me to present it to you without reservation," said Fred. "This shall be my last week under your instruction."

"Fred," said Ebenezer sardonically. "If you follow but one word I say within the next seven days, that would make this your first week under my instruction."

"I am very serious, Uncle," said Fred. "Whether you accept it or not, I have endeavored to mold myself into the kind of man who could emulate your ways. I cannot. This life where material wealth is all one can aspire to achieve is a hollow one indeed. If I continue down this path, my soul shall suffer for it. I see no passion in my future should I stay. Nor love. Nor anything of any true meaning."

"You speak as a child," Ebenezer said ruefully. "I am saddened that I was unable to help bring out the man in you."

"Oh, but Uncle, you have," Fred said. "If there is one thing that you have accomplished in these last two years, it is surely that! You have brought out the man I wish to be."

"And, pray tell, what does that man do to keep a roof over his head and food in his stomach?" asked Ebenezer.

"I will teach the young," replied Fred. "I found my years of education most exhilarating. I will mold young minds. I will do my part to make this a better world."

"You resign yourself to relative poverty," Ebenezer derided.

"Yes, perhaps my pockets will not be as full as yours, dear Uncle," said Fred. "But my soul will be rich."

"In that case, I wish you well, nephew. I hope your rich soul satisfies your monthly rental obligations," said Ebenezer, continuing to mock.

Ignoring his hostility, Fred simply smiled at his uncle, just as he had always done since he was young.

"Is there more you wish to say?" Ebenezer asked.

"Yes, Uncle. I have asked before with no success. Please, I ask now. Please tell me about my mother," implored Fred.

Ebenezer shook his head in disgust.

"We have been through this time and time again," Ebenezer snarled. "I do not wish to speak of this."

"Please, Uncle," Fred persisted. "Aunt Nancy has told me throughout my life that there were never two souls so intertwined as that of you and my mother. She told me how much my mother loved you. And you her–"

"That is enough!" Ebenezer boomed. "You have resigned your position as my apprentice. And we sit in my place of business. Those two situations are incompatible. Therefore, our conversation has come to an end. I wish you good fortune and a good day."

"But, Uncle—" began Fred.

"I said good day!" Ebenezer shouted. He then stared coldly at Fred until his nephew nodded his head in capitulation, rose, and exited Ebenezer's office and his establishment.

40

The next several years witnessed an intense escalation in the rivalry between Ebenezer and Jacob. The two engaged in a see-saw battle for dominance of the London business soul. There came a point where neither man would render a decision without first determining the chess move the other would make in response. Without realizing it, they were beginning to develop a mutual respect for one another. Both secretly viewed the other as the only worthy competitor in what had grown to be one of the largest and most prosperous cities in the world. High praise indeed.

Despite having the other on his mind at all times, Ebenezer and Jacob were rarely in the same room together. Jacob joined the Executive's Club, but the two men would not share the same space. If one entered the library, the other considered the sitting room to be more pleasant. If one secured the coveted seat by the fireplace, the other would consider that location uncomfortably warm. There was always an excuse to avoid breathing the same air.

For business growth, Ebenezer was of the philosophy that his work and his reputation spoke for itself. He found it undignified to chase business when it was obvious to him that the most valuable business would find its way to him. Or, if it did not initially do so, it would suffer as his adversary. The lesson would be learned. And soon, it would join Ebenezer's ranks.

Jacob preferred to socialize and draw the crowds to his side. He was still the smaller of the two enterprises and enjoyed actively wooing away Ebenezer's client base. He considered himself akin to a great fisherman. He cast his net wide and reeled in the catch. While only five years separated them in age, Jacob came to believe he was of a different generation than Ebenezer; one that was more nimble and more aggressive. And, of course, better.

While it was true that the two men generally avoided each other's company, on one fateful day, on the fourteenth of April, eighteen hundred and twenty, they both happened upon a conversation occurring within the Executive's Club without realizing the other was present. A crowd of gentlemen was having a lively discussion about the news of the day. The subject of power was at the fore as the country was only two and a half months into the reign of the new king, George IV, who ascended to the throne when his father passed away on the twenty-ninth of January. The general consensus was that not very much should change as he had been Prince Regent for the past nine years. But there was a minority who believed that with the weight of the crown now officially resting upon his head, he may not be the same man that he was before.

On one side of this circle of bodies stood Ebenezer. On the other, was Jacob. As should come as no surprise, they each held conflicting views on the topic at issue. At some point, the concept of power as a more general principle gripped the men as the topic of interest. This then transformed into a discussion of business power. And, of course, no discussion of the powerful businessmen among them would be complete unless the names Ebenezer Scrooge and Jacob Marley were mentioned.

Without realizing that either man was among the crowd, Adrian Graves, a banker, suggested that what the men in that room should fear most is not whether they had chosen to ally with the ultimate loser in the battle between these two business elites; what they should fear most is an alliance between these two men. In the event of a Scrooge and Marley partnership, there would likely be a virtual monopoly created in each of their currently contested industries. Who, questioned Graves, would stand a chance in such a marketplace?

Ebenezer and Jacob had never considered such a merger. They had expended far too much energy on attempting to vanquish the other that the concept of pooling resources for a common benefit never entered into either of their minds. Not until Adrian Graves planted the seed.

It would take more than a year before this hypothetical fear would materialize into reality. Both men continued their quest to dominate the other, but something had changed. They both recognized the potential that a joint venture could yield. With their most ardent competitor removed and instead of preventing business from entering their doors, being an agent who ushered it in, the riches to be made could be extraordinary. They could propel each other to heights that alone they would never achieve.

But who would approach whom? Who would humble himself and knock on the other's door? How would the division of assets be accomplished? What would be the division of power?

In the end, it was Adrian Graves himself who facilitated the union. It was well known that he had counted himself among the Marley camp. As a result, Ebenezer, ultimately considering himself to be the more pragmatic of the two, secretly went to Graves and invited him to approach his comrade with a proposal. Ebenezer paid him well but for one purpose: His silence. Whether Jacob rebuffed the opportunity or embraced it, the funds were to keep Graves' lips sealed as to the role he was asked to play.

Jacob, as it turned out, was delighted. He was pleased that in this latest contest in their battle of wills, Ebenezer approached him. In truth, he was particularly pleased that Ebenezer approached him on that specific day. This was because Jacob himself was planning to have an intermediary approach Ebenezer the following day. Jacob burned the missive he had written and never spoke of it to Ebenezer or anyone else.

The two met at a pub outside of the city limits of London. The establishment was known as The Black Horse. Neither had ever been there before and both agreed that it would be unlikely they would be recognized by any prying eyes.

Ebenezer arrived first and sat in the far corner of the room, with a view of the door. He ordered an Irish Stew. Just as it was brought to him, Jacob Marley appeared at his table. Without rising to greet his companion, Ebenezer placed his napkin upon his lap and reached for his spoon. He then spoke.

"Sit, if you intend to," Ebenezer said, blowing on his spoonful.

Jacob sat and asked the waiter to bring him a bowl of the same stew Ebenezer was enjoying.

"I received your message," Jacob said.

"So I see," Ebenezer responded, wiping his mouth.

"You called this meeting," Jacob said. "What have you to say?"

"You know what I have to say," Ebenezer responded. "It is quite simple. Either you are interested in a merger or you are not. I will not plead with you. I will not bargain with you. I will simply say that I have examined the figures multiple times and given this a great deal of consideration. I assume you have done the same or you would not be sitting here before me now. What say you?"

At that moment, the waiter reappeared and placed Jacob's bowl of stew before him.

"Is there anything else I can get you gentlemen?" asked the waiter.

"Yes," said Ebenezer. "Privacy. Please be gone and do not return until we summon you."

"As you wish, sir," the waiter said as he left.

Ebenezer returned his attention to his meal. Jacob tasted his as well. It was quite excellent.

"This is very good," Jacob said.

"Indeed," said Ebenezer.

The two men ate in silence for a few minutes before Jacob spoke.

"The merger is wise. It will benefit us both. It will harm us none. I am in favor," Jacob said.

"I as well," Ebenezer said.

"Then it is settled. Marley and Scrooge shall come to be," Jacob said, and he took a large bite of his food.

"Yes, it is settled. Scrooge and Marley will go into operation," Ebenezer said with a wry smile.

"Scrooge and Marley?" Jacob repeated. "That sounds dreadful! It must be Marley and Scrooge."

"It must be no such thing!" Ebenezer retorted. "The Scrooge name was established earlier in time, it is synonymous with quality, and it was I who was wise enough to advance this proposal. It shall be Scrooge and Marley".

"It shall?" Jacob asked with a chuckle. "The Marley name means success and as it was you who came to me and I was wise enough to accept the proposal, the name should be Marley and Scrooge."

They both looked at each other. They were no more than sixty seconds into their new partnership and they were already at an impasse. It was ironic that of all the issues that would have to be resolved for this merger to be successful, the name of the new company could derail the entire deal.

"How shall we decide this?" Ebenezer asked.

"I suggest we allow fate to play its hand," Jacob responded. "We both place our spoons down. Jointly, we both summon the waiter. Then we remain silent. Whomever the waiter first speaks to directly shall have his way. Agreed?"

"Agreed," said Ebenezer.

Their plan was initiated. Both summoned the waiter. He approached.

"Yes sirs? What can I do for you?" He was speaking to both of them. Neither responded, but both looked in his direction.

The waiter was confused by the silence. He looked back and forth between the men.

"Would you like me to remove your bowl?"

He was speaking to Ebenezer.

Thus, Scrooge and Marley was born.

41

𝔓artnership did not douse the flames of competition between Ebenezer and Jacob; if anything, it intensified them. Each was committed to the success of the new venture, but privately wished to prove to the other who was the more valuable of the pair. The union proved to be a very fruitful one, but neither was ever satisfied.

More.

This was the key for both. This was the coal that lit the furnace of their very beings. In their endless pursuit of their precious *"more"*, each pushed the other to his limits. Never were there ever two men who had so much but who believed themselves to have so little.

The two located their office in the heart of the business district. Within its walls, they housed the sum total of the departments that encompassed all of the business interests of Scrooge and Marley. The office they chose was perfect for them. It was symmetrical in its design. When one entered the door, the main working floor was laid out before one's eyes. It was divided among the various industries that comprised the giant business. In each section sat the clerks at their desks, always expected to be busy and industrious.

If one were to make an immediate left upon entry and walk down the hallway, the office of Jacob Marley would be found. To the right, an equal number of steps down that particular hallway was found the office of Ebenezer Scrooge. Both were of the exact same dimensions. Each had a large desk in its center. Facing out onto the street in each was a colossal picture window. The interior contents and decoration were unique to the two men.

One day, there was a hesitant knock at Ebenezer's door.

"I do not wish to be disturbed!" Ebenezer said, without looking up.

Despite this, his office door creaked slowly open. It was a frightened clerk, named Caleb Bentley. He worked on the Marley side of the office in the investment division. He had a young family and did not wish to be involved in anything that could harm its future. His actions at present ran contrary to his philosophy.

"I said, I do not wish to be disturbed!" Ebenezer repeated, this time looking up with an angry scowl to see who had disturbed his peace. "Was this instruction too imprecise? Perhaps the one that informs you that you have lost your situation will be more comprehensible to you!"

"I'm terribly sorry, Mr. Scrooge," Bentley said. "It is simply that Mr. Marley insisted that I bring this to you. He informed me that if I did not do so, despite any protestations you make, that will cause me to lose my situation." He then quickly scooted over to Ebenezer's desk and held out the small slip of paper he was sent to deliver.

Ebenezer made no move, but continued to glare at Bentley.

Not knowing what to do, Bentley simply placed the paper on Ebenezer's desk and beat a hasty retreat, leaving the room and gently closing the door behind him, hoping that he would still be employed by day's end.

Ebenezer stared at the closed door for a moment, aggravated that Jacob had sent Bentley in to interrupt him. Particularly when he knew it would be against Ebenezer's wishes. One more salvo in the ongoing silent war between the two men for dominance in the office. Ebenezer resolved that he would have to put that young partner of his in his place. And in short time.

Ebenezer then looked at the folded up slip of paper that Jacob found to be of so much importance that he was willing to sacrifice the career of one of his investment clerks and picked it up. He unfolded it and saw four words. At first, he did not know how to react as conflicting emotions welled up within. Then a small, almost imperceptible smile appeared on his face.

The note read:

Arthur Benson has died.

The year was eighteen hundred and twenty-two. Arthur Benson was seventy years old.

Ebenezer had never forgiven Jacob for saving Arthur's business and financial stability. Benson deserved an evil fate. Instead, he was permitted to live until a ripe old age in comfort. But at least the old man was gone at last. That defeat would not be walking around, reminding Ebenezer of all he had stolen away each time Ebenezer's eyes fell upon him. He was for the worms now. Ebenezer hoped they enjoyed their feast.

This would be a funeral Ebenezer would not attend. There were two more at which he would be compelled to appear in the next several years.

But prior to that, more tragedy struck.

"Uncle, I am getting married!" Fred announced happily. Fred was standing before Ebenezer's desk with a smile spanning from ear to ear on the twenty-fourth of March, eighteen hundred and twenty-three. "I wish for you to attend as an honored guest."

"Whom do you intend to marry?" Ebenezer asked, barely lifting his eyes from the papers before him.

"Her name is Julia Braggins. She works as a school teacher, just as I. She is beautiful and intelligent and quite wonderful! I am sure that you will love her as I do," Fred responded with a bright face, thinking about his love.

"Hmmph," Ebenezer replied, unimpressed. "A school teacher. So it is to be a modest future you have planned."

"Quite the contrary, Uncle," Fred said. "With Julia by my side, it is to be quite the extraordinary future indeed!"

"Oh? Then I suppose she is aware of your trust fund," Ebenezer said suspiciously.

"She knows all about me, as I do about her," Fred said. "But that is certainly not what I meant. We are not concerned about what our money can buy. We are only concerned about being with one another for the rest of our lives."

"Oh, Fred," Ebenezer growled. "When will you grow into a man? And stop speaking as a child?"

"Oh, Uncle," Fred retorted. "When will you stop so fearing the world that you believe you must control all of it to be content?"

"I fear nothing, nephew. I simply see things as they are, a lesson I strived mightily to instill within you. Before you rejected all such practical learning," Ebenezer said. "Just as I see this Julia more clearly than you. If she knows of your trust account, then I understand her instant attraction to you."

"Uncle!" Fred exclaimed. "That is an unacceptable and horrible assessment to make. You have not even met Julia!"

"And yet, I know her all the same," Ebenezer said dismissively.

"Uncle, I do not know what I have done all my life to cause you such disdain towards me, but nonetheless, you remain strong within my heart," Fred said. "I came here to invite you to my wedding and I continue to hope to see you there. The nuptials will take place on the twelfth of July. Prior to same, I would like to invite you to my home so that you may meet your future niece."

"I am a very busy man," Ebenezer said.

"Then we shall arrange the meeting at your convenience," Fred said.

"I shall let you know when that may be," Ebenezer said. "Now, nephew, please go. Your visit has already placed me behind on the day's responsibilities."

"Very well, Uncle," Fred said, willing himself back to cheerfulness. "Please inform me when your schedule opens so that you may meet my dear Julia."

"Good afternoon," Ebenezer said, dismissing him.

"And a very good afternoon to you!" Fred said, and he bounded out of the office.

The meeting with Julia prior to the wedding never took place.

Nor could Ebenezer find the time in his schedule to allow him to attend the marriage ceremony. He worked from dawn to midnight on the twelfth of July, eighteen hundred and twenty-three.

It would not be until the following year that Ebenezer would set eyes upon his new niece as they stood near one another at the churchyard where Uncle Laurence was laid to rest. And then not again until the year subsequent in the same spot when Aunt Nancy was deposited in the plot adjoining her husband.

For the next eleven years, Ebenezer and Jacob focused all of their energies on dominating the commercial scene of London. In that time, they added a counting house to their stable of interests. They were ruthless in competition and heartless in acquisition. Their personal, yet friendly battle for dominance of the firm continued unabated. The light from their windows was generally the last illumination to be seen from the street each night. Often, the candlelight burning when they got to their respective homes was not only for warmth, but to give them a few more hours of work so that they may get ahead of their counterpart.

Their personal rivalry kept them focused only on each other. They often took their meals together, telling the other it was for social interaction, but, in reality, it was to ensure the other was not working while he was at rest. The older they grew, the more withdrawn from the world they became. Business was their only concern. Wealth was their only prize. Victory was their only option.

42

It began in late November as a simple cough that he could not seem to dismiss. By early December, thick green mucous and blood were emanating from Jacob's lips with each hack. He then began entering the office flushed red, but complaining that he was freezing regardless of the ambient temperature. He had difficulty breathing, difficulty remaining awake and alert, and he felt great pain within his chest.

On the thirteenth of December, eighteen hundred and thirty-six, an event occurred that had no precedent. Jacob Marley was not present at work. It was a very tense day among all of the employees as they could not explain his absence. There was a question that required resolution by Jacob in the counting house department. It was time sensitive and urgent. As a result, there was only one solution to this dilemma. But it was not one that any were interested in employing. Someone would have to approach Ebenezer.

The clerks cast lots and a relative newcomer to the organization, Robert Cratchit, was the unlucky soul who was tapped for the task.

"Excuse me, please, Mr. Scrooge," Cratchit said as he knocked on Ebenezer's door. The door was slightly ajar and Cratchit's timid voice wafted in through the crack.

"What is it? What is it?" Ebenezer asked, irritated.

"May I enter, sir?" Cratchit asked.

"Is this a serious question? You have already disturbed me and now you wish to hold a conversation through a closed door?" Ebenezer asked, exasperated. This must be one of Jacob's men. Ebenezer would never hire such a tiresome fool.

Cratchit slowly entered the room and explained the situation as tersely as possible. Before he could finish, Ebenezer raised his hand.

"Why are you bringing this issue to me? Why have you not gone to Mr. Marley's office with this query?" Ebenezer asked impatiently.

"I am very sorry, Mr. Scrooge, but Mr. Marley is not in his office," Cratchit replied.

"What is that you say?" Ebenezer asked, very surprised. Jacob had no outside meetings scheduled for the day of which Ebenezer was aware.

"No, sir," Cratchit stated. "He has not been in to the office at all today."

Ebenezer thought about that for a moment. He knew that Jacob had not been feeling well of late. But that was no excuse for placing his own personal comfort above the needs of the business. Ebenezer found it to be very unbecoming. And weak.

"As for our question, Mr. Scrooge?" Cratchit reluctantly asked, attempting to get Ebenezer to focus on the problem at hand.

Ebenezer gave a dismissive and bored response. It was the clear and obvious solution and should not have taken an entire department of seemingly intelligent individuals to ponder without result. How Jacob had ever been a challenge to him in any manner was a complete mystery to Ebenezer. It spoke volumes about the poor quality of the London business mind in general.

The following day, Ebenezer was awaiting Jacob's arrival so that he may discuss with him the importance of setting the proper example for the clerks so that they should not believe themselves justified in remaining at home if they should suffer the slightest sniffle. However, that time never came. At no time did Jacob pass through the threshold at the workplace. By nine o'clock in the morning, Ebenezer was quite irritated at his partner. By eleven o'clock, he was irate. At one o'clock in the afternoon, Ebenezer seriously considered whether the appropriate duration of this partnership had run its course. Ebenezer could not have the London business establishment of the mistaken impression that the name "Scrooge" could be associated with one who chooses to be idle rather than productive.

When the third day came and went with no Jacob Marley, Ebenezer was approaching apoplexy. He did not work his entire life to be undermined by this suddenly selfish partner who was clearly placing his own desires above the requirements of the business. Ebenezer resolved that he would be forced to cut his evening hours short so that he may pay a visit to the terribly inconsiderate Jacob Marley and remind him as to where the focus of his priorities belonged.

At eight o'clock in the evening, Ebenezer rode a carriage to Jacob's home. He was stewing under his hat about how much work he was not accomplishing by being forced into this detour, but enough truly was enough. Missing three consecutive days of work just as the fourth quarter of the year was nearing its end. It was unheard of. Ebenezer struggled to remember if he had missed three days of work in total throughout his entire professional experience. At the moment, he could not recall even missing one.

When he arrived at Jacob's door, Ebenezer rapped on it with his walking stick. One of Jacob's domestics, Jensen, answered the door and allowed Ebenezer entry. Jensen took Ebenezer's coat, hat, and stick.

As he was removing his outer garment, Ebenezer ordered Jensen to fetch Jacob immediately.

"I'm sorry, sir, but Mr. Marley's physician requested that he remain in bed," Jensen replied. "I can take you to him."

"Remain in bed?!" Ebenezer exclaimed. "That is preposterous! You go and tell him to rise and greet me. He has already insulted me by remaining absent from our joint enterprise for the better part of this week. He need not compound the slight by refusing to bring himself before me here and now."

"But, sir -" Jensen began to protest.

"Go now," Ebenezer snarled.

"Very well," Jensen capitulated. He left the room to hang Ebenezer's coat and hat. He then walked up the stairs to relay Ebenezer's message to his ailing master.

A few minutes later, Jacob slowly shuffled down the stairs adorned only his nightshirt beneath a heavy robe. He trod very heavily down each step, holding on to the railing with both hands. Another servant who was attending to him in his room, named Lennox, walked alongside Jacob, holding him up under his arms to prevent him from taking an unfortunate spill. Together they took each step deliberately and carefully.

Jacob reached the landing and Lennox assisted him into the sitting room where Ebenezer was impatiently waiting. As Ebenezer watched, Lennox helped Jacob into a large, comfortable chair.

"Leave us," Jacob instructed Lennox with a rasp in his voice. Just those words alone seemed to tax all of his energy. He placed the handkerchief he was holding in his right hand to his mouth. He fought with his eyelids to keep them open.

Jacob then presented a weak smile to Ebenezer.

"Hello, my friend," Jacob greeted. "My apologizes for having been unable to join you at our office these past several days. I am pleased to see you here."

"Are you?" Ebenezer said with disdain. "What ails you to such an extent that you place your comfort over the needs of our business?"

"Again, I apologize," Jacob said. He then emitted a wet cough into his cloth. Ebenezer saw some crimson on the handkerchief when Jacob removed it from his mouth. He felt a twinge of revulsion, both from the sight of the obvious blood and due to the implications of same. Ebenezer believed that he had suffered enough loss in his life to date. He could not believe God to be so cruel as to strip him of his one friend and partner at present. His mind would not even consider the possibility. He gave in to the anger that suddenly bubbled up from within. He questioned neither its source nor its appropriateness.

"When can I expect you back at your post?" Ebenezer asked tersely.

Jacob mopped his excessively moist brow. His cheeks were an uncommonly bright shade of red. His half-opened eyes shone like glass. It is not clear that he understood the question just posed.

"So, man?" Ebenezer asked.

"I'm sorry? What was that?" Jacob asked.

Ebenezer let out a frustrated sigh.

"I asked when I can expect you back at your post. While I am fully capable of performing both of our duties, I prefer to maximize our efficiency and allow you to complete your own responsibilities," Ebenezer said.

"My hope is that this ague will abate within a day or two and I shall be back," Jacob responded. He then broke down into a fit of coughing and spasming, ejecting his sputum into the cloth in his hand.

Ignoring his partner's distress, Ebenezer nodded his head.

"See that you do," Ebenezer responded. "Now, I must depart. I have several more important issues to resolve before I may rest my head for the night. Good evening, Jacob."

"Good evening, Ebenezer," Jacob forced from himself. His throat was very sore and dry. This conversation had drained all but the last iota of energy Jacob had in reserve. He could not rise to his feet to bid Ebenezer farewell.

Jensen brought Ebenezer his coat, hat and walking stick. After assisting him with the overcoat, Jensen led the way to the front door. Ebenezer left without another word.

Jacob's prediction of his imminent return to the office did not materialize. In fact, he would never return.

43

On the twenty-fourth of December, eighteen hundred and thirty-six, shortly after the bell chimed for the tenth time that morning, there came a knock upon Ebenezer's office door.

"Come!" he called.

Jacob's domestic servant, Jensen, entered. Ebenezer did not recognize his face, despite having been greeted by Jensen at Jacob's door more times than can be counted. As Jensen could not advance Ebenezer's business interests in any manner, remembering him was simply not of importance.

"Can I help you?" Ebenezer asked. "But before you begin, if you are selling anything, I am not buying. If you are asking for something, I am not giving. I have seen enough of you seasonal do-gooders to last a lifetime!"

"Sir, Mr. Scrooge," said Jensen. "I am Jensen. I work in the home of your partner, Mr. Marley. I come asking for nothing. I come only to deliver an urgent message."

"What is it then?" Ebenezer asked impatiently. "Get on with it."

"Mr. Marley is gravely ill," Jensen reported. "His doctor fears that he may not last the day."

"And so you come seeking employment, is that it, Jensen?" Ebenezer asked.

"No, sir. Of course not. I would never dream of engaging in such a ghoulish task while my master lays dying in his bed," said Jensen, taken aback.

"You would never dream of securing your welfare at precisely the moment your financial stability is threatened?" Ebenezer asked. He chuckled darkly. "It is no wonder you cannot rise above your station as servant."

"Nonetheless, sir, I do come with a request on my master's behalf," Jensen said. "He asks that you come with me immediately to visit with him."

"Immediately?!" Ebenezer exclaimed. "My young partner must be delirious indeed. I have much to accomplish today. Once business is complete, I will make my way."

Jensen was taken by surprise.

"Sir, perhaps you do not understand the urgency," Jensen said. "Mr. Marley suffers. He may not be capable of receiving you if we do not hurry now."

"Listen, Jenkens—" Ebenezer began, staring at the man standing across his desk with a most troubled look on his face.

"It's Jensen, sir," Jensen corrected.

Ebenezer just glared at the interruption. He took a moment and then proceeded.

"I have very important business to complete. In part, because your master has chosen not to appear at this office over the course of the past two weeks. Thus, I have his work to satisfy as well as my own. He knows how crucial this is and if I were in his position at present, I would be quite put out if I discovered he had abandoned his tasks half-finished," explained Ebenezer. "Therefore, I will honor his wishes by completing my work, after which time I may pay him a social call."

"Sir –" Jensen began, trying one time more.

"That is enough," Ebenezer said. "You may go now and reassure your master that everything is well in hand. I am sure nothing would give him more peace of mind."

Jensen was forced to concede defeat and he left Ebenezer's office.

At half past four in the afternoon, a new face appeared at Ebenezer's door. This time it was Jacob's personal physician, Dr. Robards.

"Enter!" Ebenezer called from his side of the door.

An older, white-haired gentleman with spectacles perched at the end of his nose walked in.

"Mr. Scrooge, I presume?" the doctor asked.

"Of course. And you are?" Ebenezer asked.

"My name is Quincy Robards, personal physician to Jacob Marley," he replied, hoping his presence would make an impression on Ebenezer. It did not.

"Yes, doctor. What can I do for you?" Ebenezer asked.

"Well, sir," Dr. Robards began, "I am here to request your presence at the bedside of Mr. Marley."

"Why?" Ebenezer asked, continuing to work.

"Because, sir, he is dreadfully ill," the doctor replied. "Even as we speak, we may be too late in returning. I fear he will not see another day."

"I am sure you exaggerate, doctor," Ebenezer said. "As you can see, I am quite busy. I thought I made that clear earlier in the day when that servant, Jessup, was here."

"Mr. Scrooge, I assure you that I am not prone to exaggeration. To be truthful, I am amazed Mr. Marley has held on this long," said the doctor.

"If he has held on this long, a few more hours more will not try his endurance. But these constant interruptions do try my patience," Ebenezer said.

"Sir, he informs me that he has important matters to discuss with you before it is too late," Dr. Robards said.

"What are these matters?" Ebenezer asked.

"I do not know," the doctor answered. "He was quite clear that the message was for you and you alone."

"Well, is not that very convenient," Ebenezer said angrily. "If Jacob was in the dire straits such as you claim, he would send you with a proper message. I certainly would. Clearly, he has information regarding our business and he uses this to distract me from my daily duties. Even from his back, he attempts to prove that he is more worthy than I. Well, doctor, I am quite certain he will be able to reveal his information when I arrive after the proper work day is done."

"I am not so confident," the doctor responded.

"You are not paid to be confident," Ebenezer said flatly. "You are paid to be morose. If it were not so, who would seek out your services?"

The doctor's eyes conveyed clearly that he was not amused by this assessment.

"Now, doctor, please be gone and allow me to climb this mountain of work so that I may stand upon its summit before tomorrow arrives. The more interruptions I suffer, the longer it shall be before I can make my way to see the ever-so-ill Jacob Marley," Ebenezer stated.

Like Jensen before him, Dr. Robards was forced to surrender and exit Scrooge and Marley without accomplishing his task.

Several hours later, at a quarter past seven, Ebenezer finally set his quill at rest. He took his time organizing for the next day's work and finally exited his doors, putting key to lock as the bell chimed eight.

Before heading towards Jacob's home, Ebenezer was feeling quite famished and decided to quell his hunger. He chose to stop at the local pub at the corner known as The Prince and the Swan for a hot, hearty meal. He sat by himself and enjoyed the solitude. He looked about and heard most patrons wishing each other a "Merry Christmas". Ebenezer shook his head. These same people would cut the throats of their counterparts' mothers on any other day of the year. But today, everyone pretended to be of good cheer and of magnanimous personality.

Ebenezer finished his meal, wiped his mouth and paid his bill. It was too expensive in Ebenezer's opinion. Quite the "Merry Christmas" for the tavern-owner to overcharge for a simple bowl of soup.

Ebenezer then trudged out into the snow. The time was now approaching nine o'clock. He hailed a cab and gave the driver Jacob's address. Along the way, Ebenezer groused that Jacob could not simply send a proper message to save Ebenezer from this unnecessary trip. Always overdramatic, that Jacob. Always wanting everyone to come to him. Well, congratulations in that case, Ebenezer thought to himself. You have won this round, sir.

When Ebenezer arrived at Jacob's home, he alit from the carriage. The driver clearly hoped for a bit more than the standard fare due to the season. Ebenezer ensured that he would be disappointed. Everyone with their hand out at this time of year. Ebenezer was quite sure that Heaven frowned upon what had become of the yuletide. Ebenezer certainly did.

Jensen answered the door after Ebenezer knocked.

"Ah, Jergens," Ebenezer said. "You may tell your master that your journey was a success. I am here."

"Please come in, Mr. Scrooge," Jensen said somberly, without even bothering to correct Ebenezer about his name this time. "Dr. Robards would like to speak with you."

"Would he? I see that I am most popular in this house today," Ebenezer responded.

The doctor appeared.

"Mr. Scrooge, perhaps you should sit," Dr. Robards said.

"I think not, good doctor," said Ebenezer. "I understand that you have something to say and then I must discuss whatever pressing business is on the mind of Mr. Marley. So please hurry because I am quite tired and anxious to be off to my own home."

"Mr. Scrooge," the doctor began, "I am sorry to inform you of this, but Mr. Marley passed away just within the last hour. I regret that you did not arrive in time to speak with him."

Ebenezer stared at the doctor for a long moment. He then spoke.

"Did Mr. Marley impart his message intended for me to you?" Ebenezer asked.

"No, sir, I am afraid he did not," Dr. Robards said.

Ebenezer was immediately furious. Nothing should have gotten in the way of business. Not even death. This was most unprofessional of Jacob.

"Very well, then," Ebenezer said, fuming at his inconsiderate late partner. "Is there anything you wish me to do at this juncture?"

"I have prepared the death certificate," said the doctor. "If you would be so kind as to accompany me to Mr. Marley's room for an official identification of the body, I would be most grateful."

Ebenezer followed the doctor up to Jacob's bedchamber. There he lay, silent as a stone, his hands clasped together over his chest. He seemed to have lost considerable weight in just the week since Ebenezer had seen him last.

"That is him," Ebenezer confirmed. He then signed the certificate as "witness".

"I am very sorry for your loss, Mr. Scrooge," the doctor said.

"As am I," Ebenezer responded, shaking his head at Jacob's supine, still body. "Now I shall never know what that selfish lout should have conveyed through a proper and reliable messenger. I shall not forgive him if such action harms our business."

The doctor was stunned into silence by these callous words.

Later that night, Ebenezer sat by his fire, staring into it. Somewhere in the distance, the clock chimed twelve times. It was Christmas, eighteen hundred and thirty-six. The very last soul that Ebenezer had ever described as "friend" was gone. Once again, Ebenezer was alone.

Ebenezer was now fifty-eight years old.

44

The death of Jacob Marley had a profound effect on Ebenezer. Without Jacob's presence to provide Ebenezer with a modicum of a social outlet, Ebenezer retreated fully into his work. He took all of his meals alone. His patience, such that it had existed before, seemed to dissipate entirely. His tolerance for even the slightest misstep was at its nadir.

An astute observer may have diagnosed Ebenezer as a man filled with pain. But most could not get past his irascible exterior and none, save one, had the interest to delve any deeper. His nephew Fred continued relentlessly in his pursuit of Ebenezer's affection, but to no avail. The more he endeavored to bring the men together, the more Ebenezer resisted. With each passing day, Ebenezer became more and more a cantankerous old wretch.

No period of time brought out the worst in Ebenezer than did the final few weeks of every year. His thin frame was sensitive to the cold and growing more so as he aged. As a result, the onset of winter always made him of disagreeable temperament. The respiratory disorder that he acquired as a child was most present when the frosty air filled his lungs, causing him shortness of breath and painful inhalation at inopportune times. He put stress upon himself to close out the fourth business quarter with strength, although the results were never satisfactory to him. And, of course, so many of the memories he strove to suppress celebrated their anniversaries at this time of year.

His dreams betrayed him. Often, he would awaken with a sheen of icy perspiration coating his exterior. A particularly troubling recurring nightmare brought him back to the cusp of his thirteenth year. Sometimes, in the dream, he was the young man he once was; sometimes, he was in his current form. Ebenezer enters his father's bedroom on the day he was discovered dead upon the floor. He approaches the corpse, just as he had so many years ago. But unlike in reality, in the dream, Elias Scrooge's eyes snap open and look directly into Ebenezer's pale blue ones. He speaks.

"Ebenezer, I have hated you for your entire life. In granting you life, my Elizabeth sacrificed her own and I have never been able to forgive you."

It was the contents of the letter Elias had penned to his son just before he expired.

It was always at that moment that Ebenezer would awaken, shaken and frightened. Instinctually, he would look about to ensure that there were no witnesses to his weakness. But, of course, he was always alone. Ebenezer's had always been a cold, lonely bed.

Other remembrances that Ebenezer preferred to forget often surfaced when the calendar's pages ran few. The sight of his Fan hidden beneath a white bedsheet. The image of his Belle hidden beneath a white veil as she pledged her life to another, a sight he had not actually seen but one that his mind conjured for his torture nonetheless. The sound within his ears that he was sure had echoed of dear old Fezziwig cursing his name from within the crowded, dirty cell of the debtor's prison to which Ebenezer's actions had resigned him. And Jacob Marley, that young fool, with whom Ebenezer had shared so many hours, but who had his final desire of just one more meeting of the men rebuffed by Ebenezer's devotion to the business.

Ebenezer was particularly impatient with the hypocrisy he regarded as rampant at this particular time of year. Throughout the remainder of the year, Ebenezer observed man to be a grasping and clawing beast, seeking only to satisfy his base instincts without regard for the others who shared the planet. Depravity was the theme of the day. Thieves, derelicts, adulterers, sots, liars and cheats all year long. Anything to be done in an effort to take the most while producing the least.

But, for some reason, these same people believed that if they offer the trite greeting, "Merry Christmas" with a smile, or if they drop a mere shilling in a can meant for another, all other sins of the year are forgiven. For some reason, they allow themselves the fiction that they are good and decent souls. That they are among the saved and the elect.

It was enough to make Ebenezer physically ill. Each day, the periodicals revealed the true nature of mankind. The Christmas façade disgusted Ebenezer. He had no use for such falseness. He had no use for such humbug.

And it was not just the two-faced Janus that appeared on the countenance of all he met that boiled Ebenezer's stew. It was the expectation and entitlement. Somehow, by a means Ebenezer was at a loss to discern, the day of the birth of the Lord was seen by most as a celebration of idleness. Give me, without my earning it. Hand me, without my deserving it. Was it not enough that these wretched sinners were offered a place in Heaven, despite their wicked ways? Must they flaunt their unworthiness for such a gift so blatantly for all the world to see?

Even rats have the decency to remain in the corners and the shadows. Even vermin stays within the dark so that it is unseen. But he who lounges when he should work, he who loiters when he should contribute, and he who lazes about when he should be industrious has no compunction at all about extending his dirty fingers in the direction of those with means with the expectation of charity.

How had Christmas been transformed into this macabre festival of the poor and undeserving?, Ebenezer wondered each year. Was he given anything without suffering to achieve it? He thought not. Yet others believed themselves above doing what was necessary to earn. No, instead, the poor occupied their time rutting like pigs and producing litters of ragamuffins that they could not support! They waited with baited breath for this time of year when begging was a virtue and those who produced for society were made to feel guilt for their failure to resign themselves to poverty. These same people who took from the diligent at the end of a blade in a dark alleyway at all other times of the year were glad to exact additional pounds of flesh with an open hand and a wretched smile. All in the name of Christmas.

What surprised and enraged Ebenezer further was that so few recognized the season for what it truly was as he did. So few appreciated how these days that were meant to be holy had been perverted into an elaborate game of pickpocket. Ebenezer thought himself trapped within an asylum as he walked the streets during the Christmas season. The poor singing carols for coins on each street corner. The wealthy doling out their guilt-offerings and pressuring their fellow businessmen to do the same. Contests among the city's population for the prize of who can appear the most altruistic.

But where was this charity all the rest of the year? Was there something wrong with the hearts of man that prevented him from divesting himself of all worldly goods when no one else was watching if such behavior truly was a virtue? But, of course, that was the entire game, was it not? Look at me. Love me. Recognize me for the great benevolent man that I am. So that when this short season is over, you may refill my coffers to overflow. For who would not wish to do business with such a beneficent man as I? The cynicism of the corrupted season should drive all sane men to Bedlam. It was more than once that Ebenezer believed the total population of compos mentis men in London to be set at one.

On the morning of Saturday, the twenty-third of December, eighteen hundred and forty-three, Ebenezer awoke in a particularly foul mood. He had reviewed his ledgers the night before and was not content with the projections for the remainder of the year. Furthermore, he was irritated to discover that Christmas fell on a Monday during this annual cycle. Ebenezer knew what to expect before the day was done. A representative from the office, probably the Head Clerk, Bob Cratchit, would approach him and virtually demand to be free from the workplace not only the usual Sunday, but then the Monday for Christmas as well. And what was Ebenezer to do at that point? Terminate the entire staff just as the final push to the end year was needed? It was simply not fair and it was not right. No one ever appreciated the difficulties of the employer. In full truth, no one ever appreciated the employer at all.

As Ebenezer dressed and prepared himself for the day, he was quite certain he heard a rattling and scraping sound emanating from the cellar. Was there an intruder? Ebenezer grabbed his pistol and slowly made his way down the stairs.

"Who goes there?" Ebenezer cried into the darkness, holding the weapon out in front of him. "You will find nothing here that you may steal! Show yourself! Or the only asset of mine that I will share with you is the shot within this gun!"

Ebenezer crept around his cellar, with pistol cocked and ready to fire at any moment. He found nothing. He also heard no further noise that was foreign to the norm. Finally, he was satisfied that whatever had echoed within his ears earlier was nothing more than a product of his own imagination. Almost sixty-five years old and hearing that which was not there. Ebenezer scowled. Aging was unkind to the senses.

Ebenezer traveled to his office and, as always, was the first to arrive. He peered at the sign above the doorframe and found it covered in snow. He knocked his walking stick against the sign to relieve it of the precipitation so that the words "Scrooge and Marley" were clearly visible. He entered and glanced back to his left in the direction of his former partner's office, as he always did without even realizing it each day when he crossed the threshold. Ebenezer cleared out all documents of importance on the day after Jacob passed, seven years ago tomorrow, and then he locked the door. It has remained locked and untouched since that moment.

Ebenezer continued his morning routine by beginning the coal furnace in both the main workspace as well as within his own office. He used the minimum amount of coal necessary to take the chill from the air. At this temperature, the clerks were capable of performing their functions without being warmed into a state of laze. Furthermore, the cost of coal of late was far too expensive and Ebenezer was not of the opinion that profits should suffer for the sake of perspiration in December. If the clerks would prefer a warm environment, they always had the option to relocate to one of the colonies in Africa or Asia. The Empire was certainly large enough for the disgruntled to discover a new home. If, instead, the clerks arrived at Ebenezer's workplace of their own free will expecting that he reach into his pocket to compensate them for a day's work, he had no patience for protest.

As the clocks chimed, ringing in the workday, each of the departments within the office space filled. The clerks greeted each other and were of good spirits. Ebenezer's door was open so that he could look out upon the floor, as he had come to learn that productivity would be at a minimum on this day if he allowed the clerks simply to be supervised by Cratchit's permissive eye.

Outside, on the street, London was all a-bustle. The aroma of roasting chestnuts was in the air. Flocks of carolers were singing on the corners and before open shop doors. Merchants were preparing to satisfy their orders for the holiday. People were rushing to and fro, greeting each other with warm wishes for the yuletide. Among them was Fred Radcliffe, Jr., who was making his way to his uncle's business with his annual invitation, always hopeful that he would not receive his annual demurrer.

Christmas was almost here. And while he did not yet know it to be true, it would be one that would change Ebenezer Scrooge forever.

PART II

VISITS FROM THE SPIRITS

1

It was Saturday, the twenty-third of December, eighteen hundred and forty-three. Two days until Christmas.

At half past ten in the morning, the door to Scrooge and Marley burst open and in bounded Fred Radcliffe, Jr. with a wide smile on his face and a bounce in his step. From his office, Ebenezer could hear the commotion on the work floor as there were multiple exchanges of "Merry Christmas" tossed about. Footsteps clicked upon the floor heading in his direction. Ebenezer knew who approached even before seeing his face.

"Merry Christmas, Uncle!" Fred beamed, allowing himself entry into Ebenezer's open office doorway without even the courtesy of a knock.

"That phrase! I cannot tell you how it grinds upon my nerves!" Ebenezer said, with a shake of his head.

"What phrase, Uncle? 'Merry Christmas'?" Fred asked. "How can it possibly be so?"

"It is a banal greeting offered by the least of men. It signifies nothing but a celebration of humbug," Ebenezer replied.

"Christmas a humbug, Uncle? Surely you do not mean that," Fred said.

"Frederick, you exhaust me," Ebenezer said with a heavy sigh. "What is humbug is when the evil and the weak attempt to pass themselves off as the noble and the worthy. This phenomenon is never as acute as during the Christmas scourge. I find an entire season dedicated to the falseness of man to be revolting."

"If that is your position, Uncle, then perhaps you do not understand Christmas," Fred said sorrowfully.

"I understand it all too well, nephew," said Ebenezer. "Now what is it that you want?"

"I would think that after all these years that you would know the answer to that question," Fred said. "I come to invite you to dine with us on Christmas Day!"

"I am afraid that I must decline," Ebenezer said.

"But why, Uncle?" Fred asked.

"I am going to be far too busy," Ebenezer answered. "While the rest of the world may be reveling in idleness, I will be right here at my proper station completing that what must be done."

"But, Uncle, even you must eat," Fred responded.

"That is a presumption not necessarily grounded in fact," Ebenezer said.

"Please, Uncle. Each year I invite you. Each year you say no. Perhaps we could begin a new tradition. One in which you join us," Fred implored.

"No," Ebenezer said.

"Julia is an excellent cook. Do not miss such a delicious meal," Fred said.

"I'm afraid that I must," Ebenezer said, returning his attention to his desk. "Now, if there is nothing else, I must get back to work. Good day, nephew."

"Please, simply consider attending, Uncle," Fred persisted.

"I said good day," Ebenezer repeated without looking up.

"We will save a seat for you at our table," Fred said.

Now Ebenezer did raise his head and looked directly at Fred.

"Sir, I said good day. There is no reason for more discussion. You are putting me behind," Ebenezer said. "Now it is time for you to be gone."

"Very well, Uncle. A Merry Christmas to you!" Fred said with a smile.

Ebenezer ignored him.

"And a Happy New Year as well!" Fred continued.

Ebenezer looked up again, unamused. He said but one word.

"Go."

Fred left Ebenezer's office and wished all of the clerks well. He shook hands with Bob Cratchit and made for the door. When he went to reach for the knob, the door opened from the other side. Two portly gentlemen, one quite young and one considerably older, entered and asked where they could find the proprietor of this establishment. Fred pointed them down towards Ebenezer's office before heading out into the day.

The two gentlemen made their way to Ebenezer's open doorway and the younger of the two rapped on the door with his knuckles.

Ebenezer looked up. He sighed in frustration. Another interruption. It was as though all of London was conspiring to prevent him from accomplishing his day's tasks.

"Yes?" Ebenezer asked, irritated from the start.

"Scrooge and Marley's, I believe," the younger gentleman said, looking at the thin book in his hand. "Have I the pleasure of addressing Mr. Scrooge or Mr. Marley?"

Ebenezer stared at this stout young man in disbelief.

The older of the two quickly spoke.

"Of course, this is Mr. Scrooge, Garrett," the older man said, clearly embarrassed. "Please excuse him, Mr. Scrooge. He is young and new to our business community."

The young man flushed red.

"What is it that you gentlemen are seeking?" Ebenezer asked. "I am very busy and have little time."

"Well, Mr. Scrooge," the older gentleman began. "I am Horace Merryweather. This is my young colleague, Lionel Garrett. We are here on a pleasant errand. At this festive season of the year it is more than usually desirable that we should make some slight provision for the poor and the destitute who suffer greatly at the present time. A few of us are endeavoring to raise a fund to buy these souls in need some meat and drink and means of warmth. I'm sure we can rely on a successful man such as yourself to offer your assistance for the cause. What shall I put you down for?"

Ebenezer let out a disgusted sigh. More outstretched hands seeking something for nothing.

"Are there no prisons?" Ebenezer asked.

"Plenty of prisons," Merryweather replied sadly.

"And the Union workhouses?" asked Ebenezer. "Are they still in operation?"

"They are. I wish I could say they were not," Merryweather responded.

"The Treadmill and the Poor Law are in full vigor, then?" asked Ebenezer.

"Both very busy, sir," said Merryweather, becoming uncomfortable with these questions.

"Well, thank the heavens above," Ebenezer said sarcastically. "Based on your speech, I was concerned you were here because something dreadful had occurred to stop them."

"Yes, well, as I was asking," Merryweather said. "What can we put you down for?"

"I am not clear that I understand your request, sir," Ebenezer said. "You tell me that our social welfare systems are all in full operation. I help to support all of these establishments with my taxes, extracted regularly by Her Majesty's government. What more can be expected of a man?"

"Sir, while it is true all of the dreadful options created by our government are in operation, we feel it incumbent upon ourselves, as men of great blessings, to share our good fortune with those not so fortunate,"

Merryweather said.

"And you are free to do so," Ebenezer said. "Just as I am free to bid you farewell and to get back to my very important work."

"But sir," Merryweather said. "Is there nothing you can spare?"

"Yes. My advice," Ebenezer said. "Those who are badly off should take advantage of the institutions my taxes support."

"Many cannot go there," Garrett stated.

"And many would rather die," Merryweather said.

"They would rather die than work? This affliction I know all too well. Well, if they would rather die, they had better do it and decrease the surplus population. Or if not, they should cease feeling sorrowful for their circumstances and choose work over death," Ebenezer said. "Now, good day, gentlemen."

Seeing that they would not be successful in soliciting a donation at this location, the men withdrew. Just as they had begun their travels to the next business on their list, the front door of Scrooge and Marley opened and Bob Cratchit emerged.

"Gentlemen!" he cried.

They turned around.

"Here," Cratchit said, handing them a coin. "I know it is not much, but it is all I can contribute."

The two portly gentlemen beamed.

"God bless you, sir," Merryweather said.

"No, God bless you for the fine work you are doing," Cratchit said. At this, he ran back to his post before Ebenezer separated him from it permanently for having left.

The workday continued and at a quarter of six, Bob Cratchit approached Ebenezer's office door.

"Mr. Scrooge, may I speak with you?" Cratchit asked.

"Yes, Cratchit, what is it?" asked Ebenezer with a frustrated sigh. "As if I do not already know."

"The men would like to know if they may have Christmas Day to spend with their families, sir?" Cratchit inquired.

"I am not pleased," Ebenezer said. "You already have the full day tomorrow. And now you wish a second consecutive day to idle? If I agreed but chose to withhold the day's wage, you would think yourself ill-used, I'll be bound?"

"Sir, it is but once a year," Cratchit said.

"A poor excuse for picking a man's pocket every twenty-fifth of December!" exclaimed Ebenezer. "But I suppose you all must have the whole day. If but one is late or unable to satisfy all of his duties on Tuesday next, let it be known that I shall replace his entire department. And I will be in search of a new Head Clerk. Do I make myself clear?"

"Yes, sir. Thank you, sir," Cratchit said.

Shortly thereafter the workday came to a close and all present filed out into the evening. Ebenezer continued in his office for one hour further before snuffing out his candles and locking the front door for the night.

Before heading home, Ebenezer went to The Prince and the Swan and ate his customary supper at his customary table surrounded only by the periodicals he read as he ate. He was beginning to feel the development of a cold in his head, which placed him in a mood even more sour than was his usual temperament.

Following his meal, Ebenezer walked out into the cold night and made his way home. When he arrived, he resolved to get to sleep quickly so as to be fresh and ready to put in a full day's work beginning early the next morning. But a restful night's sleep was not what Ebenezer had in store.

After settling into bed and closing his eyes, he quickly dozed off. However, this sleep was short-lived as he was awakened by the sound of chains rattling in the cellar below, just as he had heard to begin his day. This time he refused to believe it. His senses were askew. It was probably just the wind, he thought to himself, coupled with the mild illness he was developing in his head.

Later in the night, Ebenezer was again awakened. This time by the sounds of doors slamming throughout the house. Ebenezer decided that the house was simply too drafty and the servants had not properly secured the doors. This also explained the moaning he heard wafting from the floor below. Ebenezer determined that the house was settling.

But then something occurred that Ebenezer could not so easily explain away.

As he lay with his eyes red from exhaustion, half opened and half shut, a fantastic light appeared from behind his bed curtains. He pulled them aside to find that the fireplace was fully ablaze. A door down the hall creaked open and then suddenly slammed shut. Ebenezer decided that he must be dreaming, but try as he may, he could not wake from this particular nightmare.

Another door slammed shut and with it, the fireplace suddenly went dark and cold. In fact, the entire room went freezing. Ebenezer began to shiver and he could see his breath as a white smoke emanating from his mouth with each exhale.

Just as quickly as the environment changed to this icy situation, the temperature returned to its chilly, but tolerable norm.

All night long, these strange phenomena persisted. Ebenezer could not remember when he had experienced such a restless night.

2

When the clock struck six, Ebenezer decided he wished to experience no more time in bed. He rose, washed, and dressed. He determined that the antidote for a poor night's sleep was a hearty day's work. His mind needed stimulation.

Ebenezer walked to his office and allowed himself entry on this cold and foggy Christmas Eve. He lit the coal furnace in his office room and set his mind to work. He remained behind his desk well into the afternoon before the disturbances began.

At approximately four o'clock, Ebenezer heard the front door open and footfalls within the main work space.

"Hello there! Who goes there?" Ebenezer called. He was confused because he was sure that he had locked the door behind him.

There was no response to his call.

"I say! Who is here?" Ebenezer called again.

Again, no response.

Irritated at being disturbed, Ebenezer got us and walked towards the noise. But when he arrived at the door, he found it closed and when he twisted the knob, he found it to be firmly locked. He looked around. Clearly, no one was there.

But then he noticed something that was very wrong.

Jacob's office door was wide open.

Ebenezer slowly walked down the hallway towards the open door.

"Who is there? How did you unlock that door?" Ebenezer cried.

No answer.

Ebenezer peered into the open doorway for the first time in seven years.

Everything was coated in a thick layer of dust. When Ebenezer looked to the floor, he saw footprints in the dust spanning from the door, leading around Jacob's desk, and terminating at his chair. The chair was facing the window looking out with the high back directed towards Ebenezer.

"Who are you?" Ebenezer called out.

He stepped into the room and walked to the chair. He put his hand on its back and tugged, turning the chair to its side.

There was no one sitting in it.

Suddenly, Jacob's door slammed shut.

Ebenezer jerked his head to find himself locked within this dusty tomb that Jacob once called his workspace. Ebenezer lunged for the doorknob and twisted it, but it would not turn. He heard a squeak and when he turned his head, he saw that Jacob's chair was once again facing out to the window as if Ebenezer had never touched it.

"This is humbug! Humbug, I say!" Ebenezer said, fruitlessly struggling with the doorknob.

Suddenly, the room was awash in light, as though it were noontime on a summer day. All of the dust was gone and the office looked as it had the day Ebenezer locked it seven years prior.

Just as suddenly, the room was once again cold, dark and dusty. But now the door was wide open.

Ebenezer scurried out and hurried down to his office. He locked his door. But as soon as the lock clicked into place, his coal furnace instantly went cold. Ebenezer went to it and attempted to relight it, but nothing he tried would make the smallest spark.

Ebenezer looked up just in time to watch as all of the candles in his office blew out one by one. He was left standing in the cold and the dark.

Ebenezer finally decided it was time to go home. He determined that he must rest his cold for he believed it was clearly wreaking havoc with his senses.

He locked his front office door and walked home. He resolved to sit by a nice roaring fire and to consume a bowl of gruel. After he did so, he would settle in and get the sleep that eluded him the night before. By Monday morning, he would be right as rain.

As he approached his front door, he removed his keys from his pocket. As he was placing the key into the lock, he felt that something was not right. When he looked up, he was horrified to discover that his doorknocker was not present where it belonged. In its place was the head of his deceased partner, Jacob Marley. It was as if a primitive shaman had shrunk poor Jacob's head down to a miniature size, removed it clean from his body, and tacked it up in place of the knocker. Unquestionably, it was Jacob's face staring ahead, unblinking.

Ebenezer leaned in.

Suddenly, Jacob's eyes shifted and looked directly into Ebenezer's. It was a most dreadful sensation.

Ebenezer screamed in fright and nearly lost his footing. Once he steadied himself, his heart pounding within his chest, he looked back at the door. But now, as he did, Jacob's head was gone and the knocker had returned.

Ebenezer rubbed his eyes and turned his head back in the direction of the knocker. It was still as he had always known it to be.

"This is absolute humbug!" Ebenezer growled.

Ebenezer quickly entered his home and affixed all of the locks behind him. He told himself to remain calm and rational.

He made his way up the stairs to his bedchamber and after he entered he locked that door as well. This may be the first time that he had ever done so. When he turned, he saw that his fire was already ablaze and the bowl of gruel he intended to make was already steaming and waiting for him upon the table beside his chair before the fireplace. He walked over to his chair. How did the fire get started?, he wondered. Who made the gruel? Perhaps one of his servants had recently done so before leaving for the night, but Ebenezer was quite cross that anyone would leave such a fire burning with no one to tend it.

Ebenezer decided that a quick meal and then sleep was what he needed to rid himself of these strange occurrences. He put on his dressing gown, his slippers and his nightcap. He then sat down before the fire to take his gruel.

As he took his first bite, he heard the chains from the night prior in the cellar again. They continued to scrape and rattle until he heard the unmistakable sound of the cellar door slamming open.

Now the scraping sound was much louder and accompanied by footsteps clearly heading up the stairs directly towards his room.

Ebenezer's eyes grew wide as they were transfixed on his locked door.

Three booming, echoing knocks fell upon the door with so much force that the entire room vibrated with each one. Ebenezer found that he could not move.

It was then the full-bodied apparition of Jacob Marley materialized through the door, dragging heavy chains that were wrapped around his torso and his arms and his legs. Ebenezer lost the strength in his arms and he dropped the bowl of gruel he was holding. It smashed on the bedroom floor and the spoon clanged down beside the bowl's remains.

Jacob's ghost trod heavily towards Ebenezer, clearly struggling against the weight of his chains. The specter was pale blue in its entirety and was emitting a faint glow. The chains were adorned with cash-boxes, keys, padlocks, ledgers, deeds and heavy purses. The ghost appeared to wince in pain with every step. But still it persisted forward until it was standing directly before Ebenezer. It said nothing. It merely stared at him, unblinking, just as it had when it was a mere head in place of the knocker on the front door.

Ebenezer was shaking. None of this could be happening, he thought to himself. He feared that he was either dreaming or in delirium.

Finally, Ebenezer could stand the silent staring no more.

"What do you want with me?" Ebenezer cried.

"Much." It was Jacob's voice with the trace of an echo.

"Are you Jacob Marley?" Ebenezer asked.

"I was."

"You are fettered," Ebenezer observed. "Tell me why."

"I wear the chain I forged in life. I made it link by link and yard by yard," the ghost replied. "I girded it on of my own free will, and of my own free will I wore it."

"Why would you do such, Jacob?" Ebenezer asked.

"Why? This is a question you should turn on yourself," the ghost replied.

"I do not understand," Ebenezer said.

"What you carry by your free will was as full and as heavy as my own seven years ago. You have labored on it since. It is a ponderous chain!" Jacob told him.

Ebenezer looked about but saw nothing.

"Tell me what this means, Jacob. I choose no chains," Ebenezer said.

"No? It is required of all men that the spirit within must look outward to contribute to the betterment of mankind. With each selfish act, with each self-serving decision, a new link was added to your coil. If you do not walk amongst your fellow man with an open heart, you will surely be doomed to walk amongst him when that heart is no more," Jacob explained. "And then you will feel the pain of loss such that you have never felt before. The longing to participate in the human experience and the everlasting denial of that desire."

"But, Jacob, you were a practical man. Surely that is no sin," Ebenezer said. "And you were a good man of business." It was no longer clear whether Ebenezer was speaking of Jacob or of himself.

"Business!?" cried the ghost. "Mankind was my business! The common welfare was my business! Charity, mercy, forbearance and benevolence were all my business! The dealings of my trade were but a grain of sand in the comprehensive desert of my business!"

The ghost let out a mighty and sorrowful wail that frightened Ebenezer, causing him to cover his ears.

"Ebenezer, I have been attempting to make contact with you from the very moment of my passing. Before it, even. Many an invisible hour have I spent by your side trying to reach out, trying to warn you, trying to save you. Only now have I been successful in materializing before you. But my time grows short. So listen carefully," Jacob's ghost said.

"Yes, Jacob. I am listening," said Ebenezer.

"I am here to tell you that you have yet a chance and hope of escaping my fate. A chance and hope of my procuring, Ebenezer," the ghost said.

"You were always a good friend to me, Jacob," Ebenezer said. "Thank you."

"You will be haunted by three spirits," said Jacob.

Ebenezer's eyes grew wide. He had quite enough of being haunted by one.

"Is there no other way?" Ebenezer asked.

"Without their visits, your sad fate will be sealed for all of eternity," said Jacob. "Tonight is Christmas Eve. Tomorrow is Christmas Day."

"Yes, Jacob," Ebenezer said. "That is true."

"Expect the first spirit at the stroke of midnight, just as Christmas arrives. The second will visit when the clock strikes one. And the third, when the bells chime two," said Jacob. "Now, look to see me no more. I shall pray for you, Ebenezer."

At that, the apparition faded from view so that Ebenezer was once again alone in the room. He was more exhausted than before and not certain if what he had just experienced was for truth or if it existed only within the confines of his mind.

In either event, he needed his rest. Ebenezer trudged over to his bed and fell heavily upon it. In seconds, he was fast asleep.

3

As the clock struck twelve, Ebenezer's eyes fluttered open. While he was enjoying a sound sleep, something within brought him out of unconsciousness very gently.

"Is it morning?" Ebenezer asked himself. But as he listened to the bells chiming one after the other, he knew that it was still the middle of the night.

Ebenezer observed that the bed curtain to his left side was open, while all of the rest were securely shut. He looked out past his bedframe and jumped in fright when he realized that there was a man sitting in a chair beside his bed, looking at Ebenezer with a smile.

The man was quite short and rotund. He was wearing a white shirt and a red tie. Over his shirt, he wore a red and green plaid vest, with matching trousers. Over the vest, he wore a green waistcoat. Atop his head was a green top hat.

"Who are you, sir, and what are you doing in my bedchamber?" Ebenezer exclaimed. "I keep nothing here worth stealing, if that is your purpose."

"Oh, Ebenezer. Poor, dear Ebenezer," the stranger said with a smile. "I come not to take anything from you. I come only to give."

"You know my name. Yet we have not been acquainted," Ebenezer observed.

"There was a time, long ago, when I was not such a stranger to you," the man said.

"Oh? You do not look familiar," Ebenezer said, holding the blanket up to his chin.

"After so many years that you have turned away from me, this does not surprise," the man said. "It saddens. But it does not surprise."

"I ask you again. Who are you?" Ebenezer demanded.

"Have you no idea after your earlier meeting this evening in this very room?" the man asked with a knowing glance.

Ebenezer was startled at the mention of his otherworldly encounter with Jacob Marley. He had convinced himself that this had been nothing but a dream. Perhaps he was still experiencing a dream at this moment.

The short, stout man leaned forward in his chair and smiled at Ebenezer.

"This is not a dream, Ebenezer," the man said with a knowing wink. "Nor was your interaction several hours ago. Although a great many men would surely dream of having the opportunity Mr. Marley procured for you."

If Ebenezer was startled before, he was entirely stunned by these words. This impish man inexplicably sitting by Ebenezer's side just swept into his mind and heard his very thoughts. His identity now seemed clear, yet impossible.

"Are you the spirit whose coming was foretold to me?" Ebenezer asked.

The man smiled, showing teeth.

"Our first miracle! He allows his eyes to open but a whit. It is a promising first step," the small man said happily. "Yes, I am he."

He stood and gave a deep bow.

"What am I to call you?" Ebenezer asked.

"I am the Ghost of Christmas Past," the petite figure stated.

Ebenezer did not understand.

"Long past?" Ebenezer asked.

"No," the spirit replied, with a twinkle in his eye. "Your past."

As Ebenezer pondered this, the small spirit reached over and touched Ebenezer's arm.

"Come. Rise and walk with me," the spirit said.

Ebenezer felt a lightness in his chest as the ghost's hand was upon him. Without realizing he was doing so, Ebenezer was alighting from his bed and sliding his feet into his slippers. He lifted himself up from the bed and stood facing the tiny spirit before him. The apparition stood no higher than Ebenezer's waistline.

As they stood there, the ghost smiled up at Ebenezer.

"Are we to take a journey?" Ebenezer asked.

"Oh, yes. We shall travel together far and wide," the spirit replied.

"Then perhaps I should dress and wear my warm coat," Ebenezer suggested. "I have been in battle with a cold for several days now."

"There is no need to dress. You will remain warm," said the spirit. "As for your illness…"

The spirit reached up and touched Ebenezer in the center of his chest. Immediately, a warm sensation began to radiate outward from the spot on which the spirit was in contact. It spread throughout Ebenezer's body. He could not remember feeling so comfortable in a room before. The nip in the air was gone. Furthermore, his head felt clear and his breathing easy. He had never felt so healthy and strong.

"What did you do?" Ebenezer asked in amazement.

"Repairing a body is not difficult because it is ultimately of no consequence. Our true task at hand is the repair of your soul. And I assure you, this cannot be accomplished by my mere touch," the spirit said. "Shall we begin?"

"I fear that I do not have the option to decline," Ebenezer replied.

"You are not a man who turns his back on opportunity. Come now," the spirit said. "Take my hand"

Ebenezer did so and at that very instant, he realized he was not in his bedchamber. He was in the foyer of a house he did not at first recognize. Suddenly, there was a mighty crack of thunder overhead. Ebenezer jumped in fright.

"Still fearful of Zeus' clap," the spirit observed.

"Spirit, where are we?" Ebenezer asked.

"You do not recognize this place?" the spirit asked with a smile.

"Well, it cannot be what I believe it to be," Ebenezer said, looking around. "Why, this looks to be my childhood home. But how can that be? Are we trespassers in another's house?"

"Ebenezer, do not doubt your instincts. As for your worry about trespass, these are but the shadows of the things that have been," said the spirit. "None we encounter will have any consciousness of us."

Another crash of thunder.

Ebenezer cringed.

At that, Ebenezer began to hear the sound of a female voice singing from one of the rooms above.

"No, it cannot be," Ebenezer said to the spirit. "Is that Fan singing to me to calm my nerves on this frightful night?"

"Let us see," said the ghost, and with a touch of Ebenezer's hand, they both floated up to the second floor and into the room from where the singing was emanating.

Ebenezer noted right away that this was not his childhood bedchamber, but was that of his father. Sitting in a chair on the far side of the room was a beautiful young woman quite far along with child. She had flowing red curly hair and tender blue eyes. She was gently rubbing her belly and singing to the baby within. The tune and words were familiar.

> *'Twas the night and the light*
> *From every little star*
> *Shone so bright at the height*
> *Of their homes so way afar.*

Now that the rain o'er the plain
Has ceased in its descent
And the sight of the night
To mine eyes is heaven sent.

The air so clear, my dear
The cool breeze upon my cheek
Free from fear, peace is near
And hope is at its peak.

"Oh my," Ebenezer said, placing his hand over his mouth. "Is that my mother?"

"It is," the spirit confirmed.

"Then that means…" Ebenezer began.

"Yes, the child within is you, Ebenezer. She sings to you," the spirit said.

"But, Spirit," Ebenezer said, unable to take his eyes from his mother. "You said you were the Ghost of Christmas Past. It is clearly not Christmas on this day."

"Ebenezer," the ghost said with a sigh. "Open your mortal mind. The spirit of Christmas is not confined to but once a year. It exists within all of us all of our days. It is for man to grasp it at any and all times. So, yes, while the calendar does not read the twenty-fifth of December here and now, the spirit of Christmas is ever present still."

Ebenezer considered this information.

"Do you know this tune?" the ghost asked.

"Yes. Fan used to sing it to me when I was in need of comfort," Ebenezer remembered. "But, in truth, I have never heard it sung so beautifully as I do now."

Trust in Me, trust in Me
All your lives are in My hands
And you'll see that you're free
If love reigns throughout your lands.

From the lea to the sea
When all is said and done
I love each of thee, said He
God bless us, everyone.

I love each of thee, said He
God Bless Us, Everyone.

Ebenezer's eyes were transfixed on his mother.

When Elizabeth finished her tune, she gently caressed her stomach. She could feel that her baby was asleep inside of her.

"That's right. Sleep my little man. I know you are a boy. I can feel it," Elizabeth said. "But do not tell your father. I wish for it to be a surprise. It will be our little secret for now. I tell you something that is no secret. I love you, even now and for always. I know you will grow to be a great man. I have seen you in my dreams. I know that you will be kind and gentle and all others will know your name for these traits. I cannot wait to meet you at last!"

"To be loved so deeply, even before one's birth is a great gift, indeed!" said the ghost. "But that man of whom she speaks. Do you know him?"

Ebenezer continued to stare at his mother, but had no response for the ghost.

Suddenly, it became quite windy and a strong breeze blew into Ebenezer's face. When he looked about, he realized he was no longer in his mother's bedroom. He was now outside in the family orchard. He was standing upon the branch of a tree, ten feet off of the ground. At his ankles was a young boy with red hair sitting on the branch and giggling with his hand over his mouth so as to muffle his sound.

Ebenezer recognized the boy as himself at approximately five or six years of age. He could feel the exhilaration of being so high off of the ground with the wind blowing through his hair. Ebenezer closed his eyes and turned his face to the heavens, soaking in this wondrous sensation.

"Ebenezer? Ebenezer, where are you?" a girl's voice called from below.

Ebenezer looked down and there below him was Fan. Young again, no more than ten years old. It had been so long since Ebenezer had laid eyes on her. A tear escaped his eye.

"It is your turn, Ebenezer," Fan said.

They were now inside the home, within Ebenezer's bedroom. The children were on the floor, playing dominos.

"Look at the fun these two are having," the ghost observed.

"Fun? Of course we had fun," Ebenezer said, watching them intently. "Fan always made sure we had fun."

The children finished and it was clear that young Ebenezer was the winner.

"Congratulations, Ebenezer!" cried Fan. "And for your prize, I shall hug you and tell you I shall love you forever!"

Young Ebenezer laughed and embraced his sister.

"You always say that, Fan," young Ebenezer said.

"And so she did," the ghost said. "A promise she kept, would you not agree?"

"Of course," said Ebenezer. "She always did."

"But even her love could not keep the two of you together always, isn't that so?" the ghost asked.

"No," Ebenezer said, his eyes growing cold. "Father hated me and he took her from me. He sent me away."

"Ah, yes," the ghost said. "Worthington."

Ebenezer's teeth ground as he spoke.

"Worthington."

4

The image of Fan and young Ebenezer shimmered away as though it were a mere reflection in a still pond being disturbed by a skipping stone. As the world around him returned to focus, Ebenezer found himself on a country road on a clear, cold winter day, with snow upon the ground.

Ebenezer recognized it instantly and he was none too pleased.

"I was bred in this place. I was a boy here," Ebenezer said somberly.

"Do you know the way?" the ghost asked.

"Sadly, I do. Up ahead is Bailey Hall," Ebenezer said.

"Let us take a closer look," the ghost said and in an instant, they were indoors, standing within the Headmaster's office. Ten-year-old Ebenezer was sitting in the hard wooden chair facing the Headmaster's desk. Headmaster Stowe was glaring at the boy as he sat in his seat.

"You spent many an hour in this room, did you not?" the spirit asked.

"Yes. Too many hours," Ebenezer responded.

"Mr. Scrooge, what must we do to convince you to take your studies here at Worthington seriously?" Headmaster Stowe was saying.

"I do take them seriously, sir," young Ebenezer responded.

"Impossible! One could not succeed less if he was making the effort to do so!" Headmaster Stowe chided.

Young Ebenezer hung his head.

"He was always very hard on you," the ghost observed.

"Yes, right from the first moment," Ebenezer agreed.

"You took from him the lesson that one must have power over others to lead a happy life," the ghost said.

"A true lesson indeed," Ebenezer said as he watched his younger counterpart absorb further verbal abuse.

"A false lesson," the ghost corrected. "One that has not served you well."

"What is that you say?" Ebenezer asked in surprise, turning his attention down to the diminutive spirit.

"Yes, Ebenezer," the ghost said. "Power is a responsibility, not a sword to wield with malice. It is sad you did not learn to shun the abuses to which you were subject but instead sought to emulate them. Not all of your authority figures treated you thusly."

"No?" Ebenezer said with an ironic laugh. "It certainly seemed so during those years."

"Cast your eyes to your left," the ghost instructed.

Ebenezer did so and was now in a classroom. Young Ebenezer was engaged in a lively discussion with a professor whose back was facing the room at the moment. When he turned, Ebenezer immediately recognized him as Professor Gerald Devereaux. Without realizing it, Ebenezer broke out into a smile.

"Tell me why you believe that to be so," Professor Devereaux asked young Ebenezer.

"He was always doing that, old Devereaux," Ebenezer said. "So many questions. So few answers. It was a wonderful way to learn."

Ebenezer and the spirit listened in as the two individuals in the room discussed a matter of religious importance as though they were colleagues and not teacher and student. It was enriching and it was stimulating.

"You see," the ghost said. "He had great power over you. But he used it to help you grow. He treated you with respect."

"It is true, to be sure," Ebenezer agreed.

"Worthington was not entirely a series of negative experiences as your memory would fool you to believe," the ghost said.

"I suppose that is true," Ebenezer conceded. "Professor Devereaux was an exception."

"Only he?" the ghost asked. "Had you no friends?"

"But a few," Ebenezer replied.

"Look," the ghost instructed.

They were now in the second floor dormitory room of Reginald Jones. Reginald was reading one of Fan's letters to young Ebenezer.

Ebenezer was captivated by his sister's words. As he listened, he was remembering how he felt to hear Fan's thoughts and her description of her love for him. Ebenezer was speechless and his eyes began to water. He had forgotten how important these letters were to him. And how grateful he felt that he had Reginald to bring Fan's words to life for him.

"It seems that there was good to be found at Worthington," the ghost said.

"Yes, well, it was quite overshadowed by the negative," Ebenezer retorted.

"Only you can cast such a shadow. And since that is so, you have the power to lift that shadow if you choose. That is real power," the ghost said. "Life is about choices. Choices dictate perspective. Perspective guides fate."

Ebenezer pondered what he had just been told.

"Where are we now?" the ghost asked.

Ebenezer turned his head and saw that he was now standing just outside of Room 3C in Kensington Hall.

"Enter," the ghost instructed.

They did so and they saw a young boy, perhaps eleven or twelve years old sitting on his bed with his bags packed all around him. He was peering out the window upon the main doorway outside. The rest of the room was vacant.

"This boy awaits a carriage that will not come," said the ghost.

"I know all too well," Ebenezer said sadly.

"Tell me, why did you pack for home each year for the Christmas holiday?" the ghost asked.

"Foolishness. The foolishness of a child," Ebenezer responded curtly.

"I tend to disagree," the ghost countered. "I do not see a foolish boy before me. I see one filled with hope."

"Hope that is dashed year after year is foolishness!" Ebenezer responded.

"It was not dashed every year," the ghost stated.

"That is true," Ebenezer admitted.

"Ebenezer! Ebenezer!"

Ebenezer turned around and observed eighteen-year-old Fan entering Room 3C. It was now morning.

Ebenezer watched as Fan walked up to twelve-year-old Ebenezer's bed and watched him sleep. He seemed to be struggling within a nightmare. She put her hand upon his shoulder.

"Ebenezer," she said as she touched him.

Young Ebenezer awoke with a start and screamed out, frightening Fan.

Ebenezer watched with a smile as he witnessed his reunion with his sister all those years ago.

"How did it come to be that Fan was permitted to bring you home from Worthington on this fateful day?" the ghost inquired.

"As I recall, she said that Father had changed. He asked her what she would desire for Christmas and she responded by asking if I may come home. He agreed," said Ebenezer.

"What made this Christmas different from all previous?" asked the ghost.

"I do not know. Nor do I care," Ebenezer said.

"I believe it is time you knew the answer to this question," the ghost stated.

At that, Ebenezer and the ghost were standing in Elias Scrooge's bedchamber. It was night and Elias was sleeping. He was not having a restful slumber.

Ebenezer looked at his father. Elias looked so much older than his mere thirty-eight years. His skin was pale with a yellow tinge and it lacked all luster. His hair was almost entirely white. He was far too thin throughout most of his frame, although his belly protruded outward. He was clearly not a well man.

"Why do we stand here before my sleeping father?" Ebenezer asked.

"Because, despite your claim that you do not care, within his dreams lies the answer to that which you have wondered your entire life," said the ghost. "Why did he summon you home? Come and we shall see."

The ghost put his hand upon Ebenezer's back and the two of them entered Elias' dream.

As Ebenezer and the ghost observed, Elias sat up in his bed within his mind's eye. The door to his room opened and there, standing before him, was his long lost Elizabeth. He leapt to his feet, tears immediately streaming down his face, and he ran to her.

"Elizabeth! Can it truly be you?" Elias asked through his tears.

"Yes, my Elias. I am here," Elizabeth responded.

Elias grabbed his wife and engulfed her in a tight embrace.

"I have missed you so, my Elizabeth," Elias cried.

Elizabeth stepped back and put her hand upon Elias' cheek.

"Elias, I do not have much time," Elizabeth said. "I have come to inquire about our children."

"Oh, Fan is wonderful. Such a beautiful young woman she has become. So intelligent. So wise. So strong. I would not have been able to survive these lonely years without you had it not been for her."

"That is wonderful," said Elizabeth. "And what of our Ebenezer?"

Elias looked to his feet.

"Elias, speak to me of our son!" Elizabeth pleaded.

"He is fine," Elias said. "He attends Worthington."

"He is fine? He attends Worthington?" repeated Elizabeth. "Why can you not tell me more?"

Elias stared at Elizabeth, but he had no further words to speak of Ebenezer.

"Elias, tell me you have cared for our son as we intended," Elizabeth implored.

"I cannot," Elias said at last. "In truth, I have never been able to look at the boy. He has your eyes. He has your smile. It pains me that he took you from me."

"Elias!" Elizabeth exclaimed. "Our Ebenezer did not take me from you! It was what was meant to be. I had to go so that you may have your son. Of course he has my eyes! It is so you may always see me looking back at you, even when I am far. I cannot accept that you did not care for our little boy!"

Elizabeth then did something she never did in life. Due to Elias' actions, she wept tears of pain.

The sight tore through Elias like an axe hewing through a tree.

"You have broken my heart, Elias," Elizabeth sobbed. "You have disappointed me. I trusted you with our children. And now I learn you used one as a crutch and you tossed the other away? All due to your selfishness and self-pity? What kind of man are you, Elias? Not the man I married to be sure! I am so ashamed!"

"No, Elizabeth. My poor, sweet Elizabeth. Do not cry. I am sorry for my wrongs. I will make amends. I will make amends," Elias cried.

"I must go now, Elias," Elizabeth said. "Repair our family. Love our children. Remove this pain you have caused me."

"Please do not go, Elizabeth! Please do not leave me again!" Elias pleaded.

"Elias, I never truly left you. Look into Ebenezer's eyes and you will see me. Listen for Fan's laugh and you will hear me," Elizabeth said as she began to fade away. "But turn your back on either of our children and you turn your back on me. Only by doing so will I truly be gone forever."

At that, Elizabeth was gone.

Elias woke up, his cheeks wet with tears.

"I will make amends, Elizabeth," Elias said as he sat up in bed. "I swear it to you."

"Your mother protected you, even from beyond the grave," the spirit noted.

"Was she real, Spirit? Or did we simply witness a guilty dream of a pickled sot?" Ebenezer asked.

"Does it matter?" the spirit replied.

"It matters," Ebenezer said. "Because if that was my mother, my father let her down yet again. Clearly, his hatred for me outweighed his love for her."

"Why do you say this?" asked the spirit.

"His own words betrayed his true thoughts," Ebenezer said.

"Ah, you speak of the missives he penned to both you and your sister," the ghost said.

"I do," said Ebenezer.

"Perhaps it is time light is shone upon that as well," the ghost said. "Things are not always as they seem."

Ebenezer and the ghost remained standing in Elias' bedchamber, but the room changed around them. It was early morning. Elias was at his desk. Upon the desk was a note wrapped in ribbon. On its face, it read, "Do not open until X-mas". This was the Christmas note Elias had written for Fan. It sat atop a portrait of Fan that Elias had drawn, his first artistic expression he attempted since his Elizabeth died all those years prior.

At his desk, Elias was endeavoring to write a proper note to Ebenezer, but he struggled for words.

He wrote:

My son Ebenezer,

I have hated you for your entire life. In granting you life, my Elizabeth sacrificed her own and I have never been able to forgive you

This was as far as he was able to pen before he stopped himself.

"What am I writing?" Elias asked himself in shock. "This is most dreadful! This is most inappropriate! This is worthy of nothing but kindling! Which is what it shall be!"

Elias then set that parchment aside and attempted to begin anew.

"So, the missive you read was intended to be consumed by flames and reduced to ash," observed the ghost.

"So it would seem," Ebenezer said, bewildered.

"Nor were these the last thoughts that passed through your father's mind on this earth," the ghost added.

Ebenezer looked at the ghost and then back at his father.

Elias dipped his quill in ink and began anew.

My dear son Ebenezer,

I have been unfair to you from the moment of your birth. You were a blessing from above, but I did not treat you as such. I was so consumed with grief due to the loss of your mother that I could not see past my pain to recognize the wonderful gift I had before me. I was wrong to blame you for my loneliness. No! It was my own foolishness and selfishness that robbed me of a full and happy life with my wonderful family.

Ebenezer

I must ask something of you that is truly unfair, but I must ask it nonetheless. I ask for your forgiveness. I ask for your benevolence in granting a thoughtless old man a second chance to be the father you deserve and have always deserved. I ask that we be permitted to begin anew.

I cannot explain to you what has happened to open my eyes after so many years of err. I doubt you could believe it if I did. But please remember this. Miracles are real. When one comes your way, embrace it with your whole heart and body and soul. You are a miracle. And this is how I intend to embrace you from now until forever.

I love you, my son. In truth, I always have. I felt too much pain to allow myself to experience said love. I will not allow such mistake to continue. As you read these words, we should be in the midst of a grand celebration. Christmas and your birthday. Two great events converged on the same day of the calendar. The two most important men in my life brought to earth on the same day of the year.

I wish you a merry, merry Christmas and a happy, happy birthday! I shall forever after show you the love your mother showed all of us all of her days – unyielding, unending and complete. You deserve nothing less. I only wish I could give more.

All my love, all my life,

Father

Ebenezer observed as Elias smiled as he read over his note to ensure that he said all that he intended.

"Your eyes," the spirit noted. "They are moist."

"Yes, I must have acquired a speck of dust," Ebenezer said quickly, wiping away the tears he could not control.

"Your father loved you," the ghost told Ebenezer.

"Spirit, if this letter was truly penned as we have seen before us, why did I not find it anywhere in the room on the day of my father's passing?" Ebenezer said skeptically.

"Watch, Ebenezer," the spirit said. "Watch. But prepare yourself."

Elias continued to read his note, but, without realizing it, began to sweat quite profusely. As his eyes scanned the page, he began to flex his left arm and pump his left fist in an effort to alleviate the stiffness and pain he was now experiencing. As he finished his last word, his eyes snapped up in fear. He knew something was dreadfully wrong.

It was then he felt a great pressure upon his chest and he brought his right hand up in a fruitless effort to quell such pain. His hand curled into a claw and he could not breathe. He looked about for the last time and then all went dark.

His body fell to the floor, upending the chair in which he was sitting. He landed with a mighty thud that shook his desk. The letter he had just written to Ebenezer floated off of the desktop and wafted to the ground. By a stroke of bad luck, when it arrived at the floor, it was positioned such that it slid directly between the wooden slats of the ground level behind Elias' now still head. In several hours, when Fan will enter the room, this letter will be nothing more than a forgotten memory of a tragic man.

Ebenezer was stunned by what he witnessed.

"This letter slid through the floor cracks?" Ebenezer asked.

"It remains there still, covered in dust but uncovered by any human eye," the spirit informed him.

Ebenezer shook his head in disbelief. He was overwhelmed by what he had just witnessed.

"Please, Spirit," Ebenezer said as his father's dead eyes stared at him from their resting place upon the floor. "Please, take me from this place."

"As you wish," the spirit stated.

At that, Elias' bedroom and him with it melted away and Ebenezer found himself standing beside the spirit in a roadway in London directly before a business establishment owned and operated by one Francis Fezziwig.

5

"You recognize this establishment, no doubt," said the ghost.

"Recognize it?" Ebenezer asked with a sad smile. "I should say so. This is old Fezziwig's counting house. I was apprenticed here."

"Tell me about Francis Fezziwig," the ghost requested.

"He was the kindest man I ever knew. Everyone who met with him came away better for it," Ebenezer said. "I wish I could say that everyone with whom he came into contact did the same for him."

"Come. Let us pay a visit on the kind man," the ghost said.

At that moment, Ebenezer and the spirit were standing in the counting house on a bright, warm day. Fourteen-year-old Ebenezer was working away as Fezziwig was leaning over his shoulder, observing his efforts. Fezziwig had a broad smile on his face and he was nodding up and down as he was praising Ebenezer's efforts.

"He encouraged you," said the spirit. "He loved the way your mind worked."

"He certainly said so," Ebenezer replied, watching the scene before him with bittersweet tears in his eyes.

"Are you moved?" asked the ghost.

"I am," admitted Ebenezer. "And pained."

"Why feel pain? All I witness is kindness," said the ghost.

"I witness a good man who will end his days cursing the name of the boy he now so affectionately encourages" Ebenezer replied.

"Come, let us see more," the ghost said, and he touched Ebenezer's hand.

Now they were in the ballroom of the Fezziwig home. Margaret Fezziwig was sitting with a book in her hand. Young Ebenezer sat across from her with a book of his own of the same title as that of Margaret's.

She was assisting him in his efforts to master reading.

Ebenezer sighed heavily as he watched. Margaret maintained her smile, even when young Ebenezer erred. She exercised endless patience with him and cheered his accomplishments, great and small. It was no wonder, Ebenezer realized, that he was capable of being such a good student for her. He wanted to please her. He wanted to make her proud. And her methods were so effective because she took the time to understand how Ebenezer would best learn. Hers was a magic the power of which could not be matched in any fairy tale she taught him to read.

"There is no doubt both Fezziwigs loved you and were proud of you," the spirit observed.

"Yes, "Ebenezer said. "I wish it were not so."

"Why, Ebenezer?" asked the spirit.

"Because had they not done so, I would not have been capable of securing for them such an unfortunate end," Ebenezer lamented.

"You speak of the investment scheme of Victor Ferguson," the ghost said.

"I do," said Ebenezer. "And bringing the plague that was Ferguson to the Fezziwigs' doorstep at the outset."

"Perhaps you should not blame yourself for the actions of an older, conniving scoundrel," said the ghost. "It was out of your hands from the start,"

"What is that you say?" Ebenezer said.

"Do you remember how you met Victor Ferguson?" asked the ghost.

"Of course. I was the victim of a pickpocket and he apprehended the perpetrator. If not for Ferguson, I would have lost all of Mr. Fezziwig's funds that he had sent with me to satisfy his ink order," Ebenezer said. "As it turns out, I would have lost a great deal less had the thief escaped on that day."

"Are you certain he did not escape with ill-gotten gains in his pocket that morning?" the ghost asked. "Look."

Ebenezer and the ghost were now in office of Victor Ferguson, a location Ebenezer recognized immediately. They were standing next to Ferguson who was busy reviewing a document when the front door to his establishment opened. Three young boys, dirty and disheveled entered.

"Do these lads look familiar to you?" the ghost asked.

"They do, Spirit, but I cannot place them at the moment," Ebenezer said, studying them carefully.

"In a moment, all will be clear," the spirit said.

Ferguson looked up from his work when the boys passed through his front door. He stood up with a wide smile as he greeted them.

"Hello, boys!" Ferguson said. "Fine work today. Fine work indeed."

"Thank you, Mr. Ferguson, sir," said one.

"I didn't hurt you too badly when I grabbed you and dragged you down to our new friend, did I, Wagner?" Ferguson asked with a smile.

"No, sir," the boy named Wagner replied. "Not a bit."

Ebenezer now recognized these three. They were the band of pickpockets who ran into him on the street on that fateful day. He identified Wagner as the boy whom Ferguson accosted and it was he who was in possession of Fezziwig's money. What was going on here?

"I suppose you are all here to collect for a hard day's work?" Ferguson asked, reaching into his desk.

"That we are, sir," the third boy responded. Ebenezer recognized him as the one who turned to apologize after the three almost knocked Ebenezer from his feet.

"It was well earned," Ferguson said, removing his hand from his desk with the remuneration intended for his three nefarious accomplices. "Here, take this with my blessing, and be prepared for more opportunities coming your way."

Wagner took the money and the three boys thanked Ferguson. They then retreated out the door and into the city.

Ferguson watched them go with a grin.

"It was well earned, to be sure. I have taken my first step with Fezziwig. And that Scrooge boy may prove to be most useful. Yes, most useful indeed," Ferguson said to the empty room, smiling to himself.

Ebenezer stared in shock as he watched as Ferguson settle back to his work.

"Spirit, I do not understand," Ebenezer said.

"I believe you do, though you may not wish to accept it quite yet," the spirit replied. "Ferguson's encounter with you was no mere accident. You were the key he used to gain entry into Fezziwig's circle. Had it not been you, it would have been another. It was not your fault."

Ebenezer walked over to where Ferguson was working and watched him for a moment with a scowl.

"So, you used me from the start, did you?" Ebenezer said. "I am only sorry that you were murdered by another so that I cannot now complete the dark task myself!"

"From that day forward, whether you realize it or not, these two men, Fezziwig and Ferguson, were engaged in a battle for your soul," the spirit said. "Come Ebenezer, allow us to witness a sample of their efforts," the spirit said.

The ghost touched Ebenezer's elbow and the room before him began to spin. When it stopped, Ebenezer was present at the Fezziwig dining room table where Fezziwig was speaking to Ebenezer's younger self, along with the other apprentices prior to enjoying a hearty meal.

"Remember, boys, why we say grace before each meal. Because

nothing is more important than recognizing that nothing can be accomplished without our Creator. His hands are involved in everything we do and His eyes are on us always. The material world is but a shadow of the greater universe in which we live. That is why it is what is inside that is paramount. Truth, honesty, goodwill. These are our true riches. Money is but a tool. It buys us what we need. It allows us certain comforts. But at the end of our days, when we are standing before the Creator, we will be proven to be nothing more than fools if we are to reach into our pockets when asked what we have brought with us from the earthly plain. Our integrity, our charity, our character will be present. Our gold will not. In Heaven, gold is nothing more than a shiny rock. Coins, nothing more than meaningless discs. Folding money, nothing more than worthless paper. Remember this boys, so that you may keep in perspective what is important all of your days and so that you may know how to measure true success. Now let us eat."

The room and all within it once again spun before Ebenezer's eyes and when it ceased its rotation, Ebenezer was standing in Ferguson's establishment. Victor Ferguson was instructing young Ebenezer.

"It is only the great fool who believes money to be of no true value. I find that those who espouse such fall into one of two categories. The first such person has so much wealth that he has forgotten the miseries of having none or was raised in riches, never having known poverty's cruel kiss. I challenge you to find such a man who claims money to be of no value to him and then voluntarily divests himself entirely so as to live among the poor and the wretched. You will sooner find a unicorn who speaks fluent French.

"The second such person who makes such a claim has little or no wealth and sees no prospect of changing his fate. He then bemoans the value of money as unnecessary to live a happy life because if he did not, he would be acknowledging his own worthlessness. In truth, as I am sure you have already discovered, although it may not be popular to voice aloud, money brings all of the advantages life has to offer. If nothing else, it brings a full belly, a warm home, comfortable clothing and, above all, dignity and respect. I challenge you to prove me false."

"You had a choice between these two conflicting philosophies," the spirit said. "More and more, you shifted your views towards that of Ferguson."

"His was the more practical," Ebenezer said simply.

"Was it?" the spirit said. "We shall see if you still believe so when our time together is through."

"What is that to mean?" Ebenezer asked.

"Ferguson convinced you that the pursuit for material wealth was the pursuit of your happiness. You learned from him that it would be the only way to win your lady love. The only way to secure a meaningful future. But was it so? No! This view of life landed Mr. Fezziwig in a debtor's prison. It sent Belle into the marriage bed of Nathaniel Weatherby. It sent Victor Ferguson to an early grave. And it sent you into a lonely existence where your business interests were your only companions through a cold and dreary life. I ask you, Ebenezer Scrooge, if money is the key to happiness, why are you not the happiest man in all of London?"

"Spirit, torment me no more!" Ebenezer cried.

"I am sorry, but for your benefit and salvation, I must continue," the ghost said calmly. "We go now to visit with the Fezziwigs after the Ferguson scheme has left them in poverty."

"No! Spirit, please no! I cannot bear it!" Ebenezer cried.

But at that moment, they found themselves within a room at Marshalsea Debtor's Prison. Margaret Fezziwig was sitting at a table, alone. The door opened and a guard brought Mr. Fezziwig in by the arm and pushed him into the room.

"You have five minutes," the guard growled, and then slammed the door shut behind him.

"Margaret, how did you accomplish this meeting?" Fezziwig said, embracing his one true love.

"I had to pay the guard for the privilege," she said.

"With what did you pay?" Fezziwig asked.

"My mother's brooch," Margaret said.

"Margaret! No! You should not have given that up!" Fezziwig cried.

"My love, it is but a thing. My mother is no less present in my heart if I do not possess her jewelry. And the feel of you in my arms at this moment is priceless!" Margaret replied.

"Oh, I do love you so!" Fezziwig said to his wife.

"Three minutes!" came an unfriendly call from beyond the door.

"How are you, Francis?" Margaret asked. "Please tell me the truth."

"I am fine, my love, except that I miss you terribly. And I feel such terrible guilt about how I let down our Ebenezer," Fezziwig said.

"I too worry about the boy," Margaret said. "He has disappeared. I cannot believe we were so rash as to throw him out into the cold. May God have mercy on our souls."

"Yes, to think that I am here, away from you, all because I allowed a wolf such as Ferguson to swallow up one of our sheep. I should have seen Ferguson for who he was from the start. Instead, I sent Ebenezer directly into the teeth of that predator. This is my punishment from God for failing to protect one of our boys, I am certain."

"Do you see what we are witnessing?" the spirit asked. "Francis Fezziwig did not curse you at the end of his days, as you have always suspected. He lamented his own failure to protect you."

Ebenezer was in shock at the conversation to which he was now witness.

"Even in poverty, look at these two. They continue to think of another – in this instance, you – rather than their own situation. Some might call this true greatness," the spirit said.

"Time!"

The surly guard re-entered the room and pulled Fezziwig away from his wife as they were in mid-embrace and mid-kiss.

"Come, Ebenezer," the spirit said, touching his arm. "It is time you confront your past as it relates to your own love."

The room in which Mrs. Fezziwig sat sad and alone began to move off into the distance until it was nothing but a speck in the darkness.

6

The speck in the darkness began to grow as it moved towards Ebenezer at great speed before it enveloped him entirely. Ebenezer and the spirit were standing in the Fezziwig garden on a calm Spring day. Fifteen-year-old Ebenezer was pacing nervously and sweating more than the outside temperature would warrant.

Belle came walking up on the path and startled young Ebenezer out of his thoughts within which he was clearly preoccupied.

"Oh, Ebenezer. There you are," Belle said.

Young Ebenezer jumped.

"I did not mean to frighten you," Belle said. She walked up to young Ebenezer and gave him a tight squeeze. He reciprocated, but was shaking slightly.

"Whatever is the matter, Ebenezer?" Belle asked, noting his perspiration. "Are you ill?"

"No, my sweet Belle," said young Ebenezer. "I just have something important on my mind. A question I have for you. No, more of a request. No, perhaps question is a better way to describe it."

"Calm down, Ebenezer," Belle said with a smile. "Whatever it is, I am sure I will be able to accommodate. What would you like to ask of me?"

"Well... what I mean to say is... that is, what I would like to ask is..." young Ebenezer stammered.

"Ebenezer," Belle said, putting her hands upon either side of his face. "Please calm yourself. You are beginning to worry me. Whatever it is, we can get through this together. I assure you. Now, what is it?"

Young Ebenezer took her hands in his and slowly lowered them from his face.

"Belle, I love you," young Ebenezer began.

"I love you as well, Ebenezer," Belle replied.

"I know it is too soon to make anything official as we are too young. But I wanted to ask you if you would agree to remain faithfully mine for the remainder of our days?" young Ebenezer finally asked.

"Are you asking me to marry you, Ebenezer?" Belle asked.

"Well, I am asking for permission to ask you to marry me when the time is right. And in the meantime, we remain promised to one another forever after," young Ebenezer explained.

"Oh yes, Ebenezer," replied Belle excitedly. "You have such permission. And I shall remain forever yours with all of my heart and soul!"

"You shall?" responded a very relieved young Ebenezer. "I am so happy to hear you say so. I am only sorry that I do not have any money so I cannot present you with a trinket to commemorate our vow. I apologize."

Belle smiled.

"I need no trinket, Ebenezer," Belle said. "Our words are ironclad and your request is as valuable to me as gold."

"She was one of a kind," the spirit said.

"She was," Ebenezer agreed.

"Why did you not follow through with this promise and marry her?" the ghost asked.

"Why?" Ebenezer asked ruefully. "Because she married another."

"She only did so when you left her no other choice," the ghost responded.

"Your information is incorrect," Ebenezer argued. "I could not marry her while I was living in virtual exile. It would not have been fair to her. She refused to understand the world for what it was."

"Perhaps you should have left this decision in her hands," the ghost suggested.

"No. I would not be responsible for having her live life in the shadows as I had been doing!" Ebenezer cried. "All she had to do was be patient and allow me to acquire enough so that I may emerge into the light. Instead she got engaged to that Weatherby fool!"

"I believe she told you that this engagement was forced upon her," said the spirit. "And she came to you so that you may avoid it by marrying her before her hand could be compelled to accept another man's ring."

"Hmph!" grunted Ebenezer. "And then she brings this man with her to my sister's home while she imposes an impossible ultimatum upon me. One she knew I would be unable to satisfy!"

"Oh, Ebenezer," the ghost said sadly. "All these years later and you still cannot see the truth. Look."

They were now at Fan and Fred's home. Belle looked at young Ebenezer with misery in her eyes. Ebenezer recognized this day immediately.

"No, Spirit," Ebenezer said. "I do not wish to see this."

"You must," the spirit insisted.

For reasons he could not explain, Ebenezer was powerless to look away.

"I do not believe that you speak the truth to me Ebenezer! It pains me to admit this, but now I know it is true. You do not intend to marry me. Another idol has replaced me in your heart," Belle said, tears in her eyes.

"What idol do you speak of?" young Ebenezer asked.

"A golden one," Belle said.

"Spirit, I will not relive this!" Ebenezer exclaimed, turning away from the scene before him and shutting his eyes. "Take me from here!"

"I cannot," the spirit said softly. "Now, watch."

The spirit lifted his hand and Ebenezer's eyelids raised against his will. Although he was certain he had turned away from the unfortunate couple in the death throes of their relationship, there they were, directly before his eyes.

Belle let out a mournful sigh.

"Very well. As you would have it," she said softly. "I release you."

"Have I ever sought your release?" young Ebenezer asked angrily.

"Not with your words," Belle said in the same sad tone as before.

"With what then?" young Ebenezer demanded.

"Ebenezer, I understand. Our promise is an old one. Made when we were but children. When you were poor and content to be so," Belle said quietly. "I see all now. Tell me true. Would you seek me out if we had met only yesterday?"

"You think I would not?" young Ebenezer asked, highly offended.

"Ah, now it is you who does not answer the query," Belle noted.

Ebenezer watched as Belle reached into the pocket of her dress. She produced the Promise Ring Ebenezer gave her the year she went on her two-month tour of Ireland with her family.

"Here, Ebenezer," Belle said, holding out the ring. "Take this. Keep it. When you gaze upon it, I hope you remember me fondly."

When young Ebenezer made no move, Belle placed the ring into young Ebenezer's hand and closed his fingers around it.

"Goodbye Ebenezer. May you be happy in the life you have chosen," Belle said, her voice cracking.

Belle then exited Fan's home, closing the door behind her and running towards the carriage that brought her from her home.

Ebenezer watched as his younger self stared down at the ring in his palm. He could stand this no longer.

"Go after her, you fool!" Ebenezer screamed into the face of his counterpart. "Wrest her from Weatherby by force if necessary!"

"But that is not what you did, is it?" the ghost said.

"No," Ebenezer replied with tears in his eyes.

Ebenezer and the spirit watched as young Ebenezer regretted his inaction and resolved to marry Belle. They saw as he opened the front door with a mighty heave and was about to speak when he saw Belle in the arms of another; the faceless man whose back was turned towards the house.

"Go to her anyway!" Ebenezer implored.

But young Ebenezer did not. His eyes narrowed, he looked down at the ring in his hand and he pressed it deep within his pocket. He then turned and stomped back into the house.

Ebenezer stood before his younger version with his arms outstretched.

"No. I will not allow you to make this mistake again!" Ebenezer cried as his younger self approached.

But when young Ebenezer reached Ebenezer's hands, he continued walking, passing directly through Ebenezer's body without slowing for even a moment.

Ebenezer turned around to witness his younger self continue down the hallway.

"Come, Ebenezer," the spirit said. "There is only one thing further you must observe before we leave this place."

"Please, Spirit, no more," Ebenezer pleaded. "I can take no more here."

"Yes, Ebenezer. One thing more," the spirit insisted.

The spirit touched Ebenezer's back and he was no longer within Fan's home. He was outside, beside the carriage. Ebenezer could now see the face of the man Belle was embracing. It was not Nathaniel Weatherby.

It was her older brother, Philip.

Ebenezer's mouth dropped open.

"Oh, Philip, it was terrible." Belle was crying into his chest. "Ebenezer and I are no more. I wished that you would act as witness as we eloped on this day. But now that shall never be!"

"Come, Belle," Philip said. "Let us go home. All will be well."

"But how can anything be well again?" Belle sobbed as Philip directed her to the waiting carriage, limping as a result of his war injury aboard Lord Nelson's ship at Corsica.

"I know it is difficult to envision right now, but it will be," Philip said. "I promise you, my sister."

She climbed into the carriage and Philip followed, with assistance from the driver.

Ebenezer stood with the ghost by his side as the carriage disappeared into the distance.

"It was her brother," Ebenezer said softly and in disbelief.

"There to act as witness to your marriage to Belle," the ghost said.

"All I had to do was call her name and all would have been revealed," Ebenezer said, still in shock.

"Yes," the spirit agreed. "But in your anger, your distrust of even those closest to you, you let her go and gave her to Nathaniel Weatherby."

"Spirit, tell me," Ebenezer said. "Has she lived a happy life?"

"Ebenezer, are you considering the welfare of another?" the spirit asked with a smile.

"Do not mock! Just answer!" Ebenezer snapped.

"Is that the question you truly intend to ask?" the spirit inquired.

"No," Ebenezer admitted, looking at his feet.

"What then?" asked the ghost.

"Has her life with Weatherby been happier than it would have been with me?" Ebenezer asked.

"That I cannot answer. For I can only see the past as it was, not as it might have been," said the spirit. "Now we must move on to the other woman in your life."

"Fan?" asked Ebenezer.

"Yes, Ebenezer," replied the spirit. "Fan."

7

As the spirit spoke her name, Fan appeared before Ebenezer's eyes. She was standing at the doorway looking out, her eyes watching as a carriage disappeared down the roadway. She was beaming. She emitted an aura of pure joy. Ebenezer studied her face, trying to memorize it for all time. It had been so long before this ghostly encounter that he had seen her and the details of her features had faded away. He did not wish for this to happen again.

There was something familiar about this day to Ebenezer, but he could not quite understand why. He watched as Fan sighed happily and then turned from her doorway and closed the door. She was alone in her house. She could not seem to stop herself from smiling. Her very skin was radiating euphoria.

"She seems so happy. Thank you, Spirit, for showing me something pleasant after what we have just witnessed with Belle," Ebenezer said, looking down at the spirit to his side. "Tell me. What day is it in Fan's life that she glows with such radiance?"

"It is the fourth of June, seventeen hundred and ninety-nine. Her third wedding anniversary," the spirit replied.

Ebenezer froze in fright. His smile vanished. He tensed at hearing the date and its significance.

"The fourth of June, seventeen hundred and ninety-nine, you say?" Ebenezer confirmed.

"Yes," replied the spirit.

"Then that means the person in the carriage my sister was just watching travel away was me," Ebenezer said.

"That is correct," the spirit stated.

"Oh no. This is a most terrible day," worried Ebenezer as he followed after Fan. "Why have you brought me here?"

"To see what you must see and nothing more," the spirit said.

"Fan, you must hear me. Leave this house. Go elsewhere for the day. Do not return until after nightfall," Ebenezer pleaded with his sister. But, of course, she heard nothing that he spoke. She simply carried on with her day.

"It is as I told you. These are but shadows of what has been. There is nothing you may do to change them," the spirit said.

"I must find a way. I must save her from what awaits," Ebenezer said desperately. "I will stay by her side all day and find some way to protect her from her fate."

"You cannot. Fate is the appropriate term to utilize. It is fate precisely because it cannot be changed. What has already occurred is immutable," explained the spirit. "Now come, we shall move several hours hence."

"No, Spirit. Allow me to remain here with Fan," Ebenezer pleaded.

But despite his plea, Fan faded from view and reappeared as she was cleaning within her dining area. Ebenezer could see by the position of the sun outside the window that they were considerably later in the day.

"Fan!" a voice called from the next room. "I am home."

It was Fred.

Fan exited the dining room and went to greet her husband.

"Oh, Fred, I am so glad you are home!" Fan said excitedly.

"Is that so?" Fred responded.

"Yes. I have wonderful news for you on this, our anniversary day," Fan said.

"And what would that be?" Fred asked.

"Fred, I learned of this several weeks ago, but I wanted to wait until today to share this news with you," Fan said.

"Yes?" Fred asked, somewhat impatiently.

"You are to be a father!" Fan squealed. "It has finally happened. After our many years of trying, I am with child!"

Fred stared at his wife, saying nothing.

"Is that not wonderful news?" Fan asked.

Still Fred said nothing.

Ebenezer tensed, sensing that something was very wrong.

"So, after three years with no success, you are suddenly with child?" Fred asked, somewhat menacingly.

Fan did not recognize his tone as hostile.

"Yes! Is it not wonderful?" Fan asked, as she ran to him and threw her arms around him. Fred did not reciprocate the embrace.

Fan stepped back.

"Fred, what is the matter? I thought you would be as thrilled about this news as I," said Fan, puzzled.

Fred looked at Fan askew.

"Whose child is this?" Fred demanded.

"What kind of question is that? Whose child could it be?" Fan asked in shock.

"You did not answer my query," Fred snarled, his anger clearly rising.

"Why, it is your child, of course," Fan said, highly offended.

"How could you do this to me, you harlot!" Fred exploded as he lashed out, striking Fan in the face with such force that it knocked her to the ground.

"Fred! Please do not do this!" Fan pleaded from her knees.

But Fred was beyond reasoning. He reached down and grabbed a handful of Fan's hair and dragged her to the bottom of the stairway where he slammed the side of her head into the newel post. It made a most unpleasant thud and Fan wailed in pain.

"Damn you, Fred!" Ebenezer screamed as he reached to grab his brother-in-law. But it was to no avail. Ebenezer's arms simply passed through Fred's body as though it were mist.

"Who has had his way with you?" Fred demanded, reaching down and grabbing Fan by the throat. "Tell me, or I will hurt you in ways you have never imagined!"

"No one," Fan choked. "I have been with no man except for you for my entire life. Please, Fred, stop this."

"Liar!" Fred spat and he struck Fan's face with the back of his hand, leaving an angry welt upon her jaw.

"Spirit, help me save her!" Ebenezer pleaded.

But the spirit just stood by with a sad look upon his face.

"This is what occurred and we cannot change it," the spirit explained.

Fred hurt his knuckle when it made contact with Fan's jaw on the prior blow. He grabbed his hand with his other.

"You bitch! You see what you have done to me!" Fred howled. He walked towards the table in his sitting room upon which were various bottles of liquor. He intended to pour himself a drink.

As he walked away, Fan scrambled up, now bruised and bleeding, and ran up the stairs towards her bedroom, with the thought that she would lock herself in. Fred saw what she was attempting and he became enraged.

"No you do not! I did not give you permission to leave!" Fred said, chasing her up the stairs.

She made it within two steps of the top when Fred overcame her. He grabbed her by the shoulders and spun her around. Because his right hand was throbbing from his most recent blow to Fan's face, he lost his grip on her. The force of his tug on her shoulders caused Fan to lose her balance.

She fell, heavily, down the staircase, crashing into each step along the way until her body thudded to the ground below.

She remained still as blood began to pool around her head.

"Fan!" Ebenezer exclaimed as he watched this terrible scene play out before him. He had always suspected that Fred was responsible for injuring Fan on this day. Why did he not remove her from his home sooner? All of Ebenezer's guilt flooded to the surface.

Fred peered down the stairs at his wife's unmoving body.

He walked slowly down the steps. When he reached her still frame, he simply stepped over her and went to prepare himself a drink. He downed a shot of whiskey and poured himself another. This too he drank quickly. He then poured himself a third, this time a full glass.

Fred walked to and sat down upon his settee and slowly sipped his drink, keeping his eyes on Fan's prone form. When he finished the libation, he walked over to Fan and squatted down to look at her closely. She appeared to have died.

"I suppose I should call the physician. Not that it appears that there will be much for him to do but to remove *this* from my home," Fred said callously.

Ebenezer glared at Fred.

"If I ever find you, I will end you!" Ebenezer said to Fred through clenched teeth.

Fred exited to call for the doctor.

Ebenezer knelt down by his sister.

"It will be okay, Fan. I will remain here with you," Ebenezer said to her.

"I am sorry, but we must move on," the spirit said.

"No! I will not leave her," Ebenezer insisted.

The spirit touched Ebenezer gently upon his back and they were now in Fan's bedchamber. She was sitting in a chair and was speaking to her belly.

"I can feel you in there, my sweet one," Fan said as she caressed her midsection. "Where did we leave off last time? Oh, yes, we were discussing your Uncle Ebenezer. He is a wonderful man and he will be a terrific uncle to you. I know if there is one person on this earth I can depend upon to love you as much as I do, it is your Uncle Ebenezer. I cannot wait to see the two of you together."

Ebenezer listened and his shame was immense.

"She really expected a wonderful relationship to develop between you and the child," the ghost stated.

"I did not know she ever even considered it," Ebenezer said softly.

"She did, and more," the ghost said. "Look."

They were still in Fan's bedchamber, but the snow outside the window told Ebenezer that several months had passed. Ebenezer looked down and observed Fan just after childbirth. She was barely clinging to life. Blood coated the bedsheets. The doctor looked down upon her with sad eyes. The midwife placed her baby into her arms. She began to speak to the infant boy, but in such low tones, her words were imperceptible.

Ebenezer looked sorrowfully at his sister.

"Spirit, I cannot hear what she says," Ebenezer lamented.

"Lean down, Ebenezer," the spirit commanded.

Ebenezer did so and the spirit placed his hands on each of Ebenezer's ears. Suddenly, all Fan was speaking was audible to Ebenezer.

"Hello, my little man. You are so beautiful. I am so glad to finally meet you. I am sorry because it seems that I must go away much sooner than I had expected. But I know you will be in good hands because your Uncle Ebenezer will always be there to look out for you and protect you," Fan said to the baby. "And so I shall name you after the most important man in my life, and who will surely be the most important in yours as well. I name you Ebenezer."

Ebenezer heard this and was taken aback in shock. What was he hearing?

"Spirit, is this correct?" Ebenezer asked.

"Just listen," the spirit said.

"I also name you Frederick, after your father. Deep down, I believe he is a kind and decent man, but on the surface I believe the drink has altered him. Do not try to live up to the greatness of your father's potential and do not try to live down his faults. You will be your own man and will follow your own path, my little Ebenezer Frederick. I will always love you, even when I am gone."

"Miss Fan," the midwife leaned in. "What would you like to name the baby?"

"Ebenezer..." Fan began in a whisper too low for the midwife to hear.

"I'm sorry. Please repeat the name again," the midwife asked gently.

"... Frederick," Fan said, just loud enough for the midwife to recognize the name.

"Frederick, you say? Very well," the midwife said softly to herself.

"Ebenezer," Fan said as her eyes began to close for the last time. "Take good care of my boy."

Those were her last words.

Ebenezer stood before his sister and began to sob as he had when he first learned she had died.

"You did not honor her dying wish," the spirit observed.

"No, I did not!" Ebenezer cried. "I am sorry, Fan. I am so very sorry. I did not know you relied on me as you did! I did not know the boy's intended name was my own! Please forgive me, Fan! Please forgive me!"

"You treated this boy as your father treated you. With disdain because of an irrational pain you felt looking at a child birthed by the most important women in your lives," the ghost noted.

"Yes, I see that now! I am so sorry, Fan!" Ebenezer said, crying uncontrollable tears.

"We must leave now. But I wish for you to look upon your sister one last time," the spirit informed Ebenezer.

The room faded away and Ebenezer was now viewing the world from a perspective he did not understand at first. It was as though he was in the arms of another. He then realized that he was looking at the world through his own infant eyes. He looked up and there, before him, was the face of five-year-old Fan examining him for the first time. Ebenezer could feel as she put her tiny hand upon his newborn forehead at which point she leaned in to him.

"I am your sister, Nancy Elizabeth Scrooge, but you may call me Fan. I shall love you all the days of my life. We do not have a Mummy, but you will always have me. I swear it."

Ebenezer's eyes then closed, the image of his big sister still fresh on the backsides of his eyelids.

"Thank you, Spirit," Ebenezer said peacefully in the darkness.

"Come, Ebenezer," the spirit's voice responded. "Our time runs short. We have but one more stop to make."

8

"Open your eyes, Ebenezer," the spirit said.

Ebenezer did so and saw that he was now in the bedchamber of Jacob Marley. Jacob was lying in his bed, his face gaunt and his blanket pulled up to his chin. His eyes were closed and his breathing shallow, but raspy and wet. Each inhale and exhale was accompanied by a grimace. He was clearly nearing the end and his was not to be a pleasant journey to the afterlife.

Ebenezer just stared at his ailing partner.

"You never saw Jacob on his dying day," the ghost said. "Not while he still lived."

"No," Ebenezer said tersely.

"Why did you not?" asked the spirit.

"I was quite busy with important tasks. Jacob would have quite understood. Had I been the unfortunate soul lying in my deathbed instead of he, I expect he would have made the same decision as I did on that day," Ebenezer said.

"Of that I have no doubt," the spirit replied. "But I believe there was more to your motivation than you choose to reveal to me here and now."

"More? What more could there be?" Ebenezer asked.

"I believe you knew what you would witness had you made haste and came to his bedside when you were first summoned early in the day. I believe you were angry with poor Jacob," said the spirit.

"Angry? Whatever for? That is preposterous!" responded Ebenezer.

"Is it? He was leaving you before you were ready to part, as others had done prior. You believed he was all you had left in this world for companionship. His was a kindred spirit," said the spirit softly.

"Nonsense. His servant came to me early in my workday and I could not abandon my tasks. To do otherwise would have been negligent and irresponsible," Ebenezer maintained.

"Ebenezer, do not forget to whom you are speaking. You may lie to yourself, but you cannot successfully do so to me. I know that there was nothing so pressing that several days of dust upon the papers that you were working would have made any difference whatever. And I know that you knew so as well," the spirit said firmly.

"That is not how I remember it," Ebenezer said stubbornly.

"You were visited twice that day by those imploring you to visit with your dying friend and partner. After the servant came Jacob's doctor. Why did you not heed his words?" the spirit asked.

"I simply recall the need to complete my work," Ebenezer said resolutely.

"Hmm. Let me ask you, Ebenezer. What occurred on the twenty-fourth of December, eighteen hundred and thirty-six?" asked the spirit.

"Jacob passed," Ebenezer replied.

"And what was the nature of the work so important that you could not visit with Jacob one last time at his request before his passing?" the spirit asked.

"I do not rightfully recall," Ebenezer stated.

"Aha. So the significance of the day remains with you as the day you lost your partner, but that which kept you from honoring his final wishes has been lost to time. It puts into perspective the importance of each," said the spirit.

Ebenezer peered silently at the spirit.

"You still could have arrived in time to speak with Jacob, even after your many delays, but instead of going to his home straightaway after you completed your very important work, the nature of which you cannot even remember at present, you made a stop to eat a meal," the spirit said.

"Yes, that is accurate," Ebenezer admitted.

"Was your denial so deep or your contempt so great that you chose to satisfy your hunger before your duty to honor a dying man's last request?" asked the ghost.

Ebenezer did not know how to answer. He simply stared at the small spirit to his right.

"Nevertheless, regardless of the reason, you never heard what Jacob called you to say," the spirit stated.

"Yes, that is true. Most unfortunate. I am sure it had something to do with our business," Ebenezer said.

"Do not be so sure," said the spirit. "Watch and see what poor, unfortunate Jacob observed on the morning of his passing."

As Jacob lay upon his bed, a great light burst forth within the room. Within the power of this light, Jacob's strength and voice returned as though his illness held no sway over his abilities. Jacob opened his eyes, struggling against the bright, searing whiteness and lifted his arm to shield his face from the light. When his eyes adjusted, he saw a figure standing before his bed.

"Father!" he cried.

"It is good that you recognize me," the bearded man replied calmly.

"Did you think I would not?" Jacob asked.

"It has been many a year since you have given me but a thought. I had feared you would not know my face."

"Why are you here?" Jacob asked.

"Your time is near. Soon you shall pass. I came to be with you."

"Ah. So we shall soon be together. I have so much to ask," Jacob said with a smile as he leaned his head back into his pillow.

"No. We shall not."

Jacob's head snapped towards his Father.

"What do you mean?" Jacob asked.

"I came to be with you at this time before you shuffle off of the mortal coil. I came to remind you that I love you, that I have always loved you and I will always love you still. But…"

"But what, Father?" Jacob asked in horror.

"But you have decided that we shall be forever separated as you enter the next dominion."

"I have made no such decision!" Jacob cried.

"You have. With the choices you made with your life and in your life."

"What is this rubbish?!" Jacob demanded.

"You see, my son, each soul is destined to walk among his fellow man in charity and goodwill. If it fails to do so during life, it must fulfill this destiny after death."

Jacob shifted his weight in his bed, but felt a great pressure holding him down. He looked at his arms and was shocked to see chains wrapped around each, with great weights attached to the many links. He looked to his legs and his torso, and around his chest and over his shoulders as well. More chains. More weights.

"Why have you bound me?" Jacob cried in despair.

"I have not."

"Lies! The evidence is right before you as I lie here chained and shackled!" Jacob accused.

"I have not," his Father repeated. "You bear the chains that you forged for yourself in your life. You have worn them for a great many years, but only now, at the end, shall you feel the weight of your decisions forevermore."

"Why have you allowed this to happen to me?" Jacob cried.

"I have never had the power to affect your decisions. You could have cast off your chains at any time during your life. Instead of removing them, you expanded upon them. You grew them. You ensured that you would be heavily laden."

With that, his Father put his hand on Jacob's forehead and looked into his eyes with compassion and love. In that instant, Jacob understood everything. The chains pressed down harder.

"A moment of understanding, and an eternity of consequences!" Jacob cried. "Woe is me!"

"You will never be alone. You shall be surrounded by humanity. And you may consider yourself grateful for your situation. Others who walk this earth still have a much worse fate in store than you."

"How can this be?" Jacob moaned.

"Can you think of no one?"

Jacob thought for a moment.

"Ebenezer! That is of whom you speak, is it not?" Jacob exclaimed.

His Father looked down, a solemn impression upon his face.

At that moment, Jacob Marley was overcome with a desire to commune with his fellow man. To save a soul, even if his was doomed to walk the earth burdened by these encumbrances. In the next moment, the realization that time may be too short to save his friend was almost too much to bear.

"I must warn him!" Jacob cried. At that moment, Jacob's Father faded away and the light that gave him his temporary vivacity faded as well.

Jacob struggled against the chains holding him down and reached for the bell sitting upon his nightstand. With all of his limited strength, he rang it softly.

The door to his bedchamber burst open and several of his servants entered, followed by his physician.

Speaking in the mortal world was a struggle for Jacob. He weakly waved Dr. Robards over to his lips. The good doctor leaned in and Jacob whispered one word.

"Ebenezer."

"Do you wish for me to summon him?" the doctor asked.

Jacob gave an almost imperceptible nod. He repeated his one word.

"Ebenezer."

The doctor turned and directed the servant Jensen to go to Jacob's place of business forthwith. Jensen was instructed to bring Mr. Scrooge back with him as soon as possible. As the doctor felt Jacob's weak pulse and listened to his slowly beating heart, he demanded that Jensen hurry. There was no telling how long Jacob Marley had to live.

The clock read half past nine and Jensen rushed out into the morning's cold air to complete his errand.

"So, it seems that you were correct, Ebenezer," the spirit said. "Jacob did have business on his mind. But the nature of that business was your welfare."

"Yes, I see that now," Ebenezer said softly.

"He was your greatest rival. But, there can be no doubt, at that moment, he was your greatest friend," the ghost said.

"No doubt," Ebenezer said.

"Come, Ebenezer," the spirit said. "It is time to return you to your own place and time. It is my fervent wish that you consider all that you have seen with me. Consider all of your perceptions of your experiences that made you the man that you have become and decide, in light of what you now know, if that is a man you wish to continue to be. Decide if something greater was meant for you. Decide if you wish to take that leap to become greater. If you but open your mind to the possibility, our time together was well spent."

The spirit then touched Ebenezer's hand and darkness enveloped him. The floor beneath his feet disappeared. He began to fall, but softly, as though being lowered into a warm bath. The next sensation Ebenezer felt was his body being cushioned within his own bed and he felt the coolness of his pillow upon his cheek. He let out a mighty yawn and stretched his arms. He was quite comfortable and his eyes fluttered open.

Ebenezer sat up in bed. He looked around and saw nothing, but the insides of his bed curtains.

Was it a dream? It was so vivid. But unlike a dream, the memories did not fade. In fact, as Ebenezer ruminated upon what he considered to be the past several hours, his memories sharpened within his mind.

Disoriented, Ebenezer pulled back his bed curtain to look to his clock. Just as he did, the bells in his home chimed once.

A great light began to shine from beneath his bedchamber door, as though just beyond a bright, sunny day awaited in his hallway.

He then heard a voice coming from just beyond the closed door.

"Come, Ebenezer. Come. Come and know me better."

Drawn to this light by an irresistible force from within, Ebenezer placed his feet into his slippers and walked to his door. He unlocked each of the latches and opened the door. He stood amid a flood of light.

He then heard the voice again.

"Come, Ebenezer. Come and know me. I am the Ghost of Christmas Present."

9

Ebenezer stepped across his bedroom door's threshold into the bright light emanating from beyond. Where he should have found his second floor hallway was a great room instead. As he looked up, the ceiling was impossibly high, extending well beyond the height at which Ebenezer knew the roof should have been. The walls were adorned in the most beautiful garland Ebenezer had ever seen. He looked all about, but could not discern the source of the brilliant light that illuminated this enormous space.

At the far side of this colossal chamber was a tall, broad-shouldered and barrel-chested man. He had long brown hair spilling to his shoulders and beyond. He had a full moustache and beard beneath sparkling green eyes. He was wearing a flowing green robe bordered with white fur extending to just above his feet. On those feet were sandals.

"Yes, Ebenezer," the man of mountainous proportions said, nodding his head with a smile on his face. "Come. Come, and know me better."

Ebenezer crossed the great floor and stood before the giant of a specimen. The self-proclaimed Ghost of Christmas Present stood more than seven-and-a-half feet tall, dwarfing Ebenezer in his shadow.

"So, you are the second of the spirits that was foretold to me?" Ebenezer asked, looking up.

"I am," the spirit said with a pleasant nod.

"And we are to travel from this place together?" asked Ebenezer.

"We are," the spirit replied.

"Where are we to go?" asked Ebenezer.

"Take my robe," the spirit instructed, holding out his arm, "and you shall see."

Ebenezer obeyed and took hold of the fringe of the spirit's robe. At that instant, the room in which Ebenezer stood melted away and in its place, an enormous compound stood before him. Four three-story buildings rose from the center in a cruciform design. They each enclosed a courtyard and the entire perimeter was enclosed within a high wall. It looked to Ebenezer as though he were in the presence of a great prison. But while this was no prison, it could easily be confused for such.

This was a workhouse.

"Spirit, why are we here?" asked Ebenezer.

"You believe yourself to have been raised in poverty. You believe those who are less fortunate than you are averse to hard work. You believe that the poor and unfortunate should simply go to a workhouse," the spirit replied. "It is time for your beliefs to be put to the test."

"I do not understand," Ebenezer said.

"Keep your eye on this family of four approaching the workhouse door and perhaps you may begin to do so," the spirit said.

The spirit directed Ebenezer's attention to a man in his early thirties, his wife and his two young children. It was clear that they had not eaten a proper meal for some time, nor had they recently, if ever, worn clothes that were not frayed and repeatedly mended. The parents shuffled slowly towards the workhouse entrance, each with a dead look in their eyes. It would be obvious to all but the most obtuse that this was a final resort that neither were the least bit interested in employing for their family.

"Who are these people, spirit?" Ebenezer asked.

"The man is Richard Sawyer. Recently, 'Lieutenant' Richard Sawyer, wounded in battle abroad during the Anglo-Chinese War. He served with distinction, but came home to find work to be difficult to secure. While still considered able-bodied, his war wounds weakened his left arm to such an extent that any task requiring heavy lifting for long periods of time was now not an option for him. For a man who worked hard at physical labor his entire life until he was called to serve his country, this was a most unfortunate situation indeed. He is now, as they say 'at the end of his rope' and is seeking refuge in this workhouse because his only other option is to watch as his children slowly starve before him," the spirit narrated.

Ebenezer and the spirit watched as the family entered, passing the porter at the gate. They were assigned to a relieving room as they waited to be examined by a medical officer. They were surrounded by others with the same frightened and desperate looks in their eyes. No one would choose to be here if other alternatives were available.

And then Ebenezer witnessed perhaps the worst aspect of workhouse life. After examination, the family was torn apart, the children screaming and crying for their parents as they were dragged away. The paupers were all separated into the appropriate ward for their category, of which included: boys under fourteen years of age (as was the son of this unfortunate family); able-bodied men between fourteen and sixty; men over sixty; girls under fourteen years of age (as was the daughter); able-bodied women between fourteen and sixty; and women over sixty. As a result of these designations, this family of four was sent to four separate destinations.

"Mama, no!" screamed the terrified young boy of six years old, as he was pulled from his mother's arms.

"All will be well, Martin," his mother tried to convincingly reassure him as tears streamed down her face. When he was taken from the room, his mother broke down entirely, sobbing in grief and shame.

Each member of the family was forced to bathe, after which they were issued a uniform as their personal possessions were taken from them. Mr. Sawyer was dressed in a striped cotton shirt with a cloth cap, a jacket, and matching trousers. Mrs. Sawyer was to wear a blue and white striped dress beneath a smock. The children wore similar garb as their parents.

Ebenezer and the spirit followed Mr. Sawyer to his ward, where the conditions were most deplorable. There was a single large room with rudimentary bedding made of straw and rags throughout. In the center of this horror was a bucket for sanitation. The smell was rancid. The fellow inmates were downtrodden. This was a room devoid of all hope. It was intentionally made as unpleasant as possible to discourage those who did not need public assistance from seeking it out. At no point, it was clear, did anyone responsible for these institutions consider the basic humanity of those who were in genuine need.

"Come, Ebenezer," the spirit said. "Let us see the important work that they have Mr. Sawyer complete in exchange for these deplorable conditions."

Ebenezer and the spirit were drawn forward in time to observe Mr. Sawyer with a pickaxe in his hand. He was given the task of breaking stones for five hours in the morning and five hours in the afternoon. His weak arm made this pointless chore a hardship even more severe than intended. He was subject to abuse by the overseers, accused of being lazy and ungrateful. Eventually, he was taken from rock crushing duty and was reassigned to picking oakum. While there, he was in proximity to those who were required to crush bones, used in the creation of fertilizer. He witnessed the dehumanizing battles that some of his starving fellow inmates engaged in with one another for possession of rotting bones so that they may suck out the marrow for sustenance. This was a most terrible fate indeed.

And then the worst of Mr. Sawyer's experiences at the workhouse. Ebenezer watched as he was given word that they had sent his son to Australia without his consent. When he demanded an explanation, he was simply told that once he entered the doors of the workhouse, he forfeited any responsibility for his family. He was now without a son forever after and he had no word of the condition of his wife and daughter. More than once, he eyed the large metal nail – his spike – that he used to pick the oakum and considered using it to open a vein so that this misery could end.

"So, Ebenezer," the spirit said. "Do you truly believe that those badly off should be sent to such a place as we have now witnessed?"

"I had no idea the conditions and the hardships," Ebenezer said softly.

"You think that you have worked hard during your lifetime? When the heaviest object you have had to haul is your quill pen?" the spirit said. "Could you break rocks for ten hours a day? Remove hemp from telegraph wires? Crush bones for fertilizer?"

"I think not," Ebenezer replied honestly.

"Yet, you advocate for such institutions that force men to be reduced to such inhumanity," the ghost observed. "It is due to men such as yourself that these workhouses continue in operation as you have seen here today."

"I did not know," Ebenezer said. "I simply did not know."

"And what, pray tell, had you done to educate yourself about these conditions before you became such a strong supporter of same?" asked the spirit.

Ebenezer had no response.

"Your silence speaks volumes. You had done nothing. So do not expect my sympathy or understanding when you express surprise or dismay upon learning the truth!" the spirit admonished.

Ebenezer's face reddened.

"We go now, Ebenezer, to visit those whose fate is worse even than what we have seen here. For at least these souls can leave this place if they choose. These people can breathe the free air. They fight their circumstances. Next, we shall see those who must fight a foe more powerful than all the rest," the spirit said. "The greed of man."

The spirit then touched Ebenezer upon his shoulder. The moment that he did so, the two were standing within a filthy hallway, with closed doors lining both sides. It did not look so very different from the workhouse. But the sense of dread and doom here, as hard as it was for Ebenezer to believe possible, was even more palpable.

10

"Spirit, where are we now?" Ebenezer asked.

"I am surprised you do not recognize this place. You have sent many an honest debtor here, and to places of the same ilk," responded the ghost.

"So, this is a prison, then?" asked Ebenezer.

"Correct," confirmed the spirit.

Ebenezer heard a baby cry from behind the door of one of the cells.

"I had no idea that children were sent to such places," Ebenezer said.

"When the breadwinner of the family is removed, where else are his wife and children to go but to join him?" asked the spirit. "Unless you feel that they should remain cold on the streets?"

"No, certainly not," said Ebenezer. "I suppose I simply had never given the matter much thought."

"Perhaps it is time that you do give the matter some thought," said the spirit. "Come. Let us observe the life of one indebted to you, Ebenezer Scrooge."

The spirit raised his arm, his robe obscuring Ebenezer's vision for a moment. When the spirit lowered his hand, they were in a cramped cell, overcrowded with men, many with red welts from flea bites. In addition, rats scurried along the floor, clearly better fed than the human prisoners among whom they ran.

One such man sat before Ebenezer. He was dressed in rags and he clearly had not been given the opportunity to shave for quite some time. Nor had his hair been trimmed. Both his beard and his hair reached down toward his chest. He scratched his bearded face absently as lice had made quite a comfortable home therein. His eyes were empty, his soul drowned in sorrow.

"Do you know this man?" asked the spirit.

"I do not," Ebenezer replied.

"You have met, in point of fact. His name is Peter Rawlings. He borrowed forty pounds from you two years ago. When he was unable to repay, you had him sent here," said the spirit. "That was over one year ago."

Ebenezer shook his head in dismay. He looked about.

"Stuck in this dreadful place for so long for a matter of only forty pounds," Ebenezer considered.

"Oh, well, it is no longer forty pounds," said the spirit.

"After one year, I should hope not," Ebenezer said.

"No, now it is fifty-one pounds!" said the ghost.

Ebenezer's head snapped up at hearing this.

"How can that be?" asked Ebenezer.

"Well, this wonderful institution that you tout so strongly has the odd policy of charging their involuntary tenants for the privilege of feeding and housing them," said the ghost. "And odd conundrum for a man confined for the crime of being unable to pay his debts. And while locked away behind these walls, our dear Mr. Rawlings has no means to earn any income to repay his creditor – you – or to pay for his meager accommodations and amenities. He has no family outside of these walls to produce an income to assist him. The best he can do is reach his arm out the window of his cell and hope that a good Samaritan passing by will deposit a coin into his outstretched hand."

Ebenezer looked at Rawlings' frame and could not escape the conclusion that his food bill could not be very substantial.

"And look at who surrounds Mr. Rawlings," said the spirit. "Murderers, thieves and more debtors like himself. All crammed together like the sardines ordered canned by the Emperor Napoleon Bonaparte himself. Would you like to see how Mr. Rawlings spends his days?"

"Not particularly," Ebenezer responded with his eyes cast down.

"Nonetheless, you shall," replied the spirit, pointing to his right. "Observe."

Ebenezer's eyes followed the spirit's extended finger and noted that he was no longer in Rawlings' tiny, overcrowded cell, but rather in a considerably larger room. Before him was an enormous treadwheel that ten men were walking upon side-by-side as though they were trapped upon an everlasting staircase. They all held on to a bar to their front to prevent them from falling. Separating each man was a wooden partition so that they could not see one another. The men completed their monotonous and arduous task in complete silence, as was required. The third man from the left was Peter Rawlings, eternally climbing but never ascending, all because he owed Ebenezer the sum of forty pounds.

"Why are these men assigned to this pointless and painful task?" asked Ebenezer.

"This is their punishment for being poor and Mr. Rawlings' punishment in particular for being indebted to you," replied the spirit. "They take their upward steps for fifteen continuous minutes before being given a mere five minutes of rest, after which they continue the cycle. They do this for eight hours each and every day. This is Mr. Rawlings' life. Climbing endlessly in place and sleeping among murderers and rats. And should he commit even a perceived offense against any of the guards, he may fall victim to the skullcap or the thumbscrew."

"I did not know of these conditions," said Ebenezer quietly.

"Look about, Ebenezer! Look at this filthy, rotten, stinking house of the destitute! Ten thousand of your fellow countrymen are imprisoned each year for debt. Twenty five percent of the people here will never exit as living men. Would you care to venture a guess as to the end fate has in store for poor Peter Rawlings?" asked the ghost. "I will express it thusly. You will never receive your forty pounds. You will receive nothing more than one pound... that would be your pound of flesh as our dearly departed William Shakespeare so eloquently described!"

"I do not wish this man's death to stain my soul," Ebenezer whispered.

"Do you think Peter Rawlings is the only debtor of yours who has succumbed or will succumb to the miseries of a debtor's prison?" the spirit asked with a rueful laugh. "Ebenezer, you can boast a body count that which any of the tsars of Russia would be proud to claim as their own!"

The pit of Ebenezer's stomach tightened upon hearing this macabre comparison. He covered his mouth with his hand, feeling more than slightly nauseated. He could say nothing.

"So now you have seen how you have impacted a stranger in a workhouse and a debtor in a prison," said the ghost. "Now we will journey to observe your influence on one you look upon every day. One of your very own employees. One of the people who toil to make and keep you rich. Come, Ebenezer. Come."

At that, the debtor's prison faded into mist around Ebenezer and the spirit. The fog hovered in the air for a moment, after which it coalesced into coherent form once again. Ebenezer and the spirit found themselves standing before a small four-room house in the poor neighborhood of Camden Town, northwest of the city of London.

11

"Do you know where we are, Ebenezer?" asked the spirit.

"I confess that I do not," admitted Ebenezer, looking about.

"This is the home of your Head Clerk, Bob Cratchit," informed the ghost.

Ebenezer took in his surroundings.

"A dismal location, to be sure," Ebenezer observed.

"But the best Mr. Cratchit could provide for his family based on the wage he earns at his place of employ," the spirit noted.

Ebenezer looked at the spirit, stung by the implied rebuke.

"Come, Ebenezer. Come and let us observe how a poor family celebrates Christmas in eighteen hundred and forty-three," the spirit said.

"So, this is today, then?" Ebenezer asked.

"It is. It is the present Christmas, simply a few hours hence, from your limited perspective," the ghost said. "Although I can understand why you did not recognize it as such, all you have seen with me has occurred on this very Christmas Day."

Ebenezer followed the spirit and they passed through the wall into the Cratchit home.

It was quite lively as the Cratchits were hurrying about, making the final preparations for the evening meal. Mrs. Cratchit was getting nervous because Christmas supper was almost ready but the entire Cratchit clan had still not arrived.

"Where is your father and Timothy? Church should have ended long ago," asked the Cratchit matriarch to no one in particular and to everyone present in general. "And where is your sister? She has never been so late in the past."

At that moment, the front door opened and the eldest Cratchit daughter, in fact the eldest Cratchit offspring, came forth.

"Here's Martha, Mother!" Belinda Cratchit, the next eldest sibling, announced.

"Martha!" the two youngest Cratchits in the room, Terrance and Susan, cried in unison, warmly embracing their oldest sister.

"My, Martha, how late you are!" said her mother, kissing her and helping her to remove her shawl and bonnet.

"We had a great deal of work to finish up last night," replied Martha. "And we had much to clear away this morning, Mother," Martha explained.

"It is a sin and nothing less that you were called in to work on the Lord's day," Mrs. Cratchit said. "And appalling by ten that you had to finish any tasks on Christmas Day!"

"Hmm. A poor girl working hard, and on Christmas, no less," the spirit noted.

"Commendable," Ebenezer said. "Commendable."

"Look, Mother! Father is coming!" Peter Cratchit, third in line of the Cratchit children, cried as he looked out the window.

"Hide, Martha! Hide!" Terrance implored, taking his sister's hand in his and pulling her away from the door.

"Yes, Martha! Hide!" giggled Susan.

To appease her younger siblings, Martha hid herself just as her father came bounding in the door with his youngest and smallest, Tim, on his shoulder. Tim was holding his crutch in one hand.

"Hello, Father!" all of the children called.

Bob put Tim down, kissed his wife and greeted his children. He noted that one was missing.

"Where's our Martha, Catherine?" he asked his wife.

"Not coming," Catherine replied, trying to keep her face from betraying the truth.

"Not coming?" Bob repeated sadly, his shoulders sagging. "Not coming on Christmas Day?"

Martha could not abide causing her father grief, even for the sake of a laugh, so she emerged from behind the closet door and ran into his arms.

"Oh, Father! Of course I am here!" Martha said.

Bob's countenance immediately brightened.

As the children were sent to complete the final tasks before supper, Catherine asked her husband how Tim behaved at church that eve.

"As good as gold. And better," said Bob. "He gets so thoughtful and thinks the strangest things you have ever heard. He told me, coming home, that he hoped the people saw him in the church because he was a cripple as it might be pleasant for them to remember upon Christmas Day who made lame beggars walk and blind men see."

"Imagine that!" Catherine gasped. "And how was he aside from his thoughts? I could not help but notice that you carried him home."

"Oh, that was for my pleasure only. He gets stronger each day. I am sure of it," Bob said, trying mightily to convince himself of the truth of his own words. "Why, I am certain it will not be long before he is carrying me to church and back!"

"I am most certain you are correct," Catherine said with a forced smile.

She then turned her attention to the kitchen. Upon surveying the feast, she announced that supper was ready. All of her children assisted in getting the food placed upon the table. They then all took their proper places, Bob spoke his yuletide prayer of hope and thanksgiving, and they all commenced to eating.

"Look at this, Ebenezer," the spirit said. "Barely enough for five, but these eight dine as though they are at the palace with a feast fit for a king."

"Yes, they do enjoy themselves," Ebenezer conceded.

"The love that heats this room, I daresay, emits more warmth than the greatest fire you can afford to set ablaze in your lonely hearth," the spirit said. "To whom are you so intently gazing upon?"

The spirit noticed that from the moment he entered the room, Ebenezer's attention was focused upon young Timothy Cratchit.

"I gaze at no one," Ebenezer said, shifting his eyes, slightly embarrassed.

"You lie, Ebenezer," the spirit said. "Your thoughts and your eyes linger on the youngest Cratchit."

"Yes, well, it is just that I am forced to wonder," Ebenezer began. "Will young Tim live?"

"I see a vacant seat in the chimney corner and a crutch without an owner, carefully preserved," the spirit said solemnly. "If no change enters young Tim's life, he will not be present for another Christmas meal."

Ebenezer hung his head.

At the end of the meal, the family gathered around the fire with warm drinks filling their mugs.

"Let us be thankful. Let us be glad. We have our family all together at Christmas. What more could we ask for at this time of year!" Bob said. "And let us not forget all those who made this possible. I begin with Mr. Scrooge, the founder of our feast!"

Ebenezer's head snapped up in surprise upon hearing his name.

"Mr. Scrooge?! The founder of the feast indeed!" cried Catherine Cratchit, fuming, her cheeks suddenly a deep crimson red. "I wish I had him here. I would give him a piece of my mind to feast upon, and I hope he would have a good appetite for it!"

"Catherine, my dear," Bob said with a wince. "The children. Christmas Day."

"It would have to be Christmas Day, to be sure, on which one thinks to drink to the health of such an odious, stingy, hard, unfeeling man as Mr. Scrooge!" Catherine spat. "You know he is, Robert. Nobody knows it better than you, poor fellow."

"My dear," Bob said quietly. "Christmas Day."

"I'll drink to his health for your sake and the day's; not for his," said Catherine. "Long life to him. A Merry Christmas and a Happy New Year. He will be very merry and very happy. Of that I have no doubt."

The family drank in uncomfortable silence.

"Why do you believe she speaks of you so, Ebenezer?" the spirit asked with a laugh. "That is the question you should be asking yourself."

"Ungrateful," Ebenezer responded.

"You are most correct. She should be grateful indeed that her husband toils six days a week at the end of which he is bestowed the grand sum of fifteen entire shillings. She should be grateful for the years that have gone by without he receiving a raise despite doing exemplary work. Grateful that it is a struggle every year for him to be permitted the day of Christmas to spend with his family," noted the ghost, his voice steeped in sarcasm. "Yes. You are most correct. She should simply be grateful."

Ebenezer looked at the ghost, but had no reply.

Bob continued with his toasts to all that made the day possible, citing many a name, none of which raised the ire of his wife. At last, he arrived at his assembled family itself.

"A Merry Christmas to us all, my dears. God bless us!" Bob cried.

The entire family repeated their father's words and they all took a hearty drink.

"A minimum of wealth, but ensconced within the greatest of riches, would you not agree, Ebenezer?" the spirit asked.

"How is that?" asked Ebenezer.

"They do not have much in terms of material gain, but their hearts are filled with love, their souls with tenderness. For all they do not have, it seems they benefit greatly nonetheless," the spirit stated. "You have all the material wealth they do not, but all you can count on to warm your heart when the day is done is the fire you fashion within the hearth of your lonely bedchamber. Poor, poor Ebenezer."

Ebenezer stared at the happy family and again his eyes drifted to young, tiny Tim, his eyes shining in the firelight.

"Come, Ebenezer," said the spirit. "We have yet another home to visit."

The sight of the Cratchits faded away and in its place, Ebenezer found himself staring into the eyes of his own nephew, Fred.

12

Ebenezer stared at Fred's smiling face and it was as though he was seeing Fan gazing back at him through his nephew's bright eyes. Ebenezer was overwhelmed with a conflicting amalgam of emotions from tenderness and joy to pain and regret. For a moment, it was as though time itself had stopped and Fan herself was standing before him, appearing as beautiful as she had ever been in life. A tear escaped Ebenezer's eye.

"Tell us more, Fred," implored the gentleman standing beside a lovely, plump young woman as he furtively snuck glances at her bosom emanating from the top of her bodice.

"Well, Topper, what more is there to say?" asked Fred as he sat down upon a comfortable, plush chair in his living room. He looked around at the modest crowd who had assembled for this soiree and took a swig from the glass in his hand. Julia came over to him and placed her hand upon his shoulder, looking down upon him with such an aspect of sincere love in her eyes. Fred immediately placed his hand upon hers and returned the gaze of affection. They held each other's stare for a moment and interlocked their fingers in a gentle, intimate clasp.

"Go on, Fred," Julia said softly to her husband. "Tell us more."

"Well, he said that Christmas was a humbug. He believed it too," recounted Fred.

"I did not say that!" Ebenezer exclaimed. "If that boy would even once listen to a word I spoke without distortion, I fear that I would swoon like a maiden!"

"Oh, Fred. He could not have said that!" Julia laughed.

"Well, more or less," said Fred, taking another sip from his glass. His countenance then became quite serious. "In truth, I feel very sorry for him. Despite everything, I could not be angry with him if I tried."

"You feel sorry for Ebenezer Scrooge?" Julia's sister asked incredulously.

"Yes, Grace, I do," replied Fred. "I must. He has all the wealth in the world, but nothing of true value. He has no wife. No children. No friends. And he rejects us for reasons I have never understood, thus depriving himself of a family eager to love him. He seems so very sad, an emotion he masks with anger to ward off anyone who threatens to get close to his heart. How, I ask all of you, could I not feel sorry for him?"

The room became silent.

Julia looked down at her pensive husband with warmth in her proud eyes. She leaned down and kissed him.

"You, Frederick Radcliffe, are the sweetest, most thoughtful man I have ever met. How I became so lucky as to have Providence's fortune bless me with you as a husband, I shall never know. I shall simply be everlastingly grateful," Julia said, and she kissed him again.

Fred beamed up at his wife and squeezed her hand tightly within his.

"Why did you object to this union?" asked the spirit.

"I did not trust the young lady," said Ebenezer.

"Yet, you had never met her," the spirit noted.

"I thought she sought my nephew's trust fund," Ebenezer admitted.

"It seems that you were in error," the spirit said. "What happened to that trust fund?"

"I have only heard rumors," Ebenezer lied.

"You heard no such things! You heard directly from Fred himself," corrected the spirit. "Tell me."

"Upon their marriage, Frederick and Julia donated it to the poor," said Ebenezer. "All of it."

"Where it did a great deal of good," stated the spirit. "But how did you react upon hearing of this generous and selfless act of charity?"

"I do not recall," Ebenezer said.

"Again, you lie!" the spirit cried. "You were enraged. You thought it to be a personal affront! You considered this to be yet one more rejection of Fred towards you. First, he spurned your values when he discontinued his apprenticeship. Then, he married against your will. Finally, he tossed away the grand sums you had procured and preserved for him and chose instead to live the life of a poor schoolteacher. Always looking inward, Ebenezer. Never outward to your fellow man. You would benefit from accepting that you could learn a great deal from your nephew and his lovely wife."

Ebenezer just looked at the spirit.

"Well I say," began Julia standing up and raising her glass, "that it is time to toast. A Merry Christmas to all of our friends and family who have graced us with their presence this evening. We love you all and are grateful to have you in our lives. And a very happy birthday to this wonderful man, my husband, my one true love, and truly the greatest man I have ever had the privilege of knowing. Without you, life would have no meaning. To my soul mate. To my Fred!"

"Cheers!" said everyone present, clinking glasses.

Fred stood up and wordlessly embraced his wife tightly. He then whispered in her ear.

"It is I who is the lucky one."

The crowd enjoyed the sight of Fred and Julia in one another's arms. Fred then broke the embrace and raised his glass once more.

"And to those who could not be with us, but who are ever-present in our hearts. To my Great Aunt Nancy and Great Uncle Laurence, who raised me as though I was their own. I miss them every day. To my mother. I only wish I could have known her. Perhaps, someday, my uncle will relent and regale me with tales of her youth. And, of course, to my Uncle Ebenezer himself. I shall never give up hoping that I may toast him while he is here in our presence one day. And to all others absent, I say, God bless them."

"God bless them!" repeated the group before all taking a drink.

"Enough of all this sentimentality! It is Christmas! Let us get to the fun!" Fred cried cheerfully.

"Do you see what you have here, Ebenezer?" asked the spirit. "Do you see what you reject?"

"I do," Ebenezer replied with a degree of reluctance in his voice.

"How can you choose your dusty workstation followed by a solitary meal to all of this?" asked the spirit. "Has any of that brought you even one fraction the joy that you witness in the hearts of those you see before you?"

Ebenezer simply stared down at his feet.

"Answer me, man!" boomed the spirit.

"Life is not always about bringing joy. It is often about being practical," replied Ebenezer.

"That, sir, is where you are wrong," retorted the spirit. "Where you always have been wrong. For there is nothing more practical than bringing joy. You exist on this earth for but a whisper in time. You forget that you were bestowed a heart as well as a head. You were meant to use both."

Ebenezer and the spirit then turned their attention to the party.

Following Fred's call to revelry, they began to play music as many in attendance were quite skilled with instruments. They sang many a Christmas carol with exuberance and delight. After this, they began playing games as though they were children again. They began with Blind Man's Bluff. Next, they moved on to How, When and Where. Finally, they began a round of Yes or No.

Without intending it, Ebenezer began to feel as though he were an active participant in the festivities and was experiencing quite the warm sensation in his heart. He endeavored to discover the secret that Fred was concealing as each clue was revealed when it was his turn at Yes or No.

"It is time for us to go now," the spirit said, after allowing Ebenezer his greatest enjoyment felt in many a year.

"Must we?" Ebenezer asked before he had a chance to consider his words.

"Remember, Ebenezer," said the spirit. "That empty chair by the table was not meant to be so. Only you prevent yourself from joining in this merriment. Your pride and your obstinance are your greatest obstacles to fully engaging in a warm, loving family. Ruminate on this carefully. And now it truly is time for us to go.

"But before we do, I urge you to consider all that you have seen. Consider how you impact others and how you wish to do so in the future. Consider your words carefully the next time you raise the subject of prisons or workhouses. Consider the lives of those who show you kindness and loyalty every day."

"I will, Spirit," Ebenezer promised.

"Good," said the spirit, pleased. "If you truly do so, you will have a better understanding of me and all of my brethren."

At that moment, the clock upon the tower above the spirit's head struck two, with two loud gongs of its bell. Ebenezer's attention was drawn to the sound.

When Ebenezer returned his gaze to the spot the Ghost of Christmas Present was standing, he was gone. In his place was a thin man of approximately the same build and proportions as Ebenezer himself. The man wore a simple black suit and an unassuming look upon his face. His skin was quite pale and his eyes were the shade of slate gray. His hair was short and black. He stared at Ebenezer without blinking or speaking for an uncomfortably long period of time.

Finally, Ebenezer broke the silence.

"I have been visited by the Ghosts of Christmas Past and Present," said Ebenezer. "I can only assume, then, that you are the Ghost of Christmas Yet to Come."

The spirit continued to stare at Ebenezer without averting his unblinking gaze for a moment more. He then nodded slowly before speaking.

"Come, Ebenezer. Come and see what awaits you."

13

Ebenezer found himself standing within the confines of a modest church. He did not recognize it, but that was of no consequence as it had been many a year since Ebenezer had entered a house of worship. His office was his cathedral where increased profits took the place of spiritual enlightenment.

The church was quite deserted, save one lone clergyman sitting upon the apse, silently reading from his Bible, and one lonely casket set before him with its lid closed to the world. Ebenezer was puzzled by what he was witnessing.

"Spirit, why are we here?" asked Ebenezer.

"For the same reason you have been brought to each location on this night, Ebenezer. For your salvation," responded the Spirit.

"Have we arrived prior to a funeral service?" asked Ebenezer.

"No."

"We are present after its conclusion, then," offered Ebenezer.

"No."

"Are you to tell me that we are witnessing a funeral in progress? A funeral with no mourners?" asked Ebenezer.

"Yes."

"That is quite the unfortunate soul, indeed. To have moved not one individual in an entire lifetime to pay final respects," Ebenezer noted.

"I quite agree," said the spirit.

"You fear I will suffer the same fate as this wretched specimen," concluded Ebenezer. "That is why we are here."

"I fear nothing, Ebenezer."

"Nor I," said Ebenezer. "For I am quite certain that when my time comes, there will be quite the crowd to see me off into oblivion."

"Why do you conclude this?" asked the spirit.

"Because I am a man of significant renown. I have many business colleagues who respect me greatly. Many a man of Parliament has benefited from my acquaintance. Many strangers wish to know me better," replied Ebenezer. "A man of business such as I will not be easily forgotten."

"I see," said the spirit.

"Do you doubt me?" asked Ebenezer.

"It is not my function to accept or to doubt. Only to accompany you on this journey," said the spirit simply. "Perhaps we should move on to witness how this decedent impacted his fellow man," said the ghost.

They were now in the main gathering room in the Executive's Club of which Ebenezer had been a member for many a year. Ebenezer immediately turned his attention to the grand chair before the fireplace, but did not see his older counterpart sitting there as he suspected he would. Charles Burbage was in Ebenezer's favored locale at the moment.

"I must be in my office hard at work," concluded Ebenezer. "I confess that I was rather hoping to observe myself at this later point in time. But I am comforted to know that my work ethic remains strong as steel."

Several men assembled near Burbage by the fire were engaged in conversation. Their voices became audible to Ebenezer.

"When did he die?" asked one. It was Stuart Brown.

"It must have been last night at some point," replied Gordon Walker. "Impossible to know exactly as he was alone when it happened."

"Well, if he was not in his office, it must have been quite late," chimed Gilbert Powell.

The group all agreed that this reasoning was sound.

"I, for one, am quite shocked that the old screw did not expire at his desk," Walker observed with a laugh. "Are any of you going to the memorial?"

"Is there one?" asked Brown. "For him, it almost seems a waste."

"Yes, well, you know the church. Memorials for saints and sinners alike," Powell said. "I suppose that I will go if there is a meal to be had."

"Yes, that would make it more appealing," noted Walker. "Although I doubt he would do the same for any of us, even if the meat were sliced and the bread warm and fresh."

"If it was free, he would be there," Brown disagreed. "Ha! He may never have given our cold frames even one glance, but he would get his grasping hands on a free lunch, to be sure!"

All of the men laughed as they had to agree that Brown described an accurate depiction of the dearly departed.

"Spirit, these men are quite cold in heart," Ebenezer observed. "I always suspected this of Walker, but Brown and Powell do surprise me. And now I know who the dead man must be," Ebenezer said. "Why, it is old Palmer Chapman. It must be. Inherited a fortune from his father and under his watchful eye and wise determinations, it grew more and more meager each year. He has an amazing knack for making just the wrong decision at just the right time. Ha! His children may see his passing as a blessing so that they may remain ensconced in the pleasures of life before the old man completely drained three generations of honest labor. Tell me true, Spirit. The dead man is Palmer Chapman, is he not?"

"I can neither confirm nor deny. I am only here to show you what you need to see," replied the spirit cryptically. "We must now move on."

Ebenezer blinked and when his eyes opened he was no longer at the Executive's Club, but instead in an obscure part of town, one where he had never penetrated before. Nonetheless, he recognized it as one he would never enter voluntarily. The streets were covered in filth and the inhabitants mulling about were no better. No doubt a great deal of crime emanated from these walls as the poor and the wretched retired to these dens of misery after a long night of accosting the contributors to society. The stench was palpable and Ebenezer could almost feel the grime upon his skin as he looked about. Without comprehension, his hands involuntarily reached for the breast pocket of his waistcoat, for had he been wearing one, that would surely be where his change purse would have been stored and, in this miserable setting, would have been vulnerable to attack. Instead, his hand merely covered his robe beside his heart, leaving him the position of one prepared to take an oath.

"Spirit, why do we come to this disconsolate place?" asked Ebenezer, not remotely comfortable to be in the presence of this strata of society, despite knowing that he could be neither seen nor heard by any of them.

The spirit said nothing, but pointed Ebenezer's attention towards a dingy shop at the corner of the street. The two entered and found it to be a patchwork of disorganized rubbish. Upon the floor was piled up heaps of rusty keys, nails, chains, hinges, files, scales, weights and refuse iron of all kinds. There were mountains of unseemly rags and tattered textiles of all sizes. As Ebenezer looked about, every corner of this grubby shop contained items to be found throughout the homes of the downtrodden and destitute. Ebenezer had a new understanding of where the underbelly of society frequented to furnish their meager abodes.

In the midst of his wares sat an old man beside a charcoal stove smoking a pipe, relaxing as though he were king of all creation. Ebenezer would soon come to identify him as "Old Joe."

The shop door opened behind Ebenezer and he turned around to spy a woman with a heavy bundle enter. He was surprised to recognize the patron of this seedy establishment to be none other than the charwoman he employed to clean his very own house, Rosemarie Beedle. As Ebenezer's eyes were focused on Mrs. Beedle, two more individuals, a man and a woman, entered the shop with wares they sought to sell. Ebenezer shifted his attention to these two new arrivals and was again surprised to recognize one. The woman was his laundress, Dorothy Dilber. The man was a stranger to Ebenezer. Ebenezer would soon learn him to be employed by the undertaker.

The three customers looked at one another and began to laugh.

"It seems that we have all come from the same house for the same purpose," Mrs. Beedle declared. "Quite the coincidence we all meet here at the same time!"

The other two heartily agreed.

"You could not have met in a better place," said Old Joe, removing the pipe from his mouth. "Come, all of you, into the parlor and let us get down to business, shall we?"

The "parlor" was nothing more than the space behind a screen of rags. Once in the old man's dealing space, the three were reluctant to share what they had brought while in the presence of the others.

"Look at this sorry display, Spirit," Ebenezer stated with a shake of his head. "All three know they are seeking to profit most deviously. I did not know that I shared a charwoman and a laundress with Chapman. Look at this! They pick at his bones! Dreadful!"

"Mr. Grunderson, is it?" Old Joe asked, addressing the man dressed in black.

"Tis," the man responded.

"It looks that you have the lightest load so why do we not begin with you. If that be pleasing to the ladies?" Old Joe asked.

"That be fine with me, Old Joe," replied Mrs. Dilber.

"Me, as well," seconded Mrs. Beedle.

Mr. Grunderson still seemed apprehensive to expose the spoils of his theft before the ladies. Mrs. Beedle noticed his hesitancy.

"Mr. Grunderson," said Mrs. Beedle. "You have nothing to fear from us. We're all paddling the same boat down the Thames. We're not going to be pushing anyone overboard on this journey, isn't that right, Mrs. Dilber?"

"Never a truer word was ever spoken, Mrs. Beedle," replied Mrs. Dilber.

"There you have it, Mr. Grunderson," said Old Joe happily. "So what does our undertaker's office have to offer on this fine day?"

As Old Joe had originally assessed, Mr. Grunderson's plunder was not very extensive. He produced a seal, a pencil case, a pair of sleeve buttons, and a brooch.

Ebenezer took note of each paltry item.

"Hmm," escaped Ebenezer's lips.

"Something troubling you, Ebenezer?" asked the spirit.

"No, not exactly," said Ebenezer, continuing to gaze at Mr. Grunderson's booty. "All of these items are quite generic. So much so that I had the strangest sensation that they had originated from my very own home."

"Interesting," noted the ghost.

"Yes, quite," agreed Ebenezer.

Old Joe totaled up the items and offered the money to Mr. Grunderson.

"That is your account," said Old Joe. "Who is next?"

Mr. Grunderson took his gains, bid farewell, and exited the shop.

After he did so, the two women looked at one another.

"Go ahead, Mrs. Dilber," offered Mrs. Beedle. "I certainly have nowhere else to be today. Go on. Make your fortune."

Mrs. Dilber thanked Mrs. Beedle for her graciousness. She then produced her offerings. She laid out several sheets and towels that she had recently laundered, two old-fashioned silver teaspoons, a pair of sugar-tongs, and a pair of boots.

"Huh," Ebenezer said, peering carefully at these items. "I must say, Spirit, I had no idea how similar items within one's home could resemble those of others."

"How do you mean, Ebenezer?" the spirit asked.

"Well, once again, I am seized with the strangest feeling that these items were not pilfered from poor Chapman's residence, but from my own!" Ebenezer said. "It is a most disturbing experience to feel as though it was I who fell victim to the looting we witness before us. To consider the absence of respect for the man as he lived and as he lay dead. I understand why we are here. Chapman's example is not lost on me, Spirit. No, indeed!"

Old Joe presented Mrs. Dilber with her funds. Out of curiosity, she chose to remain so as to observe Mrs. Beedle's offerings.

"And now undo my bundle, Old Joe," Mrs. Beedle instructed proudly.

Old Joe did so and pulled from it the first item, a heavy and bulky one indeed.

"What is this?" Old Joe asked aloud as he continued to pull the material of the item out. He then recognized it for what it was.

"Bed curtains?" he asked.

"Yes indeed, Old Joe," Mrs. Beedle declared. "Bed curtains."

"You do not mean to say that you took them down, rings and all, with him lying there?" asked Old Joe with a hint of amusement.

"I certainly do," replied Mrs. Beedle. "And why should I not have?"

Old Joe laughed as he revealed the next item.

"Are these his blankets?" asked Old Joe with a smile.

"Indeed they are. Why leave them on the bed? It is not as though his bones will grow any colder without them," replied Mrs. Beedle. "And be careful, Old Joe. You have also got ahold of his finest shirt."

Old Joe held up the white article of clothing before his eyes. He was quite clearly impressed.

"You can look through that shirt until your eyes fall from their very sockets, but you will not find one hole in it, nor even one threadbare place. To think, they almost wasted that fine garment!" exclaimed Mrs. Beedle.

"How do you mean, 'wasted', my dear lady?" asked Old Joe.

"He was to be buried in it! So I took it off of him and replaced it with something more befitting his destination," explained Mrs. Beedle.

Both Old Joe and Mrs. Dilber exploded in laughter at this response.

Ebenezer was horrified by what he was witnessing.

"Spirit, that shirt looks a great deal like one I myself own," Ebenezer observed uneasily.

"Does it?"

"And those bed curtains and blankets are of the same patterns that adorn my own bed," Ebenezer continued.

"Is that so?"

"It cannot be, Spirit," said Ebenezer, with rising horror.

"What concerns you, Ebenezer?" asked the spirit.

"Nothing. Nothing at all," responded Ebenezer quickly. "I simply allowed myself a dreadful thought. But it is nothing."

"Is there anything else that you have brought me?" Old Joe asked of Mrs. Beedle.

"Just one item more, although I doubt it is of much value," replied Mrs. Beedle.

She then recovered a book from the bottom of her sack.

When Ebenezer saw it, his eyes grew wide and his blood turned to ice. His hand gripped his face, covering his mouth, which was agape in terror.

The book was a very old, but very well preserved copy of *Gulliver's Travels*.

Ebenezer could hide from the truth no longer.

He was the dead man.

14

"Take me from this repugnant place, Spirit," Ebenezer begged in agony. "Please."

"Where is it you would prefer to go?" the spirit asked.

"Please take me to witness persons moved by my death," requested Ebenezer.

"As you wish."

The image of Old Joe's shop and the abysmal transactions taking place with such callous humor by the ghoulish participants therein faded away. In its place, Ebenezer found himself in a meager dwelling where a thin woman sat at a table. Her front door opened and a man entered, closing the door behind him. The woman rose to her feet when she saw the man come in. The two stared at each other in silence for a long moment.

She then spoke.

"So, Thomas, what have you learned?" she asked with unmasked anticipation.

"It is true, Charlotte," Thomas said soberly and quietly. "I have had it confirmed that it is indeed a fact. Ebenezer Scrooge is dead."

Another moment passed between husband and wife.

"What does this mean for us?" asked Charlotte.

Thomas broke out into a great smile. He rushed to his wife and lifted her into the air in glee.

"It means we are saved! Our debt is no more! Our certain journey to the debtor's prison to where he sent so many before us has been prevented!" Thomas cried with tears of joy streaming down his face. "We have a second chance, my love! Heaven has smiled upon us! We are saved!"

"Oh, my darling! What wonderful tidings!" cried Charlotte.

The two embraced and kissed as only two set free from certain doom can.

"Spirit! Why have you brought me here?" demanded Ebenezer.

"You asked to see those who were moved by your death," replied the spirit.

"I did not wish to see those who were moved to elation!" cried Ebenezer. "Please, Spirit, show me those for whom death is a tragedy. Where the loss is felt in their hearts as a void unable to be filled."

"As you wish."

The meager accommodations of Thomas and Charlotte were replaced with those of Bob and Catherine Cratchit.

Peter Cratchit was sitting at his father's desk reading. The two youngest Cratchits, Terrance and Susan, were sitting quietly by the fire. Catherine Cratchit, along with Martha and Belinda, were noiselessly sewing.

Suddenly, Catherine dropped her sewing into her lap. She pinched the bridge of her nose and then covered her eyes with her hand.

"What troubles you, Mother?" asked Martha.

Catherine took a deep breath.

"It is just very difficult to consider another Christmas without him," replied Catherine softly.

"We know, Mother. We all miss him terribly as well," said Martha, rising and placing her hands upon Catherine's shoulders.

"At this time of year, in particular, I feel guilt for my questioning the Almighty as to why He felt it necessary to take my son so young. I consider that He Himself gave the life of his only begotten son so that we all may be saved. When I think of such things, it makes me wonder what God was feeling when His son took His last breath before Him, as my tiny Tim took before me whilst I held him cradled in my arms on that fateful night," remembered Catherine with tears in her eyes.

At that, Peter closed his book and Belinda set aside her sewing. Every Cratchit in the room fought back the deluge of tears that urged to spring forth.

Catherine looked out the window as she endeavored to compose herself.

"It must be near your father's time to arrive home," Catherine said, wiping her eyes dry.

"Past it, rather," observed Peter.

"Come, all of you, let us get our supper upon the table so all your father must do when he enters through the door is hang his coat and sit to eat," Catherine instructed. "And let us not show him any sad eyes."

"Yes, Mother," all of the children agreed.

As the evening meal was being placed upon the table, Bob Cratchit arrived home.

"Hello, Father," the children greeted him.

"Hello, my angels from above," Bob replied. "The supper smells wonderful."

The children continued to prepare the table for the meal. Catherine walked to her husband. They gazed deeply into one another's eyes, communicating everything without but one word. Both felt moisture well within their eyes and they grasped one another tightly, as though the stronger their grip upon one another, the stronger their will to defeat this grief.

"You are late," Catherine said simply, and they each leaned back so as to look one another in the eye as they spoke.

"I am sorry. The time always seems to move more quickly when I am there," said Bob. "There is never enough time."

"So, you went again?" confirmed Catherine.

"Yes, my dear," replied Bob. "I must. I need to be near him. I wish you would come with me. You would see how peaceful and beautiful a place it is where our Tim rests."

"I cannot," said Catherine, struggling mightily to remain composed.

"Mother. Father. Supper is on the table," announced Peter.

The Cratchit parents looked to their oldest son and thanked him. The family all took their places. One seat was conspicuously empty, as it had always been since his passing. Bob offered his prayer and the family went about beginning their somber meal.

Ebenezer watched all of this with a pain squeezing at his insides.

"Spirit, I asked to see those troubled by death," said Ebenezer.

"And so I have shown you," replied the spirit simply.

"Perhaps I was not clear in my request," said Ebenezer. "I wished to see those troubled by my death."

"I apologize. That was not clear," responded the ghost.

"I wish to go where that exists, please," Ebenezer asked as he could not remove his eyes from the family before him.

"I will honor your request," said the spirit.

The Cratchits disappeared one by one until only Bob Cratchit remained seated at the head of his meager table. Ebenezer followed Bob's eyes as they drifted to the corner by the fireplace. There, in the corner, leaned tiny Tim's crutch. The last tangible reminder of that young life to whom Ebenezer was introduced just hours before.

All the rest of the home vanished away, but the crutch remained squarely focused within Ebenezer's gaze. It then too slowly faded from view. Ebenezer's trance was finally broken. He looked about, consumed by a thick fog. It was as though Ebenezer was trapped within a cloud. He expected the mist to lift and a grieving mourner, moved by his death, to appear. However, the soupy nothingness persisted.

"Spirit, where are we?" asked Ebenezer.

"We are nowhere," replied the spirit.

"I do not understand," Ebenezer said.

"You asked to go where your death was mourned," explained the spirit. "But there is not such place on earth that I can take you to witness such. Only by gazing into a mirror at this moment may you find a man distressed by your demise."

"I do not accept this," Ebenezer stated, half in fear and half in anger. "Surely someone must be moved to tears by my passing. What of my nephew? At the least, he could not but be sorrowful."

"I am sorry, Ebenezer," said the spirit. "Your accomplishments in business, great and small, did not earn you one iota of the respect you believed it to have done. Your efforts to alienate yourself from your only family were successful. While Fred was not joyous at learning of your demise, neither was he despairing. Your employees looked with hopefulness at this opportunity to serve a new master. In the end, Ebenezer, the reaction to your death is a product of your life. You chose to live it alone, surrounding yourself with no one. You will not be missed, Ebenezer. You will not be mourned. And you will not be remembered. When all is said and done, it will be as though you had never even existed at all."

"Is this future immutable?" asked Ebenezer. "I would have to think not. Otherwise, why do you bother to come to me? Why show me what cannot change? My life must have meaning. It simply must."

"We have one destination further, Ebenezer," said the spirit.

At that, the fog lifted and Ebenezer saw that he was in a churchyard. He was standing before a freshly laid grave that had recently been filled in.

"Pay your respects, Ebenezer," declared the spirit. "For no one else will."

Ebenezer looked down at the slab of granite with his name etched in stone. Ebenezer then suffered his next great shock. He saw his date of death to be coming in only two years hence.

"My time runs short," Ebenezer realized. "How can I possibly transform myself into the worthy man this spectral night has encouraged me to be in such a limited time?"

"Allow me to show you what shall happen if you do not find a way," said the spirit by his side.

Suddenly, Ebenezer was no longer standing by his graveside. He was lying upon his back, with his hands clasped upon his chest. It was dark as pitch. Ebenezer tried to sit up, but found that he was held down by a great weight.

At that moment, a brilliant light illuminated his surroundings. He was in his casket, six feet below the earth. The spirit hovered before his eyes.

"You are dead, Ebenezer," the spirit informed. "Your body is for the worms. All that is left is your soul. Now rise. Rise out of your shell and take your place among the wretched who walk the earth in disembodied, insubstantial, incorporeal form."

Ebenezer felt himself rising up through the earth, but he was in great pain. Chains engulfed him around his chest and his waist, around his arms and his legs, around his shoulders and from his ankles. When he reached the surface, he was propelled upon his feet by means he knew not. At this moment, he felt the full weight of his ponderous chain. It truly was seven years longer and mightier than the one he observed adorned by Jacob.

He tried to take a step, but every movement was a torture. Yet he was compelled by an unknown force to keep edging forward. Pain! Oh, pain! This pain that has no end!

And the pain was not limited to the physical. He saw the error of his ways. He understood the soul's need to serve his fellow man. He comprehended that he would forever after be relegated to the status of spectator instead of participant and will never have the power to satisfy this need.

Woe! Woe!

"Spirit, please let me go home. Please let me begin anew," Ebenezer pleaded. "I am not the man I was. I am not the man I was."

Ebenezer took one further painful step and then fell forward upon his face. But instead of the cold, damp soil of the churchyard, he landed softly upon his own bed in his home.

Ebenezer looked up and saw nothing but his bed curtains surrounding him. He pushed up on his hands and felt no weight of chains. He felt his face and his body only to realize he was not in ghostly form.

"Am I alive?" Ebenezer asked aloud. His heart pounded within his ears and his entire body shook with convulsions. The trauma of the night was over.

Overwhelmed, Ebenezer fainted dead away into the absolute darkness of a dreamless sleep.

PART III

AFTER THE SPIRITS

1

The bells chimed eight times. At the fifth peal of the bells, Ebenezer's eyes opened as his cheek rested upon his pillow. When the last ring died away, he sat up in his bed, not entirely confident that he knew where he was. He looked down and recognized his own blanket covering his legs. He looked about and observed that all of his bed curtains were drawn around him.

Ebenezer noticed a warm sensation radiating throughout his entire body. For reasons he could not explain, he broke out into a wide grin and felt like laughing. He felt wonderful. Taking deep breaths in and out, he was thrilled to find that the head cold raging when he went to sleep on this night last was entirely gone. Physically, emotionally and in all other ways, he felt like a new man. He wanted to Whoop! with excitement. Life had never before seemed to hold as much promise as it did for him at that very moment.

Ebenezer drew back his curtains and looked about the bed chamber. Everything seemed to be as it should have been until his eyes fell upon the shattered remnants of a bowl, cold and congealed glops of gruel interspersed among the bowl's shards, and a lonely spoon resting amid the mess. It was then that all of the events from the night previous came flooding back into his mind. Jacob Marley, the Spirits three, and all that he had seen and heard. It was overwhelming to recall in such vivid detail. But Ebenezer did not shrink in fear from these memories. Instead he reveled in their magnificence.

Ebenezer was a saved man. He knew this to be true with every fiber of his being. Never again would he be the disgruntled and gnarled despot he had been for as many years as anyone who knew his name could remember. He knew his purpose on this earth was to commune with his fellow man and to do his part to make the world a better place than the one into which he was born. He could not control his excitement. He could not wait to begin his journey immediately. So many wasted years behind him. If the visions he was blessed to have been given were true, he only had two more years before him. He had to make every moment count. Beginning right now.

He leapt out of bed, giddy as a schoolboy. He bounded over to the window and looked about at the life out on the street. He saw a young boy, no more than ten years old if he was a day, walking past. Ebenezer threw open the window and called out to the lad.

"You! Boy!" Ebenezer called. "Up here!"

The young man stopped and looked up directly at Ebenezer's smiling face.

"Me, sir?" the boy cried.

"Yes, you, you fine young lad!" Ebenezer responded. "Tell me, boy. What day is it?"

The young boy was clearly confused by the question.

"Come again, sir?" asked the child.

"Yes, yes. I know it to be an odd query. But please indulge an old, foolish man," Ebenezer said. "What day is it?"

"Why, it's Christmas Day, sir," responded the boy.

"Christmas Day! How wonderful!" Ebenezer said aloud to himself. "So the spirits did it all in one night, just as Jacob told me they would."

Ebenezer then turned his attention back to the child.

"Boy! Do you know the poulterer just around the corner?" asked Ebenezer.

"I should say that I do! He is my father!" responded the boy.

"You are Joe Miller's boy?" asked Ebenezer.

"I am," replied the child.

"Wonderful! Wonderful! What wonderful luck!" Ebenezer exclaimed. "Does he still have that prize turkey hanging in the window?"

"Do you mean the one as big as me?" asked the poulterer's son.

"Yes, my fine boy! That is the exact one of which I speak!" said Ebenezer.

"It is still there," said the boy.

"Extraordinary! Go to your father and tell him I wish to buy it," said Ebenezer. "Bring him back with the bird and I will give you a shilling. Come back with him in less than five minutes, and I will give you half a crown!"

The boy's eyes grew wide and he broke out into a great smile. He took off like a shot as though he had just been launched by a cannon.

Ebenezer laughed and closed his window. He rubbed his hands together, both in anticipation and to warm them from the frosty air he had just allowed into his room. He pulled out a sheet of parchment and, with his hands shaking in excitement, he wrote out Bob Cratchit's address and the instructions to deliver the prize bird to his residence without a mention from whom it was sent.

"Bob and his family will not have to carefully divide up that small goose tonight," Ebenezer laughed to himself. "Why, this fine animal is twice the size of young Master Tim!"

Moments later, the poulterer and his son approached Ebenezer's door. Before they could even knock, Ebenezer threw the door open and admired the magnificent turkey in Joe Miller's hand. Ebenezer paid Mr. Miller and, true to his word, gave young Master Miller half a crown for producing his father within the requested five minutes. Ebenezer, still in his nightclothes, hailed a cab for Joe Miller and paid the fare in advance to assist Mr. Miller on his way to make his very important delivery in Camden Town.

With a laugh, Ebenezer then re-entered his home to dress for the day. He smiled all throughout his morning routine as he conjured for himself the image of Bob Cratchit and his family answering their door only to find such a fine turkey to be waiting for them. Oh ho! Bob would never guess from whom it came!

Ebenezer considered everything else he must do on this day. There were a few errands that he knew must be accomplished, that was for certain. He would have to make his way to his office, but not so that he may perform any of the work he otherwise would have been engaged in all day. No, indeed! He had much more important work to accomplish!

After dressing and shaving, Ebenezer exited his home and walked briskly towards his place of business. Along the way, he surprised many a familiar face as he cried, "Merry Christmas!" to one and all whom he encountered. Ebenezer was not a stranger to these people, nor was his well-deserved reputation. To hear him spout "Merry Christmas", and with a smile upon his face no less, led many to believe Mr. Scrooge must have a twin brother who was heretofore unknown to the public or that Mr. Scrooge had gone quite mad.

In a way, one could say he had gone mad. Mad with joy. Mad with enthusiasm. Mad with the hope only one who knew his place in the world could feel.

When Ebenezer entered the front door of Scrooge and Marley, he marched directly down to Jacob's office. He unlocked the door and entered. It was as dusty as he remembered from the afternoon before and the air was just as stale and musty. Even though he was in his finest clothes, Ebenezer set about to clean the office so that Jacob's workspace could be among the living once again. No longer would it serve as shrine to the somber. Jacob inhabited this space at one time. It was time new life was breathed into its chambers.

After satisfying himself that Jacob's workspace was spotless and vibrant once more, Ebenezer walked down to his own office. He sought out very important records that would assist him in continuing his day's adventures. After leafing through his files, he discovered that which he sought. He organized the papers he removed into twelve separate piles upon his desk.

He then sought out a directory of local businesses and businessmen that he always kept close at hand. He scanned through this ream of documents until he came across the name he sought: Horace Merryweather. Ebenezer noted his business address and was pleased to see that it was only a few city blocks away. Ebenezer hoped that with a spot of luck, he would find Mr. Merryweather there or that he could at least discern where the large and generous gentlemen lived.

With his papers in hand, Ebenezer left his office and locked the door behind him. He walked the two blocks to Merryweather's establishment. Along the way, he greeted all who came across his path with a friendly tip of his hat and a kind word for Christmas. As he had experienced earlier, most who knew him or knew of him were struck speechless by this unusual behavior. Some responded with a "Merry Christmas" of their own, still unable to believe they were saying it to Ebenezer Scrooge and that he was accepting it so graciously.

Ebenezer walked up to Merryweather's shop and was pleased to find the door to be unlocked. Inside, Ebenezer found both Horace Merryweather as well as Lionel Garrett, the two portly gentlemen who came seeking donations for the poor two days prior. In addition, he found numerous other gentlemen, all preparing for a long day of distributing charity to the unfortunate.

Ebenezer was observed by Mr. Merryweather right away and the large gentleman came over to greet his unexpected guest.

"Mr. Scrooge," said Merryweather. "How may I help you?"

"I must say, Mr. Merryweather, that you have already helped me a great deal more than you can imagine," said Ebenezer with his hat in his hand. "It is now my turn to help you and your noble cause. I first must apologize for how rudely I treated you two days past. You and your young colleague came in earnest seeking only to feed and clothe those most unfortunate and I acted the complete ass. I hope you can forgive me."

Startled by the contrite words, Mr. Merryweather was struck mute for a moment. When he regained his power of speech, he could only stammer his reply.

"Y-yes. Of course, Mr. Scrooge. You are forgiven," said Merryweather. "Why, there is no other time of year when a man may request to be granted forgiveness for his transgressions and should expect the courtesy more so."

"I realize that it may be too late to do any good right now, but would you allow me to contribute five hundred pounds to the cause today?" Ebenezer asked.

"Five hundred pounds!" Merryweather gasped.

"No, you are most correct. That will not do," Ebenezer said. "Perhaps one thousand would be more appropriate."

"One thousand pounds!" Merryweather exclaimed. "Why, that is more than generous, Mr. Scrooge! More than generous!"

Merryweather reached out with his oversized hands and engulfed Ebenezer's bony fingers in a hearty and extended handshake. He then turned to the crowd of men who had stopped what they were doing as Ebenezer's conversation and donation caught their ears.

"Gentlemen! I am pleased to announce that we have just received a final donation in the incredible amount of one thousand pounds from Mr. Ebenezer Scrooge of Scrooge and Marley. Join me in thanking him most heartily!" announced Merryweather.

The group of men gasped in surprise and pleasure. They all began to make their way over to Ebenezer to shake his hand.

"No, gentlemen," Ebenezer said to the crowd of philanthropists. "Please do not thank me. For while the donation originates from the offices of Scrooge and Marley to be sure, it is not I who deserves the credit. This donation is made in the name of Jacob Marley. Never was there a finer friend or a finer man. He saved my life and, with these funds being offered, it is my hope his generosity may help to save others."

The men nodded in understanding, but all wished to shake Ebenezer's hand nonetheless in lieu of directly thanking his dearly departed partner in whose name the organization happily accepted the money.

Ebenezer then excused himself for he had other pressing business to conduct on this day that, in many respects, was the first day of his life as it was always meant to be lived.

2

Ebenezer exited Merryweather's establishment and was about to hail a cab so that he may continue on to complete the day's tasks when something interesting caught his eye. Across the street was a bookseller, known as Hardy's Books. In the window was something being advertised as a "Christmas card". Ebenezer walked across the street and into Hardy's Books to investigate.

In fact, what captured Ebenezer's attention was an item that was the world's first. Never before had Christmas cards been produced or sent to friends and loved ones. Ebenezer spoke with the proprietor of the shop, Raymond Hardy, and asked about this unusual item.

"Oh, those. They have been quite popular this year. I only have a limited number remaining," Hardy said. "It is good luck for you I am still open. I thought I would get some end of the year work done this morning before closing shop for the remainder of the day to enjoy Christmas with the family."

Ebenezer was mesmerized by the clever novelty. The card featured three generations of a family around a table raising a glass in a toast to the recipient. On either side of the family were scenes of charity. On the left side was a scene showing the distribution of food to the poor. On the right side, was a scene showing the provision of clothing to the needy. All three images sat behind a wooden trellis. Draped in front of the toasting family was a banner that read, "A Merry Christmas And A Happy New Year To You". In the center top of the card was the word, "To", where the recipient's name was to be inputted. Along the bottom right of the card was the word "From", for the sender to include his name.

"This is brilliant!" Ebenezer exclaimed. "How many still remain unsold?"

"I only have twenty," replied Hardy.

"Marvelous! I will take the lot," Ebenezer said. "How much, my good man?"

"They are one shilling each, sir," responded Hardy.

Ebenezer produced the money and exited the shop with his fortuitous find.

I know just what to do with these, Ebenezer thought to himself with a smile.

Ebenezer then hailed a cab and gave the driver his specific instructions. They were going to make several stops. All at debtor's prisons. Ebenezer had begun his day at his office so that he may retrieve the names and locations of all who were currently indebted to him who had been sent to prison. There were twelve in all. Each of the men were to be given a Christmas present, courtesy of Jacob Marley of course. They were all to be given complete pardons and an extinguishment of the entirety of their debt.

Ebenezer travelled all throughout London to the various prisons where the men were housed. He not only informed all of the wardens of each institution that the debts were satisfied, but he took from his own pocket the additional fees and costs each of the men had accumulated while in prison. They all walked out of their cells and into the fresh air of freedom unencumbered by any debt owed to any man.

Upon learning of their good fortune, some did not believe it was for truth when the guards came to remove them from captivity. None could understand how Providence could have smiled so warmly down upon them. One, Aaron Parkins, was so excited that once he accepted the truth of his situation, he ran through the streets greeting everyone he encountered with a handshake and a "Merry Christmas!"

Each man left the prisons, not only with their freedom, but also with a Christmas card made out to each one individually. They all treated these cards as though they were made of gold. It was their one tangible keepsake from the generous soul who had set them free and created for them a new chance for a happy life. When Lucas Farlane passed through the door of his home, his wife almost fainted, believing this figure to be the apparition of her surely deceased husband. After he assured her that it was, in fact, he and he explained the situation, Mrs. Farlane fell into his arms, crying tears of joy.

"Who has done this thing for us?" she asked through her sobs.

"It was no man. It was an angel to be sure!" Farlane said.

Similar scenes of rapture and relief repeated itself all throughout the city as men resigned to incarceration came home as debt-free souls. Ebenezer could not be more delighted. He once thought no experience could bring more pleasure than the acquisition of wealth, but his day spent delivering men from the evil of poverty pleased him in a way words could not describe. It was almost as if he had never been touched with happiness before this very day. That which he had done in the past so that only he may gain was pointless and meaningless. So many years heading in the wrong direction! He knew, down to the core of his being, that this, this here and now, was what was intended for his life if it was to hold any worth whatsoever. This is why he was born to this earth.

One accumulates so that one can give. One should always greet others with an open hand and an open heart. True pleasure is derived from embracing the family of man and one's place in that family. Ebenezer was overwhelmed by these truths which seemed so obvious now, but which had eluded him for so many years. Sixty five years a fool! But no more. He swore to himself and to all that was decent and good. No more!

When evening descended, Ebenezer had one more wrong to make right. He gave the driver one last address where they were to proceed. This was not a prison. Oh, so far from it! Yet, Ebenezer was more apprehensive about stepping foot into this locale than any he had done so prior throughout this extraordinary day.

When the cab arrived at the designated destination, Ebenezer took a moment, staring at the front door of the residence. His heart was beating rapidly within his chest. He was perspiring despite the coolness of the outside air of the evening.

"Everything alright, Mr. Scrooge?" asked the driver when he noticed Ebenezer's hesitancy.

"Oh, yes, Barkley. Quite alright," replied Ebenezer absently, his eyes still glued on the front door outside of the cab window. "I just worry about the reception I am about to receive."

"Oh, Mr. Scrooge, have no fear. I am sure it will be a positive one. From all you have told me, I am sure of it!" Barkley said. "Would you like some assistance climbing down?"

"No, no, Barkley. That will not be necessary. I may not be as young as I once was, but there is still life in these old legs yet," Ebenezer said, reaching for the door.

Ebenezer climbed down and paid Barkley twice what was asked.

"No, Mr. Scrooge. This is too much. I cannot accept," Barkley protested.

"Oh yes, Barkley. You are out working on Christmas Day. Take this home to your family. Wish them all a Merry Christmas," Ebenezer said, refusing to take back even one shilling. Ebenezer then handed Barkley a Christmas card.

"And this is for you as well. Enjoy the season!" Ebenezer said.

"Why, thank you, Mr. Scrooge," Barkley said, finally relenting. "For the funds, for the lovely card, and for letting me share in your day's adventures. You have a fine night, Mr. Scrooge, and a Merry Christmas!"

"You as well, Barkley," responded Ebenezer.

With that, Ebenezer turned and approached the door that so intimidated him as Barkley's cab made its way down the street.

Ebenezer took a deep breath, girded up his loins, and knocked on the door.

The door opened, and there before him, stood Julia and Fred, together.

It took Fred a moment to believe it was actually his Uncle Ebenezer standing before him. He blinked rapidly and looked down at his bride, and then back again at Ebenezer. Finally, his power of speech returned to him.

"Uncle! How wonderful to see you here!" Fred exclaimed.

"If the invitation still stands, I have come for Christmas supper," Ebenezer said tentatively.

"Why, of course it still stands!" Fred cried. "Isn't that right, Julia?"

"Of course," Julia said, perhaps twice as pleased as her husband. Once because Uncle Ebenezer had come. And twice because Fred was so happy for it.

Fred reached out and shook Ebenezer's hand most mightily and clapped him on the back.

"Come in. Come in out of the cold, Uncle!" Fred said, practically dragging his unexpected guest inside. "As promised, there is already a place set for you at the table. But I must know. What has changed your mind on this night?"

Ebenezer stared at Fred's beaming face for a long moment. He looked so like Fan.

"I cannot tell you more than this. I have taken a long, hard look at my life and did not like what I witnessed," Ebenezer said. "One such aspect for which I am most ashamed is how I have treated you. And you as well, Julia. You are a fine woman."

"Thank you, Uncle," Julia said.

"Can you both forgive an old fool? I would like to know you both better. I would like us to behave as family," Ebenezer admitted.

Fred grasped his uncle by his upper arms, his smile as bright as the sun.

"There is nothing to forgive. And, of course, we shall behave as family. We are family. I do not know what miracle has occurred between our last encounter and this one, but I get down on my knees and thank the Good Lord above for it," Fred said. "Now come! Join us. Meet our friends."

Ebenezer was swept into Fred and Julia's largest room which was teeming with people. Although Ebenezer was good at recalling names, he would be challenged to remember everyone here. Fred and Julia were quite popular indeed.

Fred introduced his Uncle to all, all of whom were at first shocked into silence at his presence. No one knew quite how to react. It was as though they had all misbehaved and an old schoolmarm was preparing to administer corporal punishment to correct their evil ways.

Ebenezer noted the apprehension throughout the room. To ease this universal sense of anxiety, he smiled and cleared his throat.

"I know you believe an ogre has infiltrated your midst. I only hope that I can disabuse you of that notion before this evening is out. A Merry Christmas to all!" Ebenezer said.

Immediately, the tension broke and everyone in the room relaxed. Ebenezer was then introduced to each individual personally. They were delighted when he handed several of them his remaining Christmas cards.

The night was enchanting. The meal was delicious. The conversation superb. The games made them all as lighthearted as children. Ebenezer could not remember a more joyful night spent.

He was reluctant to depart when the time came to make his way home. Fred and Julia accompanied him to the door to see him out.

"I can hardly believe this night to be true," Fred said as he shook hands with Ebenezer. "I fear that I will wake and this will all have been but a dream."

"It is no dream, Fred. We shall never be strangers again," Ebenezer said. "May I ask a favor of you?"

"Anything, Uncle," replied Fred.

"Come by my home tomorrow for supper. Of course, you as well, Julia," said Ebenezer. "There are things I must confide in you that I should have done long ago."

"We certainly will gladly accept," said Fred without hesitation. "If I may ask, what is the subject about which we must discuss?"

"Your mother," said Ebenezer. "I have many stories to share with you. You have asked to hear them for many years and I foolishly denied you. That all ends now. Come, sup with me and we will have a long discussion about my dear Fan, your mother."

"Thank you, Uncle. A Merry Christmas to you!" said Fred. "And a happy birthday!"

"Yes, a Merry Christmas and a happy birthday, Uncle," Julia said, giving Ebenezer a kiss on the cheek.

"A Merry Christmas to you both. Happy birthday to you, Fred," said Ebenezer as he turned to leave. "Until tomorrow, then."

Fred and Julia gently closed the door behind Ebenezer as he headed out into the lightly snowy night. He called over a waiting cab to take him home. As he climbed into the carriage, he was filled with such joy. He thought to himself that this was the day the true Ebenezer Scrooge was born.

He gave the driver his address and leaned back, allowing himself to enjoy the pleasant memories of this day. The horses were urged to begin with a gentle snap of the reins and the cab lightly lunged forward with a slight jolt, clip-clopping down the street, taking Ebenezer home.

3

The following morning, Ebenezer woke, dressed and left his home earlier than was his norm. He made his way to his office with a clever plan on his mind. He entered his office and walked up to each work station of each of his employees, leaving behind a surprise for them to discover within their desks when they arrived.

Ebenezer chuckled to himself as he formulated a plan to deceive his own Head Clerk. Old Bob Cratchit will never see this coming! No, indeed!

When the nine o'clock hour arrived, all of the employees of Scrooge and Marley came streaming in through the door. They greeted each other warmly and recounted tales from their Christmas festivities. At one minute past nine, Bob Cratchit passed through the front entrance. This minor infraction provided Ebenezer with the perfect opening for the charade he intended to perpetrate.

As Bob scurried over to his desk, Ebenezer called out to him in as gruff a voice as he could muster.

"Cratchit!" Ebenezer called from his office. "In my office! Now!"

Bob's face fell. He left his coat and hat behind upon his desk and he approached Ebenezer's workspace.

"Yes, Mr. Scrooge," said Bob tentatively from the entranceway.

"Tell the men to sit quietly at their desks, with not a soul to open so much as a drawer or to lift a pen!" Ebenezer ordered.

Bob relayed the message. Now the entire staff within the building was rigid with fear.

"Now come in, Cratchit, and close the door behind you!" Ebenezer snarled.

Bob obeyed and stood beside a chair in front of Ebenezer's desk.

"Sit," Ebenezer ordered.

Bob did so.

"Now, Cratchit, what did I explicitly say about being late on this day when you demanded not only Sunday but yesterday's Christmas Day off from work?" Ebenezer asked severely.

"You said it was impermissible, sir," Bob stated, terribly worried.

"In point of fact, I said that if even one man was late, I would replace the entire department and be in search of a new Head Clerk," Ebenezer said.

"Yes, sir," Bob conceded.

"I believe all of the men were on time, save one," Ebenezer said, his eyes flashing as much anger as he could feign.

"Sir, I was through the door but one minute past the hour," Bob pleaded.

"One minute or one hundred minutes. Late is late," Ebenezer said. "The question is what do I do about it?"

Bob sat silently, shrinking within the chair.

"And here is my decision," Ebenezer said. "For all of your work and your obvious commitment to this firm as proven by your punctuality and diligence…"

Bob gulped at what he perceived as biting sarcasm. He could not go home without employment. Finances were tight. Without an income, caring for his family would prove impossible.

"… I am," Ebenezer continued, and then broke out into a broad smile, "giving you a raise in salary!"

Bob was cringing as though he was about to be subject to a violent blow. When he heard the words, he looked up at Ebenezer, not sure he had heard correctly.

Ebenezer laughed and leaned over his desk watching Bob Cratchit carefully.

"Pardon me, sir, but did you say you were giving me a raise?" Bob asked incredulously.

"Indeed, I did! It is far past time as well," replied Ebenezer with a wide smile. "How does triple your current salary sit with you?"

"Sir, are you quite alright?" Bob asked, unable to accept what he was hearing.

"Oh, yes, Cratchit. I am more than alright," said Ebenezer. "I have recently spent some time evaluating my life and my relationship with those within it and have come to some very important realizations. One such is that my Head Clerk is woefully underpaid. So what do you say, Cratchit? Do you accept?"

Bob was having trouble believing the words emanating from the lips of his employer of so many years. He was having an equally difficult time remembering the last time he witnessed a smile on Ebenezer's face. He may never have seen one. As incredible as this all was, it made Bob somewhat uneasy. But he decided that he had better embrace this opportunity before Ebenezer changed his mind.

"Y-yes, sir. Of course I accept, sir," Bob said.

"Wonderful!" Ebenezer exclaimed, rising from his seat and coming around his desk, approaching Bob Cratchit. Bob rose as well.

Ebenezer extended his hand to Bob and when Bob lifted his own, Ebenezer shook it most forcefully.

"Bob, please accept my sincerest apologies for how I have treated you these many years. You are an integral cog here at Scrooge and Marley and a marvelous Head Clerk. I am lucky to have you," said Ebenezer, looking directly into Bob's eyes as he spoke.

"Thank you, sir," said Bob. "But, I must say that I could not provide you with any valuable service were it not for my men."

Ebenezer shook his head with pleasure.

"Look at you. Always thinking of others. I have much to learn from you, Bob," said Ebenezer. "Say no more. All of the men with be receiving healthy raises as of this day. They shall all be compensated fifty percent more today than they were yesterday. Now go and tell them to examine the top drawer of each of their desks. And do the same yourself."

Bob was not sure what awaited all of the men, and he was still not sure the surprise to be found would be a positive one. But he agreed nonetheless.

He exited Ebenezer's office and the eyes of the entire staff were fixed upon him.

"What is the matter?" asked Neil Corsett, a clerk in the investment department, concerned due to the odd look on the Head Clerk's countenance.

"Why, nothing at all gents! I have some marvelous news," Bob announced, looking back at Ebenezer's office doorway, where Ebenezer was now standing. Ebenezer smiled and gave a nod of his head to encourage Bob to proceed.

"Mr. Scrooge has offered all of you a fifty percent raise in salary!" Bob announced.

The men were left in as much shock as Bob had been when he learned of his own raise. Smiles broke out on many faces. Confusion on many more.

"Furthermore, you are instructed to examine the top drawer of your desks," Bob stated.

They all complied. Bob walked to his own desk to do the same.

There, staring at all of them were envelopes marked, "Christmas

Bonus". When they opened the seals, they were all staring down at a sum that equaled one month's salary.

By now, the reality that they were not the subjects of an elaborate hoax was beginning to dawn upon most of the men. Some laughed. Several cried. A few whoops and spontaneous cheers broke out. They all looked over at Ebenezer standing at his doorway, absolutely elated at the reaction he was observing.

"A Merry Christmas to you all!" called out Ebenezer. "Things are going to change around here. First, you, Roemer, open Mr. Marley's door. You will find it to be unlocked."

The clerk Roemer did as he was instructed.

"That door is not to be closed again! Mr. Marley is here with us every day and we shall keep his office open and in good order henceforth!" said Ebenezer. "Next, as of today, one of your job responsibilities will be to identify a charity of your liking and you are to work it. If the needs of the charity conflict with your time here, you must inform Mr. Cratchit and the charity shall take precedence. We must all make an effort to improve upon the world. So shall it be forevermore at Scrooge and Marley."

There was a general murmur of approval and delight from the crowd.

"Finally, we shall begin to take on apprentices. But not from traditional sources," instructed Ebenezer. "We shall seek out the poor, the orphan, and the needy who otherwise would not have this opportunity. These shall be the apprentices of Scrooge and Marley. We shall call them our 'Fezziwig boys'. Do you have any questions for me?"

No one spoke.

"Very well! Then let us get to work!" Ebenezer cried. "Cratchit! Tuttle! I need to see you in my office so that we may discuss modifying our policies concerning our moneylending department."

While the rest of the men settled in to the day's tasks, still unbelieving that Ebenezer Scrooge had uttered any of the words they heard that morning, Bob Cratchit returned to Ebenezer's office accompanied by Samuel Tuttle, head of the moneylending department.

Ebenezer explained to them that never again would a man be sent to a debtor's prison for failure to repay on a Scrooge and Marley loan. They sat and discussed positive alternative solutions to ensure debts were repaid, but that difficulties in doing so would not result in Draconian punishment.

When this meeting concluded, Ebenezer excused Tuttle, but asked Bob to stay a moment longer.

When they were alone, Ebenezer spoke.

"Bob, I understand that your youngest is somewhat sickly," Ebenezer said.

"Yes, sir, that is true," replied Bob, surprised that Ebenezer knew anything about his family.

"I want to help him. I have access to the finest doctors. I will send him to see them. It will cost you nothing," Ebenezer said.

Bob was overwhelmed. His first instinct was to refuse such an overly generous offer, but his sense of paternal responsibility could not allow him to turn down this opportunity.

"What do you say, Bob?" Ebenezer asked. "Would you do me a favor and allow me to do this for you?"

"Yes, Mr. Scrooge. I accept. Thank you, sir. Thank you," Bob blurted, continuing to have difficulty accepting that all of this kindness was emanating from Mr. Scrooge.

"Excellent. Tell me when the boy can be available and I will make it so," said Ebenezer.

Bob then had a thought that had no reason to occur to him earlier. The potential solution to a mystery twenty-four hours old.

"Sir, may I ask you a question?" Bob asked.

"Of course, my good man. Anything," replied Ebenezer.

"Are you responsible for sending a turkey to my home for supper yesterday?" Bob asked.

"I do not know what you are speaking of, Bob," Ebenezer said.

Ebenezer's denial solidified Bob's certainty that his employer, was, in fact, responsible for the fine meal his family enjoyed on this night last. But if his master did not wish to claim credit, Bob resolved to respect that choice.

"Very well, sir," said Bob. "Is there anything else you need at present?"

"No, Bob. You may resume your duties at your desk," Ebenezer said, dismissing him.

Bob exited Ebenezer's office. Ebenezer closed the door behind him and sat back in his chair. His mind raced with the possibilities of what more he should do. He was not finished yet.

He had only just begun.

4

The following two years were perhaps the most eventful and significant of Ebenezer's entire life. If measured by personal relationships and valuable service to the world, there can be no doubt that the extraordinary years between eighteen hundred and forty-three and eighteen hundred and forty-five met this description precisely. And from the very day Ebenezer increased the salaries, and by extension, improved the lives, of his employees, he began his close association with the Cratchit family.

Before the workday came to a close, Ebenezer once again called Bob into his office. Once seated, Ebenezer invited Bob and the entire Cratchit family to his home to sup the following night. Bob was overwhelmed by the generosity and Ebenezer was insistent in his invite.

"Bob, we have a great deal to discuss concerning your future here at Scrooge and Marley," said Ebenezer. "And we must establish a time and date that is convenient to bring my physicians to meet with your youngest. The sooner the better on that count."

"Thank you, Mr. Scrooge. You are most generous. I will discuss this with my wife, but I am certain we will attend," replied Bob.

"Excellent," said Ebenezer, delighted. "I will have a feast fit for royalty prepared so ensure you all come with healthy appetites."

"Yes, sir. We will, sir," said Bob.

With that, Ebenezer excused Bob from his office. When the hour came to depart for home, Bob's mind was swimming. He could not believe the good fortune that this day had brought. A part of him still expected to wake and learn that this was but a dream.

When he arrived at home, he had still not escaped his daze. He walked through the front door and all of the children greeted him. His wife took one look in his eyes and instantly assumed something was amiss.

"What is the matter, dear?" asked Catherine Cratchit, quite concerned.

"Not a thing," replied Bob, as he hung his coat and hat.

"Now Robert Cratchit, don't tell me there is nothing awry," scolded Catherine. "I have known you for too many years for you to think that I cannot read worry within your eyes and upon your brow. Now tell me."

"It is not worry that you read, my dear. Perhaps it is shock. Perhaps disbelief. But not worry," Bob said.

"Children. Go into the next room so that your father and I may speak privately," instructed Catherine.

"No, no. There is no need for that," said Bob, stopping the children's flight. "I have nothing but good news. And we should all be present for it. I only wish Martha was here."

"Well, what do you have to say, Bob? You are fraying my nerves," said Catherine.

"Today, I witnessed the most spectacular event these eyes have ever seen. It was like a miracle. I know of no other way to describe it," said Bob, struggling to recount the day's events. "Something has happened to Mr. Scrooge."

"Has he died?" blurted Catherine, after which she immediately placed her hand over her lips for making such a ghoulish and inappropriate query.

"Well, in a way, I would have to say 'yes'," replied Bob.

"In a way?" asked Catherine.

"Mr. Scrooge is very much alive. But something has happened to him. He is so very different now," said Bob, continuing to struggle as he heard his own words.

"How is he different?" asked Catherine.

"Well, he was kind. He was generous. Catherine, dear, he gave me a raise in salary," said Bob, smiling.

"He did? In what amount?" asked Catherine.

"My dear, he tripled my salary!" exclaimed Bob.

At that, everyone in the house began chattering excitedly.

"Triple!" exclaimed Catherine.

"Yes, and that is not all. All of the rest of the men were given fifty percent increases! And we all received Christmas bonuses!" Bob continued.

"Triple salary and a bonus!" cried Catherine.

"Yes. In an amount equal to one month's salary!" said Bob

No one in the house could believe this wonderful news. Everyone was leaping and jumping and hugging one another.

"I am not through, Catherine," Bob said. He then got down on one knee and called Tim over to him. When Tim complied, Bob spoke.

"Mr. Scrooge is going to send our Tim to the finest physicians at no cost to us to evaluate and, God willing, to cure him," Bob told the family.

"Mercy me!" called Catherine. "Can all of this be so? From such a man as Ebenezer Scrooge?"

"You can ask him yourself, my love," said Bob. "We have all been invited to dine with him at his home on this evening next. He made mention of a discussion about my future and he wished for us to have dates available for Tim to be visited by his doctors."

"This is all too much," said Catherine, sitting down in a chair and fanning herself.

"I quite agree. And one thing further," said Bob. "Although he denied it to be true, I am convinced it was Mr. Scrooge who sent us that enormous turkey for our Christmas dinner."

"Remarkable," said Catherine, still sitting. "Truly remarkable."

The Cratchit dinner meal was quite lively and ebullient that evening. Catherine promised to relay the news to Martha the next day so that she may accompany the family for supper at Mr. Scrooge's.

As requested, Fred and Julia were, at that very moment, making their way in a carriage to Ebenezer's home for supper. Fred was visibly excited.

"To what do you attribute this sudden change in attitude of your uncle?" Julia asked as they neared the Scrooge residence.

"I do not know. I wish I could say otherwise," replied Fred.

When they arrived, Fred used the very knocker that was once replaced with a diminutive version of Jacob Marley's head. Ebenezer himself answered the door with a wide smile and ushered his nephew and niece into his home. Dinner was not quite ready and so he showed them into the parlor after relieving them of their coats and hats. He brought both a pre-meal libation and then prepared one for himself. They all sat.

"Wonderful. Wonderful that you both could be here," Ebenezer said.

They then broke into a great conversation dominated by Ebenezer recounting tales from his youth featuring Fan as the star of the stories. It seemed that Fred had no end of questions and Ebenezer no end of patience in answering each.

The conversation took them into the dining room where a magnificent meal awaited them. It continued throughout the meal during which Ebenezer had questions of his own so that he may learn all about Fred and Julia, information that, had he simply allowed himself earlier, he might have known. The evening discussion continued well past the meal until Fred and Julia had to call an end to the pleasantries so that they may return home.

All had a marvelous time and they resolved to dine together at least once per week forever after so long as same was possible. This was a promise they all kept until Ebenezer's dying day.

The relationship grew and flourished in ways Fred had only dreamed could be possible ever since he was a young lad. He learned more about his mother than even he had hoped. And by so recounting, for Ebenezer, it was almost as though Fan lived again.

Ebenezer's meal with the Cratchits the next night was nearly as sublime as that he shared with Fred and Julia.

It did not start as such. It was clear that the family was apprehensive about meeting and spending the evening with Ebenezer. For the entirety of the children's lives, all they knew of the man was how penny-pinching and foul-tempered he was. And after the initial elation wore off, Catherine was once again unsure of Ebenezer and his intentions. She was fiercely protective of her Tim and was concerned as to why Ebenezer took such an interest in him, a boy that he had never met.

In fact, the only member of the Cratchit family who seemed at ease from the start was Tim himself. He accepted Ebenezer at his word and could see no ill-intent masked behind the friendly face with which Ebenezer greeted the family.

"I know this must be strange for all of you," said Ebenezer as they sat at the dining room table. "But I wish to convey my sincerest gratitude for your presence here tonight. Bob, I could not have achieved the success with which I have been blessed if not for your hard work and dedication. I wish to repay my debt to you in every way I can.

"As for you, Mrs. Cratchit. I fully understand your apprehension as it relates to me. You have no reason to accept my sincerity based upon your past impression of me, well deserved and of my own creation. I only hope I can win your trust and your friendship.

"Finally, young Master Tim. There is no reason why you should not be fully well. If money or the appropriate medical attention are the only obstacles, then there are no obstacles at all. You shall be well. I shall see to it.

"Now all, please enjoy the meal. And as my own sainted mother would say, 'God bless us, every one'."

The children thoroughly enjoyed everything set before them. The conversation flowed easily amongst them all. Ebenezer told Bob that he would like to see Bob take a more active role in the management of Scrooge and Marley.

"I realize that I am not a young man, Bob. I may not have many years left ahead of me. I would like Scrooge and Marley to live on. If you help me, perhaps we can create a future wherein the sign above our door reads, 'Scrooge, Marley and Cratchit'," said Ebenezer. "What do you say?"

Bob told Ebenezer that nothing, save the safety, security and health of his family, could make him more pleased.

"Well, let us work together to make all four a reality," said Ebenezer.

When the evening ended, Ebenezer called for the cabs that would take the Cratchit family home. Ebenezer paid the fare, with a bit extra for the drivers to ensure a comfortable and safe ride for the passengers.

The very next day, Ebenezer had his personal physician make a call on young, tiny Tim at his home in Camden Town. This visit led to others and additional doctors were called in to pool their resources and knowledge to diagnose and treat the young boy. It took time, but there was no question that Tim flourished under their care. He clearly got stronger and less reliant on his crutch as time went on. By the time the next Christmas came about, the crutch had an owner still, but one who was much less in need of it. Tim lived. Ebenezer was thrilled to witness how his efforts had lifted the dark shadow of the future that had been cast across the young boy's fate.

Ebenezer, too, flourished as Tim grew stronger. Ebenezer spent many an hour with the young boy. They spoke as friends. Ebenezer admired the child's strength of spirit. He desired to emulate the same within himself.

Catherine Cratchit was, at first, not pleased with the amount of time Bob allowed Ebenezer to spend with her youngest. While Ebenezer made good on every promise to the family, she still maintained her reservations about the man. But, as time went on, his devotion to Tim was undeniable. His commitment to Tim's recovery eventually won her over and she, too, appreciated having this newer and better version of Ebenezer Scrooge in their lives.

She was also impressed with Ebenezer's other projects. The "Fezziwig boys" apprenticeship program for underprivileged youths was proving to be a great success. Ebenezer also donated vast sums and organized and chaired a committee to construct the "Jacob Marley Memorial Children's Hospital". All of the Cratchits attended the ground-breaking ceremony on the twenty-fifth of June, eighteen hundred and forty-five, at which time Ebenezer gave a moving tribute to his late partner in whose name the hospital was forever to be known.

In addition, Ebenezer had begun a program of opening soup kitchens throughout London for the poor and the hungry. He called these locations, "Belle's Kitchens" in honor of his one and only true love. The first was opened in September, eighteen hundred and forty-four. By the date of the Marley Hospital ground-breaking, fifteen were in full operation.

Ebenezer's life had never been filled with more meaning. He truly did not believe any more good fortune could come his way.

But he was so very wrong.

One face in the crowd at the ground-breaking was beaming with a wide smile and a dimple visible on her right cheek. She approached Ebenezer from behind and spoke with a clear American accent.

"Can this really be the work of Ebenezer Scrooge?"

Ebenezer knew that voice, even with the accent.

He turned.

He knew those eyes. He knew that smile. He knew that one adorable dimple.

"Belle!" he gasped.

Annabelle Marie Benson had just re-entered Ebenezer's life.

5

Ebenezer stood staring in shock at this ghost from his past. He was beaming from ear to ear, but his mind was so overloaded with emotion that he simply could not conjure a new word to utter, and so he just remained, staring. He was thirteen years old again, entranced by this beauty before him.

"I had to come here to see for myself if all I was hearing was true," said Belle, smiling up at him. "Ebenezer Scrooge, the philanthropist? Surely, I thought, this must be some elaborate joke, or perhaps there was another Ebenezer Scrooge living in London. But, no. Look at you. The same Ebenezer that I knew, but at the same time, in no way the same Ebenezer that I knew."

Ebenezer could not take his eyes off of Belle as she spoke. He could not believe she was really here, standing before him. It had been more than forty-five years since they had last spoken, but, to Ebenezer, it was as if but one day had passed. She was still as beautiful as ever. Perhaps even more so now. It was odd to hear the American accent escape her lips, but that voice was still the sweet song that thrilled and excited him.

"Well, are you not going to say something?" asked Belle.

"Belle," Ebenezer said again.

"You know, when we first met, it seemed that he only words you could utter were those of your own name. Now, it seems that you can only say mine," Belle said, teasing him.

"You are in London," Ebenezer said.

"You noticed that. Very good, Ebenezer," Belle said, continuing to tease.

"What I mean to say is, what are you doing in London?" asked

Ebenezer. "Are you here with your husband?"

"No. Sadly, Nathaniel passed away five years ago," Belle said. "I am here with my youngest and his family."

"How long will you be here?" asked Ebenezer.

"We are scheduled to sail home one week from tomorrow," replied Belle.

"So soon," lamented Ebenezer. "Well, in that case, you must come and dine with me before you depart. Please."

"Of course, Ebenezer," Belle responded.

Ebenezer and Belle established plans for her to visit his home the following night. Ebenezer resolved to ensure the meal was the finest ever served within the walls of his abode. He then led her to a cab so that she may reunite with her family with whom she was scheduled to rendezvous in less than one hour hence.

"Until tomorrow, Ebenezer," Belle said, as the carriage pulled away.

Ebenezer's eyes watched the cab until it turned a corner and escaped from view.

"Who was that, Uncle?" asked Fred as he and Julia approached him from behind.

"That, Fred my boy, was my future until I foolishly let it slip away in my past," Ebenezer said, his eyes still on the spot where the carriage turned the corner.

The next evening could not arrive soon enough for Ebenezer. Remembering how many wonderful times were spent in the Fezziwig garden, Ebenezer had flowers of all varieties brought to adorn his home. He arranged for the most succulent meal to be served. He ordered his home cleaned from top to bottom so that not a speck of dust should mar Belle's attire when she arrived. Ebenezer restlessly flitted throughout the house to ensure all of the preparations were perfect.

When the hour arrived, Ebenezer was nervously shaking so much, he hoped he would be able to mask his excitement in having Belle – his Belle! – in his home. When he heard the rapping at the front door, he leapt from his seat and raced to admit her in, nearly knocking from his feet Stanton, the servant he had employed for the express purpose of greeting his guests and for overseeing all of the evening's preparations.

"I am so very sorry, Stanton," apologized Ebenezer. "I am aware of your instructions, having given them to you myself, but I will greet our guest tonight."

"Very good, sir," Stanton said, and he left to check on the supper.

Ebenezer opened the door and there she stood. Belle, looking as resplendent as ever. He welcomed her in and took her coat.

The evening was sublime. They spoke for hours, describing for each other the path of their lives as they had lived them since their last encounter. In truth, Ebenezer did more listening than speaking, as he was less interested in recounting the errors that had dominated his decision-making until recently.

Ebenezer learned that, after a period of adjustment, Belle came to truly enjoy her life in Boston. Nathaniel Weatherby was a kind and loving husband, and an excellent man of industry. His shipping business flourished in "the States", as Belle referred to her adopted country. She had actually returned to England on numerous occasions with him throughout the years and so she was well aware of Ebenezer's success. And of his reputation.

Belle had three children. The twins, Benjamin and Isabelle, and her youngest with whom she was now travelling, Elijah. She had eight grandchildren in all. She considered herself quite lucky that all of the children remained within a carriage ride away after they married so that she was always surrounded by family. There was nothing more important to her.

Toward the end of the evening, Belle asked the question that had been on her mind ever since she was first informed of Ebenezer's transformation.

"Ebenezer, please tell me. What happened to you? How do you account for your newfound interest in philanthropy?" asked Belle.

Ebenezer was not prepared to tell Belle the truth of his ghostly encounters for fear it would drive her away, convinced that he had gone mad.

"Have you ever truly considered the actions of your past?" Ebenezer asked in response. "Have you ever projected as to the type of future that lies ahead if you continue along your present path?"

"I don't know that I have, to be truthful," replied Belle.

"Well, I have. And I did not like what I saw," explained Ebenezer. "I know now my purpose in this life and I am now attempting to fulfill it."

"Why do I feel that there is more to this than that?" asked Belle, flashing that one incredible dimple. "But if this is what you choose to reveal, I will accept it."

"Belle, I must see you again," said Ebenezer, suddenly. "I cannot bear the thought of you walking out of that door tonight only to escape from my life once again."

Belle smiled.

"Of course, Ebenezer," agreed Belle. "How does tomorrow sound to you?"

"Wonderful!" said Ebenezer. "Just wonderful!"

Ebenezer and Belle saw each other the following night. In fact, they saw each other at some point each and every day leading up to the day of her planned departure. Ebenezer met her son, Elijah, and his wife, Abigail, and their three children, William, Robert, and Kenneth. They all got along famously.

The night before Belle's imminent departure was heartbreaking for Ebenezer. Over the course of the previous week, he learned that he had never stopped loving her and he could not stomach the thought of never seeing her again.

"Belle, I know I have no right to ask this of you, but please do not go back to America. Not yet, at least. Please stay with me a while longer. Whenever you are ready to depart, I will make all of the arrangements and will send you sailing back. But not yet," pleaded Ebenezer.

Belle blushed at the request. After what seemed like forever of her looking into Ebenezer's eyes, she softly agreed to his request. She told her children that she would be staying in London for another month hence. Although they were concerned for her, they knew her well enough to know that once she made up her mind, it was not to be unmade.

Belle's extension of time in London soon became two months, and then three. It was obvious that these two soulmates were not meant to be separated. Ebenezer made several important decisions as the summer of eighteen hundred and forty-five turned to Fall.

Ever present in his mind was his journey into the future with the Ghost of Christmas Yet to Come. Per these visions, Ebenezer was foretold that his end would come in just a few months hence. He needed to make of his life what it was meant to be with his remaining available time.

As Bob Cratchit had taken over most of the daily duties of management at Scrooge and Marley while Ebenezer busied himself wooing Belle, and had done a marvelous job of it, Ebenezer decided it was time to give him the ultimate reward. Ebenezer made Bob a partner and, as he had once suggested, modified the name of the firm so that it was forever after known as Scrooge, Marley and Cratchit. The business would live on. And Ebenezer was confident that it was in incredibly capable hands.

Ebenezer had established a solid relationship with Fred and Julia. He intended to continue his weekly suppers with them until he was prevented from doing so by whatever it was that fate held in store. He had his Will revised, leaving the lion's share of his fortune to them.

His relationship with young, tiny Tim had grown. Tim had even taken to calling him "Uncle", a moniker Ebenezer felt privileged to wear for the boy.

True, there were those in the business community who believed Ebenezer had gone daft, but Ebenezer ignored the whispers. He knew his mission. While it was certainly true that his company was not realizing the same profits as before, it still did quite well, and, more importantly to Ebenezer, the firm now did good in addition to well.

There was but one more important aspect of his life that was left to be made whole. Ebenezer confirmed plans for an intimate meal with Belle at his home on Saturday, the fourth of October, eighteen hundred and forty-five. He arranged all of the plans.

They enjoyed a quiet meal by candlelight. They drank fine wine and, as always, engaged in sparkling conversation. When the meal came to a close, Ebenezer stood up before Belle as she remained in her seat, surprised at his sudden move.

He then knelt down on one knee before her.

"Belle, these last few months have been magical," began Ebenezer.

"Yes, Ebenezer. I agree," replied Belle.

"I feel like a young man again when I am with you," continued Ebenezer. "And like that young man you once knew, I find that when I am not with you that the world is somehow less bright. That life is somehow less worth living. That all that is beautiful is more muted in your absence."

"Oh, Ebenezer. Your words are sweeter than the finest confection ever to have passed my lips," cooed Belle.

"I made a grave error in my youth. One that I cannot allow myself to repeat at this late stage of my life. I once let you go due to foolishness, hubris and pride. And my life has been the worse for it," Ebenezer said. "Now that you have re-entered my life, it is as though I have been resurrected from the depths of Hades itself and I do not wish ever to return."

"What are you saying, Ebenezer?" asked Belle.

"I am saying that I love you, Belle," said Ebenezer earnestly. "I have never stopped from the first moment I laid eyes upon you and I shall never stop until these eyes are closed forever."

"I love you, too, Ebenezer," Belle said, and she squeezed his hand which was now within hers.

Ebenezer used his free right hand to reach into his pocket and it emerged concealing something within.

"And now I must do that which I should have done long, long ago," said Ebenezer.

Belle took a sharp intake of breath.

Ebenezer pulled out an old, but perfectly preserved, small gold ring. It was the Promise Ring he had once given to her when they were young. He had secretly kept it all of these years.

He held it out in front of him and took in a deep breath. He then spoke.

"Annabelle Marie Benson. Will you marry me?" Ebenezer asked.

The tears cascaded down Belle's cheeks as she instantly recognized the ring and heard Ebenezer's proposal. She had difficulty speaking and more difficulty believing that this day she had given up as an impossibility had actually come to be true. She nodded up and down and finally found her voice.

"Yes, my Ebenezer! Yes! Yes!" cried Belle.

Ebenezer slipped the ring onto her finger, it still fitting perfectly as it once had. The two arose and embraced tightly. They kissed and when they did, Belle observed that her tears were intermingling with Ebenezer's. The two halves were finally going to form a whole.

"I do not wish to wait, my love," said Ebenezer. "I have waited my entire life. I can do so no more. Let us wed as soon as is possible."

"I agree, but I must have my children and grandchildren by my side as we do this," insisted Belle.

"Very well, my beloved. Write to them and have them sail immediately," said Ebenezer. "Let us not wait until the new year is upon us. Let us do this in one month."

"One month! That is immediate," said Belle. "But, yes, my darling. If you wish to wed in one month's time, we shall do so."

They then embraced again and promised that they would never let the other go.

6

On the twenty-fifth of November, eighteen hundred and forty-five, Ebenezer found himself standing at the front of the church before the altar, awaiting the imminent appearance of his bride. This was to be an intimate affair, as Ebenezer and Belle decided to reserve this event for the closest of family and dearest of friends. Ebenezer was flanked to his side by his nephew, Fred, as well as his two favored Cratchit men, Bob and Tim. In addition, he was joined by his two new step-sons-to-be, Benjamin and Elijah, and his new grandsons, Joshua (Benjamin's son), Adam (Isabelle's boy), and Elijah's triumvirate of sons, William, Robert and Kenneth. He was shuffling from one foot to the next in nervous anticipation. He had literally waited his entire life for this moment.

The music began to play and the rear doors opened. The women began their march down the aisle. The three granddaughters, Leslie (Isabelle's daughter), Robin (Benjamin's elder daughter) and Gayle (Benjamin's younger daughter), strolled down the aisle, one after the other. They were followed by Isabelle. All looked stunning. Finally, as all attendees watched, Belle made her appearance.

She was adorned in a gorgeous pink flowing dress, holding a beautiful bouquet of flowers in her hands and her head was ringed with a delicate flower tiara. So very her! Ebenezer took one look and he could not breathe. Her beauty literally stole his breath. Belle began her slow march to the front of the cathedral where her intended, her always intended, was waiting with a smile that could light the way through the darkest forest. She was drawn to him like a beacon from across the sea, bringing her home.

When she arrived at her beloved's side, Ebenezer took her hand and together they turned to face the priest. All but the betrothed sat back in their seats and prepared for the ceremony. Father Maloney smiled at the two standing before him and began.

"Dearly beloved, we are gathered here today…"

It was a lovely ceremony. Like a dream, but ever so much better than a dream for Ebenezer. For this was a dream from which he would never have to wake. His heart swelled with love as he heard Belle agree to be his wife. He dutifully followed his instruction to "kiss the bride". And as they turned, he could almost not believe his ears as Father Maloney announced to the small congregation that it was his great honor to introduce for the first time, Mr. and Mrs. Ebenezer Scrooge.

It was the happiest moment of Ebenezer's life.

The next several hours were as a whirlwind. A lovely reception followed the wedding for all who shared in this day. Throughout it all, Ebenezer clung tightly to his new wife. He did not wish to let her leave his sight for even a moment.

When the time came to depart, Ebenezer took his beautiful Belle home. That night, they made tender love, their bodies intermingling as though they knew exactly what the other needed and were perfectly suited to provide for the desire. When the act of love was complete, they lay naked in each other's arms, embracing as two had truly become one. Belle rested her head upon her husband's chest and told him how much she loved him. Ebenezer kissed the top of his wife's head and knew that, come what may, he could now die a happy man.

The following month was absolute bliss for Ebenezer and Belle. But as Christmas neared, Belle could sense that something significant was troubling her husband. Try as he may, he could not conceal his concern that their time together may be running out.

On the twenty-first of December, Belle could stand Ebenezer's evasions no longer.

"Ebenezer, my dear, please tell me what troubles you so," Belle pleaded.

"It is nothing, my sweet," Ebenezer insisted.

"It is most certainly not nothing. Ebenezer, the key to a healthy marriage is honesty," Belle said. "Now, please trust me enough to tell me the truth."

"Of course I trust you, Belle," said Ebenezer.

"Then reveal your secret. I know there is one," insisted Belle.

"Very well," said Ebenezer with heavy sigh. "I have had, how shall I say, a vision. A premonition. I will not see the dawning of the day four days hence on Christmas Day."

"What is that you say? You are concerned about a vision?" asked Belle. "When did you receive this vision?"

"Long ago. While I slept," Ebenezer said.

"My love, I understand your discomfort, but you speak of a dream," Belle said. "A dreadful dream, yes, but nothing more than a dream nonetheless."

"No, my sweet. It was much than that," said Ebenezer. "It will happen. Of that I am certain. But before it does, I want you to know how much I love and adore and cherish you."

"Ebenezer," said Belle more insistently. "It was but a dream."

Ebenezer saw that there was no convincing Belle. And he still could not bring himself to reveal the entire truth as to why he was so certain about his impending demise.

"Very well, my dear," said Ebenezer. "You are probably correct. I will put this grim notion out of my head."

"Yes. That is the best solution," agreed Belle.

But, of course, Ebenezer could not ignore his certainty. He had seen his own gravestone. He had seen the date chiseled into it. The twenty-fourth of December, eighteen hundred and forty-five. Three days hence.

Over the course of the next three days, Ebenezer made an effort to inform all close to him how important they were to him. He asked Fred and Julia to join he and Belle for an evening meal on Tuesday, the twenty-third, instead of simply waiting for Christmas Day or the established Friday when they always dined. Fortunately, they did not resist the earlier invitation.

The meal was very pleasant, as usual, although Ebenezer seemed a bit more sentimental than was his norm. This was the impression both Fred and Julia shared with one another during their ride home that night. Ebenezer spoke at length about Fan during the meal. He seemed to revel in her memory.

Ebenezer also used that week to spend time with Tim. The two took a walk one afternoon, at which time Ebenezer did all he could to impart as much wisdom to the boy as he could, convinced that this would be their last meeting.

"Tim, remember to always live life to the fullest. And remember that we are all members of one great family under God. Be the best member of that family as is possible," advised Ebenezer.

"Yes, Uncle," replied Tim.

"Do you remember the song I taught you that my mother used to sing?" Ebenezer asked.

"Of course, Uncle," said Tim. "It is a lovely tune."

"Remember its words. Remember its meaning. Live by it," Ebenezer said.

"I will, Uncle," Tim promised.

"Come, let us return you to your parents," said Ebenezer. "They must be wondering what the crazy old man is filing your head with."

The two shared a laugh and they headed back to the Cratchit home.

Ebenezer checked in with his charities to ensure they were all running smoothly. He visited each of "Belle's Kitchens" to ensure they were ready for the holiday needs of all they served. He visited the newly opened Marley Hospital and stopped in on several of the children in most need of care, communing with them and trying to bring them a sense of hope. He had private conversations with each of the "Fezziwig boys" and related to them how proud he was that they were members of the family at Scrooge, Marley and Cratchit. He made sure to inform Bob Cratchit how pleased he was that the two men were partners.

As night fell on the twenty-fourth of December, Ebenezer's only desire was to remain at home, embracing his wife. If tonight is to be my last, he thought, this is where I would like to meet my end. His only confusion was that he physically felt quite strong and vibrant. Aside from an increasingly nagging cough that he suspected was the result of his childhood illness catching up with him, he had no reason to complain about his health. Perhaps, he thought, death would come suddenly, as it had for his father.

Belle knew that Ebenezer only stated that he no longer feared for his own mortality in order to placate her. But she also realized that no amount of talk could convince him otherwise. Only by rising on the morning of Christmas Day would Ebenezer finally accept that his nightmare was just that and no more.

The two enjoyed an intimate supper together after which they retired to sit before a roaring fire. It was a wonderful night, just the kind Ebenezer wished Belle to have as her last memories of him.

As the bells signaled that it was eleven o'clock, Belle felt that she could remain awake and alert staring at the fire no longer. Ebenezer encouraged her to go up to bed with the promise that he would soon join her. She attempted to coax him into coming with her, but to no avail. She finally gave in to both his entreaty and her exhaustion. She kissed him lovingly on the lips while resting her hand gently upon his cheek. Belle then turned and headed up the stairs.

Ebenezer watched as she left, convinced that this had been their last encounter. He sighed deeply and then turned his attention back to the fire. He allowed himself to become mesmerized by the dancing of the flames and the intermingling of the red and the orange and the blue within the hearth. He listened to the crackling of the logs and watched as the occasional spark leapt through the air.

Without realizing it, his eyes began to close and his head began to nod. Before long, his chin was resting against his chest and Ebenezer was fast asleep.

Ebenezer was so deeply asleep that he never heard the bells echo with twelve gongs. As Ebenezer sat snoring before the dying flames, he did not realize that the twenty-fifth of December had come and brought him along with it. He would remain ignorant of this fact for fifteen minutes more. At that moment, as the clock chimed, his head happened to loll to the side and his eyes opened, at which time he noticed the time read a quarter past the first hour of the new day.

He sat up with a start and leapt to his feet. He looked around, disoriented and confused. Needing confirmation that he was truly alive, he ran up the stairs and approached his bed chamber. He swung the door open and saw Belle, lying motionless on the bed, breathing softly. Ebenezer shook her awake.

"What is it, Ebenezer?" she asked sleepily.

"It is Christmas Day!" Ebenezer exclaimed.

Belle looked through exhausted eyes at the clock.

"So it is. Merry Christmas, my love," Belle said.

"No, you do not understand," Ebenezer said excitedly. "It is the twenty-fifth of December, eighteen hundred and forty-five!"

"Yes, dear, it is," said Belle.

"I should not be here," Ebenezer said. "But I am!"

"Yes, dear, of course you are. This is your home," said Belle.

Ebenezer thought about the situation for a moment and had an epiphany.

"Belle, my love. It is a miracle!" cried Ebenezer. "I have been spared!"

"Yes, love. You have more to do on this earth. Just as I told you," said Belle.

Ebenezer took his wife's words into his heart. He certainly did have more to do on this earth. Much more.

He did not realize it, but his next opportunity to positively impact his fellow man had already been set in motion. Sadly, blight had struck the potato crop in Ireland a few months prior.

The Great Famine was about to begin.

7

Phytophthora infestans. These are Latin words that were unknown to most in Ireland even as they described a foreign invader that came upon the Emerald Isle's shores in or about eighteen hundred and forty-five. However, before the year was out, most, if not all, in Ireland were more than acquainted with this demon from Western shores. They knew it as blight and before eighteen hundred and forty-six made its appearance, over one-third of the potato crop so many depended on was infected and destroyed. Without anyone realizing it yet, the Great Famine was about to begin.

One able to recognize the danger early into the disaster was Prime Minister Robert Peel. This was the same Robert Peel who had created the Metropolitan Police Force based at Scotland Yard in eighteen hundred and twenty-nine. From that day to this, the officers employed in this capacity were known as "Bobbies" for this reason.

Understanding the devastation of his people in Ireland due to the failure of the potato crop, Peel called an emergency meeting of the Cabinet of the United Kingdom to vote on his proposal to distribute relief to the island. The Cabinet voted against the proposal.

Undaunted, in November, Peel took it upon himself to order the secret purchase of one hundred thousand pounds worth of maize and meal from the United States for Ireland. Unfortunately, this effort was rife with problems. First, poor weather conditions delayed the arrival of the first shipment until February of eighteen hundred and forty-six. Next, the initial shipments were of unground dried kernels and there were very few mills in Ireland equipped to grind the maize and meal into flour. Many people attempted to eat the uncooked corn directly, which caused extreme bowel distress. To make it edible, the cornmeal had to be cooked to excess. Even if it did not cause illness, it was neither as satisfying or filling as the potatoes the Irish were accustomed to consuming. The problems with the food, coupled with its yellow color led to its unflattering nickname, "Peel's brimstone".

After accepting that he would not only live through the day on Christmas, eighteen hundred and forty-five, but that his time on earth would continue for a reasonable period forward, Ebenezer viewed the Irish Potato Famine as an opportunity to assist his fellow man. When blight caused a similar problem in Scotland, Ebenezer was convinced of it.

He immediately made plans to extend the reach of his Belle's Kitchens to Ireland and Scotland. This proved difficult, but he persisted and was able to open five Kitchens in Ireland and three in Scotland by year's end. Still, he believed he could do more. The famine was getting worse. Three quarters of the potato crop was destroyed in eighteen hundred and forty-six.

Ebenezer's opportunity came one year after his miracle of survival.

A colleague of Ebenezer's, the banker, Baron Lionel de Rothschild, called upon some of the wealthiest and most noteworthy men in all of the kingdom to procure and manage donations to help stem the suffering. Ebenezer was happy to count himself among these men.

The first meeting of what was known as the British Association for the Relief of Distress in Ireland and the Highlands of Scotland, more commonly to be known as the British Relief Association, took place on the first of January, eighteen hundred and forty-seven at the Baron's home. The committee administering this organization was formed and Ebenezer was selected as a member. He, along with the rest of the committee members, donated one thousand pounds to the effort and he met with them almost daily to coordinate their efforts.

It was a brilliant success. Approximately five hundred thousand pounds was raised from over fifteen thousand individual contributions from around the world. They came from all avenues of life from Queen Victoria herself to a young lawyer in the United States by the name of Abraham Lincoln. Ebenezer found his role in helping to relieve some of the seemingly endless suffering of his Irish and Scottish brothers and sisters to be exhilarating. The effort continued until July of eighteen hundred and forty-eight, when the Association's funds were depleted.

In addition to focusing on assisting the needy within the British Isles, Ebenezer and Belle spent a great deal of time at travel to Boston visiting with her children and grandchildren. Family remained as important to Belle as ever and she would not allow the Atlantic Ocean to act as any real barrier to being in the presence of those she held most dear.

Ebenezer enjoyed his trips to America, but he sensed a true tension whenever he was there. This was a nation that prided itself on being conceived in liberty with justice for all. Yet, it still suffered from the scourge of slavery. And Ebenezer could see that this hateful institution was tearing at the very fabric and the soul of his wife's adopted country.

Ebenezer abhorred the very concept of slavery. The idea that one man could own another simply due to his skin color or place of origin turned Ebenezer's stomach. America was a land at war with its own founding values. Ebenezer often wondered how long it would be before that war transformed into one in which shots were fired. As he spent more and more time there, he considered an American civil war to be inevitable.

As the decade drew to a close, Ebenezer found himself reinvigorated by the written word, as he had been when he was young and Fan would read to him and then when he was a bit older and Mrs. Fezziwig gave him the tools to enjoy books on his own. Of particular interest to Ebenezer was a young writer by the name of Charles Dickens. Ebenezer was amazed at how the man could grab hold of his attention and how the words would simply not allow Ebenezer out of their grip until hours had passed and day had turned to night.

Another publication caught Ebenezer's attention in the year eighteen hundred and forty-nine, but for a significantly different reason. Ebenezer was seventy years old when his nephew, Fred, presented him with a gift during one of their Friday evening meals.

"What is this?" asked Ebenezer.

"Simply open it and you will see," said Fred with a smile.

Ebenezer removed the wrapping and held in his hand a book. He turned it over to look at the front cover and saw that the title was *Who's Who*.

"What is this publication?" Ebenezer asked. "I am not familiar with it."

"It is new, Uncle. It lists people of importance," said Fred. "Check the page that has been designated with a feather."

Ebenezer saw the feather protruding out of the book, approximately half-way between beginning and end. He opened the book at that page where the great philanthropists of the day were listed. He scanned the list until he neared the bottom of the page. His body then jolted as his eyes grew wide. Eyes that very quickly filled with tears.

"Whatever is the matter, my dear?" asked Belle, very concerned.

Ebenezer did not respond. He simply stared at the page.

"Ebenezer!" Belle cried, walking to him. "What troubles you?"

Finally, he spoke.

"Not a thing, my love," said Ebenezer softly, his hands shaking ever so noticeably. "Look at this."

Belle took the book and saw that she was viewing a page dedicated to the great philanthropists of the age. Toward the bottom of the page was printed:

Ebenezer Scrooge, age 70, of Scrooge, Marley and Cratchit

Belle looked up at her teary-eyed husband and realized that these were tears of joy. She joined him in a weep, as proud of him as was possible. The hated man who cared for nothing more than his own business was gone and the world knew it. Left behind was this wonderful man whom all recognized for his virtuous deeds.

"Oh, thank you, Fred, for bringing this to me," said Ebenezer, giving his nephew a tight hug. "And to you as well, Julia." He then held her in a mighty embrace when he released Fred.

"There is nothing to thank us for. We merely noticed this fascinating book and knew you should own a copy," said Fred.

"Truly amazing," said Ebenezer.

In the years to come, Ebenezer would find more to be amazing, but nothing so much as the Great Exhibition of the Works of Industry of All Nations in eighteen hundred and fifty-one. It was the first world's fair. The international exhibition took place in Hyde Park in London from the first of May until the eleventh of October, when Ebenezer was seventy-two years old.

Ebenezer took Belle and they were accompanied by Fred and Julia as well as the entire Cratchit family. The exhibition was housed within a massive glass building, known as "The Crystal Palace" for good reason. It looked like a giant greenhouse. Ebenezer was in awe. He did not realize that man could construct such a structure.

The group walked from room to room to observe the great wonders brought by each participating country. They saw new machinery never before conceived, jewels larger than had ever been displayed, and art so beautiful it moved one to tears. It was impossible to see it all. There were approximately one hundred thousand objects displayed over a distance of over ten miles by over fifteen thousand contributors.

Ebenezer was mesmerized by the gargantuan fountain in the middle of the building that stood over eight meters high, constructed of four tons of pink glass. Among all of the rest of the wonders, it was like stepping into the future. So much to view, so modern, so beautiful.

In the five months it was open, Ebenezer must have gone back fifteen times. He wished to explore it all. He brought Belle's children and grandchildren and great-grandchildren with him to enjoy the splendor of the place when they came for a visit in July. He especially reveled in the gleam in the eyes of the children as they wandered about.

The exhibition was an enormous success. Six million people visited from all over the world. Six million! To put this into proper perspective, there were only eighteen million people living in the entirety of the British Isles at the time. On average, more than forty two thousand people were present and when Ebenezer and Belle visited on the seventh of October, they were only two of almost one hundred and ten thousand people there! It was wondrous indeed!

It was around this time when Ebenezer accidentally discovered what would become his favorite poem of all time. Elizabeth Barrett Browning produced a collection of poems, known as *Sonnets from the Portuguese*. One day, Ebenezer was browsing in Hardy's Books when he accidentally brushed against a book on a shelf. The book fell to the floor with its pages open. Ebenezer bent to pick it up and return it to its rightful place when his eyes caught the words on the page. It was designated, simply, "Number 43".

It began:

How to I love thee? Let me count the ways.

Ebenezer was immediately entranced. As his eyes danced down the page, he felt that his heart was speaking directly to Belle. He bought the book immediately and beginning that very night, it became a common practice of his to quote from this work to his lovely Belle. And Belle loved to hear of it. Never before had Ebenezer spoken so passionately or so sincerely. It was almost as if he had written the words himself.

The remainder of the eighteen hundred and fifties were a time of ups and downs for Ebenezer. He was very pleased that Tim had decided to apprentice at Scrooge, Marley and Cratchit. They boy had a sharp mind and a warm heart. Despite almost never visiting the office anymore, on the rare occasions when he did, he always saw Tim hard at work. Bob told Ebenezer that the next generation of the company would surely be in good hands with Tim at the helm.

On a less pleasant note, time was clearly stalking Ebenezer. This much was certain. While he may have escaped death before his sixty-seventh birthday, he could not outrun it forever. As the decade progressed, Ebenezer was beginning to leave his home less and less often. His breathing became more of a struggle by the middle of eighteen hundred and fifty-five, and he was truly showing his age.

One opportunity to leave his home that Ebenezer could not pass up, however, came when Fred informed him that Charles Dickens was going on tour to read excerpts from his books and to take questions from readers. He was to be in London on the first of May, eighteen hundred and fifty-eight at none other than Hardy's Books. Fred and Julia brought Ebenezer and Belle to see Ebenezer's favorite author.

Ebenezer was seventy-nine years old, but as he sat and listened to the young man almost half his age read the words that so encaptivated his imagination for so many years, it was as though he was young again himself. He did not cough or struggle to breathe throughout the presentation. He rested his hands on his walking stick and leaned in to bask in the glow of this literature he so loved.

When the reading and the questions came to a conclusion, Ebenezer had but one request. He approached the bearded man with the wise eyes, thanked him for his time that day as well as for the joy he had brought to Ebenezer's life. He then asked Mr. Dickens if he could shake his hand, a request that Dickens gladly granted.

"Mr. Scrooge, it is I who is honored to shake your hand," said Dickens. "I scribble words on a page. You change people's lives. People you do not know. Often, people you do not even meet. And you do so without thought of personal gain or aggrandizement."

"You flatter me unnecessarily, Mr. Dickens," said Ebenezer.

"It is necessary," said Dickens. "There are those in your position who would do nothing but horde for themselves. There are others who would give, but would need all of the recognition and admiration. Yet I look around London. I do not see one monument that you have erected to yourself. Not one building that cries out, 'Ebenezer Scrooge did this'. I admire you greatly. I am very glad we have met."

"Thank you, Mr. Dickens," said Ebenezer. "Your words are kind and they are truly appreciated."

When they all left and headed home, Ebenezer leaned over to Fred.

"Thank you, my boy. That was a thrill of a lifetime," said Ebenezer.

That night, Ebenezer could not stop smiling. He sat back in his chair and reminisced about the day.

When Belle came to bring him his tea, she found him, still smiling, but fast asleep.

Rather than disturb him, she placed a blanket over him and kissed his lips gently.

"Good night, my love," she whispered. And then she blew out the candle, leaving him to rest in the darkness.

8

𝔄s eighteen hundred and fifty-nine dawned, Ebenezer was eighty years and one week old. He and Belle sat by a fire, a favorite pastime of theirs, listening as the final year of the decade entered the room. They looked into each other's eyes, gave a smile, and then leaned in for their traditional New Year's kiss.

Always begin the year with a kiss. That had become an important credo by which Ebenezer lived. Come what may, it should all begin with a kiss. It was a silent promise of love for the year ahead.

By this time in their lives, Ebenezer and Belle had taken up residence in one of the first floor bed chambers. Those stairs just kept growing longer and longer each year until Belle had had enough. She put her foot down and had all of their belongings, along with all of the furniture, moved to a main floor bedroom. Ebenezer tried to object, but relented when he could not answer her question about which of the two – his bones or the staircase – creaked more upon his ascent.

She was correct, of course. They were not getting any younger and there was no reason to risk life and limb just to reach one's own bed at night. The switch immediately make life easier for the both of them.

Ebenezer noted that he felt every one of his eighty years. His respiratory condition from his childhood illness made even short walks strenuous. He was colder than usual all winter long and even being pressed up against a roaring fire was not always enough to eliminate the chill from deep within his bones.

Ebenezer spent a great deal of time with a book in his hand. His favorite remained Dickens and one of his favorite memories was that of the eventful encounter the two men shared at Mr. Dickens' reading the previous May. Ebenezer was very excited when Dickens began publication of his new weekly circular, *All the Year Round*, on the thirtieth of April and included the first chapter of his newest work. The opening line captured Ebenezer's attention immediately.

It was the best of times, it was the worst of times...

Ebenezer eagerly awaited each new installment until the final chapter was released on the fifteenth of November.

"His best work to date," Ebenezer said aloud to no one in particular after reading the final line.

One evening in early December, Ebenezer was having a particularly difficult time falling asleep. There was tightness in his chest and, try as he may, he could not seem to inhale enough air to satisfy his lungs. He coughed relentlessly as his eyes watered from the strain.

This noise emanating from her husband had unfortunately become all too familiar to Belle. There was a time when such racket would keep her up at night, both from the sound and from worry. But no longer. If she had fallen asleep before Ebenezer's hacking had begun, she would usually remain so.

As Ebenezer attempted fruitlessly to stem the tide of his expectorations, he saw as a great light began to shine from beyond his doorframe. Suddenly his coughing ceased and his bedroom door swung open, allowing the light from beyond to pour inward like a wave crashing towards shore. Ebenezer lifted his arm, shielding his eyes with his hand. When his eyes finally adjusted to the brightness, he saw a lone figure standing in the doorway.

Ebenezer was not frightened. He was not concerned. Immediately, he recognized the face of this intruder and he smiled.

"Jacob Marley!" he gasped.

"It is good to see you, my old friend," Marley said.

As Ebenezer gazed upon his old partner, he noticed that there was something quite different about him as compared to their last encounter. Jacob was smiling, for one. And, more importantly to Ebenezer, his chains and weights were completely absent from his body. He moved freely with no trace of pain or discomfort. He simply looked like a happy man in the prime of life.

"Jacob, you are unfettered!" Ebenezer cried.

"Yes. Thanks to you, my friend," Jacob replied as he entered the room.

"Me?" Ebenezer asked.

"Yes, Ebenezer," said Jacob. "I have been watching you for these many years since we last spoke. I have been most pleased to witness the path your life has taken since that day. I watched as, with each generous deed you performed, the links of your chains began to vanish until they were no more. Miraculously, I was surprised to note that as your chains disappeared, so did my own. Day by day, I walked more freely. Until now, when I can stand before you, a free man in body, mind and spirit. So I thank you, Ebenezer! You have saved me!"

"It seems that we have saved each other!" observed Ebenezer.

"So it does," said Jacob with a smile.

Ebenezer turned to Belle sleeping gently beside him and attempted to shake her awake so that she could partake in this miracle in progress. But try as he may, she would not stir.

"You cannot awaken your lady love," Jacob said. "We have stepped outside of time. It is just you and I sharing this moment, Ebenezer."

"But I wish for Belle to meet you. After which, I can tell her the tale of when you first came to me without fear that she will conclude my mind has escaped me," Ebenezer said.

"That cannot happen. I am here only for you. And only for a short time more," said Jacob. "I have come to bid you farewell. I am now free from that which binds me to the earth. I am off to the next spiritual plane."

"I congratulate you, Jacob. I know this has been your goal and was your lament when you could not achieve such transition," Ebenezer said.

"Again, I thank you, Ebenezer. I could not accomplish this without you," Jacob said. "As for relating your tale, fear not. Trust those whom you love. They will not let you down."

"I do not know if I could share this with my Belle," said Ebenezer. "She worries about me so as it is."

"Is there no one else you can entrust the story of this miracle?" asked Jacob.

"I think there is one," said Ebenezer, with a resolute expression upon his face.

"Good," said Jacob. "And now I must go. I am very proud of you, Ebenezer. You have done what most men could not. You have changed your ways and, in so doing, you have changed the world. You are a blessing. Whereas once you were a blight upon the world, you are now a light shining bright for all to see and admire. I love you, my friend. I hope to see you again in another plane of existence."

"Thank you for all you have done for me, Jacob. You have saved me and given my life meaning beyond that which words could express," Ebenezer said.

"Farewell, Ebenezer. Farewell," Jacob said. And, with those words, Jacob Marley slowly disappeared from Ebenezer's sight.

"Farewell, Jacob," Ebenezer whispered. "And Godspeed."

When Jacob's form was no more, Ebenezer let out a wet cough and

Belle rolled over with her eyes open.

"Are you alright, Ebenezer?" she asked.

"Yes, my love. All is well," Ebenezer told her. "All is well."

As the month progressed, Ebenezer seemed to wilt. After his encounter with Jacob, he appeared to age ten years in ten days. This decline was not lost on Ebenezer. By the twentieth of December, he could no longer find the strength to exit his bed. His time was near.

Ebenezer decided the time had come to share his story with a most trusted soul. He felt that the world should know of the miracle that had transformed his life. His hope was that others could benefit from what he had learned about our meaning in this life. If others could be saved as he was, he felt that he could live on even beyond his years.

There was only one person he believed could carry this responsibility. Ebenezer summoned Tim Cratchit to his bedside.

Tim was twenty-two years old and already a vital member of Scrooge, Marley and Cratchit. He had grown into a very special young man. His slight limp was the only remnant of his childhood condition that almost ended his life before it had truly begun. There was a sweet young woman by the name of Christine Hitchens who had caught his eye and touched his heart. Ebenezer could see love in Tim's eyes as he spoke about her. It would not be long before wedding bells would ring. Ebenezer was only disappointed that he knew he would not be there to witness it.

Tim was led into Ebenezer's room by Belle. It had been approximately one week since he had last visited. It was evening after his work day was done. Belle warned Tim about what he was to see. Ebenezer looked more frail and closer to the grave than ever before. Tim steeled himself against the pain of witnessing his adopted uncle's appearance, and then walked through the door.

Immediately, Ebenezer's face brightened at seeing the boy. He attempted to sit up a bit, but his strength simply would not allow it. Tim and Belle assisted Ebenezer in his efforts and they managed to help him to a more comfortable position.

Ebenezer asked Belle to leave the men alone for a time. Ebenezer said that he had much of importance to relate to Tim. Belle nodded her head, kissed her husband on the forehead, and exited the room.

"What is it that you need to tell me, Uncle?" Tim asked, trying to hide the sadness in his soul at seeing his beloved Uncle Ebenezer in this condition.

"I have a very important favor to ask of you, Tim, my boy," Ebenezer said.

"Anything, Uncle," said Tim immediately. "Anything."

"I need to entrust in you the story of my life, including a miraculous evening that most might think me mad for believing occurred in truth," said Ebenezer.

"Of course, Uncle. I am here for you, regardless of what you need," sad Tim.

"Much of what I will tell you will be hard for you to accept. But I swear to you upon the very soul of my mother that everything I am about to say is entirely true," said Ebenezer.

"Yes, Uncle," said Tim, taking Ebenezer's hand. "I would believe anything you tell me. You can trust in me."

"Upon hearing my tale, you will then become the keeper of a miracle. One that I ask you share with the world when you believe the time is right. I only request that you refrain from doing so while I still live," Ebenezer said.

"I promise, Uncle," said Tim. "I promise."

"Then let us begin," said Ebenezer.

For the next several hours, Ebenezer related the entire tale of his life from his earliest days through his spiritual encounters on Christmas of eighteen hundred and forty-three and up until that very moment as they sat in his bed chamber. Tim sat enchanted by the story. He did not doubt the ghostly tale for even a moment. By the end of the account, Tim knew he had been given a great responsibility and a great gift.

When Ebenezer concluded, he looked deeply into Tim's eyes.

"Now, Tim, you are the keeper of this miracle. I hope it assists you in directing your life," said Ebenezer. "And I hope it helps others as well."

"There is no doubt that it will, Uncle," Tim said, in awe. "I promise to tend this tale with as much care as it deserves. I will remember it well. I will share it with the world."

"Thank you, Tim. Know this always," said Ebenezer. "I love you. Thank you for entering my life."

"I love you as well, Uncle. Without you, there would be no me," Tim said, with tears in his eyes. Something within told him with certainty that these would be the last words to pass between these two men.

He was correct.

Four days later, on the twenty-fourth of December, Ebenezer did not have even the strength to raise his head from his pillow all day. Belle remained by his bedside and she spoke softly to him about all of their wonderful times shared throughout the years. She told him she loved him again and again. Ebenezer drifted in and out of sleep, and was comforted by his wife's touch as she held his hand within hers.

As the day passed into night, Ebenezer's eyes remained open less and less often. It was clearly a struggle to remain conscious. His breathing was wet and raspy, but he did not even have the strength to cough the liquid from his lungs.

At eleven o'clock, he spoke in barely a whisper.

"What time is it?" he asked.

"It is an hour until midnight, my love," Belle replied, holding his hand.

"I must hold on to see one more Christmas," Ebenezer said. "I must."

"Just rest, my love. Just rest. Do not strain yourself," Belle told him gently.

"Tell me more about our youth," Ebenezer requested.

Belle spoke to Ebenezer about their first time they met. Ebenezer smiled as he recalled being stunned by her beauty at their initial encounter. He warmed as he was transported back to that first party at the Fezziwig's. He chuckled to himself remembering how he followed Belle around like a lost puppy dog all throughout the night. He could almost feel the sensation on his face remembering her first kiss planted upon his cheek as the new year commenced.

They were wonderful memories to envelop himself within.

He then heard the sound of the bells chiming twelve times. His eyes closed and he smiled. It was Christmas. He had made it.

Ebenezer then opened his eyes and stared directly into Belle's with more strength and conviction than he had been able to muster in weeks. He squeezed her hand within his and spoke.

"I love thee with the breath, smiles, tears, of all my life; and if God choose, I shall but love thee better after death."

Ebenezer smiled and then his head lolled back into his pillow. His grip on Belle's hand abated. His eyes closed. And then his last breath escaped his lips.

Belle placed his hand upon his chest and then buried her face within her hands, sobbing.

Ebenezer Scrooge was dead.

9

The snow fell gently upon the great cathedral in which he lay. His body rested peacefully within the coffin on the same spot where he had stood fourteen years earlier as he and his precious Belle pledged their lives to one another. Seated in every pew the house of worship could hold were mourners from all throughout the British Isles, the mainland of the European continent, and from across the sea in America. In fact, some were standing at the rear of the church because there were more wet eyes than available seats.

From the rear doors, Belle came walking in, slowly and unsteadily. She was assisted by her children and followed by her grandchildren and their children. They led the sad woman dressed all in black to the front of the church where a section had been held reserved for the immediate family. Before she sat, she walked up to the closed casket and stared at the container in which her dearly beloved lay still. She leaned in and whispered something to him that no one else could hear, a final secret shared, and then kissed the top of the coffin. She then brought her hand to her trembling lips and wept, unable to take her eyes off of it. Recognizing her distress, Benjamin approached on her left arm and Elijah on her right to lead their grieving mother to her seat.

There was a remarkable cross-section of society intermingled within the church to pay their final respects. From the wealthiest colleagues and friends at the Executive's Club to the most modest of clients who benefited from Ebenezer's generosity, they all came. Strangers fed at Belle's Kitchens during their darkest moments were in attendance, as were those who were healed at the Marley Hospital, in addition to those who only knew Ebenezer by reputation due to the good he had done for the city, the country, and to mankind in general.

Handkerchiefs were moist throughout the room. All felt a terrible sense of loss. All lamented that they had to be in this place, but none could imagine being anywhere else on this tragic day.

Father Harrison took to the podium and the congregation fell silent. He began the service with a blessing and then invited a family member up for a reading. Fred and Julia both walked up together, hand in hand. Fred looked to the page in his Bible and began to read from the Book of Wisdom of Solomon.

"A reading from the Book of Wisdom.
The souls of the righteous are in the hands of God,
   and no torment shall touch them.
They seemed, in the view of the foolish, to be dead;
   and their passing away was thought an affliction
   and their going forth from us, utter destruction.
But they are in peace.
For if to others, indeed, they seemed punished,
   yet is their hope full of immortality;
   chastised a little, they shall be greatly blessed,
   because God tried them
   and found them worthy of himself.
As gold in the furnace, he proved them,
   and as sacrificial offerings he took them to himself.
In the time of their judgment they shall shine
   and dart about as sparks through stubble;
   they shall judge nations and rule over peoples,
   and the Lord shall be their King forever.
Those who trust in Him shall understand truth,
   and the faithful shall abide with him in love:
   because grace and mercy are with his holy ones,
   and his care is with the elect."

Holding hands as they had when they approached the altar, Fred and Julia returned to their seats. Father Harrison continued the service, bidding farewell to the blessed soul lying prone before him. At the conclusion of his remarks, he invited anyone in the congregation who wished to speak to step forward and do so.

At that, a spontaneous line formed in the aisle as so many felt moved to relate their personal remembrances of Ebenezer. So many who were touched by his kindness and his generosity. So many who had never before had the opportunity to say "Thank you" to the great man. Their tributes moved Belle, causing her tears of sadness to mix with those of joy and appreciation.

The last to arise was young Timothy Cratchit. He slowly walked to the podium, his slight limp noticeable to all. He stood for a long moment, facing the audience before him, but with his eyes fixed on the casket housing his uncle's still frame. He then looked up at the sea of faces patiently waiting for him to be ready to speak.

He told the gathered crowd that had it not been for Ebenezer Scrooge, that he would not have been privileged to be among these wonderful mourners collected together on this day. He related to them how much Ebenezer had touched his life right up until their last meeting just a few short days before his death. Tim then told the assembled congregation that at that time, Ebenezer told him the wondrous tale of his life, including a miraculous encounter that changed everything for him forever. Tim revealed that Ebenezer charged him with relaying these events to the world upon his passing. And so to honor his late uncle's final wishes, he asked the crowd to indulge him in allowing him to fulfill that promise right there and then.

Tim then relayed Ebenezer's entire account. It took more than one hour, but not one soul present felt the time. Their eyes were glued to Tim's as they listened with amazement. Belle sat in the front row, nodding her head up and down as the missing details about Ebenezer's life and spiritual encounters were expressed. Fred was both shocked and delighted to learn that his intended name was actually Ebenezer Frederick. It made him feel closer to his uncle somehow.

When Tim concluded, he thanked everyone for their attention.

"And as my Uncle Ebenezer often said, 'God bless us, everyone'."

He then stepped from the podium and approached Ebenezer. He reached out and touched the top of the casket. A tear fell from his eye, moistening the box that Ebenezer would forever after call home.

"Good-bye, Uncle. I shall always love you," Tim spoke softly. He then made his way back to his seat where his dear Christine was awaiting him with a sad smile of support.

The service concluded and the entire congregation stepped out into the churchyard for the burial. As they all stood round, Ebenezer's casket was gently lowered into its final resting place. Final prayers were spoken after which earth was placed upon his coffin and used to fill his grave, allowing Ebenezer Scrooge to sleep in peace forevermore.

After the ceremony was over, a man approached Tim Cratchit. As many would do that day, he shook Tim's hand and thanked him for regaling them with Ebenezer's life story. He then introduced himself and made a request.

"Sir, my name is Charles Dickens. I was fortunate enough to meet your uncle on one occasion," said Dickens. "I found his tale as you related it to be most extraordinary. I must ask you if I may borrow it and disseminate it to the world?"

"Mr. Dickens, I do not doubt that there is anything that would have made my uncle more proud than to know that a man he held in such high esteem such as yourself would do exactly that," said Tim, agreeing at once.

"Thank you, sir. I shall endeavor to do justice to his memory," said Dickens.

"I have no doubt," replied Tim.

Within the year, a magnificent novella would be shared with the world, one that would bind Charles Dickens and Ebenezer Scrooge together forever. And even after Mr. Dickens himself was gone, the version of events as interpreted by the great author would resonate onward throughout the ages.

Never again would anyone ponder the beauty that is Christmas without also remembering a poor lost soul who was miraculously saved one fateful night by the name of Ebenezer Scrooge.

EPILOGUE

"It is time to go now, Mother," said Elijah.

Belle took one last long look at her empty house and then allowed herself to be led to the awaiting carriage. She watched out of the cab's window as the sights of London passed before her eyes for the very last time. She joined her family on the ship bound for Boston when they arrived at the pier. As the ship headed out into the Atlantic, she kept her eyes focused upon the British shore as it faded away into the distance until it was no more.

Belle had barely settled back into life in America before the great civil war Ebenezer always warned was coming broke out between the northern and southern states, tearing the country in two. She was forced to watch as the young men from her neighborhood, including two of her own great-grandchildren, marched off to war, many never to return. It was heartbreaking to Belle.

The war lasted four long years, but Belle did not live to see its conclusion. On the thirtieth of April, eighteen hundred and sixty-three, with her entire family surrounding her at her bedside, Belle gently passed from this world to the next.

Back in Britain, Fred and Julia felt Ebenezer's absence deeply. They always set an extra place at their table every Friday in memory of their dear Uncle Ebenezer. They took over responsibility for administering Belle's Kitchens as well as various of his other charities to ensure that Ebenezer's great vision for the world remained alive.

They grew old together, as they always dreamed they would. One could not live without the other. Julia passed away on a beautiful Spring afternoon. Fred joined her three days later. They were commemorated in a joint ceremony and buried side by side.

As for Tim, he married his Christine on the fifteenth of June, eighteen hundred and sixty-one. They had four children together. The first, a son, was born two years into their marriage. They named him Ebenezer Timothy Cratchit. Ebenezer Timothy would later have five children of his own, one of which would be a boy named George, who would grow to have a very special and close relationship with his grandfather.

Tim lived a long and prosperous life, always remembering the lessons his Uncle Ebenezer taught him. Shortly after Ebenezer's passing, he partnered with his father at Scrooge, Marley and Cratchit. He took sole ownership a few short years later when Bob sadly passed away at the age of fifty-nine. As Bob had accurately predicted, the company was in fine and capable hands under the leadership of Tim.

The world was a dimmer place without Ebenezer Scrooge in it. But as with all things, life went on. The number of children benefited from the Marley Hospital grew from the hundreds to the thousands to the tens of thousands. An Ebenezer Scrooge Memorial Charity was established by an admirer of his work and it raised funds each year for the needy. Belle's Kitchens continued to feed the poor. As the years progressed, Ebenezer's story as told by Charles Dickens spread throughout the world converting him from man to myth.

It is a great irony that a man who ended his life so loved would leave a legacy in which his surname would enter the common vernacular to describe a man so different than the one he became. But because of this, he was never forgotten. His tale unites us. His journey with the spirits enchants us. His redemption inspires us.

His lesson to all of us is clear.

While no one should ever allow themselves to be a Scrooge, we should all strive to be an Ebenezer.

ABOUT THE AUTHOR

First, thank you, dear Reader, for joining me on this journey that I dreamed throughout my entire life about someday being able to embark upon. The experience was actually better than the dream.

If you are reading this page, even after concluding your time with my tale, I assume that means that you would like to know a bit about me. Who am I? That's a question I have asked myself more often than I have been able to supply an answer.

I am a family man, first and foremost. I am madly in love with my beautiful wife and my three wonderful children. We live in the Finger Lakes Region of New York State.

I was an attorney for 20+ years, but it was never the right fit for me. With the love and support of my amazing family and friends, I finally made the move to get out of an unfulfilling career and I replaced it with something I love. I went back to school in my 40s and earned my Teaching Certificate and my Masters in Education in the dual areas of Secondary School Social Studies and also Special Education. I am now where I belong, finally doing a job that is "who I am", rather than simply "what I do".

As much as I love teaching, my true passion throughout my life has always been writing. I've been writing creative stories for as long as I could hold a pencil. I am very excited to have achieved my lifelong dream of becoming a published author with my debut novel, *Ebenezer: The True Life Story of Ebenezer Scrooge*, that you have just read.

I only hope my readers find as much joy in reading it as I found in writing it.

Thank you and God bless us… everyone!

Doug can be reached at ebenezerbook2017@gmail.com, and warmly welcomes correspondence from those who have read or listened to the book, which is also available as an Audiobook on Audible.com. He can also be followed on Twitter, where he goes by the handle: @LawyerNoMore.

Made in the USA
Middletown, DE
08 December 2022